FORBIDDEN VENGEANCE

A DARK, MAFIA ROMANCE

BONDS OF BETRAYAL

AJME WILLIAMS

Copyright © 2025 by Ajme Williams

All rights reserved.

No part of this book may be reproduced in any form or by any electronic or mechanical means, including information storage and retrieval systems, without written permission from the author, except for the use of brief quotations in a book review.

This is a work of fiction. Names, characters, businesses, places, events and incidents are either the products of authors imagination or used in a fictitious manner. Any resemblance to actual persons, living or dead, or actual events is purely coincidental. The following story contains mature themes, strong language and sexual situations. It is intended for mature readers only.

All characters are 18+ years of age and all sexual acts are consensual.

ABOUT THE AUTHOR

Ajme Williams writes emotional, angsty contemporary romance. All her books can be enjoyed as full length, standalone romances and are FREE to read in Kindle Unlimited.

Bonds of Betrayal (this series)
Silent Vows | Forbidden Vengeance

Mafia Lords of Sin
Tangled Loyalties | Savage Devotion | Bulletproof Baby | Cursed Confessions | Borrowed Bride

Dynasty of Deception
Merciless King | Ice Princess | Lost Prince | Stolen Queen | Triplets for the Mafia Prince | The Godfather's Christmas Twins

Shadows of Redemption
Soldier of Death | Queen of Misfortune | Prince of Darkness | Angel of Mercy

The Why Choose Haremland
Protecting Their Princess | Protecting Her Secret | Unwrapping their Christmas Present | Cupid Strikes... 3 Times | Their Easter Bunny | SEAL Daddies Next Door | Naughty Lessons | See Me After Class | Blurred Lines | Nanny for the Firefighters | Snowy Secrets

High Stakes
Bet On It | A Friendly Wager | Triple or Nothing | Press Your Luck

Heart of Hope
Our Last Chance | An Irish Affair | So Wrong | Imperfect Love | Eight Long Years | Friends to Lovers | The One and Only | Best Friend's Brother | Maybe It's Fate | Gone Too Far | Christmas with Brother's Best Friend | Fighting for US | Against All Odds | Hoping to Score | Thankful for Us | The Vegas Bluff | 365 Days | Meant to Be | Mile High

Baby | Silver Fox's Secret Baby | Snowed In with Best Friend's Dad | Secret Triplets for Christmas | Off-Limits Daddy

Billionaire Secrets
Twin Secrets | Just A Sham | Let's Start Over | The Baby Contract | Too Complicated

Dominant Bosses
His Rules | His Desires | His Needs | His Punishments | His Secret

Strong Brothers
Say Yes to Love | Giving In to Love | Wrong to Love You | Hate to Love You

Fake Marriage
Accidental Love | Accidental Baby | Accidental Affair | Accidental Meeting

Irresistible Billionaires
Admit You Miss Me | Admit You Love Me | Admit You Want Me | Admit You Need Me

Check out Ajme's full Amazon catalogue here.

Join her VIP NL here.

DESCRIPTION

HONOR OR BLOOD: She's carrying a Calabrese heir. Too bad I'm going to make her a DeLuca bride.

She was supposed to be untouchable. My brother's family.
Bella's closest friend.
Another man's woman.

But Elena Santiago isn't the sweet angel she pretends to be.
Behind that perfect smile lies a mind as ruthless as mine.
Behind those deadly eyes burns an ambition that matches my own.

Now she's pregnant with a Calabrese heir,
Playing games that could get her killed,
And looking at me like I'm the answer to her darkest prayers.

I came back to New York for revenge.
Instead, I'm going to take what was never meant to be mine.

Let them call it betrayal.
Let them start a war.

Because Elena isn't just a pawn in their game.
She's the queen who will help me burn their empire to the ground.

And I dare any man to try and stop me.

"You're playing with fire, princess."
"Maybe I want to burn."

1

ELENA

The champagne flutes chime like warning bells as I survey Bella's baby shower from my carefully chosen vantage point near the French doors. Every detail is perfect—from the hand-painted Italian cookies arranged in delicate spirals to the cascade of white roses tumbling from crystal vases.

Exactly what's expected from New York's premier event planner to the crime families.

Six months after Mario's exile, the DeLuca mansion's grand ballroom sparkles with old money and hidden tensions. Chandeliers splinter light across faces that hold more secrets than congratulations.

My phone burns in my clutch, Mario's latest text still unanswered: *Tell me everything, little planner.*

I adjust a slightly crooked place card, more from habit than necessity. Everything must appear flawless, controlled. Like me in my perfectly tailored Chanel suit, my manicured hands steady only through years of practice. The women around me chatter about nursery colors and designer baby clothes, their voices a symphony of practiced refinement masking calculation.

Bella stands at the center of it all, radiant in a cream silk maternity dress. One hand rests on her prominent baby bump while the other gestures animatedly as she shows off ultrasound photos to cooing society wives.

The DeLuca twins. Future heirs to an empire built on blood and lies.

"They're already so active," Bella laughs, her happiness genuine in a room full of manufactured emotions. "The boy especially—just like his father."

The comparison sends a ripple of polite laughter through her audience. These women, with their designer dresses and carefully maintained smiles, all know exactly what Matteo DeLuca is capable of. They've seen the news reports, heard the whispers.

Yet here they are, exclaiming over baby shower games and pretending this is just another society event.

Matteo himself hovers at the edges of the crowd, ever the protective shadow. He's traded his usual black suit for a dark navy Tom Ford, trying to look softer, more approachable.

More like a father-to-be than one of New York's most dangerous men.

But I see how his eyes constantly scan for threats while attempting to appear relaxed. How his hand occasionally brushes the spot where his shoulder holster would usually rest.

His gaze catches mine and lingers a beat too long, those gray-blue eyes x-raying me. He's cataloging my every movement, looking for signs of betrayal. Signs that his wife's best friend isn't quite as loyal as she appears.

He's right to be suspicious, of course. I've spent the last six months feeding information to his exiled brother, playing a game so dangerous it makes my previous schemes seem laughably simple.

My phone vibrates again. Another text from Mario: *Security rotation changed. Why?*

I don't respond immediately. Mario knows better than to expect instant replies during events like this. Instead, I move through the crowd with practiced ease, noting which families have aligned themselves closer to the DeLucas since Mario's exile. Who's watching whom.

Which alliances might be fracturing under the surface.

"Elena!" Bella's voice cuts through my observations. "Come see the latest ultrasound photos. Look how clear their profiles are!"

I navigate toward her, accepting air kisses and deflecting questions about when I'll finally settle down with "the right man."

If they only knew.

The irony of their matchmaking attempts almost makes me smile.

"They're beautiful," I say, studying the grainy images. And they are, in their own way. Two tiny lives that have no idea they're being born into this world of beautiful facades and lethal undercurrents. "Have you decided on names yet?"

Bella's hazel eyes sparkle. "We're thinking Giovanni for the boy, after Papa." Her voice catches slightly on her father's name, the wound still fresh even after almost a year since her father died. "And Arianna for the girl."

"Perfect choices," I murmur, ignoring the weight of Matteo's stare from across the room. He's watching our interaction like a hawk, probably wondering if I'll suddenly reveal myself as the traitor I am.

But I've learned from the best. Mario taught me how to wear masks so convincing that I sometimes forget they're there. How to turn my position as the overlooked event planner into an advantage.

After all, who pays attention to the woman arranging flowers and coordinating caterers? Who thinks twice about sharing sensitive information in front of someone they consider merely decorative?

"You've outdone yourself with everything," Bella says, squeezing my hand. Her trust makes my chest ache. "I don't know what I'd do without you."

I squeeze back, pushing down the guilt that threatens to surface. "What are best friends for?"

Another buzz from my clutch. I know without looking it's Mario again. He's probably impatient for details about the security changes, about which families are here, about every subtle shift in allegiance that this baby shower represents.

This isn't just a celebration—it's a display of power, a statement about the DeLuca family's strength even after the scandal of Mario's exile.

I excuse myself to check on the kitchen staff, using the moment alone to quickly type: *Increased security due to Calabrese movement in Brooklyn. Full details later.*

His response is immediate: *Careful, little planner. You're playing with fire.*

I almost laugh. As if I don't know that. The memory of our first meeting floods back, as vivid as if it happened yesterday instead of six months ago.

I was working late at my office, finalizing details for a charity gala. The kind of event where blood money gets laundered through silent auctions and champagne toasts. The hallway was dark except for the soft glow from my office, and I remember thinking I should call my car service instead of walking to the parking garage alone.

That's when I saw him—Mario DeLuca, emerging from the shadows like some dark angel in an expertly tailored suit. I recognized him immediately, of course, although I lied to Bella about not knowing him.

Everyone knew about Matteo's exiled brother, the DeLuca who chose revenge over family loyalty. But pictures didn't do him justice. Didn't capture the dangerous grace of his movements or the intensity of his gaze as he studied me.

"Working late, little planner?" His voice was smoke and silk, nothing like Matteo's controlled tones. He moved closer, and I caught the scent of expensive cologne mixed with something darker. "Always so efficient, so ... overlooked."

I should have been terrified. Should have called security or screamed or run. Instead, I felt something wake up inside me—something hungry and ambitious that I'd tried desperately to deny.

"What do you want?" I asked, proud that my voice didn't shake.

His smile was sin itself. "The question is ... what do you want, Elena? To keep playing the perfect society planner? Or to show them all what you're really capable of?"

He reached out, adjusting my sleeve where it had risen slightly. The touch was barely there, but it sent electricity through my entire body. "I've been watching you," he continued. "The way you gather secrets like others collect art. The way you see everything while pretending to see nothing. You're wasted on them."

"I don't know what you're talking about."

But I did. Of course I did.

"Don't you?" He leaned closer, and I caught a glimpse of a scar along his jaw—a reminder that this man was as dangerous as he was compelling. "Tell me, Elena ... don't you ever get tired of being underestimated? Of being treated like part of the decorations while you're smarter than half the men in those rooms?"

I remained silent, but something must have shown in my face because his smile widened. "Let me show you what you could really be," he whispered. "Let me show you how to turn their underestimation into power."

I should have said no. Should have walked away. Instead, I heard myself ask, "And what do you get out of it?"

"Smart girl," he praised, and the approval in his voice shouldn't have thrilled me the way it did. "I get an ally they'll never suspect. And you ... you get to become who you were always meant to be."

He pulled out a burner phone, already programmed with his number. "Your choice, little planner. Stay small and safe, or ..." His eyes traveled over me in a way that made my skin tingle. "... play with fire."

I took the phone.

Now, six months later, I'm in so deep I can barely remember what it felt like to be that other Elena—the one who was content with being overlooked. The one who hadn't yet tasted real power or felt the addictive thrill of Mario's approval.

The party continues around me, a glittering facade of normalcy. Movement near the French doors catches my eye—Bianca, Matteo's eighteen-year-old daughter, slips into the room like a shadow in Balmain jeans.

She has Matteo's striking looks—long dark hair and those piercing blue-gray eyes—despite not being biologically his.

Another secret I'm not supposed to know, though Mario made sure I understood the truth about his brother's heir.

Bella spots her stepdaughter and her whole face lights up. "Bianca! I thought you were staying at school today."

"And miss all this?" Bianca's smile is genuine, though there's still a hint of wariness in her stance. "Besides, I wanted to see the ultrasound photos of my siblings."

The word "siblings" catches slightly in her throat, and I notice how her hand tightens on her Gucci clutch.

Seven months ago, she was an only child, secure in her position as Matteo's heir. Now she's about to become a big sister to twins who will be Matteo's biological children.

It's the kind of subtle family drama I've become expert at noticing.

Bella, either oblivious to or choosing to ignore the tension, pulls Bianca into a gentle hug. "Come see—they're so clear in these new photos. The boy already has your father's profile."

I watch as Bianca's expression softens, the way it always does when someone compares her to Matteo. Blood might not bind them, but love clearly does.

The sight makes my stomach seize with guilt. These are the moments I'll be betraying—these small, precious instances of family connecting despite their complicated past.

I direct servers, adjust flower arrangements, and keep everything running smoothly while gathering intelligence that could destroy it all.

Each smile, each conversation, each perfectly executed detail is both real and fake—just like me.

When Bella catches my eye again across the room, her smile bright with friendship and trust, I force myself to smile back while ignoring the guilt that threatens to choke me. Let them think I'm just an efficient event planner, making sure everything runs smoothly.

Let them underestimate me, like they always have.

Like Mario never did.

Because that's the real danger, isn't it? Not the game itself, but the way Mario sees through every mask I wear. The way he recognized something in me that first night—something hungry and ambitious and tired of playing small.

Something that made him whisper, *"You're wasted on them, little planner. Let me show you what you could really be."*

I check my phone one last time before rejoining the party. His final message makes my pulse quicken: **Miss me yet?**

More than I should. More than is safe for either of us.

But that's a dangerous thought for another time. Right now, I have a baby shower to run, intelligence to gather, and a best friend to betray.

All in a day's work for New York's premier event planner to the criminal elite.

I smooth my suit, check my lipstick, and step back into the spotlight. The champagne flutes continue their warning chime, but I've learned to dance to more dangerous music than this.

2

MARIO

The surveillance photos spread across my mahogany desk like cards in a game I'm finally winning. Elena Santiago stares back from each glossy image—coordinating my brother's perfect baby shower with that mask of efficiency she wears so well.

Her Chanel suit is like armor, every pleat and seam a calculated defense against the world she navigates.

Only I notice the subtle tells others miss. How her fingers tremble slightly when Matteo gets too close, the way her smile never quite reaches her eyes when his precious wife shows off another ultrasound photo.

These little cracks in her performance fascinate me more than they should.

My phone buzzes with her latest intelligence: guest lists, security rotations, the quiet reshuffling of DeLuca investments that screams preparation for war.

She's thorough, my little planner. Always has been.

"O'Connor's getting impatient," my lieutenant mutters, shifting nervously by the floor-to-ceiling windows overlooking Boston Harbor. The late afternoon light catches on the water, reminding me of Elena's eyes—sharp, calculating, seeing everything while pretending to see nothing.

I'm about to respond when my office door opens. Seamus O'Connor's massive frame fills the doorway, his steel-gray hair perfectly styled despite the wind outside.

Despite his designer wares, there's something feral about him—like a wolf playing at being domesticated.

"DeLuca." His Irish brogue fills my office as he settles into the leather chair across from my desk while my lieutenant makes his escape. "Your little sparrow's been busy."

I set down the photos carefully, keeping my expression neutral. "Elena provides useful intelligence."

"Aye, that she does." His cold green eyes study me with predatory interest. "Though I'm hearing whispers she's caught other attention. Young Anthony Calabrese seems quite taken with your source."

Something dark unfurls in my chest at Anthony's name. I'd gotten similar reports, watching him circle Elena like a shark scenting blood. "Anthony's interests are irrelevant," I say with forced casualness.

"Are they?" Seamus pulls out a cigar, not bothering to ask permission before lighting it. Smoke curls between us like poison. "Word is he's been asking questions about her. About her connection to the DeLucas. About why such a pretty party planner spends so much time studying security patterns."

The door opens again, and Siobhan O'Connor glides in, her Valentino dress a stark contrast to her father's old-world menace.

I've watched her struggle these past years, trying to drag the O'Connor empire into the modern era while her father clings to tradition. Where he's all barely contained violence, she's sleek sophistication masking a razor's edge.

Siobhan's been fighting an uphill battle, her brilliant suggestions about cryptocurrency and digital banking constantly rebuffed by Seamus's stubborn adherence to "tried and true methods." She sees the future of their organization—legitimate fronts, technological innovation, untraceable transactions—but Seamus prefers handling things the old way.

With blood and broken bones.

The whispers about her are different from those about her father—where Seamus is predictably brutal, Siobhan is a storm barely contained. Everyone knows she's modernizing operations behind the scenes through her trusted captain, Sean Murphy, while maintaining the perfect image of a society darling.

She's everything the next generation of crime families should be, if only the old guard would loosen their grip on power.

But they share those cold green eyes that miss nothing—eyes I've seen turn glacial right before ordering hits as casually as ordering lunch.

"The Calabrese boy's not asking the right questions," Siobhan says, perching on the arm of her father's chair. "He sees a society planner he can seduce. He should be asking why she's so interested in the DeLucas' shipping manifests."

I keep my face carefully blank, but internally, I'm recalculating. Siobhan's always been sharper than her father, more attuned to the subtle shifts in power that most men overlook.

The fact that she's noticed Elena's particular interests is ... concerning.

The memory of my first meeting with Seamus O'Connor flashes through my mind—five years ago, fresh from my exile, burning with rage after the incident with Bianca. I'd walked into this same office—then his instead of mine—carrying nothing but hatred and a plan for revenge. Seamus had listened to my proposition while methodically breaking a man's fingers in front of me.

The poor bastard had skimmed money from one of the O'Connors' shell companies.

"You see, DeLuca," Seamus had said, his voice casual as bone snapped, "in this family, we believe in direct messages. Your brother's more ... diplomatic approach always struck me as weak."

I'd watched, understanding the display for what it was—both

warning and invitation. By the time the man started begging, Seamus had agreed to back my play against Matteo.

Within a year, I'd earned this office and Seamus's trust, though I never forgot the sound of those breaking fingers.

Now, five years later, Seamus still carries that same air of casual violence. I've seen what happens to those who cross him—the O'Connors might have modernized their operations, but they still prefer the old ways when it comes to handling problems.

"If Anthony's suspicious—" I begin, but Seamus cuts me off with a laugh that cuts like steel.

"Oh, I don't think it's suspicion driving the boy." His eyes gleam with cruel amusement. "I think he sees what we all see—a beautiful woman with access to New York's most powerful families. A way to gain influence through marriage, perhaps?"

The thought of Anthony touching Elena, claiming her, makes my hand clench around my glass. I force myself to relax, noting how Siobhan tracks the movement with interest.

"She's more valuable as an intelligence source," I say smoothly, even as my phone buzzes with another message from Elena.

"Is that all she is?" Seamus leans forward, ash dropping onto my imported carpet. A power play. One that I ignore. "Because my Siobhan's been watching her too. Says there's something different about this one. Something ... hungry."

The description is uncomfortably accurate. I remember Elena's eyes that first night outside her office—sharp, calculating, seeing right through my carefully orchestrated "chance" encounter.

She'd recognized a kindred spirit, someone else who understood what it meant to be overlooked, underestimated.

Siobhan moves to the bar, pouring herself three fingers of the rare Irish whiskey her father imports specially—another power play, treating my office like her own. I've seen her maintain that same elegant poise while ordering the execution of traitors.

Just last month, she hosted a charity gala the same evening she had three of their former associates disappear. The bodies were never found.

"The question," Siobhan interjects, her voice carrying the cultured accent of European boarding schools, "is whether your sparrow's hunger matches yours. Whether her desire for more aligns with our plans for the DeLuca empire."

"She'll play her part." The lie comes easily, though I notice Siobhan's slight smile. Truth is, I'm no longer certain what game Elena's really playing.

Her intelligence is too precise, her understanding of power dynamics too keen for a simple party planner.

My phone lights up again. Elena's message makes my blood run cold: ***Anthony asked me to dinner. Told him I'd think about it. Could be useful.***

"Going to check on your asset?" Seamus's knowing smile sets my teeth on edge.

"The Vitelli situation needs attention," I deflect, shuffling papers on my desk in a deliberate show of dismissal.

"Of course." He rises with surprising grace for his size. "Give the pretty planner my regards. And Mario?" His voice hardens. "Remember our arrangement. The DeLuca empire falls, one way or another."

He steps closer, and I catch the faint scent of blood beneath his expensive cologne. "Don't let a pair of blue eyes distract you from that goal. I'd hate to have to handle this situation ... personally."

The threat hangs heavy in the air. I've seen what happens when Seamus handles things personally. The last person who betrayed his trust ended up as a message to others—pieces of him washing up along the Boston Harbor for weeks.

It had taken me months to earn the O'Connors' trust after my exile, proving myself through increasingly violent tests of loyalty. I'd passed each one, knowing every brutal act was a step closer to my revenge against Matteo.

Siobhan lingers after her father leaves, studying me with those calculating eyes. "You should be careful," she says finally. "Elena Santiago isn't the simple pawn everyone assumes. She reminds me of myself at that age—seeing opportunities others miss, willing to do whatever it takes to claim them."

"Is that a warning or a threat?" I ask quietly, dangerously.

Her smile is all predator. "Consider it ... professional courtesy. After all, we're not so different, you and I. Both of us, fighting for recognition in a world that prefers its old hierarchies."

After she leaves, I pull up the most recent photo of Elena. She's laughing at something Bella said, head thrown back, throat exposed. Beautiful and dangerous as a blade.

Another message follows her first: *Unless you have objections?*

I stare at her words, hearing the challenge beneath them. She's testing me, seeing how I'll react to Anthony's interest. Playing her own game within our game. Just like I played the O'Connors at first, letting them think they were molding me into their perfect weapon against my brother, while I built my own network, my own power base.

The similarities aren't lost on me. Elena's doing exactly what I did —using everyone's assumptions about her to hide her true agenda.

The question is whether she's as willing to pay the price I did. Whether she understands that crossing the O'Connors isn't like crossing the DeLucas. My brother might be cruel when crossed, but Seamus?

Seamus makes cruelty into an art form.

"Careful, little planner," I murmur, already checking flights to New York. "Some games burn everyone who plays them."

I trace the scar on my shoulder where Bella's bullet struck six months ago. My brother's wife showed mercy that day, proving once again that the DeLucas' greatest weakness is their sentiment. Their belief that family means more than power.

Elena Santiago isn't the simple pawn I'd assumed. She's becoming a queen on this chessboard, moving through our world with deadly precision.

The question is: whose game is she really playing?

3

ELENA

I study my reflection in the floor-length mirror, adjusting the drape of my red Versace dress. The silk clings like a lover's touch, the neckline revealing just enough to be enticing while maintaining sophistication. My Cartier diamonds catch the light—a birthday gift from Bella last year that sends another stab of guilt through me.

Anthony Calabrese doesn't deserve this effort, but appearances matter in our world. Every dinner, every carefully orchestrated "chance" encounter is a move in a larger game. I've been sleeping with him for months, not because I feel anything when he touches me, but because his pillow talk reveals more than any surveillance ever could.

He'd asked me to dinner a few days ago. I'd texted Mario about it, testing him, wanting ... something. A reaction. A sign that this thing between us is more than strategy. But Mario had remained frustratingly professional, so I'd initially declined Anthony's invitation.

Then Anthony had been persistent, sending roses to my office, leaving messages that walked the line between charming and demanding. And Mario had gone radio silent for days.

So here I am, spending an obscene amount of time perfecting my smoky eye and ensuring every strand of my blonde hair falls exactly right.

My phone buzzes—the car service is here. I grab my Chanel clutch, checking that both phones are inside. The burner Mario gave me, and my regular iPhone that connects me to my legitimate life. Such as it is.

The elevator descends to the lobby of my Upper East Side apartment building, and I check my reflection one final time in its mirrored walls. There's been a cold front in New York and I shiver. The doorman holds the door as biting wind whips down the street.

I pull my fur-trimmed Fendi coat tighter as I step into the waiting black SUV. The streets gleam wet from an earlier rainfall, reflecting the city lights like scattered diamonds. Through the tinted windows, I watch well-heeled couples hurrying into restaurants and theaters, living their normal lives, untouched by the darkness that flows beneath this city's glittering surface.

My mind drifts to the files I discovered last week—young women arriving on tourist visas that were never used for departure, modeling agencies with more outgoing transfers than incoming profits. The pieces are there, if you know where to look. And I've spent years learning exactly where to look.

The driver's appreciation is obvious as I slide into the back seat, and I allow myself a small smile. I know exactly how good I look. The Louboutins on my feet—a Christmas gift from Matteo that I try not to think about too much—cost a small fortune. The red soles flash with each step like a warning sign.

Another buzz from my clutch. Mario this time: *Playing with fire tonight, little planner?*

My heart thrums treacherously, blood heating just from those few words. Three days of silence and now this? I resist the urge to respond immediately, instead watching the city lights blur past my window.

Eleven Madison Park rises before me, its Art Deco grandeur softened by evening shadows. Inside, the restaurant is a study in understated luxury—soaring ceilings, elegant lines, and the subtle perfume of wealth that comes from knowing you never have to discuss prices.

The restaurant's Michelin stars and impossible-to-get reservations make it the perfect setting for Manhattan's elite to see and be seen.

Anthony chose well—the Calabrese heir making a statement by dining here with the best friend of Giovanni Russo's daughter.

The maître d' greets me by name, but Anthony hasn't arrived yet. I head toward the restroom, my Louboutins silent on the thick carpet. The hallway curves past private dining rooms, each one a potential setting for deals and betrayals disguised as business dinners.

I'm about to round the corner when voices drift from the alcove ahead. I stop short, recognizing that cultured accent despite never having heard it in person before.

"The traditional methods are leaving us exposed, Sean." Siobhan O'Connor's voice carries clear frustration. "The Vietnamese connection alone could be traced through the wire transfers. We need to move to cryptocurrency, create a digital infrastructure that—"

I press myself against the wall, barely breathing. Even with her back to me, Siobhan O'Connor is instantly recognizable—that signature red hair, the Chanel suit. She's arguing with someone—Sean Murphy, I realize, remembering Mario's intelligence about her trusted captain.

"Father won't listen to reason," she continues, pacing the small space. "He's so focused on maintaining the old fucking ways that he can't see how vulnerable they make us. The DeLucas have already started digitizing their legitimate operations. If we don't adapt—"

She stops abruptly, and I slip into a shadowed alcove just as she turns. Through the ornate screen that separates the space, I watch her run a hand through her perfectly styled hair—a gesture of frustration that seems startlingly human for someone I know has ordered deaths as casually as ordering dinner.

"Just ... keep working on those accounts," she says finally. "And Sean? Be careful who you trust with this. Father has eyes everywhere."

The call ends and Siobhan stares at her phone for a long moment. I recognize that look—the same one I see in my mirror some mornings. The face of a woman trying to prove herself in a world that sees her as decorative at best, dangerous at worst.

I wait until Siobhan's heels fade down the hallway before slipping into the bathroom, mind racing. Her conversation with Sean Murphy was ... fascinating. Not just the obvious conflict with her father, but the implications beneath.

The O'Connors are modernizing their operations—or at least, Siobhan's trying to—which means the patterns I've been tracking in the Calabrese records might have an Irish connection after all.

But something doesn't add up. Mario said Seamus O'Connor was old-school, preferred handling things with violence rather than innovation. Yet the financial trails I've been following are sophisticated, modern.

Could Siobhan be operating without her father's knowledge? And if she is, what does that mean for the brewing war between the families?

I'm so lost in thought that I don't immediately register the bathroom door opening and closing. But the distinctive click of the lock sliding home has me whirling around.

Siobhan O'Connor leans against the door, looking every inch the predator who's just cornered her prey. The smile on her face looks friendly, but there's nothing soft about her. Those green eyes are pure ice.

"Elena Santiago," she says, my name rolling off her tongue like she's savoring it. "New York's most valuable event planner to the criminal elite. Though that's not all you are, is it?"

My heart pounds but I keep my voice steady. "I'm not sure what you mean."

"Please." Her laugh is musical but holds no warmth. "Don't insult us both by playing dumb. You're much more interesting than that."

She moves closer, the click of her heels echoing off marble. "Mario's little sparrow, gathering secrets for the exiled DeLuca.

Anthony's latest obsession. And of course"—her smile sharpens—"Bella DeLuca's trusted best friend. My, my ... you do like to play dangerous games."

Ice slides down my spine. How the fuck does she know about me and Mario? We've been so careful.

"The thing about eavesdropping," she continues casually, "is that you never know what other predators might be watching you while you're focused on your prey."

No point denying it. "You knew I was there."

"Of course I did. Just like I know about the discrepancies you've been investigating in the Calabrese shipping records." She examines her manicure—Louboutin rouge, I notice absently. "You're good, I'll give you that. But you're looking at the wrong pieces of the puzzle."

"And you're going to tell me the right ones?" That would be too easy, but I can't help but ask.

Her smile is all teeth. "Now why would I do that? Although ..." She steps closer, and it takes everything in me not to back away. "I will give you some free advice: be very careful which games you choose to play, Elena. Some of them have rules you don't understand yet."

"Is that a threat?"

"More like ... professional courtesy. After all, we're not so different, you and I. Both of us trying to prove ourselves in a world dominated by men. Both of us willing to do whatever it takes to claim what we deserve."

She moves to the door and unlocks it, but pauses before leaving. "Oh, and Elena? When you figure out what's really happening with those shipping manifests ... well, let's just say I'll be *very* interested in what you decide to do with that information."

The door closes behind her with a soft click that somehow sounds like a warning.

I stare at my reflection, noting how pale I've gone beneath my perfect makeup. Siobhan O'Connor just confirmed that something bigger is happening—something that connects the Calabreses, the Irish, and God knows what else.

But her warning felt less like a threat and more like … an invitation? A test?

My phone buzzes with another text from Anthony, asking where I am. I take a deep breath, check my lipstick, and straighten my shoulders.

Time to get back to work.

Anthony rises from his table near the window when he spots me, and my breath catches despite myself. He's beautiful in that polished, privileged way that defines the next generation of Mafia heirs. Nothing like Mario's dangerous edge or Matteo's controlled power.

He's inherited his uncle Johnny's devastating good looks but none of his obvious cruelty—which somehow makes him infinitely more dangerous. His Brioni suit speaks of refinement rather than flash, and his smile holds just enough warmth to be disarming.

"You look stunning as always," he murmurs, dark eyes appreciating how the Versace hugs my curves. I allow myself a calculated blush, even as Mario's warning echoes in my mind: *"Be careful with the Calabrese heir. He's more shark than his uncle ever was."*

But I need this—need the intelligence only Anthony can provide about the Irish mob's movements, about the whispers of trafficking operations that don't quite add up.

The maître d' guides us to an intimate corner table overlooking Madison Square Park. Anthony's hand rests possessively on my lower back as he pulls out my chair. His dark eyes—almost black in the restaurant's dim lighting—appreciate my body as I sit.

"I took the liberty of arranging the tasting menu," he says, adjusting his Calabrese pinky ring—a gesture I've noticed he makes when asserting authority. The ring catches the light, eighteen-karat gold with the family crest, a not-so-subtle reminder of his position. "Chef's adding some special touches just for us."

"How thoughtful." I deliberately widen my eyes, playing into his need to impress. "You always think of everything."

A sommelier materializes at Anthony's elbow. I watch Anthony's performance, the way he examines the label of the 1982 Château Lafite Rothschild with practiced expertise. Everything about him is a study in careful cultivation—from his precisely styled dark hair to the perfect cut of his suit.

Even his cruelty is refined, wrapped in layers of sophistication his uncle Johnny never mastered.

"The '82 is showing beautifully," he explains, swirling the deep red liquid with practiced ease. "Notes of cedar, graphite, and black currant. Though I doubt you know much about fine wine."

I hide my irritation behind a practiced laugh. "That's why I have you to teach me."

The first course arrives—osetra caviar on a cloud of crème fraîche, dotted with gold leaf.

"The caviar's from a small producer in Iran," Anthony explains condescendingly. "We handle their export business, among other things. The Irish have been particularly helpful with certain shipping routes."

I lean forward, letting my dress dip just enough to be distracting. "That sounds complicated. Dealing with so many international interests."

"Nothing I can't handle." He waves away my concern with the casual arrogance of a man who's never heard the word no. "Though the Irish can be ... challenging. Especially now, with their internal politics. Seamus O'Connor's daughter is making waves, trying to *modernize* their operations." He sounds disgusted at the idea.

I file away this confirmation of Siobhan's activities while pretending to be fascinated by the next course—butter-poached lobster with shaved black truffle.

"You make everything sound so exciting," I say, letting my hand brush his as I reach for my wine. "Though it must be dangerous, dealing with families like the O'Connors."

"You don't need to worry your pretty head about that." He squeezes my hand patronizingly. "I keep my business interests ... carefully segregated."

The courses flow like the wine—wagyu beef aged for 120 days, duck breast with cherry gastrique, each dish more extravagant than the last. I play my part perfectly, laughing at his jokes, hanging on his every word, while mentally recording every hint about shipping routes and Irish connections.

"The Vietnamese connections are proving particularly lucrative," he mentions over the cheese course. "Though dealing with multiple ports requires ... creative documentation."

"I can't imagine managing all those details," I say, noting the reference to Vietnam—another piece of the trafficking puzzle clicking into place.

"That's why I have people for that." His smile doesn't reach his eyes. "Speaking of which, I'm hosting a gathering next week. Several international partners will be there. You should come."

I recognize the opportunity—and the danger—in the invitation. "I'd love to, but you know how busy I am with events this time of year ..."

"Make time." His tone holds just enough edge to remind me who he is. "I want to show you off."

The dessert arrives—a gold-leafed chocolate creation that looks ridiculously expensive. Anthony places his hand over mine, his thumb tracing circles on my wrist.

"Would you like to continue this evening at my place?" His dark eyes hold that perfect mix of desire and warmth. "I have an excellent bottle of Macallan 25 I've been saving for a special occasion."

I pretend to consider it, biting my lower lip in calculated hesitation. "Well ... I really should be getting home ..."

"Please?" He brings my hand to his lips. "I've missed you these past few days."

I give him my best coy smile, ignoring the way my stomach churns at his touch. "Well, when you ask so nicely ..."

He signals for the check, never taking his eyes off me. I can feel his security team shifting into position, preparing to escort us to his penthouse. If he notices how my hand trembles slightly as he helps me with my coat, he probably attributes it to anticipation rather than the adrenaline of being so close to information I need.

Let him think I'm just another society girl dazzled by his power and charm. It's safer that way.

Hours later, in his penthouse overlooking Central Park, I let him think he's seducing me while memorizing every detail of the papers visible on his desk.

As Anthony's hands move over my body, his touch is precise, methodical, but somehow detached, as if following a routine he's done countless times before. He peels off my clothes with efficiency, as though stripping away layers of fabric rather than barriers between us. The way his fingers glide over my skin lacks any spark, any warmth—just a mechanical motion. There's no tenderness in his gaze, just a calculated focus, as if he's performing a task that has nothing to do with me.

I try to push aside the thoughts of Mario, but they sneak in like an electric current, reminding me of the connection I crave, the way his texts make my heart race, the anticipation that builds with every word he types.

A single message from Mario sends a surge of energy through me, making my pulse quicken in a way that Anthony's touch never has.

When Anthony lifts me effortlessly onto his desk, I can't help but stiffen slightly at the abruptness, the lack of care. The wood is cold against my back, the sharp edges of the desk pressing into my skin, a stark contrast to the warmth I long for. His lips finally find mine, but the kiss is clinical, without the urgency or the heat I yearn for. It's as though he's following a script, just another step in a process rather than a genuine expression of desire.

I need this access to Anthony. Three weeks ago, I discovered discrepancies in the Calabrese shipping manifests—luxury clothing imports that didn't match any known designer's production schedule, travel agencies with more outgoing flights than incoming ones, modeling contracts that led to dead ends.

The patterns were subtle, but they reminded me of something I'd seen in the DeLuca records before Mario's exile. The same careful misdirection, the same gaps that looked random unless you knew exactly what to look for.

The Irish mob's movements are tied to it somehow. Mario's mentioned the O'Connors have been expanding their operations, but their old-school methods don't align with the sophisticated financial trails I've been tracking.

Someone's modernizing their approach to human trafficking, hiding it behind legitimate businesses, and I need to know who. The DeLucas would never be involved in trafficking—it's one of Matteo's hard lines—but the Calabreses have no such scruples.

I've got a job to do—one that might finally prove I'm worth more than just planning parties and playing peacemaker. If only the guilt about betraying Bella's trust didn't feel like it was choking me with every fake moan, every calculated arch of my back.

My burner phone buzzes in my discarded clutch. I already know it's Mario, probably watching through his network of surveillance. Let him watch. Let him see exactly what this game costs.

Anthony's hands grip my hips, pulling me closer as he enters me with a slow, deliberate force. The world outside of this room fades, and all I can focus on is the lack of heat between us, the rhythm of his movements as he claims me. I try to drown out the lingering thoughts of Mario, but every kiss, every touch from Anthony is an empty echo compared to the wild connection I felt in just a few words from Mario.

I close my eyes, pretending it's someone else's touch lighting up my skin. Someone with dangerous grace and knowing eyes, who saw past my perfect facade from the very beginning.

"Some games burn everyone who plays them," Mario had warned me. Good thing I've always liked playing with fire.

4

MARIO

The surveillance photos spread across my desk like evidence of betrayal. Elena leaving Anthony's penthouse, that red Versace now wrinkled in ways that tell their own story.

Her perfectly styled hair is mussed, lipstick smeared just enough to confirm what happened behind those penthouse doors.

In one photo, she's adjusting the strap of her dress where it had clearly been hastily fixed. Another shows Anthony's hand on her lower back as he escorts her to the waiting car, his fingers splayed possessively against the silk.

Something dark and primitive rises in my chest. The desire to fly to New York and put a bullet between Anthony Calabrese's eyes is almost overwhelming.

I know this was the plan—hell, I encouraged her to gather intel through whatever means necessary. But seeing the evidence, imagining his hands on her ...

A knock at my door breaks through the red haze of my thoughts. "What?" I snarl.

Dante Moretti enters, managing to look both perfectly put together and casual in his Armani suit. My most trusted enforcer since my exile, he's the only one who knows the full scope of my plans. He's objectively handsome—all sharp angles and dark eyes—but I couldn't care less about that right now.

"Your brother has increased security around the DeLuca compound," Dante reports. "Isabella's due date is getting closer."

"How touching." I shuffle the photos into a folder, but not before Dante catches a glimpse.

"The Calabrese heir seems quite taken with your asset," he remarks wryly.

I shoot him a warning look. "What else?"

"Had to handle a situation with one of O'Connor's men. Got too curious about our shipping operations through Boston Harbor." Dante's casual tone belies the implications. "He won't be asking questions anymore."

I nod approval, but my mind is still on the photos. On Elena in Anthony's arms.

Another knock. This time it's my lieutenant—one of O'Connor's picks, which irritates me on principle. His presence is a constant reminder of my tenuous position here in Boston.

"The Irish want confirmation about the shipping routes," he drones in that nasally voice I've grown to fucking hate.

"Get me the jet." I'm already reaching for my coat. "Tell O'Connor I'll handle it personally."

My lieutenant splutters. "But Mr. O'Connor specifically requested—"

"Get. Out." I snap, and the glacial tone of my voice is enough to get the lieutenant to flee the room.

The private airfield is quiet at this hour, late fall wind whipping across the tarmac. My phone hasn't stopped buzzing with messages from O'Connor's people, but they can fuck themselves. I have more pressing matters to handle.

As we reach cruising altitude, I start reviewing intelligence reports on my tablet. Something catches my eye—a pattern in Sean Murphy's movements that I hadn't noticed before.

Over the past three months, he's been making regular trips between Boston and Singapore, always staying at hotels known for their discreet handling of cryptocurrency transactions.

The timing aligns perfectly with large transfers moving through shell companies I know Siobhan controls.

I pull up older reports, comparing them with what I already know about Siobhan's attempts to modernize the O'Connor empire behind her father's back.

Sean isn't just managing her shadow accounts—he's building an entire parallel operation. Digital banking, crypto transfers, legitimate tech companies that could launder millions without leaving a trace.

If Seamus ever discovered the full scope of what his daughter's planning ...

The implications are fascinating. Siobhan's not just trying to modernize—she's preparing for a complete takeover. Sean Murphy isn't merely her trusted captain; he's the architect of her future empire.

Which makes him either a valuable ally or a dangerous loose end.

"We're beginning our descent into New York, sir," the pilot's voice breaks through my thoughts.

I know I'm playing with fire coming back to New York. Matteo's warning was explicit: stay the fuck away or face consequences. But Elena's games with Anthony Calabrese have pushed me past caring about my brother's threats.

I look out the window as the familiar skyline comes into view. Something in my chest tightens at the sight. New York. My city. My home.

Not that fucking mausoleum in Boston where Seamus O'Connor plays at being king.

The lights of Manhattan glitter like scattered diamonds in the darkness. Each borough, each neighborhood holds memories—both the ones I cherish and the ones I've spent years trying to forget.

Somewhere down there, Elena is probably still with Anthony, playing her role perfectly while gathering intel that could destroy us all. The thought makes my hands clench.

My driver is waiting when I deplane, the black SUV's engine

already running. Let Matteo's spies report my movements. My brother's threats mean nothing compared to the game Elena's playing.

"The Midtown route," I tell the driver. Then, because I'm feeling particularly reckless, "Actually no. First, go past the DeLuca compound."

We drive through the city I still know better than my own heartbeat. Every street corner, every building holds echoes of who I used to be. Before exile. Before betrayal. Before I became the monster my brother always feared I would.

We leave the city and head towards the suburbs where old money rises with its stone walls and security gates.

The compound appears through the trees—Matteo's fortress, where he plays happy family with his wife and unborn twins. Where Bianca probably still has nightmares about the warehouse where I held her at gunpoint.

The memory triggers another, older and sharper: being eight years old, Giuseppe's latest "training session" about to begin.

"Family tradition," Giuseppe said, his gold rings catching the light as he checked the ropes binding us to our chairs. The basement air was thick with fear and anticipation. "Every DeLuca son must learn to escape any situation. To survive any trap."

Matteo sat in the chair next to mine, his face already set in that determined expression I'd grow to hate.

He was better at this—always had been. His fingers were longer, more nimble. He could work the knots faster.

"First one free gets this." Giuseppe held up a thick envelope. "Second one ..." His smile was cruel as he pulled out his belt. "Well, we need motivation, don't we?"

The ropes were tight enough to cut off circulation. Professional knots, the kind Giuseppe learned in his less legitimate business dealings. I worked them until my wrists bled, but Matteo was already slipping free.

Always fucking Matteo, perfect son, perfect heir.

The belt came down and I didn't scream. I never screamed. But later, in the darkness of the basement where losers spent the night, I promised myself that one day I'd make them all pay.

"Weakness must be burned out," Giuseppe would say while training us. The bruises and broken bones were lessons, he claimed. Making us stronger. Better. Worthy of the DeLuca name.

But somehow, it was always Matteo who earned that worthiness. Matteo who got the praise, the rewards, the recognition. I got the basement, the belt, the constant reminder that I was second best.

We return back to the city and the car drops me at Elena's Upper East Side building—all prewar luxury and old money pretension. The doorman's too easy to get past; I'll have to talk to her about security. The lobby's Mediterranean stone floors reflect the glittering chandelier, wealthy residents in designer clothes barely sparing me a glance.

They have no idea a predator walks among them, wearing civilized clothing like a costume.

In the elevator, I study my reflection in the mirrored walls. I look like them, in my custom suit and Italian leather shoes. But underneath, I'm still that boy in the basement, turning pain into power, weakness into weapon.

But I see what they don't—the street fighter Giuseppe DeLuca carved out of his bastard second son through blood and pain.

The elevator opens onto Elena's floor. The hallway stretches out in elegant cream and gold, plush carpeting muffling my steps. Her door is ridiculously easy to breach—Giuseppe's lessons still serve their purpose, even if thinking about him makes me want to put my fist through a wall.

Inside, the faint smell of Chanel No. 5 assaults my senses. My mother's signature scent, before she decided being Giuseppe DeLuca's mistress wasn't worth the consequences and abandoned her bastard son to his tender mercies.

The legitimate Mrs. DeLuca—Matteo's precious mother—had made sure I never forgot my place. The whore's son. The mistake. Right up until the day of her "tragic accident."

Giuseppe and Matteo never figured out who had tampered with

her brakes. They blamed another family, launching a war that reshaped New York's underworld.

By the time Sophia appeared in our lives, the blood had barely dried.

The apartment is exactly what I expected from surveillance photos—vast and bright, with floor-to-ceiling windows overlooking the city. Swedish furniture in cool grays and blues, original signed fashion photographs on the walls.

Very Elena—elegant but with hidden edges.

The Italian marble dining table catches my eye, specifically the bullet holes marring its surface. A souvenir from Johnny Calabrese's failed attempt to use Elena as leverage.

Shame Bella got to him first—I would have made his death so much more creative.

I run my finger over the chips in Elena's marble table, remembering how Matteo's first wife had looked at me with the same contempt as his mother. Like mother, like daughter-in-law.

Both of them so certain of their position, their superiority.

Both of them equally dead.

I pour myself a drink from Elena's bar and settle in to wait. Twenty minutes later, I hear her key in the lock.

She freezes when she spots me, but recovers quickly. Always so composed, my little planner.

"You're supposed to be in Boston," she says, kicking off her Louboutins, her toes grounding her into the floor.

"And *you're* supposed to be gathering intelligence, not fucking the enemy." The words come out harsher than intended, betraying an emotion I refuse to name. Anthony's cologne still clings to her skin, making my fingers itch for a trigger.

Her blue eyes narrow at my tone, that brilliant mind already calculating my response. Understanding dawns in her expression, followed by something that looks dangerously like satisfaction.

"Jealous, Mario?" She moves closer, all feline grace and deadly perception. "I thought that wasn't part of our arrangement."

I catch her wrist before she can retreat, feeling her pulse race beneath my fingers. "You're playing a dangerous game, Elena. Anthony Calabrese isn't just another society playboy. If he discovers what you're really after—"

"Then what?" She doesn't pull away, and the heat between us crackles like a live wire. "Isn't that exactly what we want? For them to underestimate me? To see just another ambitious society girl?"

Her free hand comes up to trace the scar on my shoulder—the one my sister-in-law's bullet left. "After all, isn't that how you taught me to play with the big shots?"

Silence.

"You want to know what *I* learned last night?" Her voice drops to a whisper, taunting. "About the Vietnamese connections? About what your Irish friends are really planning?"

I snarl, pushing her against the wall before I can stop myself. "You have no idea what game you're really playing, Elena."

"Don't I?" Her smile is razor-sharp. "Anthony was very ... informative after a few drinks. He had quite a lot to say about the O'Connors. About Seamus's daughter. About you."

My hand tightens on her wrist. "Careful."

"Or what?" She leans closer, her breath ghosting across my lips. "You'll punish me? Like Giuseppe punished your mother? Like you punished Matteo's—"

I catch her throat with one hand before she can finish that sentence. "You're playing with fire, little planner."

"Good." Her pulse races under my palm, but her eyes are triumphant. "I was starting to think Boston had made you soft."

Her words hit their mark. She knows exactly how to push my buttons, how to use my hatred of exile against me. Just like she knows mentioning my mother, mentioning Matteo's mother, will make me lose control.

The jealousy churning in my gut is a weakness Giuseppe would have beaten out of me.

But then again, Elena has always had a way of making me forget my careful controls.

5

ELENA

The tension between us coils like a serpent ready to strike. Mario's hand is still clamped around my throat, his grip possessive rather than painful. In the dim light of my apartment, he looks exactly like what he is—dangerous, devastating, and barely controlled.

His pupils are blown wide, turning his eyes almost black. A muscle ticks in his sharp jaw, and his suit can't hide the predator beneath. He's beautiful in that distinctly DeLuca way, but where Matteo's looks are classical, Mario's features have a rougher edge that makes my pulse race.

I open my mouth to push him further, to see just how far his jealousy will drive him. I want to tell him exactly what Anthony whispered in my ear last night, how his hands felt on my skin, how—

Taylor Swift's "Bad Blood" shatters the moment. Bianca's ringtone.

Mario's grip loosens just enough for me to reach my phone. "B? What's wrong?" I ask, if not a bit breathlessly.

"Bella's in labor," his niece's voice carries barely contained panic. "Dad's losing it. We need you at Mount Sinai. Now. Bella needs you."

My heart stutters. It's too soon. "How far apart are the contractions?"

"Too close. Elena, *please*. Dad's about to fucking tear this place apart, and Bella won't stop crying about it being too early."

"I'm on my way. Try to keep your father from terrorizing the hospital staff," I say hurriedly, already planning my route to the hospital.

"Hurry."

I end the call and meet Mario's intense gaze, knowing he heard the entire conversation. "Bella's in labor. The twins are coming early."

He releases me immediately, stepping back with fluid grace. We move in perfect synchronization as I head to my bedroom, years of event planning making me efficient even in crisis. I'm already dialing the hospital's chief of staff—a man who owes me several favors—while letting the red Versace pool at my feet.

"Enjoying the show?" I ask as Mario follows me into the bedroom, leaning against the doorframe like he owns the space.

"Just making sure you don't waste time reapplying that lipstick Anthony smeared off."

My pulse jumps at his tone. I step into a simple black Stella McCartney dress, deliberately ignoring how his eyes track every movement as I quickly fix my hair into a sleek ponytail.

He doesn't offer to leave, and I don't ask him to. Instead, he shadows me to my car. His hand reaches the door handle just as mine does, and electricity crackles between us as our eyes meet.

"You can't come with me," I say, hating how breathless I sound.

His dark eyes study me for a moment, something dangerous flickering in their depths. "No," he agrees, voice low and intimate. "But I'll be watching. I always am."

He walks away, leaving me unsettled and off-balance—exactly as he intended.

The city blurs past my windows as I drive like a woman possessed. Guilt churns in my stomach, mixing with the remnants of whatever just happened with Mario. Bella trusts me, loves me like a sister, and here I am sleeping with her family's enemy—the nephew of the man who killed her mother and father—while feeding information to her husband's exiled brother.

The same brother who once held her stepdaughter at gunpoint.

But it's more complicated than that. The intelligence I gathered from Anthony last night, combined with what I overheard from Siobhan O'Connor ... Something bigger is happening. Something that could destroy everything Bella and Matteo have built.

I take the corner onto Fifth Avenue too fast, my thoughts racing faster than my car. The Vietnamese shipping connections, the Irish modernization efforts, the way Siobhan watches everything from the shadows while her father clings to outdated methods.

And Mario, always Mario, pulling strings I'm only beginning to understand.

The hospital rises before me, its imposing facade a stark reminder of what's at stake. The twins weren't supposed to come for another two and a half months. If anything happens to them, to Bella ...

The hospital corridor feels endless as I rush toward the maternity ward, my Manolo Blahniks clicking against sterile tiles. Antonio materializes from the shadows, his presence a reminder that even here, the DeLuca empire never sleeps.

He buzzes me through security, and I find the waiting room full of tense DeLucas. Matteo paces like a caged predator, his usual control fractured around the edges.

His tie is loosened, dark hair disheveled from running his hands through it. He looks exactly like what he is—one of New York's most dangerous men, stripped of his power by something he can't control.

"Dad, please," Bianca pleads, her face tight with worry. "The doctors said—"

"Which room?" I cut in.

"307," Bianca says, relief evident in her voice. "Thank God you're here."

Matteo's eyes lock onto mine, studying me with an intensity that makes me wonder if he somehow knows about Mario's visit. But there's no time to analyze his suspicions.

I find Bella's room easily, but nothing prepares me for the sight of my best friend in pain. Her face is flushed, those artist's eyes bright with tears and trust I don't deserve.

"Elena," she sobs, reaching for my hand. "It's too early. The twins—they can't come yet."

"Hey, hey." I squeeze her hand, pushing down my guilt. "Everything's going to be fine. You've got the best doctors in New York."

"I kicked Matteo out," she confesses between pants. "He was driving me crazy with his hovering."

I can't help but laugh. "Only you would dare kick the great Matteo DeLuca out of anywhere."

"He was counting my contractions like he was timing a hit." A weak smile crosses her beautiful face. "I told him if he didn't stop, I'd name both babies after Mario just to spite him."

The joke hits too close to home, but I force myself to smile. "That's my girl. Always knowing exactly where to stick the knife."

"I'm so glad you're here," she whispers, squeezing my hand. "I don't know what I'd do without you, Elena. You're the sister I never had."

Before guilt can choke me completely, Bella's face contorts in pain. The monitors start screaming, and suddenly the room is full of doctors and nurses.

Matteo bursts in, his face thunderous, but I barely notice.

A nurse practically shoves me out of the room as more medical staff rush in. My whole body trembles as I lean against the wall, praying to a god I stopped believing in years ago.

Please, not Bella. Not the babies. Not when I haven't had the chance to make things right.

The sound of medical equipment and urgent voices continues to filter through, muffled but no less frightening.

My heels seem to mock me now, their confident click-click against the linoleum floor transformed into something uncertain and faltering. The hallway stretches before me like a tunnel, its fluorescent lights casting everything in that particular shade of hospital green that makes even the healthy look sick.

A janitor's cart stands abandoned near the wall, the smell of industrial cleaner mixing with the ever-present antiseptic that seems to seep from the very walls.

I pass Room 305, where a young mother cradles her newborn, her family's soft cooing and congratulations drifting out. Room 306 holds another woman in labor, the rhythmic beeping of fetal monitors a stark reminder of what's at stake.

Each step feels like walking through water, my body moving on autopilot while my mind races with possibilities I can't bear to consider.

A nurse hurries past, her scrubs brushing my arm, and I press myself against the wall to let her pass. The contact jolts me back to awareness—to the weight of my phone in my jacket pocket, to the way my hands won't stop trembling, to the copper taste of anxiety in my mouth.

I realize I've been biting my lip hard enough to draw blood.

I continue walking, each step a reminder of how far away I am from being able to help. I'm good at solving problems, at making things happen, at pulling strings and calling in favors.

But here, in this sterile corridor with its too-bright lights and whispered prayers, none of that matters. I can't plan or manipulate or scheme my way out of this. I can only walk, one foot in front of the other, back to where Bianca waits.

A cleaning cart squeaks past, and I catch my reflection in its metal surface—my carefully applied makeup still perfect, my black dress unwrinkled, my ponytail sleek and professional. I look exactly like what I am: someone playing a part, wearing clothes made of designer labels and perfect poise.

Someone whose best friend is fighting for her babies' lives while carrying the weight of too many secrets.

The waiting room appears ahead, its uncomfortable chairs and old magazines a tableau of suspended anxiety. Bianca's figure comes into view, and the sight of her—so young, so scared, trying so hard to be strong—makes my chest ache. She looks up as I approach, and I force my face into something resembling composure.

For all her attempts at being a hardened DeLuca, right now she's just a terrified eighteen-year-old. Her clothes—the Saint Laurent leather jacket she probably borrowed from Bella's closet—can't hide how young she looks huddled in the uncomfortable hospital chair.

"What's happening?" Her voice cracks. "I heard the monitors, and Dad ... I've never seen him move so fast."

I can't lie to her. Not about this. "There were complications. The monitors started screaming, and—"

"No." Bianca covers her face with trembling hands. "Dad can't lose them. He can't lose Bella."

She looks up at me, suddenly seeming so young. "You don't understand, Elena. I've never seen him like this—happy, actually *happy*. Our house finally feels like a home." Her voice catches. "It finally feels like I have a real family."

Tears well in my eyes, but I blink them back. My phone buzzes with a text from Anthony: **Missing you already. Dinner tomorrow? I have something special planned.**

I ignore it, irritation flaring. Like I care about his plans when my best friend could be losing her babies.

"I'm getting us coffee," I declare, needing to feel useful.

Bianca stares at me, as if unable to comprehend the sentence I just uttered. "The coffee here is shit," she finally manages to get out.

"I don't care," I respond, marching away.

The fluorescent-lit hallway stretches endlessly, the squeak of nurses' shoes and beeping monitors creating a symphony of anxiety. I pass other dramas unfolding—worried families huddled in corners, doctors delivering news both good and bad, a young mother crying over a newborn. The sharp scent of antiseptic can't quite mask the underlying smell of fear.

I find the coffee machine and quickly pour us two cups in white Styrofoam containers before walking back, keeping my eyes straight ahead.

Bianca accepts the terrible coffee wordlessly. Now we wait.

I pull out my phone, needing distraction. An encrypted email catches my eye—communications between Sean Murphy and several major fintech companies that my tracking algorithm flagged.

Interesting.

He's been meeting with legitimate banking institutions, discussing blockchain integration and digital payment systems. There are references to Singapore accounts, cryptocurrency wallets, everything needed to move millions without leaving a trace.

These aren't just modernization efforts; they're a complete overhaul of how the Irish handle their money. If Murphy succeeds, it could change everything about how we track their operations.

No wonder Siobhan trusts him so completely.

Time crawls by until finally, after what feels like years, Matteo emerges. His tie is completely undone now, hanging loose around his neck. I've never seen New York's most feared don look so utterly drained. The invincible Matteo DeLuca suddenly seems ... human.

Bianca and I jump up simultaneously.

"Bella?" I ask weakly, my heart pounding.

"She's stable," he says, voice rough. "They stopped the labor. She'll need to stay a few days for observation, then strict bed rest until she's closer to term."

Bianca launches herself at her father, sobbing into his chest. The relief flooding through me is so intense I have to grip the chair to stay upright.

But the hollow feeling in my chest won't leave. The weight of secrets and lies suddenly feels suffocating.

"I need air," I mumble, already moving toward the exit.

Mount Sinai's garden is one of those hidden Manhattan treasures, tucked away from the chaos of Fifth Avenue. Stone pathways wind between carefully maintained beds of roses and hydrangeas, their blooms stubbornly holding on despite the chill in the air.

A small fountain trickles nearby, its gentle sound almost masking the city noise beyond the hospital walls.

I find a quiet corner near a cluster of white roses, letting the evening air clear my head. The sun is setting behind the hospital building, painting the garden in soft golds and lengthening shadows.

For a moment, I try to sort through the tangle of emotions choking me—relief about Bella and the twins, guilt about my deceptions, that electric tension with Mario that won't leave my skin.

Movement catches my eye as I drift deeper into the garden. Of course he's here. Mario leans against one of the garden's stone pillars, cigarette smoke curling like accusation in the air.

I should be surprised to see him, but I'm not. He's always watching, always one step ahead.

"Playing the devoted friend?" His tone holds something almost gentle. Understanding, maybe. Or recognition of how complicated loyalty becomes when you're betraying the people you love.

"She trusts me," I whisper, the words tasting like ash. "They *all* trust me."

Except maybe Matteo.

Mario's laugh rings hollow as he stubs out his cigarette. "Trust is weakness in our world, little planner. You know that better than most." But when he moves closer, his hand coming up to cup my face, there's nothing weak about the electricity that surges between us. "The question is ... do you trust me?"

The kiss that's been building between us all evening hovers like smoke in the air. I lean forward, drawn by that magnetic DeLuca pull I've been fighting for months. His breath fans across my lips, and—

"Elena?" Bianca's voice cuts through the garden like a blade. "Dad's asking for you. Something about the security protocols ..."

I step back from Mario as if burned, straightening my jacket with hands that don't quite shake. His knowing smile follows me back into the hospital, a promise or a warning of what's to come.

6

MARIO

The hospital garden fades into background noise as I watch Elena disappear back inside, her Stella McCartney dress a flash of black against institutional white. The ghost of her skin beneath my palm lingers—soft but electric, like everything about her. The cool air carries a bite that does nothing to cool the heat she left behind.

Her scent stays with me too, something expensive and subtle that makes my blood heat. Not Chanel No. 5, thank fuck. She's too smart for *that* particular mistake. Too smart to wear the same perfume as half the society wives in Manhattan, the same scent my mother wore.

Elena's is something uniquely her own—lavender and danger and promises she'll probably break.

I shouldn't still be here. It's too risky, too close to the family that cast me out. But something about the way she almost kissed me keeps me rooted in place. Even through the hospital's tinted windows, I can imagine her now—smoothing my brother's ruffled feathers about security protocols while hiding how her hands still tremble from our almost moment.

Ever the efficient event planner, even with her pulse racing beneath her perfect facade.

A security guard passes nearby, his eyes sliding over me without recognition. Good. I paid enough to ensure the hospital's head of security would conveniently forget to patrol certain areas of the hospital. The same way Elena ensures certain guest lists mysteriously change at the last minute, certain conversations happen in exactly the right places.

A flash of memory hits me hard: another hospital, another night. Twelve-year-old Bianca unconscious in a warehouse, my gun pressed to her temple.

The weight of the Glock 19, the smell of sea salt from the shipping containers, the way her small body felt so fragile against my chest.

Giuseppe would have been proud of how steady my hand was.

The look in Matteo's eyes when he found her in that shipping container—that mix of rage and terror that proved blood meant nothing compared to chosen family.

My own brother was ready to put a bullet between my eyes to protect a child that wasn't even his.

The same look I saw in Elena's eyes tonight, watching Bella trust her completely while knowing she'd betrayed that trust a thousand times over.

Fascinating, really. As much as Elena plays the game, she's still soft inside. That guilt will eat her alive if she's not careful. I felt no such remorse holding Bianca at gunpoint. Giuseppe taught us early that sentiment was weakness, and for once, the old bastard was right.

Our father made sure both his sons understood that power was the only currency that mattered.

Matteo rejected those lessons. Found himself a new family, built something almost legitimate. But I learned them too well, carved them into my bones along with the scars from Giuseppe's cigars and belts.

Time to leave while I have the chance. The O'Connors will be expecting updates, and Matteo's security has probably already reported my presence. Let my brother rage about territorial violations —I have more pressing concerns. Like how Elena's skin felt beneath my touch, how her breath caught when I moved closer …

Fuck. I need to focus. The Irish situation is getting complicated, especially with Siobhan's quiet rebellion against her father's methods.

Seamus O'Connor clings to tradition while his daughter builds something new in the shadows.

Smart girl. Smarter than her father realizes.

And Elena's intelligence about Anthony's shipping operations suggests something bigger brewing beneath the surface.

The Vietnamese connections, the cryptocurrency movements, the way certain accounts keep linking back to Singapore ... It's all connected, if I can just see the fucking pattern clearly.

Numbers and codes dance behind my eyes—blockchain transactions, shipping manifests, bank accounts that appear and dissolve like smoke. Somewhere in that digital maze is the key to everything Siobhan's building.

I cut through the hospital's service corridor, muscle memory keeping me away from security cameras. The smell changes from antiseptic to motor oil and concrete dust as I approach the parking structure. My Italian leather shoes make no sound on the utilitarian flooring—a habit ingrained since childhood.

Giuseppe might have been a bastard, but he taught us well: silence is survival.

The garage entrance yawns before me, a cathedral of concrete and fluorescent light. The evening shift is ending, creating a steady stream of medical staff heading to their cars. Perfect cover.

I blend in with practiced ease, just another shadow among many. The garage holds that particular cocktail of urban scents—exhaust fumes, dried oil stains, the metallic tang of emergency stairwells, and underneath it all, that peculiar damp concrete smell that all parking structures share.

A doctor's Range Rover chirps as it's locked. An ambulance siren wails in the distance. The sounds echo off concrete pillars, creating a symphony of urban white noise. Level P2 is quieter, the lights spaced further apart, creating pockets of darkness perfect for someone who doesn't want to be seen.

That's when I catch the movement—a flash of black fabric, the whisper of expensive heels.

Elena.

She glides like silk through the shadows, seeking refuge between two concrete pillars. Even here, in this utilitarian space, she carries herself like royalty. The emergency lights cast blue-white shadows across her face, turning her into something almost otherworldly.

I adjust my stride, making each step silent despite the concrete floor. An art perfected in warehouse raids and midnight executions, now used to stalk a different kind of prey. But it doesn't matter how quiet I am—she's already sensed me. I watch her spine straighten, her shoulders squaring in that familiar way. Like a queen preparing to pass judgment, even with her back turned.

The distance between us crackles with electricity. She doesn't move, doesn't turn, but I can see the slight tension in her neck, the way her fingers curl at her sides.

Prey recognizing predator.

Or maybe predator recognizing predator—with Elena, it's hard to tell sometimes.

My little planner, who plays both sides so perfectly. Even now, probably calculating angles and exits, weighing risks and rewards. I've watched her do this dance for months through surveillance photos and encrypted messages. But nothing compares to watching her in person, especially when she thinks she's alone.

"You should be in Boston," she says without turning, but her voice holds none of its usual control. The slight tremor betrays her—desire or fear or both.

With Elena, it's always both.

I almost smile. Such bravado from my little planner, especially after our confrontation in her apartment, after our moment in the garden. The memory of her throat beneath my palm makes my fingers itch to touch her again.

"You shouldn't be playing games you can't win." I move closer, drawn by that magnetic pull that's been building since she first caught my eye outside her office. Back when she was just an event planner, before I recognized the predator behind her perfect smile.

"Anthony Calabrese, the Irish mob, my brother's empire—you're juggling lit matches, little planner."

She spins to face me then, and the fire in her eyes steals my breath. Gone is the polished professional who manages New York's elite. This is the real Elena—dangerous and desperate and so fucking beautiful it hurts.

"I learned from the best," she spits, closing the distance between us. Her perfume hits me again, mixing with the lingering scent of hospital antiseptic. "Isn't this exactly what you wanted? Someone on the inside, someone they'd never suspect—"

I cut her off with a kiss that's been six months in the making.

There's no preamble, no hesitation—just pure, raw need. Our lips crash together like a storm breaking, her sharp gasp swallowed by my hunger. It's not gentle; it's a battle of dominance, all teeth and tongue and unspoken emotions that have simmered for too long.

Her lips are soft but unyielding, matching me stroke for stroke, her hands fisting in my hair as though she's as desperate to taste me as I am to devour her.

I press her against the cold concrete wall, the unforgiving surface contrasting with the blazing heat between us. Her gasp sends a shiver down my spine, but I'm too far gone to slow down. My hands slide down to her hips, gripping them tightly as though she might vanish if I let go. The expensive fabric of her dress clings to her curves, moving against my skin as I explore every inch of her.

She tastes like cheap hospital coffee, the kind you choke down just to survive, but beneath that, there's a flavor that's all her own—dangerous and addictive, like the sharp sting of whiskey on a cold night. Something primitive in me roars at finally claiming what I've been watching for so long. Her body fits against mine perfectly, all soft curves and sharp edges.

When I bite her lower lip, dragging my teeth slowly across the plump flesh, she moans, a low, throaty sound that echoes in the empty space around us and nearly undoes me. Her nails dig into my scalp, sending sparks of pleasure-pain through me as she pulls me impossibly closer, her body molding against mine like we were made for this moment.

Her legs shift, brushing against mine, and I take the hint, lifting her effortlessly until her thighs are wrapped around my waist. She gasps against my mouth, her chest heaving as I press into her, pinning her firmly in place with the weight of my body.

My lips trail fire along her jawline, down the column of her throat. Her pulse thrums beneath my tongue, wild and frantic, matching the pounding of my heart. I drag my teeth against her skin, not hard enough to mark but enough to leave her trembling. Her hands clutch at my shoulders, pulling me closer, as though she can't bear even an inch of distance between us.

"Elena," I growl against her skin, the sound rough and unrecognizable even to myself.

Her fingers tug me back up, and our mouths collide again, fiercer this time, more desperate. Her lips are swollen now, her taste darker, richer, like something forbidden. The rhythm of our kiss turns chaotic, a mess of tongues and teeth and ragged breaths, but neither of us cares.

Her body arches into me, her curves pressing against every hard edge of mine. I grip her tighter, my fingers tracing the curve of her waist and the dip of her spine, committing her to memory as though I could forget. She moans again, softer this time, a sound that vibrates through my chest and sets my nerves on fire.

When we finally break apart for air, she's a mess of contradictions —her cheeks flushed, her perfect ponytail disheveled, strands falling around her face like a halo. Her eyes are wild, pupils blown wide with desire, and her lips—those perfect lips—are kiss-swollen and glistening.

"This wasn't part of the plan," she manages, but her body betrays her as she pulls me closer.

My laugh is dark against her throat. "Plans change, little planner. Haven't you figured that out yet?"

She shivers as I nip at her pulse point, her heart racing beneath my lips. This woman, who plays both sides so perfectly, who manipulates everyone around her with calculated grace, comes undone so beautifully under my touch.

The taste of her, the feel of her body against mine, the way she responds to every touch—it's better than any intelligence she's ever gathered, more valuable than any territory we might claim. Her hands clutch at my shoulders as I trail kisses down her neck, each gasp a victory.

This wasn't part of my plan either, but plans are made to be broken. And Elena Santiago might just be worth burning everything down for.

She pulls back slightly, those intelligent eyes studying my face. Looking for lies, for manipulation, for the game beneath the game. "Your brother will kill us both," she whispers, but there's a hint of excitement in her voice. The same thrill I hear when she passes along classified information, when she plays both sides against the middle.

"My brother," I murmur against her skin, "has forgotten what real power looks like." I capture her lips again, softer this time but no less hungry. "But you haven't, have you, little planner? You see exactly what's coming."

Her hands slide inside my jacket, warm through the thin fabric of my shirt. "The Irish modernization, Anthony's shipping routes, Siobhan's quiet coup …" She gasps as I nip at her ear. "It's all connected."

"Smart girl." My fingers trace patterns on her hip, and she shivers. "But you're missing one piece of the puzzle."

She pulls back, eyes sharp despite her swollen lips and messy hair. The strategist replacing the lover, just like that. "What piece?"

I smile against her throat, breathing in that intoxicating scent. "You'll figure it out. You always do."

A car door slams somewhere in the garage, the sound echoing off concrete walls. Elena tenses beneath my hands, reality crashing back. We break apart slowly, reluctantly, like magnets fighting their natural pull.

She smooths her dress, fixes her hair with practiced efficiency.

Within seconds, she's put herself back together—the perfect event planner, trusted confidante to New York's most dangerous family.

Only her lips, still swollen from my kisses, betray what just happened.

"I should get back," she says, voice steady now. "Bella will be asking for me."

I step back, letting her slip past. But I catch her arm at the last moment, pulling her close one more time. "Watch your back with Anthony," I murmur against her ear. "He's not as stupid as he pretends to be."

She pulls away with a smile that promises trouble. "Neither am I."

I watch her walk away, heels clicking against concrete, back straight and head high. My little planner, playing both sides like a virtuoso. The taste of her lingers on my tongue, a reminder of promises we'll both probably break.

The garage feels colder without her. I light another cigarette, watching the smoke curl in the fluorescent light. Somewhere above us, my brother paces hospital corridors while his wife fights for their unborn children.

Somewhere in Boston, Siobhan O'Connor plays her own dangerous game. And somewhere in Manhattan, Anthony Calabrese thinks he's about ten steps ahead of everyone else.

Let them all play their games. I've got the only piece that matters—the queen who can move in any direction she chooses.

The only question is whether Elena will burn everything down herself, or if I'll have to do it for her.

7

ELENA

The pregnancy test stares back at me like an accusation, two pink lines that turn my carefully orchestrated world on its axis. I shouldn't have even tested—my period's only five days late, and I've always been irregular.

But something felt different.

My breasts are tender, certain smells make me nauseous, and there's a bone-deep exhaustion I can't shake.

Still, I told myself it was stress, the weight of too many secrets finally catching up with me.

But these two pink lines don't lie.

My hands shake as I reach for the box, reading the instructions for the fourth time. Maybe I did it wrong. Maybe morning urine would show different results. But three other tests from different brands show the same damning truth.

How the fuck did this happen?

I sit on the edge of my marble bathtub, the cold stone seeping through my silk robe as memories assault me. Anthony's penthouse three weeks ago, his hands surprisingly gentle as he undressed me, while all I could think about was the shipping manifests I glimpsed on his desk.

Then Mario in the hospital parking garage just days ago, that kiss that felt like drowning and breathing all at once.

The timing makes my throat close with panic. There's no question about paternity—this is Anthony's child growing beneath my heart, conceived during one of our calculated encounters while I was hunting for information about the Irish mob's trafficking routes.

I've always been so fucking careful. Even when Anthony would whisper in my ear how much better it would feel without barriers, how he wanted to feel all of me, I never wavered. The pack of pills in my bathroom drawer is meticulously marked, each one taken at exactly the same time every morning. The calendar on my phone tracks everything—my cycle, our encounters, the lies I tell.

My mind races through every meeting with Anthony over the past five months. The night in his penthouse when a storm knocked out power across Manhattan, and we fucked by candlelight while I memorized the contents of his safe.

The quickie in his office before a board meeting, where I planted a bug under his desk. The weekend at his Hampton's estate, where I copied the contents of his laptop while he slept.

I was always protected. Always in control. The pills, the backup methods, the morning-after insurance when I felt especially paranoid—it was a system as carefully planned as every other aspect of my life.

Fuck. Fuck. *Fuck.*

My hands drift to my still-flat stomach, and bile rises in my throat. Was it the antibiotics last month for that sinus infection? Did they interact with the pills?

Or that weekend in the Hamptons when food poisoning had me vomiting for hours—did that compromise their effectiveness?

The marble is ice-cold against my thighs as I slide to the floor, mind spinning through possibilities. I've seen what pregnancy does to women in this world. How it binds them, traps them, makes them vulnerable. Look at Bella—even with Matteo's protection, her pregnancy has made her a target.

A baby wasn't part of the plan. It wasn't supposed to be possible, not with all my precautions. I press my palms against the cool marble, trying to ground myself as memories of Anthony's touch make my skin crawl.

All those careful calculations, all those meticulously planned encounters, and somehow I still lost control.

My phone buzzes on the counter, distracting me from my panicking thoughts: *Miss you, beautiful. Dinner tonight? I have something special planned. Wear that red dress I like.*

The sight of Anthony's name makes bile rise in my throat, but my mind is already racing ahead.

A baby changes everything. A Calabrese heir growing in my womb—it's leverage I never expected, access I couldn't have planned. The perfect cover for gathering deeper intelligence, for proving myself more valuable than just another society girl playing at power.

But it's also a liability. A Calabrese baby means I'll never be free of them. If Anthony claims this child as his heir …

My hand trembles as I rest it on my still-flat stomach.

I've seen what this world does to children born into power. Look at Bianca, look at Mario and Matteo—all of them scarred by their birthright in different ways.

I look again at Anthony's text. Every instinct screams to cancel, to buy myself time to think. I could claim a migraine, a last-minute event crisis, anything to avoid sitting across from him tonight while carrying this secret.

But that's exactly why I need to go.

The thought crystallizes as I watch my reflection in the bathroom mirror. I look the same—perfectly styled hair, no hint of the morning sickness that's been plaguing me for days. No one would guess that beneath my composed exterior, everything has changed.

My fingers hover over the phone screen. This is what I do, isn't it? Turn complications into advantages, find leverage in unexpected places.

I think of Bella, how her pregnancy bound her so tightly to the DeLuca family that no one questions her presence in their inner circle anymore. Even Matteo's most paranoid captains accept her now, seeing only a beloved wife carrying the next generation.

Could I play that same role in the Calabrese empire? Not just the ambitious mistress, but the mother of the heir—someone who needs to be protected, trusted, included.

The nausea rises again, but I swallow it down. This isn't the time for weakness. Mario's voice echoes in my head: *"The best cover is the one people write for themselves, little planner. Let them see what they expect to see."*

I pick up my phone, fingers steady as I type: ***Can't wait. Reservation at 8? The red dress is at the cleaners, but I have something else you'll love.***

His response is immediate: ***Car will pick you up at 7:30. Don't keep me waiting.***

The command in his tone would have irritated me before, but now it just confirms I'm making the right choice. Anthony Calabrese likes to feel in control—it's why he never questions why a high-end event planner would be so eager to warm his bed.

Men like him always underestimate women they think they own.

I stand, letting my silk robe pool at my feet as I walk to my closet. Not the red dress—that would be too obvious, too eager to please. Instead, I select a black Versace that makes me look expensive but not desperate.

The neckline is conservative enough for a business dinner, but the way it hugs my curves leaves little to imagination.

Perfect for a woman who doesn't know she's carrying his heir.

The bathroom counter is still littered with evidence—pregnancy test boxes, the tests themselves. I gather everything methodically, wrapping it in paper before burying it deep in the kitchen trash.

No one can know. Not yet.

Not until I figure out how to play this to my advantage.

My makeup routine is automatic—concealer under eyes that have seen too little sleep, contouring to sharpen cheekbones that haven't yet betrayed morning sickness, a nude lip that won't leave telling marks on wine glasses I won't actually drink from.

The irony isn't lost on me. I let Anthony take me against any surface he wants while memorizing shipping schedules visible on his desk. Now I'm carrying his child while hunting for evidence of human trafficking through his ports.

Mario would appreciate the symmetry, if nothing else.

My phone buzzes again—a message from him this time, as if my thoughts summoned him: *Watch your step, little planner. The Irish are moving pieces we don't see yet.*

I ignore the way my heart races at his name, the phantom sensation of his lips against mine in that parking garage. That's a complication I can't afford right now, not with Anthony's child growing beneath my heart and a human trafficking operation to expose.

Instead, I focus on my reflection as I fasten diamond earrings—Anthony's gift after our first month together. The woman in the mirror looks calm, collected, perfect. No one would guess at the calculations running behind her eyes, the secrets building beneath her heart.

Let them see the obvious story—the society climber, the mistress reaching above her station. The familiar tale of a beautiful woman using a baby to trap a wealthy man.

The truth is so much more dangerous.

A car horn sounds outside—Anthony's driver, right on schedule.

It's showtime.

~

THREE HOURS LATER, I let Anthony press me against his bedroom wall, his hands possessive on my waist. The silk of my dress slides against the expensive wallpaper as he pins me there. His touch is demanding but gentle—always so careful with his toys—and I force myself not to flinch, to arch into his hands like I want it, like I'm not carrying his child while hunting for evidence that could destroy him.

His cologne is too strong this close, mixing with the lingering taste of the wine I pretended to drink at dinner. But his kisses taste like victory and Macallan 25 as I play my part—the ambitious mistress, the woman who might give him an heir.

He thinks the slight trembling in my limbs is from desire, not the constant nausea I'm fighting down.

"You're so beautiful," he murmurs against my neck, his skilled fingers tracing patterns on my hip. I let my head fall back, giving him better access while my eyes scan the room behind his shoulder.

Every detail matters now—the papers scattered across his mahogany desk, the phone he left carelessly on the nightstand, the laptop glowing dimly in the corner.

New papers catch my attention—shipping manifests from Vietnam and Thailand, port authority documents that shouldn't be accessible to a "legitimate businessman." Anthony's hands slide lower, and I use the movement to angle us, letting him think he's directing our dance while I get a better view.

A phone conversation drifts in from the other room—his assistant working late, voice muffled but clear enough: "... merchandise arriving Thursday. The containers need to clear customs by ..."

Everything clicks into place: the missing piece of the investigation into the trafficking operation. The gaps in the schedules, the mysterious shipments, the untraceable payments—it all connects.

"You're distracted tonight," Anthony murmurs against my throat, his teeth grazing my pulse point. His hands tighten possessively on my hips, and I realize I've let my mask slip, let the hunter show through the illusion of prey.

I cover it with a practiced moan, sliding my hands into his perfectly styled hair. "Just thinking about how much I want you," I breathe, directing his attention lower while my eyes stay fixed on the papers.

The manifests show routes that don't match any official records—gaps where people could disappear without a trace. Ships that dock but don't exist in any database, cargo that vanishes between ports.

His hands find my zipper, drawing it down with agonizing slowness. The whisper of metal seems loud in the dim room. "Thinking about me?" he asks, and there's something dangerous in his tone that makes me focus fully on him for a moment. "Or about my business papers?"

My heart stutters, but years of practice keep my voice steady, sultry. "About that thing you did in the car," I purr, sliding my leg between his. "I've been wet for you all through dinner."

The lie tastes like ash, but it works. His eyes darken with masculine pride, and he captures my mouth in a bruising kiss. His hands are everywhere now, and I match his passion with carefully crafted desire. Every gasp, every moan, every arch of my body is calculated to make him forget that momentary suspicion.

The expensive silk of my dress pools at my feet as he undresses me with practiced precision. His mouth traces a path down my neck, across my collarbone, marking me as his property. I let my head fall back, playing into his possessiveness while my eyes remain fixed on the documents across the room. His fingers trace patterns on my skin that should feel like fire but instead leave ice in their wake.

"So beautiful," he murmurs again against my throat, and I force myself not to think of different hands, a different voice in a hospital parking garage. Anthony's touch is all technique and no passion—like everything else about him, it's a performance meant to demonstrate his power.

I wrap my arms around his neck, pulling him closer, letting him think he's conquered me completely. His kisses grow more demanding as he backs me toward the bed, and I respond with all the skill of a woman who's made deception into an art form. My fingers work at his shirt buttons, each touch a lie I tell with my body.

The mattress hits the back of my knees, and I let myself fall, pulling him with me. The weight of him should feel like desire, like victory, but all I can think about is the child growing inside me.

A child not conceived from love but from deception.

But I'm good at this part—making men see what they want to see. Anthony likes to think he's irresistible, that I can't help but melt for him. So I arch beneath him, matching his rhythm with calculated precision, letting him believe every gasp and shiver is real.

His mouth claims mine again, tasting of expensive whiskey and darker things.

All the while, my mind catalogs details: a burner phone on his desk I hadn't noticed before, files labeled with dates that match suspected trafficking incidents, a calendar showing meetings with shell companies I've been tracking.

When Anthony finally falls asleep, I'll have work to do. But for now, I arch beneath him, playing the role of the perfect mistress.

I try not to think about how different Mario's touch felt in that parking garage—electric and real in a way that makes this feel like a pale imitation. I can't afford that comparison, not now. Not with Anthony's child growing beneath my heart and evidence of human trafficking waiting to be discovered.

So I lose myself in the performance, letting Anthony claim what he thinks is his, while behind my closed eyes, I plan how to use every scrap of information to my benefit.

∼

Later, after Anthony falls asleep, I slip into his massive bathroom. Everything is marble and gold, obscenely luxurious like the rest of his penthouse. An ornate chandelier casts dancing shadows across Italian tile as morning sickness hits me like a freight train.

I barely make it to the toilet, my knees bruising against the marble as I retch. Everything burns—my throat, my eyes, my pride.

When I can finally stand, I study my reflection in the gilded mirror.

I look exactly like what I am: a woman playing too many dangerous games. My lipstick is smeared, my carefully styled hair mussed from Anthony's hands. Beneath my La Perla lingerie, his child grows like a time bomb.

Mario's warning echoes in my head: *"Be careful playing with fire, little planner. Some burns leave permanent scars."*

I rest my hand on my stomach, feeling the slight swell that might be real or might be my imagination. A baby should be a weakness—a vulnerability in a world that preys on soft things. But maybe that's exactly what I need—a weapon no one will see coming.

After all, hasn't Mario taught me how to turn weakness into strength? How to make everyone underestimate me until it's too late?

I fix my lipstick with steady hands, already calculating next moves. Anthony stirs in the other room, calling my name. Time to play my part.

Let them all think I'm just another ambitious woman who got herself pregnant by a powerful man.

They'll never see me coming.

8

MARIO

The surveillance photos spread across my desk mock me with fresh revelations. Elena leaving her ob-gyn appointment, clutching a manila envelope against her designer blazer.

The timestamp reads just two hours ago.

I flip through more recent shots—her ducking into a pharmacy, emerging with a paper bag. Stopping at a coffee shop but ordering tea instead of her usual triple espresso.

Each image adds another piece to a puzzle I should have seen coming.

"Latest report from Mount Sinai," Dante announces, striding into my office. He drops a thick folder next to the photos. "Full records from her appointment today."

I scan the medical documents, though I already know what they'll confirm. HCG levels. Gestational age estimates. Prenatal vitamin prescriptions.

Elena Santiago is pregnant with Anthony Calabrese's child.

"Have you verified this?" My voice sounds distant, controlled, though something primal and possessive claws at my chest.

Dante nods. "Three separate sources. The blood work doesn't lie."

The rational part of my brain—the part Giuseppe beat into both his sons—knows this was always a possibility. Elena's role required getting close to Anthony, gathering intelligence by any means necessary.

Yet seeing the proof makes me want to burn Boston to the ground and salt the earth.

"Any movement from the Calabrese camp?" I maintain my mask of professional interest, though Dante knows me well enough to see through it.

"Nothing yet. She hasn't told Anthony." Dante hesitates. "But there's more. Those Vietnamese shipping manifests we've been tracking? They're moving again. Three containers arriving Thursday, marked as 'specialty imports.'"

"Human cargo," I translate flatly. The trafficking operation we've been investigating for months, hidden behind legitimate business fronts. "Location?"

"Port of Boston. O'Connor's territory."

Of course. The Irish getting their cut, providing cover through their legitimate shipping operations. A perfect setup—if you don't look too closely at the paperwork.

Or at the young women who disappear between ports.

I study a photo of Elena entering Anthony's building last week. She's wearing Chanel, her golden hair caught in Manhattan's wind.

Nothing in her perfect posture betrays the secret growing inside her.

"Sir?" Dante's tone suggests he's been trying to get my attention. "O'Connor's waiting for confirmation about Thursday's shipment. And his daughter's been asking questions about our Boston holdings."

Fucking Siobhan. Another player making moves we don't fully understand yet.

But right now, I can't focus on Irish politics or shipping routes or any of it. All I see is Elena carrying Anthony's child while diving deeper into an investigation that could get her killed.

"Get me the jet," I order, already reaching for my coat. "And find out everything about that doctor's appointment. Every test, every detail."

"And O'Connor?"

"Tell him I'll get him the information he requests." I holster my gun with practiced efficiency. "Have someone track Elena's movements. I want to know everywhere she goes, everyone she talks to."

"She won't like being watched that closely," Dante warns.

"I don't give a fuck what she likes." The words come out harsher than intended. "She's carrying a ticking time bomb. Everything changes."

I catch Dante's knowing look but ignore it. Let him think what he wants. Elena's pregnancy changes all the calculations, reshuffles every card on the table.

A Calabrese heir growing in her womb—it's either the perfect cover or a death sentence.

Knowing Elena, she'll try to play it as both.

But pregnancy makes women vulnerable. Soft. And Elena Santiago has too many enemies to afford being either.

My phone buzzes with a message from her: **We need to talk.**

I study the three words, imagining her composing them in that precise way she has. Always so controlled, my little planner. Always three steps ahead.

But this time, she's miscalculated. A baby isn't just leverage or an opportunity. It's a weakness enemies will exploit. A vulnerability that can't be hidden behind designer clothes and perfect manners.

I think of Matteo's wife, how her pregnancy made her a target.

History has a way of repeating in our world.

Stay where you are, I text back. *I'm coming to you.*

Her response is immediate: *Don't do anything reckless.*

I almost smile. As if she doesn't know that everything about us—about this—has been reckless from the start.

I tuck the surveillance photos into my jacket pocket, but one catches my eye. Elena leaving the doctor's office, her hand resting protectively over her stomach. It's such a small gesture, unconscious probably, but it changes everything.

The need to protect her—to destroy anyone who might harm her or the child she carries—rises like a tide. Dark and unstoppable.

Anthony Calabrese might have put his child in her womb, but Elena Santiago belongs to me. Has since that first night outside her office, when she looked at me without fear and saw exactly what I was offering.

Time to remind her of that fact.

"Have the jet ready in twenty," I tell Dante. "And get me everything we have on Anthony's schedule for the next week."

"Planning something special?"

I check my gun one last time, Giuseppe's lessons about preparation running through my mind. "Just a conversation between future family members."

The rush of possessive violence that accompanies those words would make my father proud.

Some lessons, it seems, stick deeper than others.

~

My private jet touches down at Teterboro as twilight bleeds into darkness. The New York skyline glitters against the night sky like broken glass—beautiful but deadly. Just like her.

The drive to Elena's apartment passes in a blur of city lights and mounting tension. Each minute brings me closer to a confrontation I've been rehearsing since those surveillance photos hit my desk this morning.

I find her in her apartment, padding around her kitchen in cream silk Hermès pajamas. The fabric flows like water with each movement, making her look softer, more vulnerable than the power suits and designer dresses she usually wears.

Something primitive rises in my chest—possession, protection, rage I can't quite name. The sight of her makes my blood burn with emotions I refuse to examine too closely.

"Were you going to tell me?" The words come out in that deadly quiet tone Giuseppe taught both his sons to use—the calm before violence. "Or just let me find out through surveillance photos?"

Elena doesn't flinch—she never has, not even that first night outside her office when I emerged from the shadows like the predator I am.

Instead, she meets my gaze steadily. Her hair falls in loose waves around her shoulders, free from its usual perfect styling, and the city lights streaming through her floor-to-ceiling windows cast shadows across her face, making her look even more beautiful.

"It's an opportunity," she says smoothly, moving to pour herself water instead of her usual wine. The simple gesture confirms everything. "Access we couldn't get any other way. Anthony thinks—"

"Anthony thinks he's claiming something that's mine."

The words escape before I can stop them, raw with an emotion I refuse to name. Something dark and possessive that's been growing since that first meeting.

Her eyes widen slightly—the first crack I've seen in her perfect composure. "How many times do I have to tell you that you're playing with fire, Elena. He's more dangerous than you realize."

The Manhattan lights paint patterns across her silk pajamas as she moves, the fabric clinging and flowing in a way that makes my hands itch to touch.

To claim. To possess.

"I learned to play with fire from the best." She moves closer, that magnetic pull between us impossible to resist. Her perfume wraps around me—something expensive and subtle that makes my blood heat. "Isn't this exactly what we wanted? A way inside their operation?"

I catch her wrist before she can retreat, feeling her pulse race beneath my fingers like a trapped bird. Her skin is soft, but her bones are delicate—too delicate for what she's doing.

"Not like this," I growl, pulling her closer until we share breath, until I can see the flecks of gold in her eyes. "Never like this."

She's close enough to kiss now, close enough that I can feel the heat radiating from her body through the thin silk of her pajamas.

The fabric rustles softly with each breath, reminding me how easily it would tear under my hands.

The thought makes my grip tighten involuntarily.

The city continues its chaotic symphony below us—car horns and sirens and the endless pulse of eight million lives. But up here, in her perfect apartment with its perfect view, time seems suspended between one heartbeat and the next.

Between one lie and another. Between what we are and what we pretend to be.

And through it all, Elena watches me with those clever eyes that see too much. That have always seen too much. Meanwhile, Anthony's child grows like a time bomb set to destroy everything we've built.

9

ELENA

The Vitucci mansion glitters like a fever dream, tiered chandeliers casting diamond light across marble floors. I've outdone myself with the decorations for tonight's charity gala—benefiting children's cancer research, because even Mafia families need good PR. White roses cascade from golden vessels, their perfume making my already queasy stomach roll.

The ballroom could rival Versailles, though I doubt Marie Antoinette had to deal with five different crime families' security protocols.

My Dior gown—midnight blue silk that falls like water—hides how I've lost weight this past week, morning sickness turning every meal into a battle. I look perfect on the outside, even as I'm dying inside.

The specially ordered caviar station nearly made me vomit earlier, and now the scent of five thousand roses isn't helping.

Anthony, mercifully, is in Singapore closing a deal with potential "investors"—his code for expanding trafficking operations into new territories. His absence feels like being able to breathe properly for the first time in days.

Still, I notice his cousin's watchful gaze following me from across the room. The Calabrese family never leaves anything unobserved.

The Vituccis have spared no expense—the string quartet plays Vivaldi on instruments worth small fortunes, while waiters circulate with champagne vintages that would make sommeliers weep. Old Andrea Vitucci himself holds court near the grand staircase, his white hair gleaming like his diamond cufflinks as he discusses "import businesses" with the Rossetti underboss.

Both men's security details maintain a careful distance, close enough to intervene but far enough to pretend this is just another society gathering.

Through the crowd of designer gowns and family crests masquerading as legitimate business empires, I spot Siobhan O'Connor holding court near the champagne fountain. She moves through the space like she owns it, her Alexander McQueen dress a masterpiece of understated power. Old guard captains who would never take orders from a woman bend closer to hear her whispered comments.

She's modernizing the Irish mob whether her father likes it or not, one perfectly orchestrated social interaction at a time.

The Moretti brothers cluster near the French doors—young Enzo's hand trembling slightly as he reaches for another drink. Their father's recent "heart attack" has left them scrambling for control of the family's gambling operations. The older brother, Carlo, watches the room with sharp eyes while pretending to admire the flower arrangements. His wife Anastasia drips in Van Cleef & Arpels, but her nervous glances toward the Rossetti underboss tell their own story.

Security is a delicate dance tonight. Each family's personal detail maintains their designated zones—the Vituccis near the main entrance, the Rossettis by the east wing, the Morettis covering the garden access.

I've positioned the DeLuca men strategically around Bella, though they're good enough to make it look casual. The Irish contingent stays close to Siobhan, despite her obvious irritation at her father's outdated protocols.

My own security team—handpicked professionals who think they're just protecting an elite event planner—monitor the general space. They have no idea they're actually running interference between five different Mafia families' private armies. The art is making it all look effortless, like this is just another charity gala rather than a powder keg of ancient grudges and modern ambitions.

Through it all, I catalog every detail, every interaction. The way the younger Rossetti son's hand lingers too long on a Moretti cousin's back. How the Vitucci heir keeps checking his phone while his father negotiates territory lines disguised as property investments. The subtle shifts in alliance and loyalty that play out beneath dimmed lights and classical music.

But even my professional pride in orchestrating this spectacular event can't quite suppress the constant nausea. Five thousand roses might look stunning, but right now they're testing every ounce of my self-control.

"Elena!" Bella's voice cuts through the crowd. She looks radiant in emerald-green Valentino, her baby bump prominent. Matteo hovers nearby in a black Tom Ford suit that makes him look like a model, watching his wife like she might shatter.

"You've outdone yourself," Bella says, gesturing to the spectacular decor. "Though I'm not sure the Vituccis deserve your talent."

"You're biased." I smile, noting how pregnancy has given her skin a luminous glow. The emerald dress makes her look like a Renaissance painting come to life. "How are you feeling?"

"If one more person asks me that, I might scream." Bella rolls her eyes, but her hand instinctively rests on her bump. "Between Matteo and Bianca, I can barely breathe without someone documenting it."

"We're concerned," Matteo's deep voice joins our conversation. His hand settles protectively on Bella's lower back. "After the scare last week—"

"I'm fine," Bella cuts him off, but leans into his touch. "The doctors said moderate activity is good for me. Besides, Elena's here if anything happens."

I feel Matteo's eyes on me—that calculated DeLuca stare that seems to see through every lie. Instead of looking away, I meet his gaze. Let him look. Let him wonder.

"How's the security tonight?" he asks, his tone casual but his eyes sharp. "I noticed the Rossettis brought extra men."

"Everything's under control," I assure him, fighting back a wave of nausea as a waiter passes with something that smells like seafood. "The Vituccis agreed to my recommended protocols."

"Just like Anthony Calabrese agreed to your recommended guest list for his last event?" Matteo's voice remains pleasant, but there's an edge beneath it that makes my skin prickle. "Antonio tells me you've been ... consulting ... quite extensively with the Calabrese family lately."

Bella shoots her husband a warning look, but Matteo continues, his eyes never leaving my face. "Interesting timing, considering their recent shipping expansion. And their newfound interest in Irish partnerships."

I feel trapped under Matteo's gaze, the one that can reduce hardened criminals to confessions. But before I can craft a suitable response, a waiter glides past with a tray of stuffed mushrooms in a heavy truffle sauce. The smell—rich and earthy and absolutely revolting to my currently sensitive stomach—hits me hard.

"I need to check on something," I manage, already stepping back. My mouth floods with saliva in that telltale way. "The florist mentioned an issue with—"

"Elena?" Bella's voice holds genuine concern.

"Just a small crisis," I lie, trying not to gag. "You know how these events are."

I catch Matteo's expression as I turn away—thoughtful and dangerous, like he's assembling a puzzle he doesn't quite like the shape of.

But I can't focus on his suspicions right now. Not when my stomach is threatening immediate rebellion.

I flee down the marble hallway, my Louboutins clicking against stone as I search desperately for a private bathroom. Not the main powder room—too many socialites comparing jewelry and sharing gossip. I need somewhere private, somewhere I won't have to explain why New York's most sought-after event planner is vomiting at her own perfectly orchestrated gala.

Please, let there be another bathroom. Please, let it be empty.

I barely make it to a private bathroom before violent nausea overwhelms me. My knees hit hand-painted Italian tiles as I retch, each heave making my body shake. The caviar station, the roses, the truffles—everything I've been fighting to keep down comes up in painful waves until I'm left with nothing but bile and regret.

When it finally passes, I stay kneeling for a moment, hands trembling as I reach for toilet paper to wipe my mouth. My throat burns, and I can feel cold sweat beading at my temples. The lavish sconces cast merciless light as I slowly pull myself up, using the gold-plated towel rack for support.

My reflection makes me wince. My face is ghost pale except for two fever-bright spots on my cheeks, mascara smudged beneath my eyes. So much for the two hours my makeup artist spent perfecting this look.

"That won't do," I murmur. I dig through my Bottega Veneta clutch for lipstick and concealer, determined to salvage what I can of my appearance.

The door opens, admitting three women I recognize from the Rossetti inner circle. Their voices bounce off marble walls as they cluster around the mirrors.

"Did you see Siobhan O'Connor with the youngest Vitale brother?" one stage-whispers, adjusting her décolletage. "That dress must have cost a fortune—way too good for a simple family dinner."

"Daddy's money," another sniffs, reapplying her lipstick. "Though I heard she's been meeting with Sean Murphy more than business requires, if you know what I mean ..."

I resist rolling my eyes as I touch up my own makeup. Their

gossip is amateur hour—missing all the actually interesting details about Siobhan's expanding influence among the younger captains.

The bathroom door swings open again, and the temperature drops ten degrees. Siobhan O'Connor stands in the doorway, resplendent in Alexander McQueen, her smile sharp as a blade.

"Ladies," she purrs, making the word sound like a death sentence. "Don't let me interrupt. You were saying something about my dress? Or was it my ... business meetings?"

The women freeze like rabbits scenting a wolf. One actually backs up a step, clutching her Hermès bag like a shield.

"Though if you're so interested in my personal life," Siobhan continues, examining her manicure, "perhaps you'd like to discuss it with your husbands? I'm sure they'd be *fascinated* to hear how their wives spend their time spreading rumors about an O'Connor."

They scatter like startled birds, nearly tripping over their Louboutins in their haste to escape.

Silence falls as Siobhan moves to the mirror beside me. I continue fixing my makeup, hyperaware of her presence. She's close enough that I can smell her perfume—something exclusive and French.

"That shade of Dior suits you," she says casually, as if she hadn't just terrorized three women into fleeing. "Though you're looking a bit peaked around the edges."

I meet her eyes in the mirror, my pulse quickening. Siobhan O'Connor doesn't do casual conversation. Every word from her is calculated, even if I don't yet understand the equation.

"The hazards of event planning," I reply carefully, watching her adjust her already perfect lipstick. "Everyone wants everything to be flawless."

"Flawless," she repeats, something bitter in her tone. "Like good daughters should be, yes? Perfect little ornaments for powerful men to display."

Her words hit closer to home than I'd like. I think of Anthony's possessive touches, the way he parades me at events like a prize thoroughbred.

"Though some of us," Siobhan continues, turning to face me

directly now, "are tired of being ornamental. My father still calls me his 'little colleen,' you know."

Her laugh carries pure ice as she smooths her dress. "Even while I manage half our legitimate enterprises. Men like him and Anthony—they'll never see us as more than decorative accessories."

There it is. The real conversation beneath the pretense. I study her reflection carefully. "Then let them underestimate us."

"Has that worked well for you?" Her smile turns predatory. "Carrying Calabrese's heir while playing a much bigger game?"

Her words hit me like a blow to the face. The O'Connors know.

It's bad enough that Mario knows, but if Seamus O'Connor's daughter knows about my pregnancy ... My fingers grip the marble sink before I can stop myself.

Siobhan tracks the movement, a sly smile playing at her perfectly painted lips, and sudden horror washes through me. Had she just been fishing? Did I just confirm her theory with my reaction?

"I don't know what you're talking about," I manage, but my voice sounds weak even to my own ears.

"No?" Siobhan's smile widens. "The way you're gripping that sink suggests otherwise."

Another wave of nausea hits, more violent than before. I try to swallow it back, but Siobhan must see me struggling because she makes a thoughtful sound.

"You should probably let yourself vomit," she says casually. "It's not good for the baby to fight it, you know."

The horror spreading through me can't compete with my rebellious stomach. I barely make it back to the toilet before I'm retching again, my body betraying every secret I've tried to keep.

Strong hands gather my hair back, and Mario's familiar cologne mingles with the metallic taste in my mouth. Of course he's here. He's always watching, always one step ahead.

"How"—I gasp between heaves—"did you get past security?" The Vitucci mansion is supposed to be impenetrable. I personally vetted every guard, planned every patrol route.

The British royal family has less protection than this gala.

"You call this security?" Mario scoffs, his fingers cool against my neck. "A blind grandmother with a cane could breach the east garden entrance. Honestly, little planner, I expected better from you."

I want to kill him for that criticism, but another wave of nausea takes precedence.

"You shouldn't be here," I gasp "Your brother—"

"Is too busy hovering over his pregnant wife to notice me." Mario's voice holds none of its usual edge, his fingers stroking down the back of my neck.

"Well," Siobhan drawls from behind us, "this has been enlightening. Do try to keep your ... liaison ... discreet. Though I suspect that ship has sailed."

She pauses at the door. "Oh, and Elena? When you're ready to have a real conversation about the future of our organizations, you know where to find me. Assuming the morning sickness allows, of course."

The door closes with a soft click that sounds like a threat.

I rest my cheek against the cold porcelain, my face burning from the combination of vomiting, embarrassment, and fear. "She knows," I whisper, the words barely audible. "Mario, she knows I'm pregnant."

His jaw tightens, but his hands remain gentle as he produces a monogrammed handkerchief, the DeLuca crest mocking me with its promise of family loyalty. "Siobhan knowing changes nothing," he says, though something dangerous flashes in his eyes. "She's playing her own game."

"A game where she holds all the cards." My voice cracks. "If she tells Anthony—"

"She won't." His certainty makes me look up. "Siobhan O'Connor doesn't waste leverage this valuable on petty revelations."

He guides me to sit on the marble counter, his hands lingering on my waist. The bathroom's soft lighting catches the silver at his temples, highlighting his resemblance to Matteo—that same protective instinct barely masked by calculated control.

"The Irish are moving weapons through Anthony's shipping routes," I report, trying to change the subject, trying to ignore how his proximity makes my pulse race. "Using the legitimate business as cover for—" Another wave of nausea cuts me off.

Mario's hand finds my lower back, rubbing slow circles that somehow ease the churning in my stomach. The gesture feels startlingly intimate—more so than any of our heated moments or calculated encounters.

"The baby comes first," he says quietly. "Before intel, before revenge, before everything."

"Why?" I meet his eyes in the mirror, seeing something there that makes my breath catch. "I'm just another asset. A way to get information about your brother's empire."

His other hand comes up to my neck, thumb brushing my pulse point. "Are you trying to convince me or yourself, little planner?"

"Mario—"

"When are you going to admit that this stopped being just business a long time ago?" His voice drops lower, making heat pool in my stomach despite my nausea. "That maybe there are some games worth losing?"

His fingers brush my stomach, sending electricity through my body. "Some games change the players as much as the rules," he murmurs, his voice a husky growl.

I turn to face him, our faces inches apart. "And what happens when everyone realizes you're playing a different game entirely?" I whisper.

The sound of approaching voices and clicking heels in the hallway makes him pull back with a curse. "We're not done with this conversation." His dark eyes scan the bathroom before landing on the narrow window near the ceiling. "I'll find you later."

"How are you possibly—" But he's already moving, using the towel rack as leverage to reach the window with graceful efficiency that would be impressive if it weren't so infuriating.

"By the way," he adds, pausing at the window, turning his head back just enough so I could see an infuriating smirk on his lips, "tell my brother his security protocols need work."

Then he's gone, slipping away like a shadow just as the bathroom door begins to open.

I stare at my reflection, wondering when exactly this game stopped being just about revenge, and why that terrifies me more than anything Siobhan O'Connor might do with her newfound knowledge.

Later, as I coordinate with security about an overcrowded valet situation, I catch Siobhan watching me from across the room.

She raises her champagne glass in subtle acknowledgment before turning back to her father's business associates. I file away the interaction, knowing every alliance and observation could matter in the months to come.

But Mario's touch still burns on my skin, and for once, the game feels secondary to something far more dangerous—something that feels disturbingly like hope.

10

MARIO

I should be halfway to Boston by now. O'Connor's been blowing up my phone for hours, and Siobhan's cryptic text sits like poison in my inbox: *Congratulations on the impending addition to the DeLuca dynasty. Though I suppose it's technically the Calabrese line that's being continued ...*

Fucking Siobhan. Always too clever for her own good.

Instead of dealing with the Irish mess, I'm in Elena's apartment. The city lights paint patterns across her floors, and I find myself counting the minutes until she returns, like some lovesick fool instead of the exiled son I'm supposed to be.

The lock turns, and Elena enters—still in that midnight blue Dior that makes her look like something out of a Raphael painting. All that pale skin against dark silk, her blonde hair coming loose from its elegant twist. Even exhausted from tonight's performance, she moves flawlessly.

She doesn't startle when she sees me, which somehow makes me want her more. "I assumed you'd be here," she says, moving through her apartment like I'm just another piece of expensive furniture.

But I catch the slight tremor in her hands as she removes her diamond earrings.

"Help me with my zipper?" she asks over her shoulder, challenge clear in her voice.

I'm across the room before she finishes speaking. My hands find her back, fingers splaying across silk-covered skin. The zipper becomes a test of control—how slowly can I drag it down when everything in me wants to tear the dress apart?

The only sound is metal teeth parting and Elena's breath catching as my knuckles brush her spine. She's not wearing a bra, and the knowledge makes my blood heat.

"Careful," she whispers as the zipper reaches the small of her back. "This dress is worth—"

"I'll buy you another one." The silk parts like water under my hands, revealing inch after inch of pale skin. She's playing with fire—we both are. My little planner, flying too close to the sun like Icarus, thinking her wax wings will hold.

The Calabreses will burn her just like they burn everything they touch. Just like I burned everything when I went after Matteo.

Her hands are the only thing keeping the dress from pooling at her feet. She turns slowly to face me, and something in my chest tightens. In this light, her eyes are more gray than blue, like storm clouds gathering. Even under her perfect makeup, I can see the light dusting of freckles across the bridge of her nose—a reminder that beneath all her perfection, she's still so young, so human.

Her chest rises and falls rapidly, betraying how affected she is by my proximity.

"End it with Anthony Calabrese," I say, my voice low and controlled despite the rage building in my chest. "It's too dangerous, especially now that you're"—I can barely force out the words—"carrying his child."

One perfectly shaped eyebrow rises. "My, my ... is the great Mario DeLuca jealous?"

"Don't be ridiculous." I step back, needing distance from her intoxicating presence. "You reminded me yourself—you're an asset. And I need to ensure my assets are protected."

Pain flashes across her face before ice replaces it. The look makes me feel like I've kicked a puppy—a new and distinctly unwelcome sensation.

"I've never taken orders from men before," she says, voice arctic. "I don't plan to start now. In fact, I'm attending a Calabrese family function tomorrow night. As Anthony's *special* guest."

Red clouds my vision. "Playing the whore suits you then?"

The moment the words leave my mouth, I want to catch them, stuff them back down my throat. Elena's face crumbles for just a second before hardening into something terrible and beautiful.

"Get out." Her voice could chill the sun.

"Elena—"

"What's wrong, Mario? Worried your little asset is getting too close to the enemy?" She lets the dress fall slightly, revealing more skin. "Or worried that Anthony might not be the only one I'm playing?"

"You're going to get yourself killed," I snarl, advancing on her. "You think Anthony won't notice how often you study his papers? How convenient it is that you always need to fuck him in his office?"

"At least he doesn't treat me like a chess piece," she snaps.

"No, he treats you like a broodmare!"

Her hand cracks across my face. The slap echoes in the silence.

"Get. Out," she says through gritted teeth.

"Gladly." I move to the door but pause with my hand on the knob. "Just remember, little planner—when Anthony Calabrese shows you exactly who he is, don't come crying to me. You chose this game."

Her laugh is bitter music as she shakes her head, pieces of her golden hair moving in sync. "No, Mario. *You* chose it for me the moment you approached me outside my office. Now live with the consequences."

I leave before I can say something else I'll regret, but her words follow me into the night. She's right—I set this game in motion. I just never expected to care who got burned

MANHATTAN SPREADS out beneath the safe house windows like a glittering chess board. The penthouse takes up the entire top floor of an unmarked building in Tribeca—all steel and glass and strategic sight lines.

No paper trail connects it to me, just like none of my properties have my name attached. Giuseppe taught us that lesson early: always have somewhere to hide that even family can't find.

I stare into my coffee, black and bitter like my thoughts. I should be in Boston, dealing with O'Connor's latest demands, but Elena's apartment keeps pulling me back. The way her face crumbled before freezing over. The cruel words I can't take back.

My phone rings. I answer without checking, still lost in memories of silk and skin and regret.

"Getting comfortable in New York?" Seamus O'Connor's brogue turns the words into a threat. "Because last I checked, you fucking work for me in Boston."

Goddammit. "I'm handling—"

"You're handling fuck all except your brother's event planner." Ice crackles in his voice. "Need I remind you who owns your debt, DeLuca? Who gave you sanctuary when your own blood cast you out?"

My grip threatens to shatter the coffee mug. "I remember."

"Good. Then you'll remember our arrangement. I need you back in Boston. Tonight. I have a job that requires your ... particular insight into the DeLuca operations."

"My brother's security—"

"Your brother's security is precisely why I own you, boy. Or have you forgotten what happened the last time you tried playing both sides?"

The call ends, and rage explodes through me. The coffee mug shatters against the wall, dark liquid running down imported wallpaper like blood.

Fucking O'Connor, acting like he owns me. Like I'm still that desperate exile who showed up in Boston five years ago, burning with hatred and nowhere else to go.

But Elena's words from last night echo louder than O'Connor's threats: *"I'm attending a Calabrese family function tomorrow night. As Anthony's special guest."*

I can still see her standing there, dress barely held up by trembling hands, throwing those words at me like weapons. And they hit their mark—the thought of Anthony's hands on her, of him parading her around his family like some prize, makes me want to burn his whole empire to the ground.

My phone buzzes. A text from Dante: **Let me know when you want the jet.**

I hit dial. "I need you to get me into the Calabrese function tonight," I bark the moment Dante answers.

"Boss." Dante's voice holds carefully neutral concern. "O'Connor expects you back—"

"O'Connor can fucking wait." I move through the safe house, past the weapons cache hidden behind steel panels, toward the bedroom where a fresh suit awaits. "I have unfinished business here."

"The event planner?"

Fucking Dante being too fucking perceptive for his own goddamn good.

"Get me the security details for the Calabrese estate." I start laying out what I'll need—a ceramic knife that won't trigger metal detectors, garrote wire thin as silk. "Guest list, patrol routes, everything."

"You're going to get yourself killed." A pause. "Or worse, get her killed."

"Just get me what I need." I study my reflection as I knot my tie. "And Dante? Make sure my return ticket to Boston isn't traceable. Wouldn't want O'Connor getting any ideas about tonight's ... detour."

"This is suicide." But I hear him already typing. "The Calabreses have tripled security since Johnny's death. Even the waiting staff are vetted—"

"Then I guess we better make sure my credentials are impeccable." I check the knife's edge. "Send everything to my secure phone. I'll be dark after 8 p.m."

"Mario ..." Dante rarely uses my first name. "Is she worth it?"

I think of Elena's face when I called her a whore, of her trembling hands and steel spine. Of how she matches me move for move in this deadly game we're playing.

"Just get me in, Dante. I'll handle the rest."

~

I'VE SURVIVED PRISON, exile, and Giuseppe DeLuca's particular brand of lessons in control. But watching Elena play her role at this Calabrese gathering tests every ounce of that hard-won restraint.

Anthony parades her through the crowd like a prized thoroughbred, his hand possessively splayed across her bare back. Every touch, every whispered word in her ear is a calculated display of ownership.

Look what I have, his every gesture screams. *Look who shares my bed.*

She wears light blue silk that falls over her curves, the color making her look ethereal under the ornate chandeliers. The dress is a masterpiece of suggestion—modest from the front but dipping dangerously low in the back, leaving an expanse of creamy skin exposed to Anthony's wandering hands.

Her bare arms are elegant, shoulders touched golden by late summer sun. She moves like a goddess among mortals, all dangerous curves and intentional elegance.

Getting into the Calabrese mansion was almost insultingly easy. A service entrance with lazy guards, security cameras with predictable blind spots—it's almost amusing how these so-called crime families have gotten soft. The DeLuca exile slipping in right under their noses.

The mansion itself is exactly what you'd expect from new money trying to look old—marble everything, gold leaf dripping from coffered ceilings, artwork chosen for price tags rather than taste. Chandeliers bigger than cars hang over a ballroom that could fit a small army. Which it practically does tonight—for a "family function" there must be a hundred people here, all dripping in diamonds and designer labels.

I stick to the shadows near carved columns, watching. Always watching. Elena moves through the crowd like she was born to this world, but I see the tension in her shoulders, the way her smile never quite reaches her eyes. Anthony keeps her close, touching her constantly—a hand at her waist, fingers trailing down her spine, lips brushing her ear.

My teeth grind as she laughs at something he whispers, tilting her head to give him better access to her neck. He takes the invitation, nose skimming her bare shoulder in a gesture that looks intimate but feels possessive. Playing the besotted lover while his hands mark his territory.

The crystal tumbler in my hand cracks. Every touch, every false laugh, every moment she lets him claim her makes my blood boil. This is the game we chose—the game I taught her to play. So why does watching her excel at it feel like swallowing broken glass?

Through the crowd, I watch Elena lean close to Anthony, whispering something that makes him smile indulgently. Then she's moving away with practiced grace, her blue silk dress a beacon in the gaudy splendor of the Calabrese mansion.

I follow, keeping to shadows, my feet silent on highly polished floors—another of Giuseppe's lessons serving its purpose. Elena moves with purpose down ornate hallways, past Renaissance paintings probably bought with blood money, beneath sconces that cast her shadow in duplicate.

She stops at a heavy wooden door, glancing both ways before reaching beneath the neckline of her dress. My breath catches as she withdraws a key from God knows where. The lock clicks and she slips inside like a ghost.

I count to ten before following.

She's alone in what must be Anthony's study, her fingers dancing over file folders with practiced efficiency. "You shouldn't take such risks," I growl, emerging from the shadows.

Elena jumps, her body tensing as she spins to face me, her fingers freezing mid-motion over the stack of folders. Her eyes, wide with alarm, narrow as recognition replaces fear. Her chin tilts upwards, defiant even now.

"My condition is exactly why I can take these risks," she counters, but there's a tremor beneath her usual bite. Her gaze flickers to the space behind me, calculating exits, always ten moves ahead.

"And what the fuck are you doing here?" she snaps, though her voice loses its edge as I close the distance between us. "Shouldn't you be back in Boston, wagging your tail for O'Connor?"

I ignore the jab, stopping just short of touching her. Close enough to feel the warmth radiating off her skin. Close enough to catch the faint notes of her perfume. "You shouldn't take such risks," I repeat, softer this time, the words laden with something I can't quite name.

She huffs a laugh, shaking her head. "Anthony would never suspect—"

My control snaps like a wire under too much tension. Her words are cut off as I reach for her, unable to hold back another second. My hands close around her arms, pulling her to me, and my lips crash against hers with a ferocity that shocks even me.

There's nothing restrained about this kiss, nothing calculated. It's fire and desperation, need and fury, and she meets it all with equal force.

Her fingers twist in my hair, nails dragging deliciously across my scalp, and a low growl escapes my throat as I press her back against Anthony's desk. The edge cuts into her hips, but she doesn't seem to care—if anything, she arches toward me, her gasp soft and breathless against my lips. It's all the invitation I need.

I grip her thighs, sliding my hands up beneath the silky fabric of her dress, relishing the warmth of her skin beneath my palms. Papers cascade to the floor in a chaotic flurry as I lift her onto the polished wood.

Her legs hook around my waist with a desperate urgency, pulling me close, her body molding to mine as if it's where she's always belonged. The scent of her—floral and faintly spiced—clouds my senses, and I'm lost.

"Tell me to stop," I rasp, my lips brushing her ear before trailing down her jawline, tasting the salt of her skin. My mouth lingers on her throat, where her pulse flutters like a trapped bird, and I press open-mouthed kisses to the column of her neck.

Her response is immediate, a breathless command that sends a thrill through me. "Don't you dare," she whispers, her voice low and ragged, nails digging into my shoulders. "Don't you fucking dare stop."

Her words ignite something feral in me. My hands slide higher, exploring the soft curves of her hips, her waist. With one sharp tug, her dress slips upward, pooling around her hips and baring her to my touch.

Fuck me. She's not wearing underwear. The sight of her, disheveled and waiting, is enough to nearly unravel me.

Her hands work frantically at my shirt, pulling it free from my waistband. The scrape of her nails across my bare skin sends fire racing down my spine, and I groan as her palms flatten against my chest, exploring me with the same need I feel coursing through my veins.

The room fills with the sound of our mingled breaths, quick and shallow, and the whisper of fabric as it's shed in haste. Her skin is soft beneath my hands, impossibly warm, and I take my time mapping every inch of her, savoring the way she gasps, the way her body moves beneath mine.

Elena moans and tips her head back which is all the encouragement I need. I yank her dress up even higher before removing it entirely, leaving her completely naked in front of me. Her body is flush with arousal and her nipples harden even further under my gaze.

She lets out a shuddering gasp when my hands return to her breasts. She arches her back, which has the unintended—but not unfortunate—side effect of pushing her breasts further into my hands. Bowing my head to her chest, I lavish hot, open-mouthed kisses on her body, starting on her sternum before moving towards her left breast.

"Mario," she whimpers.

I have mercy on her, blowing over her sensitive nub before taking it into my mouth. The sharp contrast between the cool air of Calabrese's office and my mouth causes Elena to cry in pleasure. I hum in approval at the noise, the animalistic side of me wanting to hear exactly what I'm doing to her.

The pleasurable sounds. The cries. The screams. I want to hear how good I am making her feel. Her hands find their way into my hair. One hand grips and tugs to make sure my mouth stays where it is, while her free hand strokes the hairs at the nape of my neck.

But that's not allowed. *I'm* in charge. Growling, I reach out for her wrists, grabbing them and roughly pinning them against the desk.

To my delight, she is immediately pliant.

Satisfied, I gently scrape my teeth along her hardened nipple, from base to the tip. The shuddering gasps and moans of my name make it clear that she likes this. I detach my mouth from her left breast, kissing across her chest to lavish equal attention on its neglected twin.

My hips begin subconsciously rutting against the edge of the desk. Every pleasurable sound Elena makes goes straight to my dick, and I need some fucking relief.

But I hold myself back. I'm not fourteen anymore. I don't want this to end before it even begins.

Elena protests when my mouth leaves her body altogether. She looks at me, her chest heaving, her erect nipples gleaming.

"Why did you stop?" she demands.

I smirk before forcing her legs open, leaving her utterly exposed to my hungry eyes. My fingers lightly dance around her thighs and lower stomach, always dancing closer to where she clearly wants me, but never quite there.

"Mario!" Elena gasps, her hips thrusting up.

I can't resist my fingers taking an occasional teasing swipe at her clit, causing her to hiss in pleasure. Eventually, I stop my teasing as my right hand fully cups her entrance. I watch as she begins grinding herself against my hand, the heel of my hand providing the right amount of pressure and pleasure where it's needed the most.

Elena spread her legs wider, exposing herself more to me. "Mario," she exclaims in breathy moans, telling me that I was doing everything exactly right.

Slowly, I slip my index finger into her, groaning at the way she clenches around me straightaway. Fuck, she feels like heaven. Her hips move in time with me, guiding me. I curl my finger, teasing her G-spot and making her moan at the pleasure.

"Fuck, fuck, fuck!" she pants, her hands scrabbling for purchase against the top of the desk. "Mario, *please!*"

Listening to her plea, I slide another finger inside of her. I take in the moans and gasps she releases as my fingers play her like a violin, moving deeper, finding spots that drive her fucking wild.

"Fuck, Elena, that's it," I groan when I feel her clenching around my fingers. "That's it."

But before she comes, I remove my fingers from her. I want—no —*need* to taste her. The scent of her arousal overwhelms my senses. I softly nip at her inner thighs before moving my mouth to where we both want it.

My tongue laps at her clit, tasting her juices, making me moan in pleasure at her taste. I close my lips around her clit, sucking gently.

"Mario!" Elena gasps again, her hips grinding against my mouth. "I'm going to—I'm going to—"

With a shuddering cry, Elena's thighs clench around my head, trapping me against her as she rides out her high. I work her through her climax, lapping at the bit of wetness that escapes. When she collapses against the desk, I carefully withdraw my fingers, sucking the leftover juice off them.

I will never get enough of her taste. I already want more.

Shedding my pants, I allow my aching cock to spring free. Elena leans up against her elbows, her eyes glittering as she takes me in.

I smirk. "Like what you see?"

Instead of answering me, she yanks me forward, capturing my lips in a searing kiss. I press the tip of my cock against her entrance and she moans again, grinding her hips against me in a way that makes me curse.

"Don't fucking tease me," she snarls against my mouth. "I need you."

Those three words do me in—*I need you.*

When I finally enter her, the sound she makes is pure surrender—a broken cry that echoes through the dimly lit office, carving itself into my memory. I bury my face in the curve of her neck, my own restraint shattering as she meets me thrust for thrust, her body rising to mine like a wave cresting over and over again.

Her nails score my back, her legs tightening around me as if she's afraid I'll disappear, and the intensity of it all—the heat, the desperation, the way she moans my name like a benediction—drives me closer to the edge.

"Don't stop," Elena whimpers. "Faster, Mario. Faster!"

My hips stutter as I find a faster, more furious pace. The desk creaks and groans from the magnitude behind my thrusts. I feel and hear the telltale signs that she is approaching another orgasm. Her moans and cries become more and more pronounced.

Each movement feels like a claim, a vow made in the language of bodies, and I'm consumed by her—by us—until nothing else exists.

Grabbing her hand, I guide it down between us, growling, "I want to see you touch yourself."

Elena moans at my command, immediately moving her hand further down to where we're joined.

So much for her claim that she's never taken orders from a man before.

I look down, watching as her slim fingers tease and rub her clit in time with my thrusts. It's the hottest thing I've ever seen.

"Fuck, fuck, fuck!" I hiss before I tug her back, causing Elena to fully arch under me as I mark her skin, claiming her as mine.

"Mario, I ..." Elena's voice cuts off with a cry, her body shuddering.

"Come for me, baby," I growl into her ear. "Let me feel you."

That is the permission she seemingly needs. Her whole body

begins to shake as her orgasm overtakes her. Her legs tighten around me as I continue thrusting into her, seeking my own release. When it happens, I capture her lips in a kiss, my thrusts becoming sloppier as I ride out my high.

Afterward, the quiet hums with something heavy, something dangerous. I help her off the desk, helping her put her dress back into place, but my gaze lingers on the curve of her neck, the faint flush on her cheeks, the marks I've left behind.

She smooths her lipstick with a trembling hand, and her eyes meet mine in the dim light, sharp and unrelenting.

"This changes everything," I say roughly, the words tasting like a vow as they leave my lips.

Her hand drifts to her stomach—a gesture that feels like a knife to the gut—and her laugh is soft, humorless. "Everything changed the moment you noticed me outside my office," she murmurs, her voice calmer than it has any right to be.

She steps closer, her fingers brushing mine for the briefest moment before pulling away. "The question is … are you ready for what comes next?"

Her words hang in the air between us, a challenge, a promise, and I know—there's no going back.

11

ELENA

I wake to unfamiliar sheets that smell like Mario's cologne. My body aches deliciously, evidence of last night's desperation mapped across my skin in bruises and bite marks. The safe house is exactly what I'd expect from a DeLuca bolt-hole—floor-to-ceiling windows with bulletproof glass, sleek furniture positioned for optimal sight lines, everything a perfect balance of luxury and tactical consideration.

My mind drifts to that first encounter in Anthony's study days ago. The way Mario claimed me on that desk, papers scattering like confetti around us. How perfectly right it felt, how completely he consumed me.

I'd slipped back to Anthony's side afterward, lipstick carefully reapplied, not a hair out of place, playing the devoted mistress while still feeling Mario between my thighs.

"Stay tonight," Anthony had suggested—ordered, really—his hands possessive on my waist. But after having Mario, Anthony's touch felt hollow.

"Early meeting tomorrow," I'd demurred, playing shy. "Rain check?"

Mario was waiting at my apartment, and we'd spent the rest of the night claiming each other against every surface. The kitchen counter, the shower wall, the Italian marble table with its bullet holes—nowhere was safe from our hunger.

Since then, it's like a dam has broken. We're insatiable, meeting wherever and whenever we can. His car in underground parking garages, empty offices during charity galas, once in a private box at the opera while the Calabrese family sat unaware in their usual seats below.

I find his shirt on the floor and slip it on, the fabric cool. His scent envelops me—expensive cologne, coffee, that underlying hint of danger that makes my pulse race.

The kitchen doorway frames him like a painting of a fallen angel. Shirtless, dangerous, perfectly at ease as he makes coffee I can no longer stomach.

Scars map his broad back—bullet wounds, knife marks, a burn that spans his left shoulder blade. The scratches I left last night stand out red against olive skin, making something primal surge in my chest.

He turns at my approach, and his eyes darken at the sight of me in just his shirt. I can't help but stare—he's all lean muscle and deadly grace, more scars scattered across his chest telling stories I'm afraid to ask about. A tattoo in Italian script curves along his ribs, partially hidden by an old knife wound.

He reaches for a second coffee mug but I shake my head, my stomach already protesting the smell.

His chuckle is low and knowing as he produces a cup of ginger tea instead. "Thought this might sit better, little planner."

The gesture—so thoughtful, so domestic—creates an awkward tension I hate. We've crossed every line imaginable. I'm carrying Anthony Calabrese's child, betraying my best friend's family in ways that would get me killed if discovered. And yet …

Mario studies me over his coffee cup, those dark eyes probing beneath my skin. "What?" I ask, defensive.

"Come to Boston with me."

The teacup nearly slips from my fingers. "What?"

"Not permanently," he clarifies, something dark flashing in his eyes. "But O'Connor's breathing down my neck, and I need to handle some business there. You could work remotely for a few days, gather intel on the Irish operations firsthand."

The practical suggestion doesn't match the intensity of his gaze. This is about more than intelligence gathering, more than our careful game of strategy.

But admitting that would make this real in ways neither of us is ready to face.

Mario's hand finds my stomach, the gesture more intimate than anything we did last night. I force myself not to lean into his touch, even as warmth spreads from where his palm rests against me.

"Anthony's getting suspicious," he says, his voice low. "He's been asking questions about where you disappear to."

God, don't I know it. Finding excuses not to see Anthony has become increasingly difficult. I've stopped sleeping with him entirely —I can't stomach it anymore, not after Mario. Even if it means losing access to vital intelligence, the thought of Anthony's hands on me makes my skin crawl.

As if summoned by the thought, my phone buzzes with Anthony's ringtone. The sight of his name makes bile rise in my throat—or maybe that's just morning sickness.

I've been playing this game for months, letting him think he's claiming something precious while I steal his secrets. But now …

"Bella's watching too," I admit, remembering our encounter at the opera three nights ago.

I'd slipped away from the Calabrese family box, making some excuse about needing air. Mario was waiting in a darkened corridor, and within moments he had me pressed against the wall, thrusting into me while Puccini's aria soared in the background.

I'd been heading back to the box, still trembling from our tryst, when Bella emerged from the powder room. The look in her eyes stopped me cold.

"Elena?" Those artist's eyes had taken in everything—my flushed cheeks, the slight disarray of my hair, the way I couldn't quite meet her gaze. She reached out, adjusting the strap of my dress that had slipped. "What's going on with you lately?"

I'd made some excuse about feeling warm, needing air, but I saw the understanding in her expression. The hurt. Those eyes that see too much, that understand too well.

She'd grabbed my wrist as I tried to pass. "Whatever you're involved in with Anthony ... please be careful. You can come to me with anything. You know that, right?"

If she only knew.

"Then we need to be more careful." Mario moves behind me now, his chest solid against my back as his arms cage me against the counter. "No more risks. No more close calls."

But we both know it's too late for careful. The evidence grows inside me, a ticking time bomb of complicated loyalties and dangerous choices.

Every day that passes makes it harder to hide—from Anthony, from Bella, from the world. Soon, everyone will know I'm carrying a Calabrese heir. The thought makes panic rise in my throat.

What happens when Anthony finds out? When he realizes I've been sleeping with someone else while carrying his child? When Bella discovers I've betrayed not just her trust, but her entire family?

The DeLucas and Calabreses have killed for less.

When Mario's lips hover just behind my ear, I feel a shiver run through me, like electricity crackling between us. His breath is warm against my skin, a soft, steady rhythm that stirs a heat deep inside me. It's a dangerous thing, how close he is, how easily he seems to ignite something in me that I've tried so hard to keep buried.

I want to pull away, to remind myself of the weight of everything that's at stake, but my body betrays me, leaning into him instead.

The moment his lips press softly to that sensitive spot just below my earlobe, a quiet moan escapes before I can stop it, my chest tightening in response to the intimate caress. His lips move against my skin, featherlight at first, sending waves of heat cascading through my body. He knows exactly where to touch, where to tease, and how to make me forget every damn thing except the feel of him.

I can feel the faint press of his chest against my back, his breath hot and steady in the curve of my neck as his arms tighten around my waist, holding me there. I let myself fall into the moment for just a second, letting his warmth and his touch erase the world around us.

The weight of our lives, the secrets we carry, the betrayals and the choices—they all blur into the background as his lips brush along my skin, sending another shiver down my spine.

His hands tighten, pulling me impossibly closer, his body pressing against mine in a way that makes it impossible to ignore the undeniable chemistry between us. I tilt my head slightly, offering him more of my neck, more of me, feeling the tension build between us with every inch closer he draws me. The warmth of his lips deepens as he kisses me there again, his tongue grazing the soft skin at the curve of my ear.

It's a slow burn, the kind of touch that makes my pulse race and my breath catch in my throat, reminding me of how easily I've surrendered to him.

But even as my body craves more, my mind is at war. Anthony's claims, Bella's suspicion—they flash in the back of my mind, haunting me, reminding me of the danger we're in.

But for now, for this one, stolen moment, I let everything else slip away. It's just him. Just his lips against my skin, his warmth surrounding me, making everything else feel irrelevant.

～

Mario's driver drops me at my apartment building as evening shadows stretch across Fifth Avenue.

The memory of Seamus O'Connor's voice still echoes in my head from Mario's earlier phone call, each word dripping with barely contained violence.

"You test my patience, boy," O'Connor had snarled through the speaker. "I didn't give you sanctuary just to watch you fucking play house in New York."

"I'll be on the next flight," Mario had replied, his jaw tight. "The situation here needed handling."

"The only situation you need to handle is the one I've assigned you. Or have you forgotten our arrangement? Forgotten who owns you?"

The threat in O'Connor's voice had made even me shiver. I'd watched Mario's face darken, his fingers white-knuckled around the phone. For a moment, I thought he might shatter it.

My own phone hasn't stopped buzzing since this morning. The texts from Anthony grow increasingly demanding:

7:15 AM: *Missing you, beautiful. Dinner tonight?*

9:45 AM: *Elena, at least answer my calls.*

11:30 AM: *Are you feeling unwell? I can send my doctor.*

1:45 PM: *This isn't like you.*

3:20 PM: *I don't like being ignored,* cara.

4:15 PM: *We need to talk about your recent ... disappearances.*

The last one makes my stomach clench. Bella's text feels like a lifeline in comparison: *Dinner tonight? Just us girls. I feel like I never see you anymore.*

I text back a quick yes to Bella but continue ignoring Anthony. I'm not in the mood to deal with him. Maybe the radio silence will give me time to figure out how to handle this growing complexity.

"Good afternoon, Miss Santiago." The doorman tips his hat—James, who's worked here for twenty years and still brings me coffee some mornings. I can't help but smile, remembering Mario's scathing assessment of my building's security.

"A blind grandmother with a cane could breach this place," he growled during one of his recent visits. *"The doorman doesn't even carry a fucking weapon. The security cameras have three blind spots in the lobby alone. And don't get me started on the service entrance."*

I take the elevator up, my mind already on a hot shower and maybe a nap before dinner with Bella. My feet ache from the Louboutins, and morning sickness has left me exhausted. But when I step out onto my floor, something makes me pause.

A cream-colored envelope lies in front of my door, my name

written in elegant calligraphy. No return address. Curious, I pick it up, sliding my finger under the flap.

White powder explodes outward, coating my hands, my clothes, floating in the air around me. A note flutters to the ground:

Enjoying your game with both DeLuca and Calabrese? Ask Sophia how that worked out for her. Some games leave permanent scars.

The powder settles on my skin like a death sentence.

12

MARIO

I stare out the jet's window, rage building with every mile between Elena and me. Who the fuck does Seamus O'Connor think he is, summoning me like some errand boy? I'm Mario fucking DeLuca. I had Manhattan crime families trembling at my name before O'Connor ever offered his "sanctuary."

The memory of owing anyone anything burns like acid in my throat. Five years ago, I needed O'Connor's protection, his resources, his connections. But I've more than repaid that debt with blood and loyalty.

Now he treats me like a trained dog, expected to come running at his whistle.

My hands itch for a gun, for the satisfaction of violence. Instead, I watch Boston's coastline emerge through clouds, its old money mansions and historic architecture a poor substitute for New York's grandeur.

Everything about this city feels like exile—which, I suppose, was the point.

The car waiting on the tarmac delivers me straight to the O'Connor compound in Beacon Hill. The mansion sprawls across two acres of prime real estate, its red brick walls rising three stories behind wrought iron gates that could stop a tank.

Where the Calabreses flaunt their wealth with gaudy excess, the O'Connors hide theirs behind historic preservation and old-world sophistication. Guards patrol the immaculate grounds in tailored suits that barely conceal their weapons, while state-of-the-art security cameras track every movement from behind classical cornices.

The driveway curves past manicured gardens where I know landmines are buried beneath prize-winning roses. The garage alone could house thirty cars, though Seamus prefers to display his vintage collection in a separate building that used to be a carriage house. Everything about the compound screams old money, old power, old blood.

Patrick Lynch materializes in the marble foyer like the fucking cockroach he is. O'Connor's second-in-command stands just under six feet, but his bantam rooster attitude makes him seem smaller. That perfectly styled red hair and those cold green eyes—so like his cousin Seamus—broadcast his family connection, while the expensive suit can't quite hide his dockworker's build.

A badly healed broken nose mars what might otherwise be handsome features, a souvenir from his days running protection rackets on the waterfront.

"Finally decided to grace us with your presence?" His accent is thick with disdain. "The Boss has been waiting."

"Careful, Patrick." I smile, letting him see the violence behind it. "Wouldn't want to test my patience today."

"Big man in New York, were you?" He steps closer, and I catch a whiff of expensive scotch on his breath. "Playing house with your brother's event planner while real work needs doing?"

My hand finds his throat before he can blink. "Say another word about her and they'll never find all your pieces."

Lynch jerks away, straightening his tie with shaking hands. A bruise is already forming where my fingers dug in, but his eyes still glitter with satisfaction. He knows he's struck a nerve.

"The Boss is waiting in his study." His smirk widens as he rubs his throat. "Try not to keep him waiting any longer ... lackey."

The word hits like a slap. Five years I've spent building my own power base here, making myself indispensable to O'Connor's operation. Yet this dock rat still sees me as an outsider, a servant called to heel.

My fingers itch to show him exactly how sharp this dog's teeth are.

But O'Connor's waiting, and even my rage has limits. For now.

I adjust my Brioni tie before entering the lion's den. Seamus's office hits me with a wall of whiskey and Cuban cigar smoke, the scents as much a power play as the room itself. Dark wood panels line walls that have witnessed a century of violence disguised as business. A Monet hangs above a fireplace that's seen more evidence burned than it has logs.

Seamus sits behind a desk that probably belonged to some British lord before finding its way here through bloody means. He looks exactly like what he is—a predator playing at civility. His steel-gray hair is perfectly styled, but his cold eyes hold all the warmth of a shark's.

But it's Siobhan who commands my attention. She perches on the edge of her father's desk like a cat who's found the cream, and something in her expression sets my teeth on edge.

I told Elena that Siobhan wouldn't reveal her pregnancy, but watching that calculating smile, I'm less certain. Siobhan O'Connor is a loose cannon—the kind you can't read until it's too late. At least with Seamus, the violence is predictable.

I take a seat in one of the leather chairs facing the desk.

"I don't recall giving you permission to sit, DeLuca," Seamus growls.

I shrug, deliberately casual. "My feet are tired from all the running I do at your command."

"Your little planner is proving quite interesting," Siobhan drawls, tossing surveillance photos across her father's desk. Elena entering doctor's offices. Us in a compromising position against my car. Anthony's men watching her from unmarked vehicles. Another of Anthony's tongue down Elena's throat, his hand cupping her ass.

That one makes my vision blur red.

"Pregnant with Calabrese's heir while feeding you information. Quite the ambitious little thing, isn't she?"

I keep my expression neutral even as my self-control splinters in my chest. "Elena's involvement is tactical," I say smoothly. "A means to an end."

"Is it?" Siobhan's smile turns cruel as she circles the desk. "Because *our* sources say Anthony's not the only one sharing her bed these days."

She moves closer, all elegance and deadly intent. "The question is ... are you compromised, Mario? Letting a pretty face and clever mind distract you from our arrangement?"

"Enough games," Seamus cuts in, his voice like gravel. "You're here because you've forgotten your place, boy. Forgotten who owns your debt."

"I've more than repaid any debt—"

"You've repaid when I say you've repaid!" Seamus's fist crashes against the desk. "The DeLuca empire falls. That was our deal. Instead, you're fucking your brother's event planner while my interests in Manhattan suffer."

"*Your* interests?" I can't help but laugh. "Or your daughter's? I hear the younger captains are quite taken with her ... modernization efforts."

Siobhan's eyes flash. "Careful, Mario. Elena isn't the only one who can disappear in this city."

"Touch her and—"

"And what?" Seamus's smile is terrible. "You'll break our arrangement? Go running back to the brother who exiled you? Whose wife has permission to put a bullet through you if you return? Or to the Calabreses who'd love to mount your head on their wall?"

He leans forward. "You're mine, boy. Have been since you crawled to Boston with your tail between your legs. The only question is whether your little bitch pays for your disobedience."

My hands curl into fists, but it's Siobhan's interest that truly terrifies me. I recognize that look in her eyes—the same one Johnny Calabrese wore before destroying his toys. That particular gleam of anticipation, like a child who's found a new doll to dismember.

Her smile holds too many teeth, and those cold green eyes study Elena's photos with the focused intensity of someone imagining all the ways to take something apart. It's not just cruelty—Johnny had that in spades—it's the clinical fascination of someone who wants to understand exactly how much pressure it takes to break something beautiful.

The look says: I could destroy this, and I'd enjoy learning how.

"The DeLucas will fall," I say carefully. "You have my word."

"Good." Seamus sits back, seemingly satisfied. "Because if they don't, Elena's pregnancy might meet an unfortunate end. Tragic, really, how delicate women can be in their condition."

It takes everything in me not to reach across the desk and tear his throat out.

I grit my teeth and nod sharply. Seamus dismisses me with a wave, like I'm some fucking errand boy instead of the man who's kept his Boston operations running smoothly for five years.

But I'm self-aware enough to know when I'm outmatched. As an exile, I have no family backing, no one to avenge me if I disappear into Boston Harbor.

Patrick Lynch waits in the hallway, that fucking smirk still on his face. "How's the leash feel, DeLuca?"

My control snaps. My fist connects with his jaw before he can blink, the satisfying crunch of bone worth whatever consequences come. "Fuck you, you Irish piece of shit."

Back in my office overlooking the harbor, I try to focus on work, but rage keeps my hands shaking. I text Elena: **Check in. Now.** Then: **Answer your fucking phone.**

Nothing.

Growling, I shut the phone in my desk drawer. Boston's gray skyline offers no comfort as I stare out the window, imagining all the ways I could make O'Connor pay for his threats.

The door opens without a knock. Siobhan stalks in, but she's different now—gone is the arrogance from her father's office. Now she vibrates with barely contained fury, her composure cracked around the edges.

"What the fuck do you want?" I growl, not in the mood for her bullshit.

"What the fuck was that?" she snarls, stalking to my desk. I barely recognize this version of Siobhan. Gone is the polished predator from her father's office. Her perfectly styled red hair is slightly disheveled, like she's been running her hands through it. That arrogant mask has cracked, revealing something raw and desperate underneath. "Bringing up my modernization efforts to my father? Are you trying to get me *killed*?"

"Bit dramatic, even for you." I lean back, studying how her hands shake slightly. Something's off here. "Fair's fair, especially since you told Daddy Dearest about Elena's condition."

"You fucking idiot!" She slams her hands on my desk hard enough to scatter papers. "You've put *everything* at risk—my life, Sean's life—because you can't keep your goddamn mouth shut!"

I shrug, uncaring. "Not my problem if daddy doesn't approve of your little power plays."

"Little *power plays*?" She laughs, but it holds an edge of hysteria. "You think this is about impressing my father? About proving myself?"

She runs a hand through her hair, further destroying its perfect style. "This is about survival, you arrogant prick. About dragging this organization into the modern era before we all end up dead or in prison."

"What's so important about your modernization that's got you this scared, Siobhan?" I ask, curious. I've never seen Siobhan like this before.

Her face goes carefully blank, but not before I catch real fear in her eyes. "Get fucked."

My phone buzzes in the drawer. Probably Elena finally responding, but I'm not about to check with Siobhan here.

A terrible smile spreads across her face, and just like that, she's transformed again—terror replaced by vicious satisfaction. "I wouldn't expect that to be Elena," she coos.

My head snaps up. Something shifts in her expression—that clinical fascination returning, but now mixed with something almost gleeful. Like she's grateful for the distraction from her own fears.

"What the fuck does that mean?" I ask tightly, my heart hammering.

One perfectly sculpted red eyebrow rises. "You don't know?" Her voice drips with false concern. "And here I thought you kept such close tabs on your ... *asset*. All those careful arrangements, all that meticulous planning, and you still can't protect what's yours."

I'm across the room in two strides, my hand around her throat as I pin her to the wall. "What the fuck did you do to Elena?"

Instead of fear, she digs her nails into my hand until I release her, drawing blood. "Poor Elena was whisked to the hospital an hour ago."

She straightens her Prada blazer, looking far too delighted. "Seems you haven't taught her proper security protocols. Opening strange envelopes like a rookie ..." She tsks. "Especially when they're filled with what appears to be anthrax."

Siobhan's words are like a slap to the face. Anthrax? Elena? The baby ...

"You—"

"Oh no, not me." She moves toward the door, that mask of controlled calculation sliding back into place. "I have much bigger concerns than your girlfriend. But perhaps if you'd kept your mouth shut about my operations, I might have warned her about the envelope."

She pauses at the door. "Funny how actions have consequences, isn't it?"

I'm frozen, unable to speak.

"Frightening how quickly some toxins can affect pregnant women," Siobhan adds with a cruel smile before shutting the door behind her.

I nearly break the desk drawer yanking it open, my hands shaking so badly I can barely grab my phone. Please let her be lying. *Please* let this be another one of her fucking mind games.

But the buzzing notification wasn't Elena. Just a fucking spam email about dick pills.

"No, no, no ..." The word becomes a growl as I dial Elena's number.

Straight to voicemail.

I try again. And again.

Nothing.

Anthrax. The word echoes in my head.

With trembling fingers, I call Dante. I don't even wait for him to say anything. "Get the jet ready. Now."

"Boss?" Confusion colors his voice. "O'Connor made it crystal clear—"

"I don't give a FUCK what O'Connor made clear!" The roar tears from my throat as I sweep everything off my desk. Glass shatters. Papers flutter. "Get the fucking jet ready. I'm going back to New York."

Dante sucks in a deep breath. "Mario, he'll kill you—"

"Permanently." The word comes out like a death warrant. "I'm done being O'Connor's bitch. Done playing these fucking games. Get the jet ready or I'll fly commercial."

There's a long pause as Dante tries to make sense of what I'm saying. "Mario, what happened?"

"Elena ..." My voice cracks. "Someone sent her anthrax. She's ... I need to—"

"Fuck." Dante understands immediately. "I'll have the jet ready in forty minutes. But Boss? This means war with O'Connor."

I think of Elena opening that envelope. Of the baby growing inside her. Of all the ways I've failed to protect them both. "Let them come."

13

ELENA

The hospital room is sterile white and oppressively quiet except for the steady beep of monitors. I close my eyes, but all I can see is that white powder settling on my skin like death made tangible.

The last three hours replay in my mind like a nightmare. The powder exploding outward, coating my hands, my clothes, floating in the air around me. The note fluttering to the ground. My hands shaking so badly I could barely dial 911.

"Please," I begged the operator, my voice breaking. "I'm pregnant. There's white powder everywhere."

What followed was like something from a disaster movie. First responders flooding my building within minutes. The screech of sirens, the flash of emergency lights turning Fifth Avenue into a carnival of red and blue. Men in hazmat suits materializing in my hallway like astronauts, their voices muffled behind protective masks as they ordered me not to move, not to touch anything.

"Try not to brush off the powder," one had instructed while another took photos. "Keep your hands away from your face. Breathe normally."

Breathe normally. Right. With potentially lethal powder coating my skin and a baby to protect.

James the doorman's face had been ghost white as they evacuated the building. "Miss Santiago ..." he'd started to say, but hazmat-suited figures had pushed him back. I watched my neighbors being hurried out—the hedge fund manager from 12B still in his silk pajamas, the society widow from 9A clutching her Pomeranian.

All of them staring at me like I was already dead.

The ambulance ride felt like a blur of terror and clinical questions. Paramedics in protective gear asking about my medical history, my pregnancy, any symptoms. "How far along are you?" one had asked, her eyes kind behind her mask.

"Ten weeks," I'd whispered, tears finally breaking free. "Will my baby ... ?" I couldn't finish the question.

Now, hours later, that fear claws at my throat. If this is anthrax, what does that mean for my child? The doctors speak in careful terms about "monitoring the situation" and "preventative antibiotics," but I see the concern in their eyes when they look at my chart.

"Is there anyone we should call? Family?" A nurse asks me.

Mario's face flashes in my mind immediately. My hand actually twitches toward my phone before I stop myself. I can't call him. Not with O'Connor's threats hanging over his head. If he comes rushing back to New York, Matteo will know within hours. The DeLucas have eyes everywhere—in hospitals, police stations, even emergency dispatch.

One call to Mario could be his death.

"Ms. Santiago?" The nurse prompts gently. "Perhaps Mrs. DeLuca? We have her listed as your emergency contact."

My throat tightens. Bella would come immediately, dropping everything to be here. But she'd bring Matteo's protective fury with her, and then would come the questions—about the envelope, about the note mentioning Sophia.

Questions I'm not ready to answer. Questions that could get us all killed.

As for my biological family ... I cut them off years ago. They're dead to me, just like I'm dead to them. The nurse's suggestion about contacting them almost makes me laugh. They wouldn't come anyway.

"No," I manage. "There's no one to call."

The lie tastes bitter, but it's safer than the truth. Safer than admitting I'm carrying Anthony Calabrese's child while sleeping with his enemy. Safer than explaining why someone might want to send me anthrax in the first place.

The nurse's expression holds pity as she notes "No family contacts" in my chart. If she only knew that my real family is too dangerous to involve. That the people I love most are the ones I have to protect by staying away.

My hand drifts to my stomach. Somewhere inside me, a child grows—a child who might already be in danger because of my choices, my games, my lies. Tears slip down my cheeks before I can stop them.

For the first time since I started playing this dangerous game, I feel truly alone.

My solitude lasts exactly twenty-eight minutes before Bella bursts through the door like an avenging angel, Matteo's tall frame filling the space behind her. My heart plummets.

Of course HIPAA means nothing when your best friend is married to one of New York's most powerful men.

"Elena!" Bella rushes forward, her face pale with worry. "Why didn't you call me? Are you okay? Have the test results—"

"Don't." Matteo's command stops her inches from my bed. His eyes never leave my face, cold and calculating. "Step back, *piccola*. We don't know if it's anthrax yet."

"I feel fine," I say quickly, hating how my voice shakes. "No symptoms. It's probably nothing—"

"Anthrax symptoms can develop over days." Matteo's tone is icy. "Sometimes weeks."

Bella wrings her hands, and guilt churns in my stomach. "The doctors are running tests," I tell her. "But really, I'm okay."

"What *I* want to know," Matteo cuts in, moving to stand at the foot of my bed, "is why someone would target my wife's best friend with a biological weapon."

The question hangs heavy in the air. I force myself to meet his gaze. "I don't know."

"No?" His smile doesn't reach his eyes. "Then perhaps you can explain how they got past your building's security. Or why you didn't immediately call us when you arrived at the hospital."

"I didn't want to worry anyone—"

"Bullshit." The word cracks like a whip. "You're hiding something, Elena. The only question is what."

"Matteo," Bella warns, but he continues.

"First the disappearing acts. Then the missed calls. Now this?" He leans forward, his hands gripping the bed rail. "What game are you playing?"

My heart pounds so loud I'm sure he can hear it. "No game," I manage. "I was just ... scared."

"Elena." Bella's voice is soft, hurt. "We're family. You should have called us."

Family. The word feels like a knife twisting in my chest. If they knew about Mario, about the baby, about all my lies ...

"I'm sorry," I whisper, and at least that's not a lie. "I wasn't thinking clearly."

Matteo studies me for a long moment. "Antonio," he calls, and his captain materializes in the doorway. "Post guards. No one in or out without my approval."

"That's not necessary—" I start, panic rising.

"It wasn't a suggestion." Matteo's tone brooks no argument. "Someone targeted you, which means they targeted my family. Until we know why, you don't leave our sight."

The words feel like a prison sentence. Or a death warrant, if Mario tries to come to me now.

The doctor returns hours later with results that make my knees weak with relief. Not anthrax—just powdered sugar mixed with chalk dust. A scare tactic, not a death sentence. I nearly burst into tears.

"Follow up with your primary care physician," he says, carefully not mentioning my pregnancy. "But you should be fine to go home."

"She'll be coming home with us," Matteo interjects smoothly. "For monitoring and safety."

"Like hell I will." The words slip out before I can stop them. "I'm going to my own home."

Matteo's expression could cut glass. "That wasn't a request, Elena."

"And that wasn't an acceptance, Matteo," I respond coolly.

The doctor looks between us, clearly sensing the mounting tension. "I'll ... just get those discharge papers ready." He practically runs from the room. Coward.

A knock interrupts our standoff. One of Matteo's men appears, his face grim. "Boss, there's a young woman here. Claims she's Ms. Santiago's cousin."

Cousin? My heart skips. I'm an only child, my mother was an only child, and we never saw my father's side—

A girl bursts into the room, all wild brown curls and huge doe eyes. She can't be more than nineteen, dressed in ripped jeans and a cropped NYU sweatshirt. Before anyone can stop her, she's at my bedside.

"Oh my God, Elena!" Her words tumble out in a rush of tears and relief. "We were so worried! The hospital called Mom and she completely freaked out, saying we needed to bring you home right away. Why didn't you call us?"

I stare at her face—heart-shaped, earnest, those big brown eyes silently pleading with me to play along. Something in her expression makes me trust her, though I couldn't say why.

"Jenna," I manage, though I'm certain that's not her name, but I know it's a distant cousin's name. "Tell your mother I'm fine. Really."

"I thought you didn't have any family," Bella says slowly, confusion evident in her voice.

"Jenna" turns to face Matteo's scrutiny. "My mother is her father's sister," she says smoothly. "We lost touch after Uncle Richard died, but—"

"Convenient timing," Matteo cuts in, his eyes narrowed. "Showing up now."

"Not convenient," she counters, meeting his gaze without flinching. "Family." She produces a driver's license that looks perfectly real, the name Jenna Santiago clear beneath her photo.

Something about her composure, her careful answers ... this girl is more than she appears. But right now, she might be my only chance at avoiding Matteo's fortress.

"Elena's coming home with me," Jenna announces, gathering my belongings.

"Absolutely not." Matteo's voice is forbidding. "She's coming to the compound where we can protect her. We haven't even verified your identity."

Jenna rolls her eyes before turning to me. "Who the fuck does this guy think he is?"

The temperature in the room drops ten degrees. Nobody talks to Matteo DeLuca like that.

"Elena," Bella interjects quickly, sensing danger. "*Please*. It would be safer with us until we figure out who tried to hurt you."

But I've made my decision. Whatever game this girl is playing, it's better than being under Matteo's thumb. "I'm going with my cousin."

Jenna beams triumphantly. The hurt that flashes across Bella's face makes me hate myself, but I can't take it back now.

"Nobody leaves until we verify her identity." Matteo's tone brooks no argument.

"Fine by me." Jenna drops into a chair, crossing her ankles with exaggerated patience. "I've got nowhere to be."

It takes less than an hour for Matteo's men to confirm that Jenna Santiago exists and is, apparently, actually related to my father through his sister. I keep my face carefully blank at this news.

"Finally," Jenna sighs. "Can we leave now?"

The discharge process seems to take forever. Before I can escape, Bella pulls me into a careful hug. "Call me, okay? Promise?"

"I promise," I whisper, the lie tasting like ash.

Matteo catches my arm as I pass. "Whatever game you're playing," he says softly, his blue eyes cold, "remember that my wife considers you family. If anything happens to her because of your ... choices, there won't be anywhere safe for you to hide."

I meet his gaze steadily. "I'd never hurt Bella."

"No?" His smile is cruel. "You already are."

His words are like a knife to my chest, but I keep my face impassive, cold. Professional. I jerk my arm from his grip and walk away, refusing to let him see how deeply that cut.

The air slaps my face as we exit the hospital, making my eyes water. Or at least that's what I tell myself as I blink back tears. A sleek black SUV idles at the curb, its dark-tinted windows reflecting the hospital's harsh fluorescent lights. A broad-shouldered man in tactical gear sits in the driver's seat, his eyes constantly scanning our surroundings through mirrored sunglasses.

Jenna—or whoever she is—collapses into the leather seat beside me with a dramatic sigh. "Take us away, Manolo," she says, and the car jerks slightly as it pulls away from the hospital.

The innocent, bubbly cousin act vanishes as she pulls out her phone, her fingers flying across the screen with fierce concentration.

The transformation is jarring.

"Cut the shit." My patience snaps like a brittle twig. "Who are you and why did you just risk your life lying to Matteo DeLuca?"

She winks, those innocent doe eyes suddenly sharp with intelligence. "Sofia Renaldi. And Mario DeLuca sent me to get you to the safe house in Tribeca."

My heart stops. "Mario—"

"My brother Marco is one of his closest friends." She grins, looking pleased with herself. "Pretty good act, right? Though I thought that DeLuca asshole was going to have me disappeared when I rolled my eyes at him."

14

MARIO

I wear a path in the safe house's hardwood floors, my footsteps echoing off floor-to-ceiling windows that overlook Manhattan's glittering skyline. Marco Renaldi sprawls on the leather couch, looking infuriatingly calm as he scrolls through his phone. His dark curls—almost black in this light—fall across his forehead, and that perpetual stubble does nothing to hide his angular jaw.

Even after twenty-five years of friendship, he still looks like the scrappy kid who used to have my back in schoolyard fights.

We met when we were eight—both of us trying to steal the same car on Giuseppe's orders. Instead of fighting over it, we'd worked together.

That kind of thing creates a bond that even exile can't break. Marco was there the night I held a gun to Bianca's head. He and Dante helped me land in Boston afterward. His father might run a smaller operation, but the Renaldis have always understood loyalty better than the DeLucas.

"Relax," he drawls, not looking up. "Sofia's got this."

"If your sister gets caught—"

"She won't." He finally meets my gaze, those dark eyes holding the same sharp intelligence that got us both out of countless situations. "Sofia's better at this shit than both of us combined."

He's not wrong. His sister started running cons when she was ten, proving herself more valuable to their father's organization than half of his made men. By fifteen, she was the one handling their more delicate extraction operations.

Now at nineteen, she's developed a reputation for getting people out of impossible situations—usually while making their enemies look like idiots in the process.

I resume pacing. The moment Siobhan told me about Elena, I knew I couldn't go to the hospital myself. Matteo would have men crawling all over it—probably already did.

Going there would be suicide, and I couldn't help Elena if I was dead.

"Your sister's really up for this?" I'd asked Marco three hours ago while I was on the jet, after calling in a twenty-year favor.

"Sofia?" He'd laughed. "That girl could convince the Pope he's Jewish. Besides ..." His expression had darkened. "After O'Connor's men tried to take over our Brooklyn territory last month, she's been looking for ways to stick it to the old guard. Getting one over on Matteo DeLuca? That's just bonus points."

It had been Marco's idea to use his sister. "Think about it," he'd said. "Matteo's looking for threats. He's watching for rival families, the Calabreses, for my father's people, for you. But a teenage girl claiming to be Elena's long-lost cousin? That's so far out of left field it might work."

He'd been right. Marco's always been the strategic one—probably why his father thought I should have led the DeLuca family instead of Matteo. Old man Renaldi had seen something in me that Giuseppe never did. Had even offered to back my claim after Giuseppe's death, but by then I was already deep into my revenge against Matteo. Already sealed my fate.

Marco had put Sofia on speaker when we were brainstorming how to get Elena out.

"Does she have any family?" Sofia had asked. "Anyone I could impersonate?"

I'd drawn a blank, realizing I knew almost nothing about Elena's background. Her family had never seemed relevant to our plans. "I ... don't know."

"Are you fucking kidding me?" Sofia's disgust had crackled through the phone. "You're sleeping with her and you don't even know her family history?"

"Just find something," I'd growled, annoyed at how Sofia had twisted this.

"Give me five minutes." Keys had clicked rapidly in the background. "Got it. Her father—Richard Santiago, deceased five years ago—had a sister named Maria. Maria has a nineteen-year-old daughter, Jenna Santiago, currently enrolled at NYU." More typing. "Well, what do you know? Little Jenna's got brown curly hair, brown eyes ... I could pass for her."

"You found this how?" I'd asked, unsure if I should be impressed or concerned.

"Please." Sofia's eye roll had been audible. "Social media, death records, college enrollment ... it's not exactly Fort Knox. The real Jenna Santiago is currently posting Instagram stories from Central Park."

"It won't be enough," Marco had warned. "Matteo won't let Elena leave without proof."

"Already on it. Marco, call your guy at the DMV. I need a driver's license that'll pass inspection. And find me everything you can about this family—birth records, old photos, any detail that could trip me up."

Now, waiting for them to arrive, I have to admit the plan was brilliant. Sofia had memorized the Santiago family tree in under an hour, created a backstory that matched public records, even studied Jenna's social media to perfect her mannerisms.

"Your sister's terrifying," I tell Marco.

He grins. "You have no idea. Remember when she convinced that cop she was the mayor's niece?"

"She was twelve," I say fondly. Sofia was the sister I never had.

"Exactly. Now imagine what she can do at nineteen. She's going to run circles around Matteo."

I resume pacing the penthouse when both Marco's phone and mine buzz simultaneously. We dive for them, opening the group chat from Sofia:

Mission accomplished! Got her out easy peasy. No anthrax btw (duh). You should have seen me work Matteo DeLuca. Oscar-worthy performance if I do say so myself :-)

Marco whoops. "What did I tell you? My sister's the best."

Good work. Get here quickly, I text back.

Wow, try to contain your enthusiasm there, old man. I'll take that as a thank you.

My hands shake slightly as I wait for the elevator. When it finally dings, my knees nearly buckle at the sight of Elena—pale but alive, still wearing that hospital gown under a borrowed coat. Sofia stands next to her, practically vibrating with self-satisfaction.

"What the hell are you doing in New York again?" Elena demands, her relief at seeing me quickly morphing into anger. "If O'Connor finds out—"

"I left him." The words come out like a declaration of war. "Permanently."

Elena's eyes go wide. Even Sofia's smug expression falters.

"Are you insane?" Elena's voice rises. "He'll kill you. He'll—"

"Let him try." I move closer, unable to stop myself from touching her face, needing to feel that she's real. "I'm done being his attack dog."

"Well, this is getting spicy," Sofia stage-whispers to her brother.

Marco grabs her arm. "And that's our cue. We'll talk later," he tells me, dragging his protesting sister toward the elevator.

"But I want to see how this plays out!" Sofia whines.

"Out. Now." Marco's voice fades as the elevator doors close on them.

The moment the elevator doors close, Elena whirls on me. "What the fuck were you thinking?" Her voice shakes with rage. "You just threw away everything—all our intel, all our plans—because what? You got spooked?"

"I got *spooked*?" I advance on her. "*You're* the one who opened a fucking unmarked envelope like some amateur. What happened to all that security protocol you're so proud of?"

"Don't you dare lecture me about protocols." She backs up until she hits the window, Manhattan's lights creating a halo around her fury. "You just declared war on Seamus O'Connor. Do you have any idea what he'll do to you?"

"Better than watching you get yourself killed! Christ, Elena, you could have—" The words stick in my throat. "The baby could have—"

"Oh, *now* you care about the baby?" She jams a finger into my chest, color flooding her too-pale face. "This isn't about me or the baby. This is about your ego. Your need to control everything, to—"

"My *ego*?" I grab her wrist before she can poke me again. "You think I left O'Connor because of my fucking ego? I left because the thought of you in that hospital, of not being able to get to you—"

"I didn't ask you to come charging in like some knight in bloodstained armor!" She tries to yank her hand free, but I hold tight. "I had it under control."

"Under control?" My laugh is sharp and bitter, the sound cutting through the tension between us. "You could have died. And for what? Some half-baked plan to—"

She doesn't let me finish. With a fierce growl, she surges up on her toes, her lips parting like she's about to unleash every fiery accusation bottled inside her. But before the words can escape, I'm done waiting. I claim her mouth with mine, crushing her protests under the weight of everything I'm too afraid to say aloud.

The kiss is wild, untamed, a collision of anger and desperation. Her teeth nip at my bottom lip, sharp enough to sting, drawing blood that mixes with the taste of her, sharp and intoxicating. A low growl rumbles in my chest as I retaliate, driving her backward until her spine meets the cold glass of the window with a soft thud.

My hands travel down her sides, fingers splayed wide as if I need to map every inch of her, anchoring her hips against mine. She lets out a sound—half-gasp, half-moan—as I press closer, the heat between us scorching. Her fingers knot into my shirt, pulling me even nearer, her nails scraping my chest as if she's trying to find some way to crawl under my skin.

She breaks the kiss only to drag in a ragged breath, but I'm not done. My mouth moves to her neck, finding the soft, sensitive hollow just below her jaw. I nip at it, earning a gasp that makes my blood sing. Her hands are in my hair now, nails raking my scalp as I tease that spot again, pulling another breathless moan from her lips.

"You drive me crazy," I murmur against her skin, my voice rough with emotion. I let my teeth graze the delicate line of her throat, savoring the way she shivers against me, the way she arches into my touch like she can't stand even a sliver of space between us.

My hand threads into her hair, gripping gently but firmly as I tug her head back to expose more of her throat. The way she looks at me, her lips parted, her eyes dark and glassy with a mix of fury and need—it undoes me.

Her body molds against mine, pliant and demanding all at once, and I press harder, the cold glass behind her a stark contrast to the heat between us. The sound she makes—a raw, desperate cry—ignites something primal in me. I kiss her again, harder this time, pouring every ounce of fear, relief, and hunger into it.

When we finally break apart, we're both gasping for air, her lips swollen and her cheeks flushed. Her eyes are locked on mine, daring me to look away, but I don't. I can't.

"Don't you ever," I rasp, my voice like gravel as I press my forehead against hers, "open another unmarked envelope."

"What can I say?" Her lips curve into that smile that drives me fucking crazy. "I like to live dangerously. Why do you think I'm sleeping with you?"

The sass in her tone makes my blood boil. I silence her with another kiss, this one harder, more demanding. She responds instantly, melting against me even as she fights for control.

My hands slide down to cup her ass, lifting her against me as I start walking us backward toward the bedroom. She clings to me, her legs wrapping around my waist, her lips never breaking from mine except for the occasional gasp.

"Besides," she murmurs against my mouth, her voice a teasing whisper, "your security protocols could use some work—"

That's enough of that. I pin her against the cool surface of the hallway wall, her gasp swallowed by my mouth. She squirms in my grip, half-hearted in her resistance, and I press my hips harder against hers, reminding her exactly who's in charge.

We stumble into the bedroom, her breath hitching as I finally let her feet touch the floor. The room is massive, bathed in soft moonlight streaming through floor-to-ceiling windows. The city sparkles below, a sprawling sea of lights that fade into the inky horizon. The bed dominates the space, its oversized frame dressed in crisp white linens that look almost too clean for what's about to happen.

But I'm not interested in the view.

I'm on her in an instant, my hands tugging at her coat, sliding it off her shoulders and tossing it carelessly aside. She laughs breathlessly, the sound turning into a soft moan as I unbutton her hospital gown and drag it down in one smooth motion. It pools at her feet, leaving her standing before me in nothing but her bra and underwear.

And she's breathtaking.

Her body trembles slightly, whether from the cool air or the intensity between us, I don't know. My gaze sweeps over her, lingering on the soft swell of her stomach where her baby grows, a tiny curve that makes my chest tighten.

"Beautiful," I murmur, my voice low and reverent. My hands find her hips, tracing the curve of her waist with my thumbs before sliding up to cradle her stomach. She watches me, her lips parted, her eyes wide with a mix of vulnerability and heat.

"Mario," she whispers, her voice trembling as she places her hands over mine, holding them against her belly.

I can't hold back any longer. My lips crash into hers, fierce and claiming, as I back her toward the bed. She falls onto the soft mattress, her hair fanning out around her like a halo, and I follow her down, intent on showing her just how much she drives me crazy—how much I need her.

Her lips curve into that maddening smirk again, her hands sliding up my chest to grip the lapels of my jacket. "Not so fast, Mario," she murmurs. "If you're going to strip me down, it's only fair I return the favor."

Her fingers make quick work of the buttons on my shirt, pulling it open with a sharp tug that sends one flying to the floor. She bites her lip, her eyes gleaming with amusement and heat, and I can't help but laugh, low and rough.

"Elena," I growl, grabbing her wrists to slow her down, but she shakes her head, her grin defiant.

"No interruptions," she says, her tone as commanding as it is playful.

She tugs the shirt off my shoulders, her fingers skimming over my skin, leaving a trail of fire in their wake. My breath hitches as her touch dips lower, finding the buckle of my belt. Her movements are slow, deliberate, as she unfastens it and slides it free, the soft whisper of leather making the tension between us even thicker.

"Enjoying yourself?" I ask, my voice rough with restraint.

She looks up at me through her lashes, her hands moving to the button of my pants. "Immensely."

Her voice is a husky purr that sends a jolt of heat straight through me. She pushes my pants down, her knuckles brushing against me in a way that has my control unraveling. When I'm left in nothing but my boxer briefs, she leans back slightly, her gaze raking over me with unhidden appreciation.

"Not bad," she says, her tone light but her eyes betraying her hunger.

"Not bad?" I echo, grabbing her hips and pulling her flush against me. "You're playing with fire, Elena."

"Good thing I like getting burned," she whispers, her hands finding their way into my hair as she pulls me down into a searing kiss.

My lips find hers again, my hands tracing the curves of her body as I press her into the sheets. Her touch is everywhere, her fingers skimming over my shoulders and down my back, her nails digging in just enough to leave marks.

Her soft gasp, the way her body arches into mine—it's everything. And as I pull back just enough to meet her gaze, I see it: the trust, the desire, the connection that binds us.

Elena's hands skim over my back, her nails grazing my skin as I trail kisses down her neck, over her collarbone, and across the swell of her bra-covered breasts.

Well, that won't do. I unhook her bra and throw it across the room.

Her breath hitches when my mouth finds her nipple, and I take it between my lips, rolling it gently with my tongue. She arches beneath me, her fingers tangling in my hair, urging me closer, and I respond by lavishing the same attention on her other breast, wanting to give her everything she desires.

Elena's skin is warm and soft, and the feel of her beneath me, the way her body responds to every touch, every kiss, drives me to the edge of control. But I hold back, wanting to savor this moment, to make it last as long as possible. I slide my hand down her side, feeling the curve of her waist, the dip of her hip, until I reach the softness between her thighs.

She gasps when I touch her, her body trembling beneath my hand as I stroke her gently, feeling the wet heat of her arousal. Her hips move in time with my hand, her breath coming in short, quick bursts as I explore her, learning what makes her shudder, what makes her moan my name in that breathless, desperate way that makes my blood pound in my ears.

"Mario," she whispers, her voice a plea, and I know she's ready. I'm barely holding on myself, the need to be inside her, to claim her, so strong it's nearly overwhelming.

Our underwear is quickly shed and I position myself between her legs. As I push into her, a groan escapes my lips at the feel of her surrounding me, warm and tight and perfect.

Elena's back arches, her nails digging into my shoulders as I fill her, slowly, completely. I hold still for a moment, letting us both adjust to the feeling of being so connected. Her breath mingles with mine, our foreheads pressed together as we savor the moment, the intensity of it making my heart race.

I start to move, slowly at first, the rhythm of our bodies perfectly in sync, a dance as old as time itself. Each thrust is deliberate, controlled, a blend of passion and tenderness that leaves us both breathless. Elena's moans grow louder, her body moving in time with mine, meeting me with each thrust, her legs wrapping around my waist to draw me closer.

The mattress beneath us is soft, but nothing compares to the softness of Elena's skin, the way she feels beneath me, around me. I watch her face, the way her eyes flutter shut, her lips parting with each gasp of pleasure.

I lean down, capturing her lips in a searing kiss, pouring every ounce of my feelings into it. Elena responds with equal fervor, her hands clutching at me as if I'm the only thing keeping her grounded. I can feel her tightening around me, the telltale signs that she's close, and I increase the pace, driven by the need to bring her to the edge.

When she finally cries out, her body convulsing in the throes of her orgasm, I follow her, the sensation of her release pulling me over the edge. I spill into her, a shuddering groan escaping my lips as I bury myself deep, my body trembling with the intensity of it all.

For a long moment, we stay like that, tangled together on the bed, our breaths mingling as we come down from the high. I hold her close, pressing a gentle kiss to her forehead, feeling her heartbeat gradually slow beneath my palm.

As sweat cools on our skin, I allow myself to admit what I've been denying for weeks: I'm falling for her. Not just the refinement or brilliant mind that first caught my attention, but everything—her sharp wit, her quiet strength, the way she matches me move for move in this dangerous game we're playing.

"I'm starting to think you're more dangerous than any of them," I murmur against her throat, feeling her pulse jump beneath my lips.

"The Irish, the Calabrese family, even my brother—none of them see what I see."

"And what's that?" She turns in my arms, those eyes that miss nothing searching my face.

"A queen," I admit, the words feeling like surrender. "Not just another piece on the board."

She goes still in my arms, and for a moment I think I've said too much, revealed too many of my cards. But then her hand comes up to trace the scar Bella's bullet left, her touch featherlight but burning.

"Dangerous words," she whispers, but I catch the slight tremor in her voice. "Especially for a man who just declared war on Seamus O'Connor."

I catch her hand, pressing it flat against my chest where my heart beats too fast, too hard. "Some wars are worth fighting."

The look she gives me is equal parts wonder and terror, like she's finally realizing this stopped being a game a long time ago.

15

ELENA

I grip the arms of the waiting room chair, my Cartier bracelet catching fluorescent light as another wave of anxiety hits. The private clinic Mario arranged is a study in understated wealth—all cream walls and mahogany trim, abstract art worth small fortunes hanging above Italian leather chairs. The kind of place that treats gunshot wounds without police reports and writes prescriptions for people who don't officially exist.

The reception desk is staffed by women who look more like models than medical professionals, but their eyes hold the sharp intelligence of people who know how to keep secrets. A man in an expertly tailored suit sits in the corner, pretending to read *The Wall Street Journal* while actually watching the door. Private security, clearly—the gun beneath his jacket making that extremely evident.

Still, my heart races every time the door opens, expecting Anthony's men or worse—Bella. I can't shake her hurt expression from yesterday, or Matteo's cutting words: *"You're already hurting her."*

"Ms. Santiago?"

The nurse—middle-aged and elegant in clean scrubs—calls my real name rather than one of my carefully crafted aliases. Mario's influence, no doubt. I rise on shaky legs, surprised when a familiar hand steadies my elbow.

"What are you doing here?" I hiss, even as something warm unfurls in my chest at Mario's presence. He looks devastating in a casual Armani charcoal suit, the material molding to his broad shoulders like a lover's touch. With his dark hair slightly tousled and those dark eyes intense, he plays the role of supportive partner perfectly.

"We already discussed this," I whisper furiously. "It's not safe for you to be seen here. If Anthony, Matteo, and O'Connor have people watching—"

"I told you last night," he murmurs, his hand warm on my back as he guides me forward. "I'm done hiding."

"This isn't about hiding," I insist. "It's about survival. You can't just—"

"I can't, huh?" His smile holds an edge. "Too bad, little planner. You're stuck with me."

"Mario—"

"Shut up and let me do this," he growls, but his hand is gentle at my lower back as we follow the nurse down a hallway lined with more expensive art. Each door we pass is numbered in discreet gold lettering, no names, no specialties listed. A place designed for people who need to disappear.

The nurse leads us into an examination room that looks more like a luxury hotel suite than a medical facility. The ultrasound machine is plated in gold, and even the examination table is covered in what looks like Egyptian cotton.

"The doctor will be right in," the nurse says, closing the door with practiced discretion.

"You're insane," I tell Mario, but my hand finds his anyway. "Being here together ... it's like painting a target on both our backs."

His fingers interlace with mine. "Let them try."

My phone buzzes and I fish it out of my Chanel clutch, grimacing when I see Anthony's name on the screen. I hit decline before stuffing it away again.

With everything that happened yesterday, I completely forgot about Anthony. Probably not my smartest move.

"Who was it?" Mario's voice is deceptively casual.

"Anthony."

His face darkens, jaw tightening in that way that makes his scar more prominent. The muscle in his cheek ticks—a tell he probably doesn't realize he has. Jealousy looks good on him, though he'd rather die than admit that's what this is.

Something warm and smug unfurls in my chest. It's nice to feel wanted.

My phone starts dinging rapidly—the sound of multiple incoming texts. I pull it out again, biting my lip as I read:

Where are you? I heard about the hospital.

Answer your phone Elena.

My men saw you leave with a girl claiming to be family.

We both know you don't have family.

You're making dangerous choices, cara.

Remember what happened to the last person who betrayed my trust.

No one disappears from me without consequences.

I will find you. And we'll have a long discussion about loyalty.

"What's he saying, Elena?" Mario's voice has gone dangerously soft.

"None of your business," I retort, moving to put the phone away.

"Like hell it isn't." He snatches the phone from my hand before I can react.

"Don't you ever," I snarl, fury making my voice shake, "grab my phone without permission again. I'm not one of your soldiers to command."

His eyes scan the messages, and I watch something lethal awaken in his expression. His whole body goes preternaturally still—the kind of stillness that precedes violence.

"He's threatening you," he says, each word precise and sharp as a blade. "Making promises about loyalty lessons."

"Give. Me. My. Phone." Each word drips with ice. "I've handled

Anthony Calabrese for months without your help. I don't need you to—"

We're on the verge of nuclear war when a knock interrupts us. The doctor enters—tall, blond, looking like he walked off a soap opera set in designer scrubs. His easy smile falters slightly when he catches the tension crackling between us, no doubt recognizing the particular brand of danger radiating off Mario.

"Ms. Santiago?" he says carefully, looking between us like he's calculating the odds of violence erupting in his examination room. "I'm Dr. Matthews. Should we ... perhaps reschedule?"

I take a deep breath, smoothing my expression into something professional. "No need to reschedule, Dr. Matthews. Someone," I shoot Mario a pointed look, "just needs a lesson in boundaries."

The doctor's gaze flicks between us again. I hop onto the examination table, flashing him my most dazzling smile—the one that gets me past security checkpoints and into private files. "Besides, I'm sure you're very busy. We wouldn't want to waste your valuable time."

Mario's jaw ticks at my obvious flirting. Good.

"So," Dr. Matthews pulls up my chart, "I understand there was an incident yesterday involving potential toxic exposure?"

"Just a scare," I assure him. "The substance turned out to be harmless."

"Nevertheless, we should run a full panel." He glances at Mario. "And this is ... ?"

"Not the father," I say loudly, satisfaction blooming at Mario's barely concealed flinch. "Just a ... friend."

"I see." The doctor's expression remains professionally neutral. "Would you prefer to continue the examination privately?"

Some petty part of me wants to say yes, to punish Mario for grabbing my phone, for thinking he can control me like one of his people.

But then I look at him—the way his shoulders are rigid with tension, how his fingers grip the arm of his chair just a little too tightly. For all his dangerous grace, there's something almost vulnerable in the way he's trying so hard to appear calm.

"He can stay," I finally say.

Something flickers across Mario's face—a crack in that perfect mask of control. His eyes, when they meet mine, hold something that makes my chest tight.

"Alright then," the doctor says, reaching for the ultrasound equipment. "Let's check on your little one. This might be cold."

I inhale sharply as gel hits my stomach, my heart racing as the wand moves across my skin. For a moment, there's nothing but static, and then—

On the monitor, a grainy black and white image appears. The most beautiful sound I've ever heard fills the room. Quick, strong, like galloping horses or hummingbird wings.

My baby's heartbeat.

"Is that normal?" I ask anxiously as the heart continues its rapid flutter. "The heart rate?"

"Perfectly normal," Dr. Matthews assures me. "Would you like to know the sex? Our equipment can detect it earlier than standard machines."

I nod, unable to form words. A sharp intake of breath draws my attention to Mario, who's standing, transfixed by the monitor. He moves closer, his eyes never leaving the screen, until he's standing beside me. His usual predatory grace is gone, replaced by something almost reverent as he watches this tiny life dance across the screen.

"It's a girl," the doctor announces.

A daughter. The word echoes in my chest like a bell. I'm having a little girl. Emotions I can't even name surge through me—fierce love, bone-deep terror, wild joy. I imagine a tiny face, wonder whose features she'll have. Will she have Anthony's dark eyes? My blonde hair?

Will she be as calculating as her father, as ambitious as her mother?

Dr. Matthews points out her features—the dark curve of her head, the bright spot of her beating heart, tiny arms and legs that look like delicate butterfly wings.

She's still so small—barely over an inch long—but already I can see she's perfect. As we watch, she shifts position, her tiny legs kicking out in a flutter of movement that makes my eyes burn with unexpected tears.

"That's her spine," the doctor says, tracing a curved line. "And here—" he moves the wand slightly, "you can see her profile. That's her nose, her forehead. At ten weeks, she's starting to look more like a tiny baby."

Mario's hand finds mine, his fingers intertwining with my own. When I look up, I see his carefully constructed walls crumbling. The dangerous man who makes hardened criminals tremble looks utterly undone by this grainy image of new life. His throat works as he swallows, and for a moment, I catch a glimpse of raw emotion in his eyes before he can hide it.

It's the first time I've ever seen Mario DeLuca look afraid.

The baby shifts again—a complete somersault this time, like she's showing off for her audience—and his grip on my hand tightens.

I understand his fear. This little girl, barely formed but already so real, will be born with a target on her back. A Calabrese heir. The child of a woman who betrayed her father. The daughter of a man who would burn the world to claim what's his, being watched by another man who would die to protect her despite having no claim to her at all.

"Would you like to hear the heartbeat again?" Dr. Matthews asks softly, clearly reading the emotion in the room.

I nod, and that magical sound fills the space once more. Mario's hand trembles slightly in mine, and I pretend not to notice when he quickly wipes his other hand across his eyes.

Dr. Matthews prints out several ultrasound photos, each one capturing my daughter from different angles. "Take it easy," he instructs, handing me the prints. "Prenatals daily, moderate exercise, and—" his eyes flick to Mario with something like recognition, "try to keep stress levels down."

I tuck the photos into my clutch, promising to follow his instructions. The moment he leaves, silence fills the room.

But I catch Mario's eyes darting toward my bag for the third time in as many minutes. Something warm and liquid unfurls in my chest, like honey spreading through my veins. The dangerous Mario DeLuca, who made his name putting bullets in people's heads, wants to see baby pictures.

I undo the clasp of my clutch. "Would you like one?" I ask softly. "To keep?"

He startles, though he covers it quickly with that practiced DeLuca control. "Why would I want photos of another man's child?"

But there's no bite to his words, no real resistance. I saw his face when that tiny heartbeat filled the room. Saw how his hands shook when she moved on screen.

I roll my eyes and select one of the clearer images—the one where you can see her profile perfectly, her tiny hand raised like she's waving. Moving deliberately, I cross to where he stands and pull open his suit jacket.

"Elena—" he warns.

I slip the photo into his breast pocket, but leave my hand there, pressed against his heart. It's racing beneath my palm, betraying everything his carefully blank expression tries to hide. His cologne mingles with the antiseptic smell of the clinic, and this close, I can see the gold flecks in his eyes, the way his pupils dilate as I lean in.

"Tell me again," I whisper against his jaw, "how you don't want pictures of her."

His hand comes up to cover mine, pressing the photo more firmly against his heart.

His Adam's apple bobs as he swallows hard, his heart still racing beneath my palm. For a moment, I think he might kiss me—his eyes darken in the way that usually precedes him backing me against the nearest surface. But then he clears his throat, and the DeLuca mask slides firmly back into place.

"We should get back to the safe house," he says shortly, hand finding the doorknob.

I roll my eyes at his attempt at coldness. This is what Mario does —retreats behind walls the moment vulnerability threatens to crack his perfect control. But I saw his face when he heard my daughter's heartbeat.

He can play the untouchable don all he wants, but I know better now.

We're halfway to the lobby when movement outside the window catches my attention. A flash of tactical gear that's too high-end for regular security, too precise in their movements to be random. I recognize the formation—it's how Anthony's elite team operates, the way they fan out to cover exits.

The same pattern they used when eliminating the Russian faction last spring.

"Mario," I warn, but he's already seen them. His body shifts subtly, transforming him from the man who just got emotional over ultrasound photos into something deadly. My hand moves instinctively to my stomach as he positions himself between me and the window.

"Time to go, little planner," he says softly, fingers flying over his phone as he alerts his security team. "Seems we're not the only ones interested in your appointment today."

16

MARIO

Well, fuck.

I should have known Calabrese would pull this shit, especially after those texts he sent Elena. The memory of his threats still makes my blood boil. But I've got my own problems burning a hole in my pocket—Dante's been blowing up my phone all morning:

O'Connor's losing his shit. Says he'll put you down like the traitor you are.

Boss, this isn't like you.

What the fuck is going on?

He's calling in markers. The Irish are mobilizing.

Even Siobhan had to get her dig in: *Running after a pregnant girl? How the mighty have fallen.*

But I'd managed to forget all about O'Connor's threats the moment that baby appeared on screen. Her heartbeat filled the room like music, and something in my chest had seized up, grown two sizes too big. That tiny profile, those butterfly-wing hands—fuck, is this what Matteo felt when he first saw Bianca? When he decided to claim another man's child as his own?

The doctor had printed those pictures and Elena tucked them

away in her clutch. Every fiber of my being wanted to snatch one, to keep that image of perfection close.

But I have Giuseppe's lessons branded into my bones—never show weakness, never reveal what matters to you. I couldn't let Elena see how much that tiny life affected me.

But somehow she knew. Fucking knew exactly what I was thinking when she slipped that photo into my breast pocket, her hand pressed against my heart like she could feel every crack in my carefully constructed walls. Fucking Elena.

But I have bigger problems right now. Like how the fuck Anthony Calabrese knew Elena would be at this supposedly discreet clinic. The rent-a-cop who'd been pretending to read *The Wall Street Journal* springs to his feet, hand moving to his concealed weapon. I roll my eyes.

This amateur would piss himself if he actually had to face Calabrese's men.

I text my security team while retrieving my arsenal—Glock 19 from my shoulder holster, Sig Sauer from my ankle, ceramic blade from beneath my tie. Each weapon a comfort, each placement learned at Giuseppe's knee. My phone lights up with intel:

Four men at south entrance.
Two in stairwell B.
Three covering parking garage.
Sniper on roof of building across street —northeast corner.
Two more incoming from west side.

My mind's already mapping our next steps. The clinic's glass walls are both advantage and liability—clear sight lines, but no cover. We'll need a distraction, something to draw the sniper's attention.

"Ladies," I call to the reception staff, keeping my voice gentle. No need to terrify them more than necessary. "You might want to find somewhere safe to wait this out."

They scatter, heels clicking against marble as they flee. Smart girls.

I turn back to Elena, expecting fear, maybe panic. Instead, she watches with cool calculation, those blue eyes taking in every detail.

She's not the same woman who trembled when Johnny Calabrese held her hostage. That Elena would have frozen.

This one's probably already counting exits and cataloging weapons.

"Here's how this plays," I explain, checking my magazine. "My team's setting up a kill box in the parking garage. We'll use the service elevator—they'll be watching the main ones. Car's waiting in the underground tunnel that connects to the building next door."

"And the sniper?" she asks.

Fuck, I love that she caught that detail. "He's about to have a very bad day. But it's going to get messy. People will die." I meet her eyes. "Once we leave here together, there's no going back. Anthony will know you're with me. Word will reach Matteo within hours."

She hesitates, one hand drifting to her stomach. For a moment, I think she'll choose the safer path—return to Anthony, play the dutiful mistress. But then her lips curve into that smile that drives me crazy.

"Please," she scoffs. "Like I didn't burn that bridge the moment I let you fuck me in Anthony's study."

My heart definitely doesn't skip at her casual claim of choosing me. My phone buzzes: *In position. Awaiting signal.*

"Ready?" I ask, offering her my spare Glock.

Those blue eyes meet mine, sharp as blades. "Ready."

I give the signal and all hell breaks loose.

My security team creates the perfect distraction—an explosion in the east wing that has Calabrese's men spinning toward the noise. The sniper's attention diverts just long enough for my counter-sniper to take him out. Clean shot, straight through the scope. Glass shatters somewhere in the distance.

"Move," I order, keeping Elena close as we head for the service elevator. Two of Calabrese's men appear at the end of the hall—both drop before they can raise their weapons, my shots perfect between their eyes. The muscle memory Giuseppe beat into me serving its purpose.

Elena doesn't flinch at the blood spray. She flows through the space beside me, that Glock held with surprising steadiness in her perfectly manicured hands. When another of Anthony's men bursts through a side door, she puts two in his chest without hesitation.

The blood splatter across her face doesn't even make her blink.

"Behind!" she calls, and I spin, taking out the man trying to flank us. But something catches my attention—he was aiming for my legs, not center mass. The same with the others.

They're shooting to disable, not kill.

We reach the service elevator just as Dante's voice crackles through my earpiece. "Boss, they're trying to funnel you toward the garage."

The pieces click together as we descend. I watch two more of Anthony's men attempt to grab Elena rather than shoot her. They're not here to kill us—they're here to separate us. To take her.

Rage pours through me, hot and familiar. Nobody is taking what's mine.

The elevator opens to chaos. My men have created the kill box as planned, but Calabrese's team is more focused on reaching Elena than engaging them. One manages to get close enough to grab her arm—I remove his hand at the wrist with my ceramic blade.

"Change of plans," I growl into my comm. "They're after her. Formation Echo."

My team shifts instantly, creating a tighter circle around Elena as we move toward the tunnel. She proves herself again, shooting a man trying to breach our perimeter. But they keep coming, more focused on grabbing her than stopping me.

"Mario!" Her warning comes just as someone manages to get an arm around her waist. I don't even think—my knife finds his throat before he can pull her away. The sight of another man's hands on her makes something feral rise in my chest.

We're almost to the tunnel when I hear it—the distinctive three-tone radio signal that's been Matteo's security signature since we were kids. I'd know that sound anywhere—used to use it myself.

Fucking Antonio must have called him. That fucking man has eyes everywhere.

Fucking perfect.

"Run," I tell Elena, already formulating my next move. "Car's through the tunnel, second left. Go!"

Her blue eyes widen in shock. "I'm not leaving you—"

"Trust me," I growl, pushing her toward one of my men. "I'll be right behind you."

She hesitates for just a moment before nodding. I watch her disappear into the tunnel as I turn to face the approaching storm. Let them try to take her. I've spent a lifetime being the DeLuca son everyone underestimated.

Time to remind them why that was a mistake.

The moment Elena disappears into the tunnel, I let the mask slip. The careful control, the precision—all of it falls away. What emerges is the creature Giuseppe crafted through years of basement "lessons" and brutal punishments.

The beast that caught Seamus O'Connor's eye, that held a gun to Bianca's head and felt nothing.

Blood sings in my veins as I move. Two Calabrese men go down before they can blink, their necks snapped with mechanical efficiency. A third loses his eyes to my blade. I don't bother with clean kills anymore—let them suffer. Let them carry the scars back to Anthony as a reminder of what happens when you try to take what's mine.

Matteo's men pour in from the west entrance, but they've forgotten what I'm capable of. They know the Mario who lost to Matteo, who went into exile. They don't know this version—the one Giuseppe *really* created.

"You shouldn't have come back." Antonio's voice cuts through the chaos. He emerges from the shadows like the ghost of my past sins, still moving with deadly grace despite his age. "Matteo knows you're in New York."

I laugh, the sound sharp as broken glass. "Come to put me down, old man?"

"Those are my orders." He shifts his weight, and I recognize the stance—he taught it to me, after all. "Permanent this time."

"Not fucking likely," I sneer, cocking my gun.

He moves faster than a man his age should be able to, blade appearing from nowhere. I counter, muscle memory from a thousand training sessions guiding my response. But he's always been craftier than most give him credit for. The blade is a feint—his real attack comes from the left, a strike that would have crushed my throat if I hadn't seen it coming.

"You were always sloppy with your left side," he growls, pressing the advantage.

"And you were always too confident in your tricks." I drive my knee into his solar plexus, following with an elbow to his temple. But the old bastard rolls with it, coming up with his gun drawn.

Around us, my men engage with the mixed forces of Calabrese and DeLuca soldiers. The garage echoes with gunfire and breaking bones. Blood makes the concrete slick beneath our feet.

"Matteo should have killed you after what you did to Bianca," Antonio snarls, circling me like the predator he is. "Or after you tried to kill the donna."

"Matteo should have seen me for what I really am." I match his movements, waiting for the tell in his left shoulder that always precedes his favorite combination. "The son Giuseppe really wanted."

The words hit their mark. Antonio's shoulder twitches and I'm already moving, flowing around his strike like water. My blade finds the nerve cluster in his arm—not a killing blow, but enough to drop him to his knees.

"Get up," I growl, kicking his gun away. "You're going to take a message back to my brother."

I lean close to Antonio's ear. "Tell my brother that if he wants me, he can come himself. And tell him that if anyone—Calabrese, DeLuca, or fucking O'Connor—tries to take Elena from me again, I'll burn this whole city to the ground."

The screech of tires announces my ride. The armored Mercedes slides to a stop, door flying open. I dive in just as bullets pepper the side panels, the reinforced metal absorbing impacts that would have turned me into Swiss cheese.

Elena's hands find me immediately, pulling me fully inside. "Are you hit?" she asks anxiously.

"Take us to the Clinton house," I order Vincent, the driver, ignoring her question as I check her for injuries. "Now."

"Another safe house?" She sounds almost impressed. "How many do you have?"

"Sweetheart, I've got more houses than you have shoes." I wink, but then Vincent's voice cuts through from the driver's seat.

"We've got company."

I spin in my seat. Three black Escalades tear around the corner behind us—Calabrese cars, judging by the way they move in formation. "Fuck me."

Elena's eyes go wide as bullets spiderweb the rear window. That cool mask she's worn all morning finally cracks. "Mario—"

"Hold on." I grab my Glock as Vincent takes a hard right, cutting off a delivery truck and sending us into oncoming traffic. Horns blare as he weaves between cars at speeds that would make professional drivers shit themselves. A bullet makes it through the back window.

Without thinking, I grab Elena and shove her down. "Stay low."

Then I'm moving, rolling down the window and pulling myself halfway out. The wind hits me like a fist as I line up my shot. The first bullet takes out the lead Escalade's front tire. It fishtails, forcing the second car to swerve.

The third car's windshield explodes as I put two rounds through it.

"Mario!" Elena's scream makes me duck back inside just as we take a corner on two wheels. A bus horn blares as Vincent cuts across four lanes of traffic.

"You good?" I check Elena again, noting how she's gone pale beneath the blood spray on her face.

"Been better," she manages through clenched teeth.

"Your driving's worse than your mood swings." I bark out a laugh, but more headlights in the side mirror cut it short. Two more cars joining the chase.

"Vincent!"

"Working on it, boss!" He takes another corner so sharp I have to brace against the ceiling. "But we've got a problem."

"Besides the obvious?" I ask sarcastically.

"They're herding us toward the bridge." His voice is grim. "Where Matteo's men will be."

"Fuck that." I grab Elena's purse, ignoring her protest as I dig out her iPhone. Without hesitation, I chuck it out the window.

"Are you insane?" she shrieks, wind whipping her golden hair across her face. "That was my—"

"They can track your GPS," I snap, pulling her down as more bullets shatter what's left of our back window. "Use the burner I gave you."

"You could have just turned it off!" Elena argues, her face red with anger.

"You really want to argue about this now?" I fire three more shots at our pursuers. One catches a driver in the shoulder, sending his Escalade careening into a hot dog cart. "I'll buy you ten new phones later."

Vincent takes us down a service alley, scraping paint off both sides of the car. The move cuts off two of our pursuers, but three more are still on our tail. Bullets rain against the car's armored panels like lethal hail. Elena clutches the overhead handle as Vincent executes a move that sends us up on two wheels.

"If we survive this," she grits out, "we're having a long discussion about your definition of 'discreet clinic visit.'"

I can't help but grin at her attempt at sass even while pale with fear. But then more headlights appear ahead of us—Matteo's signature black SUVs blocking the bridge approach.

"Options?" I demand, reloading my Glock.

"I'm thinking," Vincent mutters, then suddenly yanks the wheel hard right. We crash through a construction barrier, sending workers diving for cover. "Boss, you're really not going to like this next part."

"What—" Elena's question cuts off in a scream as Vincent aims our car straight for the river. "Mario!"

I grab her close as Vincent accelerates toward the water. "When I say so, take a deep breath!"

"You have lost your fucking mind!" Elena screams but she's already yanking off her Louboutins, ready to follow my lead despite her terror.

Bullets pepper our car from both directions now—Calabrese behind, DeLuca ahead. The river rushes up to meet us as Vincent floors it, and I notice Elena's hand has found mine, squeezing hard enough to break bones.

"Now!" I shout, and we all gulp air just as the Mercedes becomes a submarine. The impact hits like a concrete wall. Water rushes in through the bullet holes as we sink into the murky Hudson.

But Vincent's already triggering the emergency releases, and the doors pop open against the pressure. Elena kicks free like she was born to it, proving once again she's more than just a society planner.

I follow her sleek form toward the surface, toward the boat I know Marco has waiting nearby. We break the surface gasping, the sounds of chaos on the bridge above us oddly muted by the water in our ears.

"I'm going to kill you," she sputters, but lets me pull her toward the waiting boat. "Slowly. Painfully."

"Get in line, little planner." I hoist her onto the deck where Marco rushes towards us, face pale as he throws a blanket at Elena. "Your ex is trying to kidnap you, my brother wants me dead, and O'Connor's probably got a price on both our heads by now."

Her laugh holds a touch of hysteria as she wraps the blanket tightly around her, her teeth starting to chatter. "Just another Tuesday then?"

17

MARIO

Marco guides the boat through the choppy water while I watch the chaos unfold on the bridge. Through the mist of water and gun smoke, I spot Matteo. He stands at the railing like the devil himself—his black coat whipping in the wind, hair wild, hands gripping the metal barrier.

Even from this distance, I can see the cold fury in his eyes, the way his mouth is set in that particular line that always meant someone was about to die.

He looks exactly like Giuseppe in that moment, and my stomach bottoms out.

"Get us out of here," I tell Marco, already pulling out my waterproof phone to arrange another car. The Clinton house is still our best bet—it's the one safe house Matteo and O'Connor don't know about. "We need transport at point Charlie."

. . .

Elena shivers beside me, her wet clothes clinging to curves that would be distracting if I wasn't so focused on getting us to safety. I move closer, offering body heat while I coordinate with my team.

"You doing okay?" I ask, noting how her lips have started to turn blue.

The look she gives me could chill the sun. Water drips from her ruined hair, mascara runs down her cheeks, and she's still the most beautiful thing I've ever seen.

Also possibly the most pissed off.

"Let me think," she says through chattering teeth. "In the past hour, I've been shot at, chased through Manhattan, and driven into the Hudson River. My phone is probably crushed on some street, my Louboutins are somewhere at the bottom of said river, and this outfit?" She plucks at the soaked Versace. "Was *couture*."

I shrug off my jacket—also ruined, but at least it's dry on the inside—and wrap it around her shoulders over the blanket to provide her some additional warmth. "I'll buy you new shoes."

"That's not the point and you know it." But she burrows into the blanket and jacket anyway, her shoulder pressing against mine. "Your brother is going to hunt us down."

"If he can find us." I keep my eyes on the bridge where Matteo still stands, his figure growing smaller as Marco guides us downstream. My brother's stance is pure Giuseppe—the way he holds himself, like violence barely contained in an expensive suit. "We've got bigger problems."

"Bigger than Matteo DeLuca?" Elena asks dubiously.

"Anthony won't stop until he has you back." I try to keep my voice neutral, but something must show because she turns to study my face. "And O'Connor ... well, let's just say Boston's about to get very interesting."

Marco calls back from the helm. "Car's waiting two clicks south. But Mario? We've got company on the water."

Sure enough, the distinctive rumble of police boats echoes across the river. Because this day just keeps getting better.

"Any chance those are regular harbor patrol?" Elena asks without much hope.

"Not with my brother making calls." I check my weapon—waterlogged but still functional. "Marco?"

He grins, hitting something on the console that makes the boat's engine roar to life with new purpose. "Hold onto something."

Marco opens up the throttle and the boat leaps forward like a living thing. The police boats fall behind as he expertly weaves between cargo ships and river traffic, using the larger vessels as cover.

"Just like Monaco," he shouts over the engine's roar, taking us through a turn that sends spray everywhere.

"Except with fewer supermodels," I call back, steadying Elena as she sways. Her face has taken on a greenish tint that has nothing to do with fear.

"Very James Bond, wouldn't you say?" I can't help teasing her. "You make quite the Bond girl."

She shoots me a look that could curdle milk. "If you're Bond, we're all definitely going to die. And I'm nothing like those idiots who fall for his bullshit."

"Says the woman who just drove into the Hudson with me," I shoot back.

"If you two are done flirting," Marco cuts in, "we've got company."

Another police boat appears ahead. Marco just smirks and cuts the engine, letting us drift into the shadow of a container ship. The patrol boat roars past, missing us completely.

"Your sister is going to be pissed she missed this," I tell Marco as he restarts the engine.

"Already got six angry texts." He takes us through another series of moves that has Elena looking decidedly ill. "Says this beats anything she did at the hospital."

Finally, we reach the pickup point—a discreet dock tucked away from prying eyes. A black Mercedes waits in the shadows, engine idling.

"You good from here?" I ask Marco as we climb out.

He waves me off. "Heading to Jersey, then ditching the boat. Already got my exit planned. This is the most fun I've had since that thing in Prague."

Elena stumbles slightly as we make our way to the car, her wet skirt hampering movement. "Where exactly are we going?"

"Clinton house," I say shortly as I open the car door.

"And Matteo doesn't know about this one because ... ?"

I help her into the backseat before sliding in beside her. "Because I bought it with money Giuseppe left me. The old man had accounts even Matteo didn't know about."

She raises a brow. "And O'Connor?"

"Let's just say there are some things I kept to myself." I give the driver an address as we pull away from the dock. "Even demons need backup plans."

My phone rings—Dante on the secured line.

"Tell me you're not dead, you stupid fuck," he demands the moment I pick up.

"Would I be answering the phone if I was dead?" I ask dryly.

Elena snorts and covers her mouth, turning to look out the window. Even through the phone, I can hear Dante's teeth grinding.

"You're a jackass." A pause. "How the hell did you get away from both families?"

I detail our escape, earning an appreciative whistle from Dante. "Fucking Marco saving the day," he responds laughingly.

The three of us go way back. We've shed blood together, buried bodies together.

"How bad is it in Boston?" I ask, changing the subject.

Dante's voice goes grim, all traces of amusement gone. "Bad. I told you that O'Connor's gone nuclear. Already called in markers from Philadelphia to Montreal. He's got a million-dollar bounty on your head. Two million if they bring you back breathing so he can kill you himself."

"Charming." A bead of water trails into my eye and I impatiently wipe it away.

"He's burning every connection looking for you. Says no one walks away from him, especially not his pet Italian." Dante lowers his voice. "But that's not the interesting part. Got some intel about Siobhan you need to see. Already sent it over."

I pull up the files on my phone. Surveillance photos show Siobhan holding court at Murphy's Pub—the real seat of Irish power in Boston. She's surrounded by younger captains, all of them leaning in like moths to flame. Her red hair glows under vintage lights, her father's cold eyes scanning the room as she speaks.

The timestamps catch my attention. Three weeks of late-night meetings, increasing in frequency. Always the same core group, but with new faces being added strategically.

"They're calling it modernization talks," Dante reports. "But it looks more like succession planning. She's gathered most of the younger leadership—Sean Murphy, the O'Brien cousins, even old man Flaherty's grandson."

I study the hungry look in those young faces—the same expression I used to see in the mirror during Giuseppe's reign. That particular mix of ambition and resentment that breeds revolution.

"And Seamus?" I ask carefully.

"Blind to it. Still running things like it's 1980." Dante's voice holds dark amusement. "She's transformed her father's social club into a war room. While he's focused on traditional smuggling routes, she's building a network of tech-savvy operators. Cryptocurrency, digital money laundering, cybersecurity."

Elena shifts closer, clearly listening. Her wet hair drips onto my shoulder as she studies the photos with sharp interest.

After more details about Siobhan's power plays, I end the call. Elena's been quiet, but I can practically hear her mind working.

"A million-dollar bounty," she says finally. "That's quite the price tag."

"Worried about me, little planner?"

"I'm worried about the fact that the O'Connors and Calabreses will work together now," she says, rolling her eyes. "They both want the same thing—you dead and me back with Anthony."

"Don't forget my brother." I watch her face in the passing streetlights. "Matteo would make a deal with the devil himself if it meant getting rid of me for good."

She doesn't like that—I can see it in the way her jaw ticks.

The car turns onto a quiet street in Clinton Hill, Brooklyn, pulling up to what looks like a restored brownstone. But the historic facade hides cutting-edge security that would make the CIA jealous. I guide Elena through three separate checkpoints before we reach the main floor.

Inside, it's all clean lines and tactical considerations masked as luxury. Sight lines to every entrance, reinforced walls hidden behind expensive art, weapons caches disguised as modern decor. The furniture is minimal but high-end, everything positioned for maximum defensive advantage.

I nod toward the stairs. "Shower's up there if you want it."

"And what exactly am I supposed to wear after a shower?" She gestures at her soaked Versace. "Planning to have me parade around in my underwear?"

"I wouldn't object," I answer honestly.

She scowls, throwing my wet jacket at my head. "You're impossible."

"There are clothes upstairs you can use."

One perfect blonde eyebrow rises. "You have women's clothes in your secret safe house? Interesting for someone who's supposed to be in exile."

"First of all, they're my clothes. And second," I can't help but smirk, "did you really think I spent five years actually staying away from New York just because my brother said so?"

"You're impossible," she repeats, but I catch her smile as she heads upstairs.

Once Elena disappears upstairs, I look down at the jacket she threw at me. The ultrasound photo. My heart lodges in my throat as I thrust my hand into the breast pocket, already knowing what I'll find.

The photo comes out in pieces, the river water having turned it into wet pulp. The image of that tiny profile, those butterfly-wing hands, now just a ruined mess of paper and ink.

Something in my chest constricts painfully.

It shouldn't matter—it's just a photo, and not even of my child. But seeing it destroyed hits harder than any of Seamus O'Connor's threats.

Fucking Matteo. Fucking Anthony Calabrese. Always destroying everything they touch.

The stench of the Hudson suddenly hits me—a lovely mixture of industrial waste and God knows what else. I grimace, realizing I smell like I took a swim in Satan's bathtub.

The sound of the shower in the master bath cuts off, and unbidden images of Elena fill my mind—water running down her curves, her wet hair slicked back, droplets trailing down her throat ...

I curl my hand into a fist, nails biting into my palm. No. I can't go there right now. Not with the enemy closing in from all sides, not with her carrying another man's child, not with the memory of that ruined ultrasound photo burning a hole in my pocket.

I force myself toward the guest bathroom, away from temptation. Away from the dangerous way she makes me feel things I can't afford to feel.

After a shower and change of clothes, I feel human again. Black slacks, charcoal cashmere sweater, Italian leather shoes—a DeLuca never looks anything less than perfect, even in a safe house. Even in exile.

I head to the master bedroom to check on Elena and stop dead in my tracks. She's wearing one of my old Columbia T-shirts, the soft gray fabric falling to mid-thigh. Her freshly washed hair falls in dark gold waves as she runs a towel through it, making her look younger, more vulnerable somehow.

Something catches in my chest at the sight of her in my clothes, in my space. She must hear my sharp intake of breath because she looks over her shoulder, those blue eyes bright without makeup, questioning.

"Is this okay?" she asks, gesturing at the shirt. "I know you said I could use your clothes, but I probably should have asked which ones and—"

I cross the room in three strides, drawn like a magnet. "Elena."

She bites her lip. "Yes?"

"Stop talking."

I cup her face in my hands and kiss her, pouring everything I can't say into it. All my fears about O'Connor, about Anthony, about this baby that isn't mine but that I already want to protect. She melts into me, her hands sliding up my chest, into my hair, and for a moment, nothing else matters. Heat burrows its way through the space between my ribs and pools at the center of my chest.

Elena pulls back and scowls at me. "I'll talk whenever I damn well please. And I sure as hell don't take orders from *you*."

Her expression is furious and glorious.

"Orders?" I can't keep the dark delight from my voice, wouldn't even if I tried. "Careful, little planner. I can think of some orders you might enjoy."

She only glares, her fingers tugging sharply at my hair—and the pain sends electricity down my spine, making me instantly hard.

"Unless you'd rather go back to Anthony," I say, voice trailing off —no longer caring how obvious my want for her is, because the fire in her eyes is intoxicating. Like the finest whiskey, burning through my veins.

"Shut up," she snarls through her teeth.

My hands rise to anchor themselves on her hips. As my fingers slide under the T-shirt to brush against bare skin, she slowly releases my hair, her wrists draping around my neck.

"Then turn around, little planner," I growl. My fingers curl around her waist, and I push so that she begins to turn. "And put your hands flat on the dresser."

She scoffs, but she plants her feet apart as I gently press her towards the dresser with a hand on the small of her back. She rolls her eyes but then deliberately raises one hand to set it upon the dresser. The other in front of her.

I wrap myself around her, chest against her shoulder blades and her arms bracketed by mine. I tuck my chin into the curve between her shoulder and neck, eyes falling to where my hands cover hers, and our fingers interlock.

Elena sighs, leaning back against me, and then my lips drag across her neck, desperate to coax out more of that sound. My tongue sweeps across her pulse and she leans her head to the side, allowing me more access.

"Good girl," I whisper, voice falling across the bit of skin glistening in front of my lips.

One of my hands drifts—two fingertips tracing up over the back of her hand, her wrist, up her arm until it meets her elbow, and then wraps around to her waist. I gather the fabric of her shirt in one hand, teeth and tongue scraping across her neck and the corner of her jaw, and I begin to lift her shirt up.

Elena's hand jerks, going to help me pull at the hem of her shirt, but then I press my teeth into the side of her neck. Just enough that the heel of her palm falls back down against the surface of the dresser. I continue, this time using both hands, and inch my fingers beneath her shirt. Across her stomach. The fabric bunches up around my wrists as I lift them higher.

My fingertips have just touched the underside of her breasts when a low whimper bursts from her lips, unbidden. Her hands are shaking from just how hard she is pressing the pads of her fingers into the wood.

I scrape my thumb along the line of her ribs, and when she shivers, I press my hips forward. Her mouth falls open in a gasp.

"Let me touch you," she rushes out. She turns her head, trying to catch my eye, but my lips are still pressing against her neck, my eyes downcast. Watching as one of my fingers trails up the center of her body towards her breasts.

"I sure as hell don't take orders from you," I whisper, throwing her words back at her.

She either glares at me or rolls her eyes but then my hand curves around her bare breast, fingers brushing over the peach-colored nipple and a freckle just beneath it. I grind my hips against her ass again, and she groans.

Beneath my touch, her nipple hardens and then both my hands are over her breasts, kneading them while my mouth lavishes attention to her neck. Her hips begin to roll, ricocheting off the edge of the dresser and back against me. My pants are *uncomfortably* tight as my dick hardens.

I can almost feel it—a thread fraying and all too close to snapping. I'd come in my pants if I don't get myself under fucking control soon.

But control is an unattainable thing. I'm growing feverish, my thoughts increasingly more difficult to decipher and I feel sure that my grip on her breasts is bruising. But Elena certainly doesn't seem to mind by the way she is moaning.

I have her voice in my ears, the taste of her on my tongue, her breasts in my hands, and it still isn't enough.

I lift one hand, roughly grabbing her chin to jerk her head to the side and then press my mouth against hers to capture the sounds of her pleasure. Still rolling her nipple between my fingers, I grind my cock against her ass but now I swirl my tongue in her mouth.

And it's fucking indelicate and messy, but I keep kissing her. Until I can't breathe and my head is spinning and I have to tear my mouth away.

I stare down at her, panting as she looks up at me, her chest heaving. Lips swollen and red and her lashes wet. But her hands don't move. Her back is arched against me, and my hand falls from her chin to curve gently around the front of her throat before moving them up to her mouth.

Pressing my two fingers against her bottom lip, my lips curve into a smirk. "Suck."

Eyes flashing, Elena takes my fingers into her mouth as her tongue swirls around the digits, her cheeks hollowing out. She releases my fingers with a *pop* and when they fall back against her nipple, her eyes close and she has to bite down on her lip to keep herself from moaning.

"Good girl," I whisper into her ear. "Just like that."

I trail my wet fingers over the curve of the top of her breast, down her sternum and towards her navel. And that's when I realize she's wearing a pair of my boxer briefs.

She notices where my gaze is and her face flushes. "I couldn't just rewear my old underwear," she protests. "They were disgusting."

Her hands begin to slip towards the edge of the dresser and she twists like she's trying to face me.

I tear my hands off her again and slam them down against hers, pressing them back into the dresser.

"Mario—"

Instead of answering her, I roll my hips forward, pressing myself against her, but it offers no relief. My hands move to her hips, pulling her back against me each time my hips roll forward.

"That's good, Elena," I say, watching as her eyes begin to close again. I sigh, my own eyes sliding shut as I press my forehead against her shoulder. "So good."

I let loose one, shuddering sigh before I sink to my knees. Elena is panting above me, feet shifting as she tries to look down to see me, but with my arms on either side of her and her hands on the dresser, she can't quite get a glimpse of me.

Which is for the best because I can feel my eyes going wide, tongue swiping out to wet my lips. I'm ravenous, and my hands go to the backs of her legs, pressing my palms to her calves and coasting up. My thumbs trace circles on the backs of her knees.

"This is fucking *rude*," Elena hisses. "You're taunting me."

"Such a fast learner," I murmur, hands rising to curve over her ass. I squeeze at the rounded curve in front of me before I hook my fingers into the briefs and slowly tug them down.

"That's not fair," Elena says breathlessly. "You still have your pants on."

"Life isn't fair," is all I say before I get up and grab her, moving her towards the bed. She shrieks and clutches onto me, but it's not long before I've crossed the room and deposited her onto the king-sized mattress.

She's bare in front of me, her thighs spread. I lower myself again onto my knees, my mouth on the inside of her thigh. My lips inch up towards the juncture of her thigh as her hips begin to shift.

I press a soft kiss against her before allowing my tongue to stroke up against her clit. Elena gasps, heels digging into the bed as she almost jolts away from the contact, but my arm wraps around her one thigh and the other comes down across the front of her stomach to keep her still.

The light *smack* from the impact sends my pulse into a frenzy.

Fuck, she tastes so good. Nothing has ever come close to this, to lapping at the very stars with the blade of my tongue as I begin to pleasure her with my mouth.

Flicking my tongue across her or sucking at her clit, I didn't care as long as I could get that *exact* moan from her again. My cheeks are wet as I let go of her thigh to use my fingers to spread her even further. So I can press my face closer.

Her thighs squeeze against both sides of my head as I slip a finger back inside her. I look up so I can see her. She has a hand over her mouth as she writhes underneath my touch.

That won't do.

"Let me hear you," I say, removing my mouth from her.

Elena's heels dig into my shoulders as she lifts a shaking hand from her mouth and thrusts it through my hair. She pulls so hard that it smarts but the sound of a trembling moan from her mouth is reward enough so I place my mouth back on her pussy.

She bucks up into me, hips rocking against my face as I stroke my fingers inside her, my tongue swirling against her. The sound of her moans is dulled by her thighs pressing against my ears, but it's so *good*. The taste of her and the feel of her makes me feel like I'm drowning in a sea of stars.

My hips begin to thrust against the bed as if I'm no fucking better than a teenager. All I want is more, would gladly suffer my own destruction if it tastes *this* sweet.

I keep licking at her until her voice breaks and her head is thrown back. I can't keep my eyes off her as her thighs begin to shake around me and her back arches off the bed.

Elena comes, and even as my fingers slow inside her and I rake my tongue over her to taste her orgasm all I can think is that I want to see it a million more times.

Her head snaps up as I reluctantly pull away from her, and she looks down at me. Her chest heaves from her breaths, and I smooth my hands over her thighs as her breath returns to a normal rate.

"Stop smiling," she orders, but with how breathless it sounds, all of the bite is gone.

I smirk and brush a finger over her clit. Her knee jerks up.

"Still so sensitive," I murmur, but I slowly lower her legs back onto the bed and crawl over her. I press a soft kiss to her lips and delight blooms in my chest when she moans against my mouth.

"Take off your clothes," she says into the kiss.

"Say please," I murmur, though my tongue is already on the side of her throat and my hand is already undoing my belt.

"No," she snaps before she reaches down to help me.

I toss my pants and briefs off the edge of the bed and quickly shuck off my shirt. I grip myself in my hand, stroking my length slowly a few times. Fuck me, I'm so *tense*—every one of my nerves alight with that same, glimmering haze.

I better fucking last but from the way she's looking at me, I don't think I will. Her chin tips up, eyes narrowing at me in challenge.

"Where are your manners?" I click my tongue even as I hook my arms beneath her thigh, moving it up and to the side. I lean over onto one forearm and look down between our bodies. Where her skin is covered in a thin sheen of sweat, and I can still see wetness smeared between her thighs.

"Nonexistent," Elena retorts. "Fuck me."

I nearly come undone at just the first press of my cock against her, but I bite down on my tongue and press my forehead against her shoulder in order to collect myself. Elena slips her arm around me, fingers pressing into my shoulder blades and then smoothing up to the hair at the nape of my neck.

"*God*, Mario," she murmurs, voice somewhere near my temple.

I press deeper into her in one long stroke, gasping against her skin. I kiss her shoulder, then her mouth before I begin thrusting into her.

Every particle in my body has a tenuous grasp on the other, the spaces between us filled with electricity. I moan against her mouth, thrusting into her slowly at first until I feel both of her arms wrap around me.

"Fuck, Elena," I manage to groan, my mouth somewhere between the corner of her jaw and the front of her throat. My hand falls back down somewhere near her waist, gripping her.

Elena whimpers and I collapse against her, the thrust of my hips quickening. Stars burst behind my eyes and my fingertips are going numb whenever they graze her skin. I can't fucking *breathe* and the only reason my lungs continue to fill is because Elena is moaning my name back into me.

"Mario," she says. A chorus of it, "*Mario. Mario. Mario.*"

My hips snap against hers as I press another bruising kiss to her mouth. I hook one of her legs over my shoulder, and then another as I thrust into her. I feel her pulse around me as she comes.

Once, and then I am still kissing her and fucking her and *God*—what is this? Because she comes again, and only then do I whisper them.

The dreams and the fantasies and the things I'd never let myself voice—I fucking say them against her lips, her collarbone. Words I didn't even know lived inside me until they spill out like blood from a wound.

I come and it is with Elena's arms around me and Elena's name on my lips, like a prayer, like salvation. I pull out of her and gather her into my arms. We don't say anything until both our pulses calm, mirroring each other in the quiet dark.

"What did you say? Earlier?" she whispers against my chest.

I shake my head, tucking her head beneath my chin. "Nothing, I think."

After, as she dozes in my arms, I finally allow myself to admit the truth I've been fighting, the words I whispered into her skin: I'm in love with her. With her brilliant mind and calculated grace, with her ability to match me move for move in this deadly game.

Even with that perfect baby growing inside her—Anthony's child, a complication I never saw coming.

The realization should terrify me. Instead, it feels like coming home. Like finding something I didn't even know I was missing until it was already under my skin, in my blood.

Giuseppe would call it weakness. O'Connor would call it stupidity.

But holding Elena in my arms, feeling her heartbeat against my chest, I finally understand why my brother chose Bianca over blood. Why he'd burn the world to protect what's his.

Because I would do the same for her. For them both.

18

ELENA

The morning sickness hits like clockwork at exactly 10:37 a.m., a cruel reminder that my body is no longer entirely my own. Twelve weeks pregnant and it hasn't eased—if anything, it's gotten worse.

I barely make it to the bathroom, marble cold against my knees as I heave up the ginger tea and bland toast that was all I could manage for breakfast. My hair—still damp from this morning's shower—falls forward, but familiar hands gather it back before it can get in the way.

"Can I get you anything?"

Mario hovers behind me, his usual dangerous grace replaced by awkward concern. It's almost endearing, seeing New York's most feared exiled son looking so uncertain, like he's facing an enemy he can't shoot or threaten into submission.

His hands are gentle as they hold my hair, and I catch his reflection in the mirror—jaw tight with helpless frustration, those piercing eyes dark with worry.

"I'm fine," I manage, wiping my mouth with trembling hands. The taste of bile burns my throat, making my eyes water. "The doctor said this was normal. It should go away in a few weeks."

He doesn't look convinced. One of his hands moves to my back, rubbing slow circles that ease some of the tension. It's these moments that undo me—when the calculated killer transforms into something almost tender.

When I forget that this isn't real, that I'm carrying another man's child while playing a game that could get us both killed.

Before he can argue, my burner phone rings. The number belongs to Kate, my assistant of three years who handles the children's hospital account.

Sweet, efficient Kate, who probably thinks I've lost my mind.

The charity gala was supposed to be my masterpiece—reimagining their annual fundraiser to double donations through meticulously planned silent auctions and strategic seating arrangements. Over three hundred sick kids depending on my ability to squeeze every possible dollar from Manhattan's elite.

Even in exile, even in hiding, that responsibility weighs on me like a stone in my chest.

"Let it go to voicemail," Mario says, his voice rough with concern, but I'm already answering. Three weeks before everything imploded, I'd promised the hospital director we'd break fundraising records this year.

Some promises should be kept, even when your whole world is burning down.

"Kate? What's the emergency?" I ask urgently.

The silence on the other end makes my skin prickle. Then:

"How long?"

My heart stops. Bella's voice is soft, controlled—more dangerous than if she were shouting. Ice spreads through my veins as Mario goes perfectly still behind me, no doubt reading the change in my expression.

His hand tightens on my shoulder, and I catch our reflection in the mirror—both of us frozen like prey in the moment before the predator strikes.

"Bella—" My fingers grip the phone so hard the plastic creaks. The taste of bile rises again, but this time it has nothing to do with morning sickness.

"How long have you been sleeping with the man who tried to kill me?"

Mario goes still behind me, his body vibrating as if he's checking for violence. But there's no enemy to fight here, no threat he can eliminate with practiced expertise.

This is emotional shrapnel, and all his protection is useless against it.

"It's not what you think," I whisper, though we both know that's a lie. The words taste like ash in my mouth.

"Really?" Her laugh holds no warmth—it's all ice and steel, the sound of the donna she was always meant to become. "Because what I think is that my best friend—the woman I trusted with everything—has been fucking the monster who held my stepdaughter at gunpoint. The man who tried to destroy my family. Who tried to kill me, remember?"

My burner phone chimes with an incoming message. Photos fill the screen, each one a knife to the heart: Mario and me at the clinic, his hand protective on my stomach as if he has any right to that tenderness. Our kiss in the parking garage, desperate and raw. Us on the boat, Mario's jacket around my shoulders like some twisted fairytale.

Every betrayal captured in high-resolution clarity.

"Did you help him?" Her voice cracks, and the sound breaks something in my chest. "Have you been with him this whole time? When he tried to kill me? God, Elena—he threatened my babies. And you've been feeding him information this whole time?"

"No!" The denial bursts out, tasting like desperation. "Bella, I swear, I would never—"

"Don't." The word slices through me like a blade made of ice. Gone is my sweet, artistic friend. In her place is Matteo DeLuca's wife, the donna of New York's most powerful family. Her voice holds all the authority of her position, all the cold fury of a woman betrayed. "Don't you dare lie to me. Not after everything we've been through. Johnny, the nights you held me while I cried about losing my father and mother—was any of it real? Or was I just another mark in your game?"

Tears blur my vision, hot and unstoppable. This was inevitable, wasn't it? You can't live in two worlds without one of them burning. And now everything is going up in flames.

"Of course it was real. You're my best friend—" My voice breaks on the words, memories flooding in: holding Bella through panic attacks, helping her plan her wedding, the way she squeezed my hand when she first showed me her twins on the ultrasound.

A thousand moments of genuine love and friendship, now tainted by betrayal.

"Friends don't betray each other like this!" Her voice rises, raw with pregnancy hormones and hurt. "Friends don't sleep with the man who—who—"

She breaks off, and I hear the telltale gasping that signals a panic attack. Years of friendship means I know exactly what she's experiencing—the tightness in her chest, the way the world starts to spin.

My hands itch to comfort her, the way I have countless times before. Muscle memory screaming at me to help, even as the impossible distance between us grows wider with every breath.

"The man who what?" Mario's voice cuts through my guilt like a blade. He's moved closer, pressed against my back now, close enough that Bella can probably hear him. "The man who saw through Giuseppe's lies? Who tried to stop Matteo from becoming exactly what the old man wanted?"

"Mario, don't—" I try to pull the phone away but he catches my wrist, his touch gentler than his voice.

"You want to talk about monsters, Bella?" he continues, and I feel the tension thrumming through him. "Ask your precious husband what really happened the night Sophia died. Why he's so desperate to protect Bianca."

"You fucking bastard," Bella snarls, and I hear the raw fury beneath her tears. The sound of her transformation from my sweet artist friend into Matteo's donna. "You think I don't know what you are? What you've done? Elena might be fooled by your act, but I know better."

"Bella, please," I beg, tears falling freely now. "It's not that simple—"

But it is that simple, isn't it? I've betrayed my best friend. Slept with the man who tried to destroy her family. Carried Anthony's child while falling for her family's greatest enemy.

There's no coming back from this, no way to make her understand that both versions of me were real—the loyal friend and the woman who chose Mario anyway.

"It *is* that simple!" Bella's voice breaks. "You chose *him*. After everything he's done, everything he's still doing, you chose *him*. And now you're carrying Anthony's baby—oh yes, Elena, I know all about that and so does Anthony—while sleeping with the man who—"

She stops abruptly. The silence that follows is deafening, pregnant with realization. I stop breathing entirely, knowing what's coming.

When Bella speaks again, her voice has gone cold. "That wasn't really your cousin at the hospital, was it? The night we tried to take you home?"

I clutch at the toilet bowl, fingers white-knuckled against the porcelain, searching for anything to anchor me in this moment. Mario's breathing stills.

"Bella, you have to understand. I couldn't—"

"Yes or no." Each word falls like an executioner's blade. "Was that your cousin?"

I close my eyes. "No."

"You fucking bitch." The words explode from her. "You let some stranger walk into that hospital—into my husband's territory—and lie to our faces? Do you have any idea what could have happened? What if she'd been sent by our enemies? What if—"

She cuts herself off again, and her voice is pure ice when she speaks again. "Matteo's on his way to you right now."

The world tilts sideways. Black spots dance at the edges of my vision as panic claws up my throat.

"What? How—"

"The Cartier bracelet," she says flatly. "The one Anthony gave you for your birthday. Did you really think those diamonds were just diamonds?"

My hand flies to my wrist where the bracelet gleams innocently in the morning light. I'd been wearing it for months, so used to its weight I barely noticed it anymore. Anthony's voice echoes in my memory: *"Every beautiful thing deserves protection,* cara.*"*

Protection. Or surveillance.

Mario's already moving, that lethal DeLuca grace returning as he shifts into tactical mode. His gun appears in his hand like magic, and he's already speaking rapid-fire Italian into his phone. The transformation from the man who held my hair minutes ago to this deadly predator is jarring.

With trembling fingers, I unclasp the bracelet. The diamonds mock me as I hurl it across the room like it's burned me. Such a beautiful cage I've been wearing all this time.

"Bella," I try one last time, desperation making my voice crack, "I never meant—"

"To what? To betray me? To help the man who tried to destroy everything I love?" Her words cut deeper than any knife. "Save your explanations, Elena. I trusted you with my life, my family, my children. And you—" Her voice breaks, and the sound shatters something inside me. "You were the one person I thought would never hurt me like this."

A sob tears through her words, raw and broken. Then her voice hardens into something terrible. "I hope you and Mario get exactly what you deserve."

The line goes dead.

My knees buckle as the magnitude of our exposure hits. The bracelet. Such a simple oversight. Such a deadly mistake.

And then another realization slams into me—Bella knows about my pregnancy. Which means Anthony knows. Because Bella confirmed it.

The room starts to spin as panic claws at my chest, stealing my breath. My heart hammers against my ribs like it's trying to escape.

"Elena?" Mario's voice sounds far away, underwater. Dark spots crowd my vision as I gasp for air that won't come. The last thing I feel is him catching me, that familiar cologne mixing with the metallic taste of fear in my mouth.

～

I wake in a different room, monitors beeping steadily beside me. Not a hospital—too luxurious, too private. The walls are a soft cream, original art hanging between bulletproof windows. Another safe house, I realize. Probably one of Mario's many contingency plans.

Mario sits beside me, his usual dangerous grace softened by what looks suspiciously like fear. His hand hasn't left mine since I passed out, if the warmth of his grip is any indication.

"The baby?" I ask immediately, hand flying to my stomach.

"Is fine," he assures me, but his voice holds an edge I've never heard before—something raw and protective that makes my stomach tighten with something other than morning sickness. "But you're not leaving this bed until the doctor clears you. No more games, no more risks."

"We have to move," I argue weakly. "If Matteo—"

His kiss silences me, gentler than our usual desperate encounters. "The only thing that matters right now is keeping you safe," he growls against my lips. "Both of you."

My hand finds his, pressing it against my stomach where his enemy's child grows. The gesture feels impossibly intimate, impossibly right.

"I'm sorry," I whisper, though I'm not sure what exactly I'm apologizing for. The bracelet? Bella? Every choice that led us here?

"Don't." His voice is rough with emotion I've never heard from him before. "Don't apologize for choosing me."

But as sirens wail in the distance, growing closer with every heartbeat, I wonder if we'll live long enough to regret our choices.

If this baby will ever have a chance to grow up in a world where her mother's decisions haven't damned her before she's even born.

19

MARIO

The beeping of medical monitors fills the safe house bedroom as I watch Elena sleep, her hand curled protectively over her growing stomach even in rest. She looks almost ethereal in the predawn light—golden hair spread across the pillow, long lashes casting shadows on too-pale cheeks.

Even exhausted and hunted, she maintains that meticulous composure that first caught my attention.

The past twenty-four hours have stripped away every carefully constructed layer of our game. The Clinton House is probably in pieces by now—Matteo's men, O'Connor's thugs, and Calabrese's soldiers all tearing through my carefully curated sanctuary.

My phone hasn't stopped vibrating:

O'Connor wants your head on his desk by morning.
Calabrese offering five mil for her location.
Your brother's men spotted in Brooklyn.
Boss, they're closing in from all sides.

But for once, I don't care about the implications. All I can focus on is how Elena looked when she collapsed—her skin gray, lips blue, one hand pressed to her stomach as if she could protect the baby through sheer will.

My heart had seemed to stop until the doctor confirmed they were both stable.

The phone buzzes again. Siobhan's number. Goddammit. What does she want?

"What?" I snap, answering the phone against my better judgment.

"Now, now." Her voice holds none of its usual mocking edge. "Is that any way to talk to someone asking after Elena's health?"

I go still. "What game are you playing?"

"Game? I just find her ... interesting." Siobhan's tone changes. "A simple party planner, they all said. Just another pretty face organizing galas. And yet here she is, bringing three of the most powerful families to their knees."

"If you're threatening her—"

"Quite the opposite." Siobhan's laugh is surprisingly genuine. "I admire her style. Using their assumptions against them, playing the role they expect while building something entirely different. Very ... clever."

The penny drops. "Like using social events to modernize your father's empire?"

"Finally catching up, are we?" I can hear her smile. "Who would suspect the vapid socialite daughter of revolution? The party planner of espionage?"

"Speak fucking English for once," I snap, rubbing my temples. I can feel the start of a headache brewing.

"Fine. Here it is in simple terms: Elena reminds me of myself. And I protect what I recognize." She pauses. "Especially when they're carrying the next generation of our world."

"Cut the cryptic bullshit, Siobhan." I move away from Elena's bed, keeping my voice low. "You building a shadow empire behind daddy's back isn't exactly news. What I want to know is what the fuck you want with Elena."

"Direct as always." She sighs, as if I'm a particularly slow student. "I'm proposing an alliance. With her, not you—though unfortunately, you seem to be part of the package now."

"An alliance." The word tastes bitter. "And what exactly would that entail?"

"Elena has a particular talent for operating in plain sight. Moving through spaces the old guard doesn't think to watch. Building networks they don't even know exist." There's something like admiration in her voice. "Honestly, I wish she hadn't gotten herself tangled up with you. You really do piss me off, Mario."

I scoff. "Feeling's mutual, princess."

"But we can't all have what we want, can we?" Her tone sharpens. "Your brother on some level, Calabrese, even my father—they're dinosaurs fighting over territory while the world changes around them. Elena understands that. She's been quietly revolutionizing how money moves through this city for years, all under the guise of charity galas and society events."

I think of Elena's meticulously planned fundraisers, her strategic seating arrangements that have brokered more peace deals than any formal sit-down. "And you want to what? Combine forces?"

"Like I said, I want to ensure the next generation has a future worth inheriting. The question is: are you going to stand in the way of that future, or help protect it?"

"I protect what matters," I tell Siobhan flatly. "You know that after everything that's happened."

"Mmm, yes. Quite the show you've put on recently." Her amusement grates on my nerves. "I'll be in touch."

She hangs up before I can respond. I stare at my phone, imagining all the ways I could make her regret her games and double meanings.

But then Elena stirs on the bed, and suddenly Siobhan O'Connor's machinations seem irrelevant.

Those eyes focus on me—blue as ice but somehow warm, seeing everything I try to hide. Even exhausted, even hunted, they miss nothing. It's what first drew me to her—that perfect balance of beauty and calculation.

"How are you feeling?" I ask, sitting down beside her.

"Fine." She shifts, one hand still protective over her stomach. "But

I need to know something. Something that's been bothering me since Bella brought it up." She takes a breath. "Tell me about Bianca. About that night. I need to understand."

Dread pools in my belly. I've never talked about it—not to anyone, not even Marco or Dante. The memory lives like poison in my blood, a reminder of everything Giuseppe said I would become.

But Elena deserves the truth, especially now.

"I was so angry," I begin, the words feeling like glass in my throat. "You don't understand what it was like, growing up as Giuseppe's mistake. His bastard. The son who should never have been born."

I move to the window, unable to face Elena as the memories surface. "Matteo was perfect—legitimate, pure-blooded, everything a DeLuca heir should be. When we failed Giuseppe's tests, I got the basement, the belt. Matteo got second chances. Private tutors. Understanding."

My laugh carries an arctic chill. "Do you know what it's like, watching your brother inherit an empire while you get table scraps? Knowing that no matter how hard you work, how loyal you are, you'll never be more than the whore's son?"

The words taste like copper and rage. "I planned it for months. The warehouse by the pier—where the rotting fish and diesel fuel would mask any screams. A shipping container modified just so ... and sweet little Bianca in her navy school uniform, walking the same route home every day."

My hands clench as I remember that night. "I called Matteo at midnight. Told him it was his turn to lose something precious. 'Your empire or your daughter,' I said. 'Choose quickly—she's running out of air.'"

I close my eyes, but the images come anyway. Bianca tied to that chair, her small wrists raw from fighting. She'd tried so hard to be brave, just like Matteo taught her. *"Uncle Mario,"* she'd whispered, *"why are we playing this game?"*

"I made sure to smile when I pressed the gun to her head," I continue. "Made sure the camera caught every detail—the rope burns, her tears, my finger on the trigger. I wanted Matteo to see exactly what his perfect life had cost. What his *bastard* brother was capable of."

The confession burns like acid. "I became exactly what Giuseppe always said I was. A monster wearing a DeLuca face. But when I saw her there, so small, so afraid of disappointing everyone ... she looked just like I used to, after Giuseppe's 'lessons.' And I realized I'd become him. The thing I hated most."

Elena's silence feels like a physical weight. I can't bear to look at her, to see disgust or worse—pity—in those clever eyes.

"Why Bella?" she asks finally. "After five years of exile, why come after her?"

The laugh that tears from my throat sounds unhinged even to my ears. "How do you not see it? Perfect Matteo got everything. Again. A loving wife, a baby on the way, the fairy tale ending he never deserved." My voice cracks on the words. "He took a girl who wasn't even his own child and made her his heir. Built himself the perfect family while I rotted in Boston, dancing to O'Connor's tune."

I don't tell her about those first months after the failed attempt on Bella. How O'Connor's men held me down in that basement while Seamus reminded me what happens to dogs who bite the wrong hand. Three days in that cold room, chains biting into my wrists while O'Connor systematically broke every promise of protection he'd made.

The scars on my back still ache in cold weather—a gift from his favorite brass knuckles.

"You think exile was my only punishment?" The words taste like copper. "A year of absolute loyalty. Taking the jobs even O'Connor's most hardened men wouldn't touch. Building my worth back piece by bloody piece until he trusted me to breathe without permission."

The bitterness I've carried for years pours out like poison. "Meanwhile, my brother, the great Matteo DeLuca, who claims to value chosen family over blood—where was that sentiment when Giuseppe cast me out? When I needed a brother instead of an heir?"

My hands shake as memories surface—Matteo teaching Bianca to shoot, the way he looks at Bella like she hung the moon, how tenderly he touched her stomach when they announced the twins.

All the soft moments a monster like me doesn't deserve.

"So yes," I continue, the words bitter as ash. "I came for his wife. His unborn children. Everything he loves, just like he took everything from me. And I had the backing of the Irish mob to do it."

I finally turn to face Elena, letting her see exactly what kind of creature she's gotten involved with. "Giuseppe always said I was born wrong. Twisted. A monster." My laugh holds no humor. "Guess fathers do know best after all."

"You're not a monster." Elena's voice carries quiet conviction as she struggles to sit up. The movement makes the monitors beep in protest, but her eyes never leave my face. "Damaged, yes. Dangerous, absolutely. But monsters don't change. They don't grow. They don't care for complicated women carrying another man's child."

The last words hang between us like smoke, heavy with implication. Something in my chest cracks open at her steady gaze, her complete lack of horror at my confessions.

I turn back to her slowly, waiting for the other shoe to drop—for the disgust to surface, for her to realize exactly what kind of creature she's let into her bed. Into her life.

But there's no judgment in those clever eyes. No fear. No rejection. Only understanding, wrapped in something that looks terrifyingly like love.

The acceptance hits harder than any of O'Connor's punishments, than any of Giuseppe's lessons.

"How—" My voice breaks. I clear my throat and try again. "How can you look at me like that? After everything I just told you?"

She reaches for my hand, and I move back to her bedside. I let her take it, marveling at how steady her grip is. How sure.

"I'll never forgive myself for that night," I admit roughly, the words scraping my throat raw. Each syllable feels like confessing to a priest, like laying my sins bare before something holy. "For becoming everything I hated about our father. For letting revenge poison everything."

My hand finds her stomach where Anthony's daughter grows, and the contact burns like confession, like possibility. Like everything I never thought I could have. "But this? You? It's changing everything."

"I know," she whispers, pulling me down into a kiss that tastes like redemption. Like forgiveness I never thought I deserved.

When we break apart, her eyes hold assurance beneath the softness. "So let's make sure our choices moving forward are better than our choices in the past."

The words hit like absolution. Like a chance at something more than revenge and violence and living up to Giuseppe's worst expectations.

She pulls me down for another kiss, this one harder, hungrier. Her fingers tangle in my hair as she arches up from the bed, making the heart monitor spike erratically.

"Elena," I warn against her mouth, even as my body responds to her need. "You need to be careful. The monitors—"

"Shut up," she hisses, nipping at my lower lip. "Help me get these damn things off."

Her hands are already moving to the electrodes on her chest. I catch her wrists gently. "Let me."

She shivers as I carefully peel each electrode from her skin, the heart monitor giving one final protest before falling silent. The moment the last one comes off, she's pulling me back down, kissing me like she can erase every dark confession with the press of her lips.

"You sure about this?" I ask, even as my hands slip beneath her nightgown. "The doctor said—"

She silences me with another fierce kiss. "I said shut up, Mario."

Who am I to argue with that?

Moving my hands away from her warm body, I slip them beneath her ass to pull her forward, wrapping her legs around my torso. I push her down onto the bed, grinding my hips into her.

Let her feel how much I want her.

I slide my fingers up along the outside of her thighs, her nightgown bunching up around my wrists. Growling, I tug at the sides of her panties. It's a fucking joke that she still has them on.

"Someone's impatient," Elena says as she pulls back, giggling lightly.

My gaze falls on her kiss-swollen lips and her darkened eyes and the hunger I feel for her grows, evolving into something bottomless.

"Shut up," I say dumbly.

Elena laughs again before leaning back onto both elbows. She pulls one leg up so it's bent at the knee against the side of the bed. The other leg is pulled up to the mattress, creating more space between her thighs, and revealing the soft pink of her panties beneath the hem of her nightgown.

"I'm going to fuck you with my mouth," I growl before I lower myself down onto my hands and knees.

"Such dirty words," Elena murmurs as her fingers spear through my hair. She slides forward enough so she can rest one of her heels against my shoulder blade and then gently guides my face forward.

Hooking a finger around her panties, I shove them aside and stroke my tongue along her pussy from her entrance to her clit. The taste of her spreads over my tongue and it takes everything in me to not fucking finish right there.

Fuck, she feels so good.

I do it again as my hands spread over the outside of her thighs, pulling her flush to my face. My tongue strokes over her a few more times before I begin to suck at her clit, flicking the tip of my tongue over it just to hear her sigh above me.

"Fuck, Mario," Elena says, sinking back onto her elbows. Her head falls back and I look up to see how the arch of her back pulls the nightgown taut over her breasts. My lips close over her clit and I lave at it until her hips are rocking up against my mouth. "So *good*."

Those words are my unleashing. I haul her forward in one swift pull, my fingertips creating indentations in her skin. She yelps and falls back against the bed. Normally, I would ask if she's okay, but I'm too fucking gone at this point. I lift her ass up off the bed so I can shove my face right up against her. Elena swings her other leg up and over my shoulder so both heels dig into my skin.

But I don't care because she tastes so *fucking* good. The room is filled with Elena moaning my name, singing my praises. Her moans come first as these little whines, but she tries to press them between her lips like flowers in the page of a book. Then, her breath comes as enchanting little pants and the muscles in her belly tense.

I wrap one arm around the back of her thigh to spread my palm over her abdomen, just to feel. The flutter of her muscles when I drive my tongue into her dripping pussy and roll my head from one side to the other so her clit catches on the ridge of my nose drives me crazy.

Elena groans above me, one hand gripping the mattress while the other searches clumsily for my own hand, where it rests over her navel. Her fingernails rake over my wrist before she grabs it tightly in her fist.

"Holy shit," Elena gasps.

I can't help it. I grin against her pussy and her heels dig sharply into my back. I wince and I think I see a flicker of a smile on her face. I hum then, all humor leaving me as I continue to work her pussy. Her wetness spreads across my cheeks and drips down my chin.

Elena may be saying something, but I'm not able to make it out. All I focus on is sucking and licking at her like she's the last drop of water in a desert. I feel the first shake of her thighs as they squeeze around my ears. Her fingers pull sharply at my hair and her voice is a high, a keening moan as she comes against my mouth.

I lick through each rolling wave of her orgasm and don't stop until I feel her try to push me away. I pull away like coming up from the crest of the ocean for air. My breath comes out of me in little huffs as I tilt my face back to look at her, but my gaze keeps getting pulled back in the direction of her pretty pussy—soaking wet and swollen with need.

Elena yanks on my shirt, and I allow myself to rise up and sit on the bed. She reaches for my shirt and roughly tugs it over my head, tossing it somewhere else. Then she pushes me back until I'm laying against the bed and she's crawling over me.

"How did I taste?" Elena asks, her eyes practically glittering.

"Like honey," I answer honestly, stroking my hands up and down the back of her thighs.

Elena snorts. "Such a corny answer," she teases, but then she pushes herself up onto her knees and tugs her nightgown over her head, exposing her beautiful breasts to me. She tosses the nightgown over my face, and then I feel her fingers tugging at my pants and boxers as she tugs them down, down, down.

She wraps her hand around my cock and I hiss, tearing her nightgown away from my face.

"What's it like?" Elena asks, almost offhandedly as she watches herself lazily stroke me from base to tip. Her thumb presses against the slit of my cock and I bite back a curse. Fuck me.

"What?" I ask, fingers raking over my own abdomen as I watch that languid roll of her wrist over my cock.

Elena grips me harder, her hand halting somewhere towards my base and I thrust upward into her unmoving palm, wanting friction she doesn't grant me. I growl.

"Wanting me so badly," she answers me, "I had to push you off me."

"I can show you," I respond, hissing as she strokes my cock again.

She laughs and leans forward slightly, her breasts pressing against my chest. The tip of my cock taps against her belly with each stroke.

"That's so cute," she hums as her pace quickens over my cock. I start to rock my hips up into her touch.

"*Cute?*" I repeat roughly, my voice breaking slightly from how I try to keep back a moan. "I'll fucking show you cute. And I've had enough of those panties too."

I rip her panties away from her and throw the scraps onto the ground. She makes a low noise of dismay as she looks at the tiny lace pieces scattered on the hardwood floors.

"I liked that pair!" she complains.

"I'll buy you thirty more," I promise. My thoughts are getting away from me. All I can think about is burying myself deep inside her.

Elena looks satisfied at that and lifts my cock so that it's notched right against her entrance.

"That's better," she says. "And since you promised ..."

She sinks down onto me, the delicious slide of her so divine I think I see God. Or God is her. I can't tell anymore. She rocks slowly back and forth over me and I reach around to grab handfuls of her ass as she rides me, bouncing up and down lightly on her knees.

Her breasts lift and drop with her movements and I remove one hand from her ass to hold one of her breasts, squeezing it and flicking my thumb over her nipple. I drive my hips up into her and she gasps, throwing her head back. I can feel her pussy flutter around me, and then she slowly stops, hips rolling lazily against me instead.

Very patiently—I think, at least—I release her breast and press a hand between her shoulder blades, pushing her down so that her hands are above my head. I shift down so she has the proper angle to rock her hips back onto my cock. I gently trace my fingers up and down the back of her thighs before capturing her nipple in my mouth.

"*Mario!*" She cries out as she starts to move again. I only moan in response.

Closing my eyes, I lose myself to just how wonderful this is, feeling her slide around me over and over until that needy, urgent feeling builds low in my abdomen. My mouth is on her breasts, my hands grip her thighs and her ass and I'm so fucking full of her—her perfume, her taste.

Elena pushes back into me wantonly, the wet smack of her skin punctuating each thrust, the breath rushing out of her in moans and little pants. I groan, wrapping both arms tightly around her so I can get my mouth on her breasts again. She circles her hips over me and I hiss in response.

She's making me feel so fucking good and without prompting, I bring my fingers between us, playing with her clit. Stars begin to dot my vision as she rolls her hips against mine at a stuttering pace now. Uneven, really, as if she's losing a tenuous grip on reality.

Or it might be me, with how I keep thrusting up into her. Thrust after heavenly thrust.

"Fucking come, baby," I growl, my fingers continuing to flick over her clit. I can feel myself start to lose control. I don't know how much longer I'll last but I want her to come first. "Come all over my cock."

Elena cries out before she presses her mouth against mine. Our kiss is messy, tongues stroking languidly against each other as her hips pause and then still over mine. But I don't allow for any pause and start punching up into her, back arching up and off the bed.

She cries out again and then I feel a rush of wetness, her pussy pulsing rapidly around my cock.

My eyes fucking roll into the back of my head as I spill into her, my cry muffled by her kiss. My entire body is a live wire, and I don't think my mind fully comes back into myself until she's lying against me, toes tracing up and down my calves with her ear pressed to my chest.

For the first time in a long time, I feel something dangerous spark in my chest.

Hope.

20

ELENA

I'm going to lose my fucking mind in this place.

Two weeks since moving to the new safe house, and the walls feel like they're closing in. They have since day three.

Mario moves freely, conducting business and coordinating with his network while I'm expected to stay hidden away like some fairy tale princess in her tower. I spend my days in an endless cycle of restless activity—swimming laps in the private pool until my arms burn, practicing yoga to keep the morning sickness at bay, obsessively reviewing hospital fundraiser details I can no longer execute.

By midafternoon, I'm usually reorganizing the walk-in closet or rearranging the library for the third time that week. Anything to keep my mind off the fact that my entire world has shrunk to these four walls. I refresh news sites compulsively, searching for any mention of the manhunt I know is still ongoing. My fingers itch to be doing something real—planning events, moving money, playing the game that's become as natural as breathing.

The fact that the "tower" is a luxury penthouse with better security than Fort Knox doesn't make it any less suffocating.

The irony isn't lost on me.

"I'll be back in a few hours," Mario says, adjusting his shoulder holster. He looks devastating in that charcoal Armani suit, the material molding to his broad shoulders like it was made especially for him. The silver at his temples catches the morning light, and three days of stubble does nothing to hide the sharp cut of his jaw. Those dark eyes that miss nothing sweep over me, cataloging every detail like he always does before leaving.

"Don't leave the apartment," he warns. "The Calabreses—"

"Have eyes everywhere, I know." The words come out sharper than I intended, jagged with frustration. "Just like they had yesterday, and the day before that. Go. Handle your business. I'll just sit here getting fat and useless."

Am I bitter? Is it that obvious?

His jaw tightens—that tell he probably doesn't realize he has. "Elena—"

"Don't." I wave him off, turning back to my laptop where more intel from Siobhan's operation fills the screen. She'd somehow gotten my burner number two days after we had to move from the Clinton House, her first text typically cryptic: *Not all cages are meant to hold us.*

Since then, we've developed an odd rapport. Our conversations range from cryptocurrency integration strategies to the psychology of men who underestimate women in power. She sends me intelligence about Anthony's movements, coded in references to social events we both know will never happen. I feed her information about old guard banking practices that need modernizing, disguised as charity gala planning.

We're building something, though neither of us quite admits what.

This morning's text was particularly interesting: *The old men play chess while the world turns digital. Ready to show them how queens really move?*

Mario moves closer, and I hate how my body responds to his proximity even when I'm furious with him. Heat pools low in my belly as his cologne—expensive and subtle and uniquely him—

wraps around me. My skin prickles with awareness, remembering his hands on me this morning, how he'd kissed me awake with that perfect mix of tenderness and possession. His hand finds my chin, calloused fingers gentle despite their strength, tilting my face up until I meet his eyes.

"You're carrying precious cargo," he says softly. "Everything else is secondary."

I jerk away from his touch, ignoring the flash of hurt that crosses his face before that perfect DeLuca control slides back into place. "Go. Your empire won't run itself."

The moment the door closes behind him, I'm already moving. Two weeks of watching these walls, of being treated like spun glass instead of the strategist I am.

Through the penthouse windows, I spot Mario's men trying to maintain cover—one pretending to read a newspaper at the cafe across the street, another "walking his dog" for the third time this hour, two more poorly disguised as maintenance workers.

But they're watching for threats coming in, not a pregnant woman slipping out. I've spent days studying their patterns, noting the seven-minute gap in coverage when they change shifts. The blind spot in their surveillance where the building's art deco architecture creates the perfect shadow.

I change quickly, trading Mario's borrowed clothes for the emergency outfit I'd insisted he buy me. The Chanel suit feels like home—a navy wool crepe that skims over my barely showing baby bump, the jacket's clean lines making me feel powerful again. More like the woman who runs Manhattan's social scene rather than someone's precious secret to protect.

My office isn't far. Just a quick trip to grab critical files, check on time-sensitive contracts. What's the point of all our precautions if I can't maintain the legitimate business that makes them possible?

I've planned this escape for over a week—watching the security rotations, timing the service elevator's maintenance schedule, noting which guard takes an extra long coffee break at exactly 10:15. The service entrance sees constant deliveries, and I've memorized today's schedule.

Right now, a catering van should be unloading for the law firm's lunch meeting at twelve.

Sure enough, when I slip into the service corridor, workers are too busy with stacks of sandwiches to notice another well-dressed woman hurrying past. I keep my head down, letting my hair fall forward as I join the flow of office workers heading out for early lunch.

The street swallows me into its rhythm, and for the first time in weeks, I feel like I can breathe. Let Mario play protector—I have an empire of my own to maintain.

The journey to my office feels blessedly ordinary. Just another day in Manhattan, joining the river of people heading to work. The familiarity of it makes my throat tight—how many times have I walked this exact route with Bella? Her arm linked through mine as she chatted about her latest painting, both of us stopping for coffee at that little place on Fifty-Third that makes the best almond croissants.

My chest aches remembering how she used to surprise me with lunch, showing up with takeout from our favorite Thai place, her hands usually stained with paint. We'd eat cross-legged on my office floor, planning galas and dreaming up ways to squeeze more money from Manhattan's elite.

The security guard greets me with a warm smile as I scan my keycard. "Welcome back, Ms. Santiago. Mrs. DeLuca was asking after you last week."

The smile on my face nearly falls at those words. Of course Bella would be asking if I showed up. After she warned me last time that Matteo was on his way, she wouldn't be making that mistake again. She would want to catch me in the act.

My chest caves in. My best friend wouldn't be doing this if I hadn't betrayed her.

My office feels like stepping into another life. Everything is exactly as I left it—the wall of windows overlooking Madison

Avenue, fresh flowers on my desk (probably Kate trying to maintain normalcy), the framed photo of Bella and me at her wedding.

I have to turn it face down, unable to bear her radiant smile.

The space reflects my carefully crafted image—sophisticated but approachable, everything chosen to make wealthy clients feel comfortable writing large checks for good causes. Abstract art in soothing colors, comfortable seating arranged for intimate conversations, awards for fundraising excellence displayed with calculated modesty.

A half-finished painting leans against one wall—Bella's work. She'd been so excited to surprise me with it, showing up one afternoon with her easel and determination to "add some soul to this corporate maze."

Now it sits abandoned, another casualty of my choices.

I sink into my chair, muscle memory taking over as I begin sorting through urgent emails. But my eyes keep drifting to the empty cream leather sofa where Bella used to curl up with her sketchbook, planning artwork for charity auctions while I worked.

So many lazy afternoons spent like that—me arranging seating charts while she filled canvas after canvas with color and life.

I miss her. God, I miss her so much it feels like bleeding.

My phone buzzes with encrypted intelligence from Boston, pulling me back to my current reality. I focus on analyzing Siobhan's latest power plays, letting the familiar work of gathering intel distract me from memories I can't afford to dwell on.

I'm so absorbed in piecing together the patterns of Irish money movement that I don't hear him approach.

"You've been avoiding me," Anthony's voice carries from my office doorway, making my blood run cold.

I gasp and look up, my heart nearly stopping. Anthony Calabrese fills the doorway like a predator, so much like his uncle Johnny it makes my skin crawl. The same danger, the same cold eyes that catalog every detail while revealing nothing. His Armani suit is immaculate, not a dark hair out of place, but there's something sinister in his perfect polish now. Something that reminds me why the Calabrese name inspires terror.

He moves toward me with lethal fluidity as I reach for my phone, but he's faster. His fingers close around my wrist, the touch gentle but immovable as he takes the phone from my trembling hand. The gesture is almost tender, which makes it infinitely more frightening.

"You're not calling him," he says softly, placing my phone in his jacket pocket. "Your DeLuca exile can't help you now."

"This was never about you," I try, my mind racing through escape scenarios even as my hand instinctively covers my stomach. "The baby—"

"Is a Calabrese." Anthony's smile shows too many teeth as he perches on my desk, close enough that his cologne—sharp and expensive—makes my head spin. "Just like you'll be, once we handle this ... unfortunate situation with Mario."

He straightens his already perfect cuffs, the gesture casual but somehow menacing. "The Irish are *quite* interested in helping me secure what's mine. So is Matteo DeLuca. Why, I have them fighting over who gets to deal with the exile first."

My throat goes dry at the calculated pleasure in his voice. This isn't the polished society heir I've been playing all these months. This is Johnny Calabrese's true successor—someone who enjoys the game of breaking things.

The threat hangs in the air between us, heavy with implications. My pulse thunders against my ribs as I realize how thoroughly I've been outplayed. Every calculated risk, every careful move, leading to this moment.

Stupid, stupid, *stupid*. God, what was I thinking? One moment of rebellion, of wanting to feel normal, and I've endangered everyone. Mario warned me. He fucking *warned* me and I was too proud, too frustrated, too goddamn selfish to listen.

My skin crawls with self-loathing as I remember how easily I slipped past the security meant to protect me. Protect our baby.

Our baby. The thought sends fresh panic through me. I won't let Anthony anywhere near her. I won't let that monster—that creature wearing expensive suits and a practiced smile—taint the most pure thing in my life. I'd rather die.

"You really think I'll just go along with this?" I keep my voice steady despite the fear clawing at my throat. My hands curl into fists beneath the desk where he can't see them shaking. "That I'll let you—"

"Let me?" His laugh holds no warmth as he pulls out his phone. "You don't have a choice, *cara*." He turns the screen toward me—surveillance photos of Sofia Renaldi entering our safe house with supplies, then Marco coordinating with Mario's security team. "The Renaldis have been very helpful to you and Mario, haven't they? Sweet little Sofia, playing the perfect undercover agent. It would be a shame if something happened to her. Or perhaps her brother? I hear their niece just started kindergarten."

My heart plummets to my feet. The Renaldis are one of Mario's only real allies—the only people who've helped us survive this long. Sofia with her brilliant schemes and unfailing loyalty. Marco who's stood by Mario through everything.

Their innocent niece who has nothing to do with any of this.

I've endangered them all because I couldn't stand being confined for a few more weeks. Because my pride was more important than their safety.

The realization makes me want to vomit.

"What do you want from me?" My voice comes out steady, surprising me.

Anthony chuckles and slides his phone away. "You're going to come with me," he says, moving closer. "You're going to make such a wonderful Calabrese bride." His eyes gleam as he continues, making my stomach turn. "And when my heir is born, I'll take over his training. Raise him to be the next don our family deserves."

I don't bother correcting him about the baby's gender. I've seen how Calabrese men treat their women—like decorative possessions to be displayed and controlled.

"And you," he reaches out to stroke my cheek, making my skin crawl, "will be my pretty little plaything. Something beautiful to bring out for events, to fill with more children."

"And if I refuse?" I ask, though I already know the answer.

Anthony's chuckle turns dark as he closes the remaining distance between us. His hand shoots out, grabbing my wrist and squeezing until I feel bones grinding together. I bite back a cry, refusing to give him the satisfaction.

"Either you play your part as the devoted mother and wife-to-be," he says softly, "or your lover joins his father in an early grave."

But I hear the lie in his words. Anthony will never let Mario live, no matter what I do. He's too much like his uncle Johnny—he enjoys breaking things too much to show mercy.

My only choice is whether I want to watch it happen.

I hear my phone buzzing in Anthony's pocket—Mario, most likely, having discovered my absence. Horror floods through me as I picture him tearing apart the penthouse, that careful DeLuca self-control splintering as he realizes I'm gone.

That I've put myself—put my baby—directly in harm's way.

The emotions must play across my face because Anthony laughs, the sound echoing off my office walls. "Ah, there it is," he taunts, squeezing my wrist harder. "That moment when you realize just how thoroughly you've fucked up. Did you really think you could play in our world without consequences, little party planner? That you could whore yourself out to a DeLuca exile and not pay the price?"

He yanks me to my feet. "Time to go home, *cara*. I have such plans for breaking that spirit of yours."

The door explodes inward before he can move me further, and Mario fills the frame. Rage has transformed his features into something terrifying, something that reminds me exactly who raised him. His eyes are pure Giuseppe DeLuca, promising violence with a precision that makes even me shiver. Blood spatters his immaculate suit, evidence that he's already carved through Anthony's men to reach me.

Behind him, I catch glimpses of Dante's team engaging with

Anthony's security in the hallway. The sounds of fighting echo off marble floors—flesh meeting flesh, bodies hitting walls.

"Get away from her," Mario growls, and I've never heard that tone from him before. It's pure violence barely contained, a promise of exactly how many ways he knows to make a man suffer.

Anthony's smile widens as Irish accents fill the hallway. "Perfect timing," he says smoothly, rising from the desk. "We were just discussing family arrangements."

My world turns sideways as I realize what the true point of this was—this wasn't just about catching me.

It was about luring Mario into a trap.

21

ELENA

The tension in my office crackles like a live wire as I watch Mario catalog threats with lethal efficiency. Three Irish enforcers in the hallway, Anthony's smug smile, my own carefully controlled fear as I shield our unborn child with my body.

No—not our child. Anthony's daughter, a complication that's become the center of everything.

"Perfect timing," Anthony says smoothly, rising from the desk. "We were just discussing family arrangements."

"The only arrangement you need to worry about is your funeral," Mario snarls, but I catch the slight tension in his shoulders. He's counting exits, calculating odds. His hands are already stained with blood from fighting his way to me, but more enemies are coming. I can hear them in the hallway.

"Always so dramatic." Anthony adjusts his cuff links with deliberate casualness. "But you might want to see what I found in Elena's private server first." He turns his phone screen toward us, and my heart stops. "*Fascinating* collection of shipping manifests, bank records, surveillance photos of my operations. The kind of evidence that could put someone away for a very long time—especially if they're carrying my child."

My blood runs cold as I recognize my own meticulous notes about the trafficking operation. Every piece of intelligence I've gathered, every connection I've documented—all of it leading back to me. Months of carefully crafted evidence that could destroy not just Anthony, but the entire Calabrese empire.

And now he has it all.

The look Mario gives me is pure fury—not at my investigating, but at the danger I've put myself in. His jaw clenches so hard I hear teeth grinding. "You're not walking away from this," he tells Anthony, his voice promising violence.

"No?" Anthony's smile widens as more Irish voices join the chaos in the hallway. "I think you'll find *I* hold all the cards. Elena's evidence. Her baby. Her life." He shifts closer to me, his hand finding my throat in a gesture that's both possessive and threatening. "The question is: what are *you* willing to sacrifice to save her?"

Mario's expression transforms into something terrifying—pure danger emerging from behind his careful control. I've never seen him look so lethal, so capable of absolute destruction. It should frighten me, but instead I feel oddly safe.

Because that rage? It's not directed at me.

It's aimed at the man foolish enough to threaten what Mario considers his.

"The FBI would be very interested in how deeply you've infiltrated our organization," Anthony continues, satisfaction dripping from every word. "Corporate espionage, conspiracy, maybe even RICO charges. Imagine our child being born in prison."

Mario shifts subtly, positioning himself between me and the Irish enforcers. Even with blood splattering his suit and rage burning in his eyes, his movements are calculated. Precise. "You wouldn't risk exposing your own operation."

"Wouldn't I?" Anthony's smile is anything but kind. "Everything leads back to Elena's private investigations. Such a shame—an ambitious event planner getting in over her head, working alone to expose things she shouldn't have seen. Nothing connecting to me or my legitimate businesses at all."

"None of it connects *directly* to you," I say, fighting to keep my voice steady while my mind races through possibilities. "Just like Johnny's operation didn't connect to you. You're very good at keeping your hands clean."

"While *you've* been quite sloppy lately." Anthony's gaze drops pointedly to my stomach, making my skin crawl. "Hormones affecting your judgment, perhaps? The old Elena would never have left such an obvious trail. Coming to your office alone, carrying evidence that could destroy you …"

A gun appears in his hand—not pointed at us, just resting casually on the desk. A reminder of power rather than an immediate threat. The metal gleams in the afternoon light streaming through my office windows, and I catch Mario's minute flinch.

Not from fear—Mario DeLuca has never feared guns—but from the effort of restraining himself from tearing Anthony apart with his bare hands.

"You really think I came alone?" I ask, stalling for time as I catch movement in the hallway behind Mario. More of Mario's men, strategically positioned. "That pregnancy has made me stupid?"

Anthony just laughs. "I think you've been very stupid lately, *cara*. Sleeping with a dead man walking, carrying evidence that could destroy you …" His eyes gleam with cruel amusement. "Coming to an office my family has owned since before you started playing in our world."

My breath hitches involuntarily. Of course. I've been so focused on maintaining my independence that I forgot the most basic rule—always know who really owns the ground you're standing on.

"So here's how this ends," Anthony continues, ignoring my horror. "You come home. Play your part as my child's mother *and* my wife. All this evidence disappears, and you get to raise our son in luxury instead of from behind bars."

"And Mario?" I ask, though I already know the answer. Mario's look could incinerate me where I stand—furious that I'm even entertaining this conversation.

"Gets to live." Anthony shrugs elegantly. Liar. "Isn't that generous of me? He goes back to Boston, you stay where you belong, and everyone survives. Unless of course," his smile turns cruel, "you'd prefer to test how maternal instincts develop in federal prison."

I feel Mario coiling like a spring beside me, rage radiating off him in waves. The Irish enforcers respond instantly—O'Connor's best men shifting their stances as weapons appear in practiced hands. The hallway crackles with lethal tension.

One wrong move and this becomes a bloodbath.

But Anthony has miscalculated. He's so focused on Mario that he doesn't see my hand sliding into my desk drawer, doesn't notice how I've positioned myself during this conversation—angling my body so my movements are hidden by the desk while keeping his attention on my face.

"You're right about one thing," I say calmly, though my heart slams against my chest so hard I'm sure everyone can hear it. "I have been sloppy lately. Pregnancy brain, probably."

The flash drive arcs through the air before anyone can react. One of the Irish enforcers catches it reflexively—Sean Murphy, I realize with a flash of recognition. Tall and imposing in his tactical gear, but with cold blue eyes. I've seen him in enough surveillance photos, standing at Siobhan's right hand while she builds her shadow empire.

The same Sean Murphy who's been helping her modernize the Irish mob behind her father's back.

The same Sean Murphy whose cryptocurrency wallets I've been tracking for weeks.

"That's everything I have on the trafficking operation," I continue as Anthony's face transforms with pure rage. The sophisticated mask shatters, revealing something terrifying beneath—raw fury that makes my skin crawl. "Every manifest, every bank record, every connection. Insurance, you might say. And now it's in Irish hands."

"You stupid bitch," Anthony snarls. "You have no idea what you've just done."

"I know exactly what I've done." I keep my voice steady despite my pounding heart. "Your arrangement with the Irish was always fragile. How do you think Seamus will react when he sees proof that you've been running trafficking operations through his legitimate shipping routes?"

Something angry flashes in Anthony's eyes. The gun lifts slightly—not quite pointed at me, but the threat is crystal clear.

"You're bluffing," he says softly, that dangerous calm more frightening than his rage. "That drive is empty. You wouldn't risk—"

"Risk what? My life?" I laugh, though I feel Mario coiling tighter beside me, ready to explode into violence. "You've already threatened that. My freedom? Also threatened. My child's future? Let's add that to the list. Seems I have nothing left to lose."

Sean Murphy examines the drive with careful interest, his Irish lilt deceptively casual. "Interesting insurance policy you've got here, lass."

"Kill them both," Anthony orders sharply, control completely abandoned. "Get that drive—"

The windows explode inward as rappelling ropes appear. Mario moves with inhuman speed, tackling me behind my heavy desk as gunfire erupts. Through the chaos, I hear familiar voices—Marco's team, perfectly timed.

The world dissolves into violence and breaking glass.

"You okay?" Mario's body shields me completely, one hand protective over my stomach while the other aims his gun around the desk's edge. His breath is warm against my neck, his heartbeat steady despite the chaos.

"Other than dying to throw up? Perfect." I try to peer around him, but he presses me more firmly down, his body a wall between me and danger.

"Stay down," he growls. "Marco's team has the office covered but the hallway—"

A fresh explosion rocks the building. Sofia's delighted laugh carries over the gunfire: "Hallway's clear, boys! Anthony's running!"

"What the *fuck* is she doing here?" Mario snarls, his body tensing with fresh rage. "I'm going to kill her. Then I'm going to kill Marco for letting her anywhere near this."

But I have more pressing matters to address rather than worry about a nineteen-year-old having the time of her life. "Shouldn't we go after him? He's getting away."

"Let him," Mario says grimly as the gunfire dies down. He helps me up, hands checking me for injuries with practiced efficiency. "We've got what we need."

Sean Murphy holds up the drive, his gear splattered with evidence of the fight. "This what you wanted them to see, then?"

"That depends," I say carefully, watching his face. "On whether you're really here under Seamus's orders, or if someone else sent you."

His smile is sharp as a blade. "Smart lass. The lady O'Connor sends her regards." He tucks the drive into his vest. "Said you might need some backup today."

"So Siobhan's finally making her move," Mario says beside me, his arm still protective around my waist.

"The old ways are dying," Murphy says simply. "Lady O'Connor thinks it's time for new alliances. New ways of doing business."

Relief floods through me. Siobhan had come through after all.

Through my broken office windows, I hear sirens approaching.

"We need to move," Marco calls from the shattered window. "DeLuca security is incoming—someone finally called them."

Sofia pokes her head through the doorway, blood splattered across her face like war paint. Her grin is fierce and wild.

"I told you I'd be useful," she says cheerfully.

"You had no fucking business being here," Mario snarls, but his arm stays steady around me. "We'll discuss your suicidal tendencies later."

Sofia just sticks out her tongue, looking far too pleased with herself.

Mario turns to me, his body angled protectively as more sirens join the chorus outside. "Ready to get out of here?"

I look around my destroyed office—papers scattered like snow, windows blown out, everything I've built lying in chaos around us.

But my hand finds Mario's, squeezing tight. For the first time since discovering my pregnancy, since watching my carefully constructed world start to crumble, I feel steady.

"Take me home."

⁓

BACK IN THE SAFE HOUSE, Mario's rage finally explodes. His careful control shatters as he rounds on me.

"What the *fuck* were you thinking?" His voice vibrates with fury. "Going to your office alone? After everything we discussed?"

"I was thinking I have a business to run," I snap back, refusing to be cowed by his anger. "That I can't just disappear into your protective bubble forever."

"A business?" He laughs, the sound sharp and bitter. "You almost got yourself killed over fucking *paperwork*?"

"It's not just paperwork and you know it!" I match his volume, weeks of frustration pouring out. "It's my life's work. My independence. Everything I've built!"

"Your independence?" He stalks closer until he's only inches from me. "And what about our safety? What about the baby?"

"Don't you dare use her against me," I snarl, jabbing a finger into his chest. "I've been protecting her since before you even knew she existed."

"Protecting her?" His eyes flash dangerously. "By walking straight into Anthony's trap? By carrying evidence that could get you killed or imprisoned?"

"I had it under control!" I shout.

"Under *control*?" He grabs my shoulders, fingers digging in almost painfully. "He had you cornered! If I hadn't—"

"If you hadn't what?" I wrench away from his grip. "Come charging in like a bull in a china shop? I handled it! I got the evidence to Murphy, I made the connection with Siobhan—"

"You got *lucky*!" The words explode from him. "One wrong move and you'd be in Anthony's hands right now. Or dead. Is that what you want?"

"What I want," I say through gritted teeth, "is to not be treated like some fragile thing that needs to be locked away! I'm still *me*, Mario. Still the woman who's been playing this game since before you noticed me."

"And what happens when the game gets you killed?" His voice cracks slightly, revealing the fear beneath his rage. "When Anthony decides you're more trouble than you're worth?"

"That's not—" I start to say, but Mario cuts me off.

"I can't lose you!" The words tear from him like they're being ripped from his chest. "*Either* of you. Don't you understand that?"

We stare at each other, both breathing hard. The anger still crackles between us, but something else too.

"I won't be caged," I say finally, my voice softer but no less firm. "Not even by you."

"And I won't watch you die because you're too stubborn to let me protect you." He backs me up into the wall.

My breath is shallow, my chest rising and falling against his. Mario's hands grip my waist, pulling me closer, as if touching me is the only thing keeping him grounded. I can feel the heat of his body, the tension that radiates from him—an electric pulse that matches my own racing heart.

The confrontation with Anthony, the gunfire, the way we nearly lost everything … it leaves me raw, desperate, like I can't breathe until I know *he's* okay.

I don't think. I don't hesitate. My body moves of its own accord, driven by the ache deep inside me, the need to *feel* him, to confirm we're both still here. I lean forward, pressing myself against him, and capture his lips in a heated kiss. It's urgent, all teeth and fire, as if we can erase the fear, the chaos, through this touch.

His mouth is on mine almost violently, and I meet him with equal desperation. There's no sweetness in it—just raw, unrestrained need, as if we're trying to anchor ourselves in each other. His hands slide over my body, rough and possessive, claiming every inch of me, making sure I'm real, making sure I'm here, safe.

"I need you," he growls against my neck, his voice ragged. His words send a shiver through me, igniting something deep inside. I can feel it—*he needs me* just as much as I need him. My hands tangle in his hair, pulling him closer, deepening the kiss, matching his urgency. His leg rests between my legs and my body arches in response when it brushes against my heated core.

We don't wait. There's no gentleness, no softness—just the frantic need to hold onto each other, to assure ourselves that we're alive, that we survived this. He presses me harder against the wall, his body a furnace against mine.

I can feel his pulse, fast and frantic, matching my own. The world outside doesn't exist in this moment. Only him. Only us.

Our mouths clash again, forceful and claiming, as if we're trying to erase the weight of everything that's happened. Every desperate kiss, every possessive touch, is a promise to survive, to stay together. To fight for each other.

Mario's hands slide up my body to plunge underneath the silk blouse, grasping my breast, his thumb flicking over my peaked nipple. I gasp, arching into his touch.

He works my breasts, his fingers kneading them softly until I grind my hips against the leg that is still in between mine. Mario growls and presses his body flush against mine, the hard length of him pressing into my stomach. I try to move my hand in between us to touch him through his pants, but he grabs my wrists and pins them over my head.

"I don't think so," he murmurs into my collarbone. He uses one of his hands to continue to pin my wrists while the other pulls my skirt up to my hips. He moves my hands down to grip my skirt as he kneels down before me, hands on both of my thighs.

With a wink at me, he spreads my legs and licks me.

A low moan rips from my chest at the feeling of his tongue against my heat. He circles the apex of my thighs, his teeth scraping slightly and huffs a laugh against me when my hips buck and yet another moan escapes me.

"I'll never get sick of hearing you make those noises," he says before continuing.

My fingers grip his hair as his tongue works me in long strokes. He slips a finger into me and I whimper, biting my lip in an effort to be quiet. He adds a second finger and I feel the heat pooling in my stomach, begging for release. I grip his hair harder when his fingers begin pumping faster inside me, sensing how close I am.

Mario sucks my clit and I look down at him on his knees before me. The sight of him undoes me and I arch off the wall as my orgasm rocks through me, my legs quivering.

Mario stands up, his lips shiny, and his hands go to my hips to support me while I finish coming down from my orgasm. My lips crash against his and I can taste myself on him. He groans deeply into my mouth as he pushes me back up against the wall, a hand coming between us to undo his pants.

I pull them down myself and they pool around his ankles, the full length of him springing free. I can feel my slickness against my thighs and I place my hands around his neck as he lifts me up, his strong hands gripping either thigh.

My legs wrap around his waist as he slides into me. I cry out as he hisses through his teeth at how wet I am before he begins moving slowly inside me.

"Faster," I whimper, unable to handle just how *good* this feels. Holding his face in my hands, I kiss him as I start to move against him, wanting to feel that delicious friction. I meet him thrust for thrust as he slides a hand up to squeeze my breast, rolling my sensitive nipple between his fingers.

My head falls back against the wall and a moan escapes me before I can stop myself. The sound seems to spur Mario on because he thrusts rougher into me, his hips smacking into mine. His breath comes in huffs as he adjusts his grip on my hips and pounds deeper into me. His lips crash against mine to devour my moan as release shudders through me, my walls clenching and squeezing him as he spills into me.

Mario continues thrusting, his movements wild and unrestrained as we both come down from our high. His hips finally slow before he buries his face in the crook of my neck, his breaths coming in pants. I brush his hair off his sweaty forehead and kiss the top of his head.

"Bed?" I remark, my legs shaking.

After, as we lay tangled in sheets, I trace the many scars mapping Mario's chest—each one telling its own story of survival. "You were going to let them kill you," I whisper, the realization hitting me fully. "If it meant keeping me safe."

"There was no 'letting' about it." His voice is rough as he pulls me closer, his hand gentle on my hip. "I told you before—you and this baby are all that matter now."

"Even though she's his?" The question that's been haunting me finally slips out.

Mario's hand finds my stomach, slightly rounded and holding such complicated promise. His touch is reverent, protective. "She's *yours*," he says firmly. "That's all that matters."

I turn to face him fully, seeing my own desperate choices reflected in his eyes. The violence and tenderness there, the capacity for both destruction and protection that drew me to him from the start. "What happens now? Anthony won't stop. And the evidence I gave Sean ..."

"Now we fight smarter." He kisses my temple, my cheek, my lips —each touch an anchor in this storm we've created. "Together. No more solo missions to your office."

I laugh against his mouth, some of our earlier tension finally dissolving. "No promises."

His growl of frustration makes me smile. We're both too stubborn, too used to fighting our own battles.

But maybe that's what makes us work—two broken pieces fitting together in all the wrong ways to make something stronger.

Something worth protecting.

22

ELENA

I force myself to stay busy in this gilded cage, analyzing intelligence and building new alliances while trying not to feel trapped. My conversations with Siobhan have become increasingly frequent—encrypted messages flying back and forth as we reshape the landscape of power.

Your little insurance policy is paying dividends, she texts. *Sean says the shipping records alone are worth their weight in gold. And the banking trails? Pure poetry.*

"The old men are scrambling," she'd purred during our last call, delight dripping from every word. "They don't understand how deeply you've mapped their networks. Using their own digital footprints against them—it's beautiful really."

"Your father's traditional routes are particularly vulnerable," I'd replied, pulling up files I've been compiling for months. "The way he moves money through shell companies ... it's so outdated it's almost quaint."

Her laugh had been sharp with ambition. "Oh, we're going to have such fun rebuilding this empire, you and I."

I spend my days coordinating multiple operations from behind bulletproof glass—managing my legitimate business remotely through Kate (who deserves a massive raise for handling this "family emergency" so smoothly), analyzing Siobhan's modernization efforts, tracking the ripple effects of Anthony's exposed trafficking routes.

And when that's not enough to keep the walls from closing in, I research preschools. Baby gear. Birthing plans. All the normal things expectant mothers are supposed to care about, as if there's anything normal about my situation.

My phone buzzes constantly with updates from Siobhan's network. The Irish are moving digital currency through new channels. The younger captains are aligning behind her. The old guard is starting to notice something's shifting, but they can't quite see the pattern yet.

I try not to think about Bella, now thirty-two weeks pregnant with twins who could arrive any day. But it's impossible to avoid her completely—she's everywhere in the society pages I shouldn't be reading. Photos of her at charity events, her belly huge but her smile radiant. Matteo hovering protectively behind her, one hand always resting where his children grow.

I was supposed to be there. To hold her hand through delivery, to meet my godchildren, to share every moment of this journey with my best friend. Instead, I'm hiding in a safe house, carrying another man's child while helping dismantle the very world Bella's children will inherit.

The irony is bitter enough to choke on.

My phone chimes again—not one of my usual contacts. The number isn't familiar, but the message makes my blood turn to ice:

Code Blue in L&D. Preeclampsia confirmed, BP critical. Twin B showing severe decels. Dr. Chen requesting emergency team.

Then another:

You should know—it's bad. Really bad.

"No, no, no ..." The phone slips from my trembling fingers, clattering against imported marble. The sound echoes through the safe house like a gunshot.

Mario materializes instantly, elegance forgotten in his concern. "Elena?"

"Bella's in trouble." My voice breaks as I scramble for my coat, hands shaking so badly I can barely manage the buttons. "The twins—their heartbeats are unstable. Preeclampsia. I have to—"

"Are you out of your *fucking* mind?" He blocks the door, his expression thunderous. "You can't go anywhere near that hospital. Matteo will have it locked down tighter than the Pentagon."

"Get out of my way." The words come out desperate, raw. But even as I say them, I know he's right. The logical part of my brain—the part that's kept me alive in this world—knows I can't just storm Mount Sinai like I would have before.

That doesn't stop me from trying to help remotely. My fingers fly over my phone as I contact trusted hospital staff, making sure the right specialists are called. Each update makes my chest tighter.

Status updates flood in, each one worse than the last:

BP 160/100 and rising.

Twin A showing decreased movement.

Protein in urine confirming preeclampsia diagnosis.

Preparing OR for emergency intervention.

Every message makes breathing harder, guilt and fear warring in my chest until I feel like I might shatter.

"They're saying she might need an emergency C-section," I report, refreshing messages compulsively as I pace the living room. "The boy's heartbeat keeps dropping and—" Another text appears. "Fuck. She's hemorrhaging."

Mario watches from the doorway, his face carefully blank. "Your contacts have it handled. The best doctors are already there."

"But what if they're not enough?" My hand drifts to my own swollen belly, terror clawing at my throat. "What if she—" I can't finish the sentence.

My best friend could be dying, and I can't even be there to hold her hand. All because I chose Mario. Chose love over loyalty.

The guilt threatens to suffocate me.

"Going there is suicide," Mario says quietly, his tone gentler than I've ever heard it. "After what just happened with Anthony? The hospital will be locked down tight. Every family in New York watching to see if the DeLuca twins survive. The Calabreses and Irish will be watching too. They know you'll try to make a move."

I shouldn't care anymore. Shouldn't feel this crushing weight of responsibility, this desperate need to help the woman I betrayed. Bella made her position clear—I'm dead to her, just like Mario is dead to his family.

But old loyalties die hard, especially ones forged through years of shared secrets and midnight confessions.

"You think I don't know that?" But I'm already moving, grabbing my coat. My hands shake as I reach for my bag. "She's my best friend, Mario, even if she hates me. The only real friend I've ever had. If she dies thinking I abandoned her completely ..."

"*Elena.*" His voice cracks slightly, an edge of desperation I've never heard from him before. The sound makes my chest ache—Mario DeLuca, who fears nothing, sounds terrified. "Please. Don't do this."

I cup his face in my hands, feeling the stubble rough against my palms, the tension in his jaw. His eyes hold a fear he's trying desperately to hide—the same look he had when Anthony held that gun in my office. "I have to. You understand that, right? After everything that's happened, all my betrayals ... I have to try to do one thing right."

He mutters something about me putting him in an early grave, but I can see the resignation in his eyes. He knows he can't stop me. I kiss him quickly before rushing out to where his most trusted guard waits with a car.

The drive to Mount Sinai feels endless. Manhattan scrolls past my window—streets I used to walk freely are now full of potential threats. Every red light feels like torture as another update comes in about Bella's failing condition.

I make it three levels into the parking garage before Matteo's security spots me. Just as I knew they would. The guards' hands move to their weapons, but it's Matteo himself who emerges from the shadows, fury radiating from every line of his body.

My breath catches at the sight of him. Those blue-gray eyes are pure ice, promising revenge. For the first time, I truly understand why men fear him—why even Mario speaks of his brother's rage with grudging respect.

"Give me one reason," he says softly, that deadly quiet tone sending chills down my spine, "why I shouldn't have you shot where you stand. After what you and my brother have done."

"Because I know things about this hospital your men don't," I respond, lifting my chin even as fear makes my heart race. "Which doctors are compromised. Which nurses report to rival families. And right now, your wife and children need every advantage they can get."

"You want to talk about advantages?" Bianca's voice cuts through the tension like a blade. She emerges from behind her father, still a Mafia princess despite her obvious exhaustion. Dark circles ring her eyes, but her fury burns bright enough to scorch. "Like how you used your position to spy on us? How you betrayed Bella's trust while pretending to be her friend?"

I force myself not to flinch at the raw hatred in those blue-gray eyes—so like Matteo's, but the same shape as Mario's. "Bianca—"

"*Don't.*" Her hand twitches toward her hip where I know she carries a gun—a habit she started after Mario's reappearance nearly a year ago. The gesture holds a promise of violence that makes my throat constrict. "Don't you *dare* act like we mean anything to you. Not after what you and *he* did."

"You're right." I keep my voice steady despite my pounding heart. "I betrayed your trust. *All* of you. But right now, Bella needs every ally she can get. Even ones you hate."

"She's not wrong." Antonio materializes from the shadows, his usual stoic expression troubled. "Three different families have tried placing people on staff since Mrs. DeLuca was admitted. The Rossettis alone—"

"I don't give a *fuck* about rival families right now!" Bianca's voice cracks with rage, her hands trembling with barely contained fury. The perfect DeLuca composure fractures as she advances on me. "I care about the woman who's been feeding information to the monster who held me at gunpoint. Who chose him over us. Over *Bella*."

"Then care about this," I cut in sharply. "Dr. Marcus Hansen—Bella's current ob-gyn? He has gambling debts to the Vituccis. The charge nurse on the maternity ward reports to the Calabreses. And the anesthesiologist on call? His brother disappeared three months ago. The Rossettis are holding him as leverage."

I watch Matteo process this information, that brilliant tactical mind working behind his carefully blank expression. His head tilts slightly—a gesture I've seen a thousand times when he's evaluating a threat.

"You have proof?" he asks finally, skepticism warring with necessity in his voice.

"Everything's on my phone. Staff schedules, financial records, proof of compromised personnel. It's yours—along with my network of trusted contacts who can replace them. All I'm asking is a chance to help. One last time," I say as I fumble for my phone.

Relief courses through me as I pull up the files. Just let me do this one thing right.

The silence stretches like a wire about to snap. Finally, Matteo speaks into his comm: "Get me new staff. Full background checks. Use Ms. Santiago's information to—"

"Dad, you can't trust her!" Bianca's voice cracks with fury and fear. She stares at her father with wide eyes, looking suddenly young and vulnerable. "After everything she's done—"

"No." Matteo's eyes never leave my face, cold and assessing. "But right now, your stepmother and siblings need every advantage. Even dangerous ones."

He steps closer, close enough that I catch the familiar scent of his cologne—the same one he's worn since I first met him. His stubble is more pronounced than usual, evidence of hours spent worrying. "But understand this: the moment this is over, if I ever see you near my family again ..."

He doesn't finish the threat. He doesn't need to.

I nod once, sharply. "Understood."

What follows is a carefully choreographed dance. I work through

Antonio, never getting close enough to actually see Bella. My phone becomes command central as I coordinate replacements.

"Dr. Sarah Chen is clean," I tell Antonio. "Harvard trained, no family connections, and she specializes in high-risk multiples. Get her here now."

"The Vituccis have someone in radiology," he reports back twenty minutes later.

"Use Marcus Thompson instead—he's on call at Presbyterian. His wife just had twins last year, he'll understand the urgency."

Every person who comes near the DeLuca family gets triple-vetted. I check credentials, financial records, family connections. One nurse gets pulled when I discover her cousin works for the Calabreses. An orderly is replaced after I find suspicious deposits in his account.

"The anesthesiologist from Mount Sinai Brooklyn," I tell Matteo's captain. "He's clean and he's the best with compromised patients. I'll have him here in thirty minutes."

Hours pass in a blur of coordination and careful maneuvering. Then finally, my phone buzzes with the update I've been praying for: *Twins delivered safely. Boy 4lbs 2oz, girl 3lbs 11oz. Mother stable.*

My knees nearly buckle with relief. I find an empty waiting area, needing a moment to process. My hand drifts to my own stomach, to my daughter who will never know her cousins. Who will never play with Bella's children or hear them called family.

More family lost to choices I can't take back.

Another text: *They're naming them Giovanni and Arianna. Both breathing on their own. Father hasn't left their side.*

Tears burn behind my eyes as memories flood back—late nights with Bella, planning the nursery while sharing gelato and dreams. How she'd grabbed my hands, eyes bright with joy, when asking me to be godmother. "You're the only one I trust with them," she'd said. "The only one who's always been there."

Now I'll never even get to hold them.

My phone buzzes with a text from Mario: *Tell me you're alive.*

They're all safe, I reply. *The twins are beautiful. Perfect.*

His response makes my breath catch in my throat: *You did the right thing, little planner. Even if they never know. Now get out of there before Matteo remembers he's supposed to kill you.*

I start to rise, to walk away from everything I've lost, when Bianca's voice freezes me in place.

"I thought you'd still be here."

I turn slowly. Bianca stands in the doorway, her face a battlefield of complicated emotions. For a moment, I see her as that scared twelve-year-old in the warehouse. Before any of us knew how choices could destroy everything we love.

"I was just leaving," I say quietly.

"Good." Bianca's voice drips hatred. "But first—she asked for you. When she woke up. Even after everything, even knowing what you've done, her first thought was still to ask if you were here."

She says that on purpose. To hurt me.

And it works.

I feel each word crack against my ribs, stealing my breath. Of course Bella would ask for me. Even after my betrayal, even after everything—that's who she is. Who she's always been. Better than all of us.

I force myself to breathe through the pain. "Tell her ..." But what can I possibly say? What words could ever bridge this chasm I've created? "Tell her I'm glad they're healthy. That I—" My voice breaks. "That I'm sorry. For everything."

"Sorry doesn't fix what you and *he* did." Bianca's hand drifts to her gun again. "If I ever see you near my family again ..."

"You won't." I straighten my shoulders, squaring myself against the weight of all my choices. "Take care of them, B. Those babies are lucky to have you as their big sister."

I walk away before she can respond, my heels clicking against hospital tiles for what I know will be the last time. The sound echoes through empty corridors like a funeral march. Everything I've built, every relationship I've cultivated, all of it sacrificed for a love that both saves and damns me.

My phone buzzes one final time—a photo from one of the nurses

I trusted. The twins in their separate NICU incubators, tiny but fighting. Giovanni, slightly larger, dark hair visible beneath his breathing tubes. Arianna, smaller but already showing her mother's determination in the way she grips her father's finger.

Matteo stands between them, his usual controlled expression cracked with worry as he watches his children fight for every breath.

Bella isn't in the photo—she'd still be in recovery after the emergency C-section. But I know she's probably demanding updates every few minutes, refusing to rest until she can see them.

I delete the photo immediately, but the image burns behind my eyes. Those tiny babies, so fragile yet so loved, fighting to survive their early arrival into this dangerous world.

Babies I'll never get to hold, never get to watch grow up.

In the parking garage, Mario waits in a borrowed car, his face tight with worry. He doesn't speak as I slide into the passenger seat, just reaches for my hand. His fingers are warm against mine, an anchor in the storm of loss threatening to drown me.

"Take me home," I whisper, and feel him squeeze my fingers in silent support.

I don't look back as we drive away. I made my choice the moment I let Mario into my life, trading one family for another. The weight of it sits heavy in my chest.

A reminder that every choice has consequences, that love and loss are two sides of the same blade.

Now I have to learn to live with the scars.

23

MARIO

It's been three weeks since Matteo and Bella's twins were born, and the silence is driving me insane. Even the Irish have gone dark—no threats from O'Connor, no cryptic messages from Siobhan. My sources are stumped by the sudden quiet.

I pace the safe house, muscles coiled tight with anticipation. Elena watches me from the couch where she reviews intelligence reports, one hand absently stroking her growing belly. The sight still hits me in ways I can't quite name—this fierce, brilliant woman carrying new life while helping me navigate a war.

My phone buzzes—Sofia's name lighting up the screen. The message makes my blood run cold: *Anthony has my brother. Meeting at the old St. Patrick's church in one hour or Marco dies. Come alone.*

"No." My voice cuts through the quiet room. "It's obviously a trap."

"Marco helped us escape Anthony at my office," Elena says, already reaching for her coat after she quickly scanned the text. "He's given us intelligence, protection, support. We can't just—"

"*We* aren't doing anything." I move to block her path, panic clawing at my throat. Not her. Not again. "You're staying here while I handle this."

"Like hell I am." Her blue eyes flash with that dangerous fire that first drew me to her—that perfect blend of calculation and courage. "Marco and Sofia risked everything to help us. I won't abandon them now."

"You're four months pregnant!" The words come out harsher than intended, fear making my voice sharp.

"Which is exactly why Anthony won't risk harming me." She meets my gaze steadily, that brilliant mind already working through angles. "He wants his heir too badly. We can use that."

I study her face—the determination in those blue eyes, the slight lift of her chin that means she's already decided. My little planner, always three steps ahead, always willing to risk everything for what matters.

Giuseppe would call it weakness. This need to protect people who've helped us, this refusal to sacrifice pawns for tactical advantage.

But I'm not Giuseppe. And Elena isn't some pawn to be sacrificed.

"Fine," I growl, already calculating exit routes and backup plans. "But we do this my way."

The smile she gives me is pure danger—a reminder that she's as dangerous as anyone. God help me, but I love her for it.

Even if she's probably going to get us both killed.

∽

THE ABANDONED church looms like a gothic nightmare against Manhattan's skyline. Crumbling gargoyles peer down from weathered stone, their grotesque faces casting monstrous shadows in the streetlights. The rose window above the entrance is broken, jagged glass teeth catching moonlight like an open wound.

Through surveillance cameras, I watch Elena approach those massive wooden doors. Her black dress can't hide her growing belly, but she moves with that purposeful elegance that's become second nature. Even now, walking into danger, she maintains the image we've crafted—the ambitious society planner caught between powerful men.

She plays her role perfectly as she enters the church. That precise mix of fear and defiance as she surveys the space, one hand resting protectively over our child—Anthony's child, I correct myself bitterly. Every gesture calculated to draw attention exactly where she wants it.

Then Anthony emerges from the shadows like a demon from hell, and my blood runs cold.

"Such a clever little thing," he muses, circling Elena like a shark scenting blood. Marco kneels nearby, his face a mess of bruises and dried blood. His left eye is swollen shut, but his good eye meets mine through the camera with steady determination. Two of Anthony's men hold guns to his head with practiced ease.

"Playing both sides so beautifully," Anthony continues. "But did you really think I wouldn't figure it out?"

More of his men materialize from the darkness between stone pillars, their weapons glinting in the dim light filtering through broken stained glass. "Did you enjoy it?" Anthony asks Elena. "Using my bed to steal our secrets? Carrying my child while plotting with the DeLuca bastard?"

"Actually," Elena says with deadly calm that makes my chest tight with pride and terror, "I did enjoy it. Every moment I spent gathering evidence of your trafficking operation. Every piece of intelligence I fed to Mario. Watching you think you were so clever while I dismantled everything piece by piece."

Anthony's hand flashes out, catching her chin. Every muscle in my body screams to move, to tear him apart for daring to touch her. "Careful, *cara*. You seem to have forgotten who holds the power here."

"No." Elena's smile is cruel. "*You* have."

Sofia appears from behind an ornate confessional, her gun trained on Anthony's head with rock-steady aim. "Let my brother go," she says pleasantly, as if discussing the weather, "or I paint these lovely stained glass windows with your brains."

My finger tightens on my own trigger as I watch through my scope. One signal from Elena, and this becomes a bloodbath.

But Anthony just laughs—a cruel sound that makes the hairs on my neck rise. It's the same laugh Johnny used before destroying things he considered his property. "Did you *really* think I'd come without insurance?"

He pulls out his phone, showing them a video feed. "That's your father's house, isn't it Sofia? Such a shame about the gas leak they haven't discovered yet. One phone call and—"

The explosion of stained glass sends rainbow shards raining down as my team breaches through the windows. Fury ignites through my veins at his threat to Marco and Sofia's father. I move with the lethal precision Giuseppe beat into me, each movement calculated for maximum damage.

The first man goes down before he can raise his weapon—my elbow crushing his windpipe as I use his body as a shield. Two more rush me with knives, but years of training make their movements seem slow. I redirect one blade into his partner's chest while snapping the other's knee with a precise kick.

The crack of bone echoes off stone walls.

A fourth man gets his gun up, but I'm already inside his reach. My ceramic blade finds the soft spot beneath his jaw as I spin past, my other hand relieving him of his weapon. Three shots take down the men trying to flank me—center mass, just like Giuseppe taught us. No wasted movement, no hesitation.

I find Elena backed against the altar, one hand protective over our child—no, *Anthony's* child—while she holds a gun on her former lover with rock-steady aim. My little planner, dangerous to the end.

"Touch her again," I say quietly as I approach, letting that deadly DeLuca tone fill the space, "and there won't be enough left of you to bury."

"You still don't understand, do you?" Anthony spits blood onto consecrated ground. "She's carrying my heir. My blood. You really think I'll let a bastard son raise my child? That I'll let my child grow up with Giuseppe DeLuca's reject?"

The words hit their mark—I feel that old rage rising, that need to prove myself more than my father's cast-off son. But then Elena's hand finds mine, her touch anchoring me to the present.

"The baby is not your child," Elena says softly. "This child is mine. And they'll never know you existed."

Rage twists Anthony's handsome features into something monstrous. What happens next seems to unfold in slow motion.

I catch the slight shift of his weight, the telltale movement toward his jacket. My body moves on instinct, tackling Elena behind a carved wooden pew as steel glints in candlelight. The thunder of gunfire echoes off sacred walls, making angels weep from their perches above.

Sofia's aim proves true—two rounds tearing through Anthony's shoulder in a spray of red that stains his perfect suit. The impact spins him like a dancer, his own shot going wide to shatter the last intact window.

"Rather poetic," Sofia muses as Anthony crumples, her gun still trained on him. "The mighty Calabrese heir, bleeding out in a house of God."

But Anthony advances like a specter—rolling behind a pew as more of his security team pours in through the side doors. The sacred space erupts in chaos, bullets splintering wood and shattering what remains of the stained glass. Colored shards rain down like deadly jewels as gunfire echoes off stone walls.

"You really think I came alone?" Anthony's laugh carries over the mayhem as I shove Elena behind a stone pillar, my body covering hers. "My family built this power while you were playing dress-up with society wives, Elena. Did you forget who taught you about contingency plans?"

An explosion rocks the church's foundation, the blast making my teeth rattle. Through the thickening smoke, I watch Sofia dragging her injured brother toward cover. Marco leaves a trail of blood across hardwood floors as Anthony's men advance from multiple directions, their movements precise and coordinated.

My mind races through scenarios, calculating odds and exits.

We're outnumbered, but I've survived worse. Giuseppe made sure of that, drilling tactics into us until they became instinct.

"This isn't over," Anthony calls out, his voice carrying that deadly calm that reminds me too much of his uncle Johnny. "You've just ensured I'll take everything from you piece by piece. Starting with our child."

The threat makes something primitive rise in my chest—pure rage mixing with a protectiveness I've never felt before. Elena presses against me, one hand on her stomach where Anthony's child grows.

But in this moment, watching her face set with determination even as death closes in, I know the truth.

This baby is ours. And I'll die before I let Anthony Calabrese near either of them.

Through the smoke, I count at least fifteen of his men moving into position. We're surrounded, outgunned, with nowhere left to run.

Time to remind them why the DeLuca name used to make men tremble.

I return fire, each shot finding its mark with the precision Giuseppe drilled into us. Two of Anthony's men drop before they can reach new cover, my bullets catching them in the soft spots their tactical gear doesn't protect. But more keep coming, pushing us back toward the altar with coordinated precision.

I feel Elena behind me, her breath steady despite the chaos. One hand holds her gun with practiced ease while the other shields her stomach. The sight makes something primal rise in my chest—a need to protect that burns hotter than any rage Giuseppe ever beat into me.

"When I find you again," Anthony promises as he backs toward an exit, blood staining his body but his composure never wavering, "and I *will* find you—you're going to find out what happens to people who betray the Calabrese name. Ask your friend Bella what happens when someone crosses me. Ask her about her father's last moments."

I feel Elena flinch against my back. But there's no time to process the implications as the church's rear wall explodes inward, showering us with centuries-old stone and mortar. Anthony's extraction team moves with military precision, covering his retreat with synchronized efficiency.

The last thing we see through the thickening smoke is his smile—cold and promising, exactly like Johnny's. A reminder that this isn't over.

※

Later, back at the safe house in the safety of our bedroom, my hands shake as I check Elena for injuries, needing the physical reassurance that she's truly unharmed. The confrontation with Anthony left us both raw, emotions too close to the surface. Every shadow of a bruise, every slight wince as she moves, sends rage coursing through me.

"I'm fine," she insists, but lets me continue my inspection, removing her clothes piece by piece until she's only in her underwear. Her own fingers trace the cuts on my face from the exploding stained glass, her touch gentle despite the tremor I pretend not to notice.

The adrenaline crash hits us both hard. Every near miss, every bullet that could have found its mark, every threat Anthony made—it all catches up at once. I pull her closer, needing to feel her heartbeat against mine, to know she's really here. Safe. Alive.

Elena leans in, seeking my lips. It's clear she needs this connection, this moment of feeling something other than guilt and fear. I hesitate for a moment, my eyes searching hers.

"Are you sure?" I whisper, my voice rough.

Elena's answer is to pull me closer. The kiss is gentle at first, almost tentative. Then something shifts, and suddenly it's all heat and urgency. Her touch erases Anthony's threats, Matteo's condemnation, every scar Giuseppe left on my soul. For these moments, nothing exists but us.

Her hand cups the back of my head, fingers tangling in my hair. My own hands explore the soft roundness of her body. Every touch, every sensation, pushes the horror of the day further away.

As we lose ourselves in each other, I feel a spark of warmth cutting through the cold dread that's been consuming me.

I deepen the kiss, my tongue exploring hers with a hunger that leaves both of us breathless. My hands move lower, skimming over her waist, her hips, and she arches into me, craving more. Our breaths mingle, our movements frantic as we lose ourselves in each other.

My lips trail down her neck, nipping at her skin, and she moans in response. The sound is raw, needy, and it only spurs me on.

"Mario," Elena gasps, tilting her head back to give me better access. "I want you."

I pull back just enough to look at her, eyes dark with desire. "You sure?" I ask again, my voice husky.

"Yes," she breathes, her voice trembling with need. "I want you, Mario. I *need* you."

A wicked smile curves my lips, and I step back, my eyes never leaving hers. The air between us crackles with tension, with the promise of what's to come.

I remove my own clothes until I'm just in my underwear, my cock straining against the resistance. I palm myself through the material and groan. The urge to take her right now is overwhelming.

"Turn around," I murmur to her as I guide her towards the bed. "Do exactly what I say, Elena."

For once, Elena obliges without argument. She turns and leans against the bed, her hands splayed against the mattress. The sight of her like this, willingly submitting to me, sends a jolt of desire straight to my dick.

My hands move over her shoulders, down the smooth expanse of her arms, my touch light, teasing. Her skin is so soft under my fingertips, and I can't help but lean in, my lips brushing the shell of her ear.

"You're beautiful," I whisper, my voice thick with desire. "I won't let him take you," I growl against her throat, feeling her pulse race beneath my lips. My hand finds her stomach, where our daughter grows strong despite everything. "Either of you."

The words feel like a vow, like a prayer to a god I stopped

believing in years ago. A promise I'm not sure I can keep, but one I'll die trying to fulfill.

I press my body against hers, feeling the heat of her through our naked bodies. She shivers, and I can feel her pushing back against me, seeking more contact. My hands slide up her bare torso and I cup her breasts, my thumbs brushing over her nipples, and she moans softly, her back arching against me.

The sound of her moan, the feel of her in my hands, makes my cock throb with need. I grind my hips against her, letting her feel just how hard she's made me. "Fuck, Elena," I groan, my mouth hovering by her ear. "You're driving me crazy."

I run my hands over her curves, my touch becoming more possessive, more demanding. I turn her around to face me, my eyes locking onto hers, blazing with desire. She looks up at me, her eyes filled with need.

I slide my hand between her legs, pressing it against her pussy. She's already wet, her arousal soaking through my hand, and the knowledge that she's this turned on because of me sends a thrill through my veins. I rub my thumb over her clit, watching her face as her eyes flutter closed, her lips parting in a soft moan.

Her head falls back, a needy whimper escaping her lips, and I take that as my cue to slide one finger inside her. She gasps, her hips bucking against my hand, and I smirk, loving the way she responds to my touch. I add another finger, pumping in and out of her slowly, my thumb still working her clit.

"Mario," she moans, her voice breathless, filled with desire. "Please ..."

"Please what, Elena?" I ask, my fingers curling inside her, finding that spot that makes her cry out every time. "Tell me what you want."

"I want ... I want you," she pants, her hips rocking against my hand. "I want to feel you inside me."

Her words nearly undo me, but I hold onto my control, wanting to drag this out a little longer. I withdraw my fingers, bringing them to my lips, tasting her on my tongue. She watches me, her chest heaving, eyes dark with lust.

"That's it, Elena," I murmur, my thumb circling her clit with deliberate slowness. "Let me hear you. I want to know how much you like this."

I move behind her again, pressing my body against her back, my hands sliding up to cup her breasts once more. I pinch her nipples between my fingers, rolling them gently, and she moans, her head falling back against my shoulder.

"You like that, don't you?" I whisper, my voice low and rough. "You like being at my mercy, feeling my hands on you, my cock pressing against you."

"Yes," she breathes, her voice trembling. "I love it. I love the way you make me feel."

I groan, my cock throbbing against her lower back, aching to be inside her. But I want to make this last, to push her to the edge and watch her fall apart before I take her. I turn her around again and push her down onto the mattress. I crawl on top of her, my mouth finding hers in a deep, hungry kiss.

I trail kisses down her neck, her chest, taking one nipple into my mouth, sucking gently. Her back arches off the bed, a keening moan slipping from her lips, and I move to the other nipple, giving it the same attention.

My hands roam over her body, exploring every curve, every inch of skin.

I move lower, kissing my way down her stomach, my hands gripping her hips. I spread her legs wide, settling between them, my mouth hovering over her core. I can see how wet she is, her arousal glistening in the moonlight, and I can't resist teasing her just a little longer.

"Tell me what you want, Elena," I murmur, my breath warm against her. "Do you want my mouth on you? Do you want to come on my tongue?"

"Yes," she moans, her voice desperate. "Please, Mario. I need you."

I grin, satisfied with her response, and finally lower my mouth to her. I start with a slow, deliberate lick, tasting her, savoring the way she moans, her hips lifting off the bed. I circle her clit with my tongue, flicking it gently, then harder, sucking it into my mouth. Her moans grow louder, more frantic, her body trembling beneath me.

"Fuck, you taste so good," I murmur against her, my fingers sliding inside her once more, thrusting in time with the movements of my tongue. "I could do this all night, make you come over and over again on my tongue."

Her hips buck, her moans turning into cries, and I know she's close. I increase the pace, my fingers pumping harder, my tongue flicking faster over her clit. She's writhing beneath me, her breath coming in short, ragged gasps, and then she's coming, her body arching off the bed, a loud, needy moan tearing from her throat.

I don't stop, drawing out her orgasm, loving the way she falls apart beneath me, the way she cries out my name. When she finally comes down, her body trembling, her breath shaky, I pull back, looking up at her. Her eyes are glazed with pleasure, her lips parted, and she looks absolutely wrecked.

"Holy shit," she whispers, her voice hoarse, and I can't help but smirk.

"I'm not done with you, Elena. Not even close," I say, my voice low.

I'm so turned on, I can hardly think straight. Her taste is still on my lips, the memory of her coming undone beneath me seared into my mind. Her scent fills the air, mixed with the faint trace of sweat and sex, and it drives me wild. I sit back on my heels, staring down at Elena, her body sprawled across the bed.

Her chest rises and falls with each shaky breath, her eyes half lidded and heavy with desire. I know I should take a moment to breathe, but I can't help it. I want her again.

I lean down, kissing her deeply, letting her taste herself on my tongue before my hand slips in between her legs again, finding her still wet and ready. I slide two fingers inside her, curling them against that spot that makes her whimper.

"You're so wet," I murmur against her lips, thrusting my fingers in and out, my thumb brushing her clit. "You love this, don't you?"

She moans, her hips rocking against my hand, her breath coming in short, needy gasps. "Mario ... please ..."

I release her clit, my hand moving to her hip, flipping her over onto her stomach. I pull her up onto her knees, spreading her legs. I slide my hands over her ass, gripping it, kneading it, before bringing one hand down in a sharp smack. She gasps, her head jerking up, and I do it again, loving the red mark that blooms on her skin.

I kiss my way down her back, my hands roaming over her body, teasing her nipples, stroking her thighs. I can feel her trembling under my touch, her breath hitching with each caress as I press my body against hers, my cock sliding between her legs, brushing against her wetness.

"You feel that?" I growl in her ear. "That's what you do to me. You make me so hard, Elena. I can't wait to be inside you."

I slide inside her in one smooth thrust, filling her completely. She cries out, her body arching, and I hold her there, buried deep, savoring the way she feels around me. I start to move, slow at first, then harder, faster, my hand gripping her hip, pulling her back against me.

"Fuck, you're tight," I groan, my hips slamming into hers, the sound of our bodies colliding filling the room. "You were made for this, Elena. Made to take my cock. You're so fucking perfect."

Her moans are loud, desperate, each one sending a jolt of pleasure through me. I tighten my grip on her, loving the way she gasps for breath, her body clenching around me. I reach down, finding her clit, rubbing it in time with my thrusts. Her moans turn into cries, her body shaking, and I know she's close.

"Come for me, Elena," I command, my voice harsh, demanding. "Come on my cock."

She lets out a scream, her body tensing, her muscles clenching around me as she comes. The sight, the sound, the feel of her falling apart under me is too much, and I let myself go, thrusting into her hard, chasing my own release. I come with a groan, holding her still as I empty myself inside her.

We collapse onto the bed, both of us breathing heavily, her body still trembling beneath me. I wrap my arms around her, pulling her close. Even though we're both damp with sweat, I hold her tightly, feeling her snuggle into me. There's nowhere else I'd rather be, no one else I'd rather be with.

My hand returns to her stomach. The gesture feels different now —less protective and more defiant. A challenge to fate, to family, to everyone who says I don't deserve this. Her fingers intertwine with mine over the slight swell of her belly, anchoring me to this moment.

"What now?" she asks softly. Even exhausted, her mind never stops working—always three steps ahead, always calculating angles. Anthony's threats echo between us.

"Now we fight smarter," I say grimly, pulling her closer until I can feel her heartbeat against my chest. "We find his weaknesses before he finds ours." I kiss her with an edge of violence, tasting her desperation and matching it with my own. "And we make him regret ever threatening what's mine."

The words hang in the air between us—a declaration of war, a promise of protection, a confession I still can't quite voice.

Because this fierce, brilliant woman and the child she carries *are* mine, regardless of blood or circumstance. And I'll burn the world to keep them safe.

Giuseppe always said love was weakness. That it would get me killed faster than any bullet.

Looking at Elena now, I finally understand—he was wrong about that too.

Love isn't weakness. It's armor. It's a weapon. It's everything I never knew I needed until she crashed into my life with her perfect masks and calculating mind.

And I'll be damned if I let Anthony Calabrese take it from me.

24

ELENA

I can't sleep. Beside me, Mario sprawls across the bed, one muscled arm flung wide. Moonlight streams through bulletproof glass, bathing him in silver that catches on old scars and new bruises. Even in sleep, he looks ready to move at the slightest threat.

I study the man everyone sneers at. The sharp cut of his jaw, softened slightly in sleep. The scar that curves along his collarbone—a souvenir from some long-ago violence. His face holds none of its usual careful control, making him look younger, almost peaceful. It's hard to reconcile this version of him with the deadly precision I witnessed in the church.

But that's who he is—both the man who kills without hesitation and the one who traces my growing belly with reverent hands. The exile who would burn the world to protect what's his.

Anthony's words echo in my head: *"Ask your friend Bella what happens when someone crosses me. Ask her about her father's last moments."* That cold smile before he disappeared into the smoke—he knows something. Something that makes him certain of victory despite tonight's chaos.

I slip from bed, pulling on some leggings and a long-sleeved shirt.

The soft material comfortingly settles around me as I move to the window. One hand finds my stomach, hoping beyond hope that today would be the day I feel our daughter move.

"I'll keep you safe," I whisper to her. "I promise you'll grow up knowing how fiercely you're loved."

Manhattan sprawls before me, a glittering maze of light and shadow. But something feels wrong—an instinct screaming that we've missed something vital.

My phone buzzes and my heart nearly stops. It's almost 1 a.m. No one should be messaging me at this time.

With shaking hands, I grab my phone and look to see who it is.

It's a message from Siobhan through our secure channel: *Anthony just left a meeting with my father. Somehow he found your safe house location. They're moving tonight. Father wants Mario delivered alive—says he has "unfinished business" with him. Anthony has permission to handle you however he sees fit—Calabrese's exact words were "retrieve what's mine by any means necessary." They're already positioning men around the building.*

Another message follows quickly: *This isn't just about territory anymore, Elena. Father wants to make an example of Mario's betrayal. And Anthony ... the way he smiled when discussing his plans for you ... Be careful.*

Horror solidifies in my gut as my mind races through possibilities. The garage exit would be watched. The service entrance is too obvious. But the building next door shares a maintenance tunnel—if we can reach it before they close the gap ...

My hand tightens protectively over my stomach as I move to wake Mario. We've got maybe twenty minutes before they breach the perimeter.

Before I can get to him, the first shots shatter the windows, sending glass raining across my bare feet as I scramble towards the bed.

By the time I reach the bed, Mario is already dressed and armed, yanking me behind cover in seconds. "Down!" he barks, his body shielding mine as more bullets tear through the safe house. "Stay low and move!"

The hardwood floor is cold against my knees as I army crawl toward the panic room, my growing belly making the movement awkward but manageable. "Anthony met with O'Connor," I gasp out between breaths. "They found us somehow. O'Connor wants you alive—something about unfinished business. Anthony has permission to take me by any means necessary."

"Fucking hell." Mario's phone lights up with security alerts, his face hardening with fury. "They've got all exits covered. Multiple teams, coordinated assault." He grabs my arm. "Follow me. Stay close."

We move through the safe house as windows explode inward, glass crunching under our feet. The beautiful apartment we've called home becomes a tactical nightmare of broken furniture and bullet holes.

The elevator shaft looms before us—our best chance at reaching the basement exit. Mario secures the harness around me with practiced hands, double-checking every strap. "Hold onto me," he orders. "Let me take your weight."

The descent is terrifying. Mario keeps me pressed against him, one arm secure around my waist while the other holds his weapon ready. Each floor we pass brings new threats—voices echoing through the darkness.

"Check the north stairwell!"

"Nothing on twelve!"

"They're moving down, lads!" The Irish accent carries clearly. "Don't let them reach the garage!"

We're three floors from the basement when I spot movement below—flashlight beams sweeping the shaft. My mind races as I pull up building schematics on my phone, already calculating alternatives. Always have an escape route—the first lesson Mario taught me.

"The maintenance tunnel," I whisper against his neck. "If we can reach the access panel on the next floor …"

The sound of boots on metal stairs grows closer. Time's running out.

Mario's answering smile is proud as he helps me swing toward the maintenance tunnel. I'm not just some society girl anymore. I've learned too much, survived too much, to let them win now.

"I'm sorry," I whisper as we navigate the dark service corridors, suddenly feeling guilty. "I'm so sorry I got us into this. That I played games with people's lives. That I—"

He cuts me off with a heated kiss, his hands cradling my face with a gentleness that belies his dangerous nature. "Stop apologizing," he growls against my mouth. "You're the best game I ever played. The only one that matters."

The words hit me harder than any bullet could. Because that's when I realize—*truly* realize—that I love him. Not just the dangerous exile or the tactical genius, but all of him. The damaged son trying to prove himself better than his father's legacy. The man who keeps choosing me, again and again, even knowing the child I carry isn't his. Who cried when he saw my baby on the ultrasound screen.

"I love you," I say for the first time, the words feeling like freedom in my mouth. Like finally admitting a truth I've known for months. "Whatever happens next—I love you."

His smile is fierce as he reloads his weapon, that perfect blend of danger and tenderness that first drew me to him. "Then let's make sure something happens next. Ready to fight for our future, little planner?"

My answering smile matches his own as I pull up building schematics again. Because that's what we do best—find angles others miss, turn weakness into strength, choose each other despite every reason not to. I feel a tiny flutter in my belly, as if my daughter is adding her own determination to survive.

Siobhan's warning had given us precious preparation time—another example of how the world was changing, women working together to survive in this male-dominated realm.

The old guard's power was already slipping, even if they didn't know it yet.

"Fuck yes," I promise. Whatever comes next, we face it as one.

We make our way through the maintenance tunnel, Mario pausing every few feet to assess threats. His fingers fly across his phone. "Dante's coming," he whispers. "Just need to hold position until—"

The tunnel opens to a deserted alley, and my skin prickles with unease. It's too quiet—the kind of silence that precedes violence. Mario scans our surroundings, his body coiled tight as he checks angles and sight lines.

The first shots come from nowhere and everywhere. Anthony's men materialize from the shadows, but Mario moves faster. His gun barks in precise three-shot bursts, each one finding its mark with devastating efficiency. Blood sprays across brick walls in abstract patterns that make my stomach turn. Bodies drop with sickening thuds that will haunt my dreams.

"Hide!" he roars, already engaging three more attackers.

I dive behind a dumpster, one hand protective over my bump as I watch the man I love become death incarnate. He moves with terrifying grace—each motion calculated for maximum damage. Two men rush him with knives; he disarms one with a brutal twist that ends in a wet crack of bone through flesh. The sound makes bile rise in my throat as he uses the man's body as a shield while dispatching his partner with a shot that turns the brick wall behind him red.

More men pour into the alley. Mario's elbow crushes one's throat —the gurgling sound making me gag—while his other hand sends another flying into a wall with force that leaves brain matter splattered like modern art. His expression is pure predator, all calculated savagery, and I'm torn between awe and horror at what he's capable of.

A young soldier—he can't be more than twenty—raises his gun with shaking hands. Mario doesn't hesitate. The boy's face disappears in a spray of red that paints the alley like some twisted Jackson Pollock.

I bite back a scream, knowing we can't afford the distraction, but tears blur my vision. How many mothers will get phone calls tonight about sons who aren't coming home?

Suddenly headlights blind us as a car comes screaming down the alley. Bodies crunch under its wheels—the sound like overripe fruit being crushed, wet and terrible. The vehicle skids to a stop beside us, and a man that I assume to be Dante is behind the wheel—his handsome face ghost pale, dark eyes wide with the kind of adrenaline that comes from taking lives.

"Get in!" Mario roars.

I fling myself into the backseat. Mario dives in after me as Dante floors it, the car bouncing sickeningly over bodies as we tear out of the alley. My hands shake as I try to process what just happened—the violence, the death, how many lives were just snuffed out in that narrow space.

"Where to?" Dante asks, taking a corner so sharp I slam into Mario. The smell of gunpowder and blood clings to him, making my stomach roll.

"Take us to the Thompson Street location," Mario responds, checking me for injuries with gentle hands that moments ago dealt death with surgical precision.

"Seriously, how many safe houses do you have?" I ask incredulously, still trembling from adrenaline and the weight of all those deaths. My voice cracks slightly, betraying how close I am to breaking down.

Mario smiles as he pulls me closer, his heartbeat steady against my back despite the chaos we just escaped. "Like I told you before. More than you have shoes, little planner."

25

MARIO

The Thompson Street safe house occupies the top three floors of a prewar building in Greenwich Village, hidden behind the facade of a tech start-up. I disarm multiple security systems, ushering Elena inside as Dante peels away into the night.

The space is industrial modern—exposed brick and steel beams, floor-to-ceiling windows with bulletproof glass. Less luxurious than our last place, more tactical. Every piece of furniture positioned for defensive advantage, weapons caches disguised as art installations.

Elena moves through the space like a ghost, her usual elegance replaced by something fragile. Her hands haven't stopped shaking since we left the alley, and she flinches at every car horn from the street below. Blood stains her clothes—evidence of lives I took to keep her safe.

"How are you doing?" I ask softly, watching her catalog exits with the tactical awareness I taught her. But her eyes are distant, seeing things I wish I could protect her from.

"I ..." She swallows hard, wrapping her arms around herself. "That boy. He was so young. And the sound when the car ..." Her voice breaks. "There was so much blood."

I clench my fists, rage and fear warring in my chest. This is what I was afraid of—that she'd finally see exactly what kind of monster Giuseppe created. That the violence would be too much, that she'd realize loving me means wading through rivers of blood.

But then she's there, her hands gentle on my face. "Hey," she whispers, "I'm not going anywhere. It was just ... a lot. All at once." Her fingers trace the scar along my jaw. "This is the world we live in. I knew that when I chose you."

I swallow, feeling something heavy in my throat. "Elena—"

"No." She cuts me off with a fierce kiss. "I chose this. Chose you. The violence, the danger—it's part of who you are. Who we are." Her hand finds mine, pressing it to her stomach where our daughter grows. "I just need time to process."

I pull her closer, breathing in her scent beneath the gunpowder and blood. My little planner, always surprising me with her strength.

"Let's get you cleaned up," I say finally. "Then we figure out our next move."

She nods against my chest, but neither of us moves. For now, we just hold each other, letting the night's horror wash over us like baptism by blood.

Elena's phone rings, making her jump while I immediately shift into a defensive stance. She fishes it out of her pocket, frowning at the display.

"It's Siobhan."

"Put her on speaker," I demand, still not trusting the O'Connor princess despite her earlier warning. Elena obliges, holding the phone between us.

"Hello?" Elena says into the receiver.

"Oh good, you're still alive," Siobhan drawls, sounding entirely too pleased with herself. "Now, about the meeting happening in two days—"

"What fucking meeting?" I cut in, making Elena roll her eyes at my tone.

"If you'd let me finish," Siobhan sighs with exaggerated patience,

"I was about to tell you that the five Irish families are gathering. First time in twenty years they've all agreed to meet."

My body goes rigid. The five Irish families never meet unless something massive is about to shift. "Why?"

"Because, darling, the old guard is losing their grip and they know it. My father's called them all in—trying to shore up support against the modernization movement. Against me." Her voice holds a dangerous edge. "I want you both there."

"How the fuck do you expect that to happen?" I demand, amazed at her stupidity. "In case you haven't noticed, we're public enemy number one and two right now."

"Christ," Siobhan sighs loudly. "Elena, how do you stand being with such a fucking moron?"

Elena grins while I scowl. "Sometimes I wonder," she teases, squeezing my hand to take the sting out.

"You'll be joining remotely," Siobhan explains like she's talking to a particularly slow child. "Only Sean and I will know you're listening in. Think of it as ... insurance. For all of us."

I study Elena's face, seeing that brilliant mind already working through possibilities. Always thinking ahead, my little planner.

"What exactly are you planning, Siobhan?" I ask, though I'm starting to see the shape of it.

Mirth bleeds from her words. "Revolution, DeLuca. Care to help?"

∼

Two days later, the five Irish families gather at Boston's Fairmont Copley Plaza, the images crisp on Elena's laptop screen thanks to Siobhan's carefully hidden cameras.

"Sound check," Siobhan's voice comes through their encrypted channel. She stands behind her father's chair in Chanel, her red hair softly framing her face. Everything about her radiates careful submission—the perfect daughter hiding revolution behind her smile. Sean

Murphy hovers nearby, his tactical awareness masked by a perfectly tailored suit.

I catalog the players as they enter—faces I know from years of navigating Irish politics. Seamus O'Connor sits at the head of the table, his steel-gray hair and cold eyes commanding respect even as his power base erodes. Declan Flaherty, whose dock workers' unions control the port. Michael Gallagher, construction trades giving him a stranglehold on development. Patrick Brady with his politicians in his pocket. And finally Kevin O'Brien, whose South Boston territory makes him kingmaker in any power shift.

Each family head brings their chosen successor—sons and nephews who eye their elders with barely concealed ambition. The generational tension crackles even through the digital feed.

Elena adjusts camera angles on her laptop while I pace, unable to stay still. Just forty-eight hours since bullets tore through our safe house, since I killed all those people in the alley, and here we are—watching through hidden lenses while planning revolution with the daughter of the man who wants me dead.

The irony would be amusing if the stakes weren't so high.

"They're all here," Sean murmurs through our earpieces. "Let the games begin."

"The old ways are dying," Siobhan announces, her voice carrying authority that belies her youth. Through the feed, Elena can see how the younger family members keep glancing her way, seeking direction. "While we cling to outdated vendettas, our legitimate profits drop 60 percent. Meanwhile, modernized operations like the DeLucas in New York have doubled their earnings."

"Legitimate?" Seamus sneers, his contempt obvious even through the digital feed. "Since when do we care about—"

"Since RICO investigations started targeting traditional operations," she cuts in smoothly. "Since blockchain made old-school money laundering obsolete. Since we realized survival means adaptation."

My hand rests on Elena's shoulder as she documents reactions—the younger O'Briens nodding in agreement, the Gallagher heir's carefully blank expression, the way the Bradys shift almost imperceptibly closer to Siobhan in silent support. The battle lines being drawn between old and new couldn't be clearer.

"She's playing it perfectly," I murmur, watching power shift in real time. "Setting up exactly what we need."

Elena nods, already compiling intelligence through their secure channel. Every outdated scheme Seamus clings to, every digital vulnerability in his operation, every piece of evidence showing how his stubbornness has cost the Irish families millions.

"Your father's refusal to modernize has left them vulnerable to federal investigation," Elena types to Siobhan. "Show them the digital trails."

Through the feed, we watch Siobhan pull up records on the meeting room's screens—documentation Elena spent months gathering, now deployed like precision-guided missiles.

"These banking records," Siobhan announces, displaying files Elena discovered months ago, "show how our traditional money laundering methods leave digital footprints that might as well be neon signs for federal investigators."

Seamus's face darkens dangerously as his daughter systematically dismantles everything he's built. Every weakness Elena found, every vulnerability she cataloged while playing the perfect society planner, now becoming weapons in Siobhan's hands.

"Your own daughter had to create shadow accounts to protect family assets," young Patrick Brady speaks up, his voice carrying the weight of his family's political connections. "While you were busy fighting modernization, she was keeping us from financial collapse."

Elena squeezes my hand as we watch the old guard's power crumbling in real time. The revolution we helped plan unfolding through hidden cameras and careful manipulation.

This is how empires fall—not with gunfire and blood, but with spreadsheets and digital footprints.

My hand tightens on Elena's shoulder as we watch Seamus realize he's losing control. "He'll make a move soon," I murmur against her ear. "Men like him always do when cornered."

As if on cue, Seamus stands, his chair scraping against hardwood with a sound like breaking bones. "This modernization you're all so eager for," he spits, face mottling with rage, "it's what let that DeLuca exile and his pregnant whore spy on us for months. Let them steal our secrets while pretending to plan our parties."

"Interesting choice of example," Siobhan says smoothly, and I have to admire her delivery. "Since Elena Santiago's intelligence gathering proved exactly how vulnerable your old methods are. She walked right through our security because you refused to update it. Gathered evidence because you insisted on paper records. Used your own stubborn adherence to tradition against you."

Elena's fingers fly across the keyboard: *Show them the shipping manifests. The ones that don't match the digital records.*

Through the feed, we watch Siobhan pull up document after document, each one demonstrating how Seamus's outdated methods have left the Irish families exposed. Not just to law enforcement, but to rival families, to ambitious upstarts, to anyone smart enough to exploit their weaknesses.

"Jesus," I breathe as the younger family members start openly challenging Seamus. "You really did catalog everything."

"Knowledge is power," Elena responds, her hand drifting to her stomach. "And I needed enough power to protect what matters."

The meeting descends into barely controlled chaos. Decades of resentment explode as sons face fathers across the polished table. The Brady heir slams his fist down, demanding access to digital operations. Michael O'Brien lists millions in lost revenue due to outdated methods. The Flaherty successor reviews federal investigations that could have been avoided with proper cybersecurity.

"Mark my words," Seamus growls at his daughter as the old guard storms out, "you'll regret this betrayal. Family is everything."

"Yes," Siobhan responds coolly. "That's exactly why I'm saving ours."

The door slams shut and there's silence for a heartbeat.

"It's done," her voice comes through our private channel once the dust settles. "The families are with us now. Time for phase two?"

Elena and I look at each other, satisfaction clear in her blue eyes. "Phase two," Elena confirms, already pulling up our carefully gathered evidence about Anthony's operation. "Let's show them exactly what modern warfare looks like," I say.

Through the feed, we watch a revolution unfold. The next generation replacing brute force with precision strikes, fear with calculated strategy.

Elena pulls up new files while the younger Irish leaders convene through Siobhan's feed. "Anthony's been playing both sides," she explains, sending documents to Siobhan. "Using the old guard's shipping routes while secretly building his own digital infrastructure."

"Show them," I say, already mapping implications. "Show them how he's been undercutting both factions."

Pride swells in my chest as I watch Elena's months of intelligence gathering deployed through Siobhan's presentation. Every double cross, every manipulation, every way Anthony played both sides while building his own power base laid bare before the Irish heirs.

"The trafficking operation was just the beginning," Siobhan tells her allies. "While we fought amongst ourselves, Anthony built a parallel infrastructure. Using our internal warfare as cover to steal what's ours."

Elena feeds Siobhan more ammunition. My little planner, dismantling empires with keystrokes instead of bullets. Giuseppe would never understand this kind of power—would call it weakness to fight without blood.

But watching understanding dawn on those young faces as they realize how thoroughly they've been played? This is power of a different kind.

"Perfect," I murmur, rubbing Elena's back as we watch our carefully laid trap spring shut. "Now Anthony loses support from both factions."

"We have a proposal," Siobhan announces, and I feel tension coil through me as our plan enters its most crucial phase. "A way to deal with both the old guard and the Calabrese problem."

Michael O'Brien leans forward. "We're listening."

Siobhan presents the strategy Elena spent many hours crafting—using Anthony's own methods against him. Every digital trail he created while modernizing his operation now becomes a vulnerability. Every alliance he built while playing both sides now becomes a weapon.

"He won't see it coming," I say quietly, unable to hide my pride as we watch Elena's plan unfold. "He'll be so focused on hunting us directly that he won't notice his support system crumbling."

But Elena keeps typing, feeding Siobhan more ammunition: *Show them the shipping manifests from Singapore. The ones that prove he's been circumventing their ports entirely.*

The reaction is immediate—angry murmurs from the Irish heirs as they realize how thoroughly Anthony has been undermining their control of the waterfront.

My smile is lethal as we watch the Irish heirs begin coordinating their response. We watch the next generation of Irish leadership disperse with new purpose—each one carrying pieces of Elena's strategy to dismantle Anthony's power base.

Siobhan's final message makes Elena smile: *Let the games begin, sister.*

But I keep my eyes on Elena, knowing the real war is just beginning. Because Anthony Calabrese isn't just going to roll over and die. When he realizes how thoroughly he's been outplayed ...

Well, Giuseppe taught me what cornered animals do.

"He'll retaliate hard," I say as Elena shuts down the laptop. "When he realizes what's happening ..."

"He'll come straight for us," she finishes. "Too angry to see the larger trap until it's too late." She turns to face me fully, and I see my own dangerous satisfaction reflected in those clever eyes. "That's what makes it perfect."

I can't help but stare at her—this fierce, calculating woman who turns everyone's assumptions into weapons. The supposed society planner who just orchestrated a revolution. Carrying another man's child but fighting with a savage grace that matches my own.

The urge to claim her overwhelms me. I sweep her into my arms and carry her into our bedroom as my mouth finds hers. The kiss is equal parts pride and possession—celebrating not just our victory, but everything she is. Everything we've become together.

The exile and the party planner, underestimated by everyone until it's too late.

Perfect for each other in all the wrong ways.

I place her onto the mattress but before I can lower myself onto her, she grins and flips us so she's on top. "I like to one up you sometimes," she says, her hair tickling my face as she leans over me.

But I have other things on my mind. I bring my hand up to cup the back of her head and bring her lips to mine. She sighs and I let my tongue sweep into her mouth. She gasps as she feels the hard length of my cock against her and I feel my skin break into goosebumps.

My fingers slip back under her hair and in between one kiss and the next, my hand curls into a fist and her head is pulled back in her grip. Elena gasps before I kiss down her neck, nipping and sucking at the delicate skin there. A contorted, breathy moan escapes her and I growl in approval.

I fucking love that she likes this.

I roll us over so I'm on top, my erection pressed in between her legs. She moans at the sensation and twists. The skin of her stomach is hot against mine as my lips move to her jaw. To her neck, to the hollow in her throat.

"God, Mario, I love you," Elena moans. I roll my hips into hers and her back arches into it.

"I love you too," I murmur, my mouth moving back up to her ear before an idea comes to me. "Do you trust me?"

"Yes," Elena answers honestly without hesitation.

Before she can ask me what I'm doing, I flip her so she's on her stomach and I'm straddling her knees. My fingers spear through her hair, using it to drag her head towards me. It forces an arch in her back so she can't move. Perfect.

"Do you trust me enough to do this?" I ask in a low hiss.

"Yes," Elena gasps.

I hum as my fingers trace down her spine, then catch in the waistband of her pants. I tug them down and press a kiss just above her tailbone and her whole body shivers in my grasp. I softly laugh at how much I affect her as she affects me in the same way.

"Clothes off now," I croon, palming myself through my pants. Elena smirks but obeys. She lifts her hips so I can help her pull her pants off and she quickly takes off her shirt, leaving her only in a matching black bra and panties. My mouth waters as I push her back down, hand between her shoulder blades.

"Good girl," I say roughly as I unclip her bra, my fingers moving down to the band of her lacy underwear. I pause over her tailbone, letting one finger swirl over her tailbone before I turn my wrist and continue over the tiny scrap of material, following the seam all the way to her clit.

She's soaking wet. I suck in a deep breath.

"You're wet from having your hair pulled?" I ask incredulously, my heart hammering with excitement. But I don't wait for her answer. I gather her hair in my hand and move her head in a slow circle before I yank her back once more. She moans and my other hand is pressing against the wet patch on her underwear.

"Oh, we're going to have so much fun, Elena," I murmur into her ear before nibbling on her earlobe. "I want to hear you moan my name. Hear you cry out."

My fingers get rougher over her clit and she cries out. I chuckle. "Yes," I say. "Those ones."

Elena's breathing is coming fast and shallow now. Wanting to at least relieve her from her agony, I push her underwear to the side and stroke her bare pussy. She's properly moaning now as I slide my fingers through her slickness.

"God, Mario," she rasps as she tries to move her hips, but because of the position I've forced her into there's little she can do. I will not give her an inch. I slowly push my fingers inside of her, biting back my moan at how wet she is, how her walls clamp around my fingers.

"That's it," I say softly. "You're so tight and it's just my fingers." I slide them in and out, feeling wetness trickle down my hand. "God I could do this all fucking day."

Elena starts to shake a little, her moans coming in short, broken cries. I pick up my pace and I can feel her clench around my fingers.

"Close already, Elena?" I laugh huskily. "Are you going to come for me? Come like a good girl?" I use her hair to tilt her face up to me and viciously kiss her. I gently bite her lip while Elena moans. My tongue slips into her mouth again and it's then when her climax rips through her. I swallow her screams and moans in another deep kiss.

Once she stops trembling, I pull back and let her hair go so she can collapse against the bed. But I'm not done with her yet.

"Not bad for the first one," I comment as I roll her onto her back and kiss her again. Her hands are suddenly everywhere as she unbuttons my shirt and I yank it off before letting it fall onto the ground. The rest of my clothes follow in quick succession, and then her bra and panties join mine on the ground.

"Beautiful," I murmur as I bend down to kiss her, my cock straining against her stomach. She shivers, but I can't tell if it's from my cock or how it feels to be skin on skin.

"Do you want to come again, Elena?" I ask her, looking down at her beautiful body, her breasts heaving. "Do you want to come on my cock?"

"Yes," she breathes, squirming a bit, and I have to bite my lip to stop from moaning. I hook one of her legs over my shoulder, then I lean over her again so the head of my cock is at her entrance. Elena is moaning again as my fingers tangle with hers, bringing them above her head and pinning them there.

"Good girl," I say, then push into her.

She and I both moan at this first slide. It's the most delicious feeling and I exhale slowly against her lips. Elena squeezes my fingers, and I can feel her body try to make room for my length. I withdraw and she whimpers.

"Just a little more," I murmur and then I'm sliding in again. She jerks when I slide in deeper and I groan as I fully seat myself inside her. "Fuck, Elena. That's it." I start moving and I lose myself in the sensation of her wet, tight heat around me and the sounds of her moans.

I pick up the pace and release one of her hands, but she doesn't move it. I lick my thumb and circle it over her wet clit. Elena arches at the contact but my other hand splays over her sternum, holding her down. I fuck her harder now and her face is contorted into ecstasy, her lips clearly trying to form words that she cannot utter.

"Fuck, Elena," I gasp. The hand on her chest slides up and moves to her throat. "That's a girl, that's my fucking girl." I increase the pressure on her clit at the same time as I press down on the soft skin of her throat. "That's a good fucking girl. You look so fucking good like this, did you know that?"

My words only seem to encourage her as her hips slam into mine and she's moaning wildly. "I'm going to come, Mario," she gasps, her hands fisting into the sheets.

"Oh yeah?" I purposefully slow down my movements—one ... two ... three languid slides and then it's hard and fast again. My fingers are relentless against her clit. "Fucking come all over my cock, Elena." My hips move erratically as I feel my own orgasm start to build.

"Do it now, Elena," I snarl as I slam into her one more time. That seems to be her undoing as she screams and spasms over my cock. It's so fucking hot and I have no problem following her over that cliff, my own body jerking as I ride out my wave of pleasure.

I collapse against her and she brings her arms up to wrap them around me, rubbing soothing circles into my back as I come back down to earth.

"Good?" she whispers after we've been still for a few minutes. My heartbeat is still thundering in my chest and I'm still wrapped around her. The question is so ridiculous I can't help but laugh and roll onto my back, tugging her with me.

"You're seriously going to ask me that while you're full of my cum?" I ask, laughing at the scandalized look on her face. "But yes, Elena," I say, kissing her head. "That was fucking perfect."

I tilt her chin up, smirking at the blush forming on her cheeks.

"You are more than I deserve. You are everything I don't believe I can have."

∼

Hours later, I realize we've become something I never expected—true equals, perfect partners in this deadly game we've chosen to play together. She catches me staring.

"What?" she asks, her eyes narrowing as she works to decode my expression.

"Just thinking about how perfectly you've surpassed every expectation," I admit, pulling her closer until I can feel her heartbeat against my chest. "You're not just playing the game anymore, little planner. You're rewriting all the rules."

Her answering kiss holds promises of more victories to come. Because we're no longer exile and society girl, no longer predator and prey. We're partners now—equally dangerous, equally brilliant, equally committed to burning down anyone who tries to come between us.

26

ELENA

Four months of calculated silence. Four months of watching Anthony's empire crumble piece by piece while he searches frantically for external enemies. He's too focused on hunting Mario and me to see how thoroughly we've turned his own infrastructure against him.

The young Irish families have proven masterful at dismantling his operation from within. Ships mysteriously redirected. Digital payments vanishing into cryptocurrency mazes. Security teams compromised by better offers. Each small cut precisely placed to bleed him dry while maintaining plausible deniability.

"Another shipping contract lost," Siobhan reports through our secure channel. "Poor Anthony seems to be having terrible luck with port authorities lately."

I smile, rubbing my now-prominent belly as I review her latest intelligence. At eight months pregnant, I've turned this safe house into a command center—coordinating with Siobhan and the other Irish heirs while Mario handles the physical security.

Sean Murphy visited last week, bringing detailed reports of how thoroughly Anthony's support system is disintegrating. "He's too proud to admit he needs the old guard's help," Sean had explained smugly. "And too suspicious of modernization. Prefers to cling to the old ways, like his grandfather and uncle. He's isolating himself perfectly."

Seamus O'Connor remains a looming threat—his rage at Mario's betrayal only intensified by his daughter's growing defiance. But Siobhan insists we focus on Anthony first. "One war at a time," she'd said during our last call. "Let's destroy the Calabrese heir before we deal with my father's outdated vendetta."

My phone buzzes with another update from Siobhan: *Anthony just lost his Singapore connections. Apparently someone showed them proof he's been skimming profits. Such a shame.*

I grin, remembering how carefully we planted that evidence. Death by a thousand cuts, each one precisely placed to ensure he never suspects the real architects of his downfall.

"Something amusing?" Mario asks, coming up behind me to massage my shoulders.

"Just watching Anthony's world burn," I reply, leaning back into his touch. "One digital transaction at a time."

Sometimes the best revenge isn't swift or violent. Sometimes it's watching your enemy destroy himself while searching for shadows in all the wrong places.

∽

I STUDY my reflection in the safe house mirror, smoothing my Carolina Herrera dress over my eight-month bump. The baby has been active all day, kicking and rolling as if sensing the tension in the air. The letter sits beside my makeup bag, Bella's familiar handwriting making my heart ache:

I know what you did at the hospital that night. How you made sure the right doctors were there. Please come home. Matteo has agreed to a temporary truce—proof attached.

The proof and letter came through one of my most trusted hospital contacts—someone even Matteo's extensive network doesn't know about. The video shows Matteo himself making the formal declaration of sanctuary: "For twenty-four hours, I invoke the old laws. The DeLuca compound is neutral ground, protected by traditions older than our grudges. Any violation will be met with total war."

"You don't have to do this," Mario says from the doorway. I catch his reflection—devastating in a charcoal Stefano Ricci suit that emphasizes how handsome he is. His eyes linger on my stomach before quickly looking away, that shadow I've come to recognize crossing his face. These moments have become more frequent as my pregnancy progresses—the slight hesitation before he touches my bump, the way he pulls back when the baby kicks.

"It's actually perfect," I say, turning to face him. "Anthony's watching every hotel, restaurant, and safe house in Manhattan. But the DeLuca compound? He'd never expect us to walk right into what he thinks is enemy territory."

"Unless that's exactly what he expects us to think," Mario says.

"No. He knows Matteo would burn the city down before letting anyone violate sanctuary in his home. Even Anthony won't risk breaking that kind of old world tradition—not when he's trying to convince the conservative families to back him." I turn back around to finish my makeup.

"Besides," I add, watching his reflection carefully, "this might be our only chance to secure real protection. If I can make Bella understand why I did what I did, if Matteo sees that helping us hurts Anthony and the Irish ..."

"That's a lot of 'ifs,' little planner." But I can see him considering the advantages. The DeLucas might hate Mario, but they hate Anthony more. And with the Irish families fracturing, new alliances become possible.

My daughter kicks hard, as if adding her vote to this dangerous gamble. Mario's hand twitches toward my belly before dropping away—another moment of wanting to connect but holding back.

Some battles, I realize, are fought with guns and blood. Others with computers and bank accounts.

But the hardest ones? Those are fought with truth and trust and the hope that love might be stronger than betrayal.

My hand drifts to my stomach as the baby kicks again. These moments still catch me off guard—the fierce protectiveness that floods through me. Everything I do now isn't just about survival or revenge—it's about creating a future where my daughter won't have to play these deadly games.

"Antonio will be watching every move we make," Mario says, finally meeting my eyes in the mirror. "If this is a trap ..."

"Antonio is old school." I turn to face him fully. "He may hate you, but he respects the old traditions even more than Matteo does. For twenty-four hours, we'll be untouchable under his protection."

The weight of Bella's message seems to fill the room: *Come home.* The words make my eyes water because that's what the DeLuca mansion had been, before everything. Before Mario, before Anthony, before I started playing games with people's lives.

"What aren't you telling me?" Mario asks softly, reading something in my expression that I can't quite hide.

I hesitate, then pull out my phone, showing him another part of Bella's message I hadn't shared: *After what you did at the hospital— making sure the right doctors were there, protecting the twins even after everything ... maybe it's time we both stopped letting the men in our lives dictate who we can trust.*

"She was my best friend," I say quietly, the words tasting like regret. "Before the games, before the schemes ... she was the only person who saw me as more than just a party planner or someone to be used. And I betrayed that trust completely."

The baby kicks again, as if sensing my turmoil. I remember Bianca's words in the hospital—how even after everything, Bella's first instinct was to ask for me. To trust me one last time.

Maybe it's time to earn that trust back.

"And now?" Mario raises a dark eyebrow.

"Now I'm eight months pregnant, hiding in safe houses, watching my daughter's future get decided by other people's wars. Maybe it's time to try building bridges instead of burning them. The DeLucas might hate you, but they understand choosing love over family loyalty better than anyone."

Mario moves closer, his reflection joining mine in the mirror. "You really think they'll understand? After what I did to Bianca?"

"Matteo chose Bianca," I remind him. "Chose love over the DeLuca name. And Bella ..." I sigh. "Bella chose Matteo even after learning what he'd done to Sophia. To countless others. She understands better than anyone how love forces us to make impossible choices."

The baby kicks again, harder this time, making me wince. Mario's hand comes up automatically to steady me, and I notice he doesn't pull away from my bump as quickly as usual. That slight hesitation becoming less pronounced each time.

"Still," he says, voice rough. "Walking into the DeLuca compound ..."

"Is exactly what Anthony would never expect." I check my reflection one final time. "Besides, I have it on good authority that he's got men watching every restaurant and hotel where Bella and I used to meet. He'd never believe we'd risk going there."

"And if it *is* a trap?" Mario repeats.

"Then we'll handle it like we handle everything else." I turn to face him fully. "Together."

His answering smile holds equal parts pride and concern as he grasps my hands, his callused thumbs rubbing over my knuckles. "Just promise me something, little planner."

"What's that?"

"If anything feels wrong—anything at all—we leave. Immediately. No games, no clever plans. Just getting you both out safely."

The use of "both" doesn't escape my notice. I reach up to cup his face, seeing all his carefully hidden fears in his eyes. "I promise."

27

MARIO

Antonio meets us at the DeLuca compound gates himself—a deliberate choice that doesn't escape my notice. His presence is both warning and reassurance: for twenty-four hours, sanctuary will be honored, but one wrong move and Matteo's most loyal soldier will remind me exactly why people still fear the DeLuca name.

"You'll both be searched," Antonio says without preamble. His eyes linger on Elena's pregnant belly before meeting my gaze with barely concealed hostility. The look says everything—he hasn't forgotten how I held Bianca at gunpoint, how I tried to destroy the family he's protected for over two decades. "Even with sanctuary granted, we're not stupid."

The security sweep is thorough but professional. They let Elena keep the small gun in her thigh holster—another calculated message about trust and limits. I catch Antonio's slight nod of approval at our acceptance of the procedure. Some traditions still matter, even between enemies. Even after everything.

The mansion hasn't changed since my exile—still all old money and careful power. Diamond-filtered light danced across Italian stone, priceless art hiding security cameras. Every corner holds memories: there's the study where Giuseppe first taught us to clean guns, the staircase I fell down during one of his "lessons," the basement door that still makes my hands shake.

Elena's fingers tremble slightly in mine as we follow Maria through familiar corridors. The housekeeper who once bandaged my wounds after Giuseppe's rage now looks at me like I'm a stranger—worse, like I'm the piece of shit Giuseppe always said I would become. Her eyes linger on Elena's obvious pregnancy, something like pity crossing her usually stoic features.

Matteo and Bella wait in the formal dining room, the space deliberately chosen for its lack of personal connection. Pure business, no sentiment allowed to cloud the negotiations. My brother looks exactly like Giuseppe in this light—that same cruel perfection in his features, that same calculated control. Only the protective way he angles himself toward Bella betrays any humanity.

Bella herself is a study in contradictions—still radiant with new motherhood, but with shadows under her eyes that speak of sleepless nights. Her gaze remains fixed on Elena's stomach, something complicated flickering across her expression.

Recognition? Sympathy? Or just remembering her own recent pregnancy?

Bianca stands slightly behind them, more ice princess than teenage girl now. Her hand drifts toward her concealed weapon when she sees me—muscle memory from that night in the warehouse. My niece's composure cracks momentarily at the sight of Elena's bump before ice replaces shock.

The tension in the room could stop hearts. Matteo's face gives nothing away, but I recognize the slight tension in his jaw—the same tell we both inherited from Giuseppe. That barely contained violence that made the DeLuca name feared across continents.

For a moment, I'm ten years old again, standing in this same room while Giuseppe decided which son deserved punishment. The chandelier still catches light the same way, creating patterns like broken glass on the ceiling. I can almost smell his cigars, feel the weight of his rings against my skin.

But Elena's grip on my hand anchors me to the present, her bump pressing against my arm as she shifts closer. Reminding me why we're here, what we're fighting for.

This isn't about old wounds or family vendettas anymore.

This is about making sure our daughter never knows the kind of pain this room has witnessed.

"You searched them?" Bianca demands, her hand still hovering near her weapon.

"Thoroughly," Antonio confirms from his position by the door. His men take up strategic positions around the room—protecting the DeLuca family while enforcing the sanctuary's terms. I recognize their formation from years of training beside them.

Elena starts to speak, her voice carrying that perfect society polish: "Thank you for—"

"Save the social niceties," Bella cuts in, her tone arctic. "We both know you're excellent at playing roles."

I raise an eyebrow at the hostility—so different from the understanding tone of her letter to Elena. Something's changed. Something we missed.

Dinner is excruciating—all careful manners masking deadly intent. Each course arrives with perfect timing, served on the same Wedgwood china Giuseppe used to smash when his temper broke. The conversation is sharp enough to draw blood, served with the same precision as the wine.

"Interesting choice," Bianca says as Elena declines the offered Bordeaux. "Though I suppose you've had plenty of practice playing the perfect mother-to-be with Anthony."

Elena's hand tightens on her water glass but her voice stays steady. "I've made my choices, B."

I watch my brother's face for reactions, seeing the mind working behind his carefully blank expression. He's evaluating every word, every gesture, just like Giuseppe taught us. Looking for weakness, for advantage, for any sign this sanctuary was a mistake.

The weight of old memories presses down like the chandelier above us—ready to shatter at the slightest provocation.

Elena asks about the twins, and I catch the slight tremor in her voice that others might miss. Something in Bella's expression softens fractionally—that same warmth I remember from before I destroyed everything.

"They're fine," Bella says stiffly. "Growing stronger every day."

"That's ... that's good." Elena's fingers twist in her napkin. "I'm glad they're—"

"They're perfect," Bella cuts in, but there's less ice in her tone now. "Giovanni has Matteo's eyes."

I watch Elena struggle not to react to the small bits of information Bella feeds her. The pain on her face is raw, unguarded. She wants desperately to see these babies she helped save, these children who would have been her godchildren in another life.

Matteo must see it too. A muscle jumps along his jawline.

"The twins won't be joining us," my brother says unnecessarily, his eyes cold as they track my every movement. "Some bridges can't be rebuilt."

"Like the bridge of trust you burned?" Bianca adds, her fingers drumming against the table in a rhythm that reminds me too much of Giuseppe's rings. "Or just the ones that don't serve your purposes anymore?"

I feel Elena flinch beside me, the words hitting their mark. But beneath the table, her other hand rests protectively over our daughter—never Anthony's daughter—as if shielding her from these poisoned words.

The crystal glasses catch candlelight like tears we're all too proud to shed.

After dinner, Bianca storms off, the door slamming behind her with finality. The tension in the room thickens—Bella studying her wine glass with too much intensity, Matteo's fingers tapping that familiar pattern on the table, Elena's hands twisting in her lap.

Suddenly, Bella breaks the suffocating silence. "We should walk in the gardens," she tells Elena. "Get some air."

Matteo shoots his wife a warning look, but Bella meets his gaze with surprising defiance. I watch their silent communication with interest—something's shifted in their dynamic since the twins were born. Finally, my brother sighs and gives a single sharp nod.

Elena hesitates beside me, but I see the naked longing on her face—the desperate need to reconnect with her best friend, to bridge the chasm between them. She follows Bella outside like someone walking toward execution.

"There are guards everywhere," Matteo says casually, watching them through the window. "If she tries anything—"

I can't help but scoff. "Yes, because the eight-months-pregnant woman is clearly a physical threat."

He leads me to the smoking room—Giuseppe's old sanctuary, now stripped of his presence but not his shadow. Guards line every corner, making me roll my eyes. Always so dramatic, my perfect brother.

"What exactly are you planning with Elena and her baby?" Matteo asks, pouring scotch with deliberate precision. "After all, she's carrying Anthony Calabrese's child."

I'm immediately on edge. "What's that supposed to mean?"

"The child isn't yours," he says bluntly. "I saw how you watched her tonight, how carefully you attended to her needs. You can't seriously be planning to raise a Calabrese bastard as your own?"

The word hits like a physical blow. *Bastard.* The same word Giuseppe spat at me for years, the label that marked me as less than Matteo, less than worthy. How fucking dare he use that word about my daughter? About the innocent child I've already sworn to protect?

Anger blazes through my veins—the same fury that made me hold Bianca at gunpoint, that drove me to try destroying everything my perfect brother built. For a moment, I imagine throwing the crystal tumbler at his head, watching that carefully controlled expression shatter like glass.

But then I catch the slight tension in Matteo's posture, the way he's angled for quick movement. He's waiting for exactly that reaction—wanting proof that I'm still Giuseppe's savage second son, still the man he banished over a year ago.

I won't give him the satisfaction.

I force myself to breathe through the fury, to push down decades of pain and resentment. "Biology doesn't matter," I say, the words surprising us both with their conviction. I see Matteo's eyebrow lift at my uncharacteristic composure, at this evidence that maybe I've grown beyond our father's poison. "You taught me that with Bianca."

Matteo's composure changes to understanding or recognition, I'm not sure which. "Anthony won't stop claiming what he thinks is his."

"I know." I accept the scotch he offers—a peace offering neither of us acknowledges. "That's why I need your help. Not for me. For them."

The silence stretches between us, heavy with decades of rivalry and pain. Finally, Matteo speaks: "You love her. The way I love Bella."

"More." The admission costs nothing now, not when Elena and our daughter's safety hangs in the balance. Every protective instinct Giuseppe tried to beat out of me rises when I think of them. "Enough to raise another man's child. To be better than our father's lessons about blood and power."

Understanding passes between us—something deeper than blood or loyalty or the games Giuseppe beat into us. I see it in the way Matteo's shoulders relax slightly, how his grip on the tumbler eases.

Because we both know what it means to choose love over revenge, to protect a child regardless of biology. To break the cycle of violence our father created.

The smoking room holds too many memories—Giuseppe's cigars, the sting of his rings, lessons taught with blood and broken bones. But now my brother and I stand here as men who survived, who chose different paths than the ones carved into our skin.

"I'll help," Matteo says finally, swirling the amber liquid in his glass. The glass catches lamplight like memories we'd rather forget. "Not for you. For her. For the baby."

He pauses, something almost gentle crossing his face—an expression I haven't seen since we were boys, before Giuseppe's lessons turned us into weapons. "And because our father would hate it."

A brittle laugh escapes me as I raise my glass, but something lighter than revenge stirs in my chest. "To spite the old man?"

"To being better than him," Matteo corrects, and for the first time in decades, we share a real smile. Not the calculated ones Giuseppe taught us to use as weapons, but something genuine. Something that tastes like redemption.

28

ELENA

The DeLuca mansion's terrace feels colder than I remember, though maybe that's just the ice in Bella's eyes as we face each other. The woman who once shared every secret, every dream, every moment of joy and pain, now stands like a stranger. My heart twists painfully at the distance between us—remembering late nights talking about everything and anything, celebrating when we found out she was pregnant, our lunch dates ...

All of it gone because of my choices.

The awkward silence stretches between us like a physical thing. I resist the urge to fill it with excuses or explanations. We were closer than sisters once—sharing clothes and secrets and dreams.

Now we can barely look at each other.

"Why?" Bella asks finally, the single word carrying months of betrayal. "After everything we've been through together—after Johnny, after all of it. Why *Mario*?"

I force myself to maintain eye contact, knowing I owe my former best friend at least this much honesty. "It started as a game," I admit. "A way to prove I was more than just the society party planner everyone underestimated. But then ..."

"Then you fell in love with the man who terrorized my stepdaughter? Who tried to kill my husband? Who would have killed my babies given the chance?" Bella's voice shakes with barely contained emotion. "Do you have any idea what Bianca went through? The nightmares, the therapy—"

"I know what he did was unforgivable—" I start but Bella interrupts me, her nostrils flaring with anger.

"Unforgivable?" She laughs bitterly. "He tried to kill Bianca when she was twelve years old! And you seem to find that acceptable? So what were you doing? Planning parties and gathering intel while fucking Mario? Playing both sides while pretending to be my friend?"

"It wasn't like that," I protest, but the words sound hollow even to me.

"Then what was it like?" Her eyes flash with that Russo fire I used to admire. "Explain it to me, Elena. Explain how my best friend—the woman I trusted with *everything*—could betray me so completely."

"He's different now," I start, but her bitter laugh cuts me off.

"Different? Like every man in our world who claims to change but just finds new ways to destroy things?"

"No." My hand rests on my bump, drawing strength from my daughter's movements. "Different because he's choosing to be better than their father's legacy. Different because he's willing to raise another man's child, like Matteo did. To protect us both from Anthony, from the Irish, from everything."

Bella scoffs. "And I'm supposed to just forgive everything because he's decided to play hero?"

"I'm not asking for forgiveness," I say quietly even though I desperately want it. "I don't deserve it. But I am asking you to understand. You of all people know what it's like to love someone others call a monster."

Her expression transforms—not forgiveness, not yet, but understanding maybe. "You really love him?"

"Like you love Matteo." I meet her eyes steadily. "Enough to risk everything. To choose something bigger than revenge or power or proving ourselves."

Silence stretches between us, broken only by the distant sound of security teams patrolling the grounds. Finally, Bella reaches into her pocket, withdrawing her phone. "The twins," she says softly, pulling up photos. "Giovanni is Matteo's spitting image. It's uncanny. But Arianna ... she's got my father's eyes."

My breath catches at this small olive branch. The babies are beautiful—four months old and thriving despite their early arrival. Giovanni already has Matteo's serious expression, even with his chubby cheeks and toothless grin. Arianna is smaller but fiercer, dark eyes looking so much like Giovanni Russo's it makes my chest ache.

"I'm having a girl," I offer quietly. "Her name will be Stella. It means star."

"Like something bright in the darkness?" Bella's voice holds no judgment now, just wary acceptance.

"Like hope," I correct, meeting her eyes. "For something better than what we came from."

Bella studies me for a long moment before nodding once. "I'm not ready for you to meet them," she says honestly. "Maybe I never will be. But ..." She pauses, choosing her words carefully. "I hope Stella has an easier path than any of us did."

She slips back inside the mansion, leaving me alone with the weight of everything we've lost. It's not forgiveness. It's not even really reconciliation.

But as I watch my former best friend disappear into the warmth of the house, I realize it's something almost more important.

It's understanding.

~

THE DRIVE HOME from the DeLuca mansion feels surreal, the weight of what just happened settling over me like a blanket. Mario sits beside me in the back of the armored Mercedes, his hand never leaving mine as his security team takes a deliberately circuitous route back to our safe house.

Neither of us speaks—there's too much to process, too many implications to consider.

My mind replays the photos of Bella's twins. Beautiful, healthy babies. My niece and nephew in another life.

Giovanni with his father's face but his mother's chin. Arianna with her grandfather's fighting spirit clear in that toothless grin. The fact that Bella showed me at all—that she let me glimpse this precious part of her life after everything I've done—makes my throat close up with emotion.

It's more than I deserve, this tentative olive branch. More than I had any right to hope for after betraying her trust so completely.

Matteo's agreement to limited protection complicates things further. Having DeLuca security coordinating with Mario's teams will help against Anthony's increasingly erratic moves, but it also means navigating decades of distrust and betrayal. I caught the looks exchanged between Antonio and Mario's men—old wounds don't heal easily in our world.

My phone buzzes again—another report that makes me wince.

"What's wrong?" Mario asks sharply, noticing my distress. I hand him my phone.

Photos of a warehouse in Brooklyn, walls painted red with what used to be Anthony's most trusted captain. "He tortured him for hours," I tell Mario quietly. "Made an example of him in front of the other crews."

"Fuck," he curses, handing me my phone back. "Why this one?" Mario asks, though I suspect he already knows.

"Caught him talking to one of Siobhan's people." I swipe through more photos that turn my stomach. "He's getting paranoid. Two more captains found in the East River last week. One of them ..." I swallow hard. "One of them had a pregnant wife."

Mario sucks in a breath and I can't help but agree. The message couldn't be clearer.

Stella kicks hard, causing me to wince. Mario's hand immediately covers mine where it rests on my bump, his touch gentle despite the violence I know those hands are capable of.

"He's seeing threats everywhere," I continue, forcing myself to study the intelligence reports. "Lashing out at his own people. He doesn't realize the real damage comes from how we've systematically dismantled his support system."

"Good." Mario's voice holds no mercy. "Let him destroy himself from within. Makes our job easier."

Sometimes the most dangerous wounds aren't the ones that bleed. Sometimes they're the ones we inflict on ourselves while searching for enemies in all the wrong places.

"He's unraveling," I tell Mario as we enter the safe house. The tension in my shoulders eases as the security system engages behind us. It's ironic how this temporary shelter has become more home than anywhere I've lived before—maybe because it's the first place I've been truly myself, not playing some calculated role.

"My sources say he executed his own cousin yesterday for suggesting they modernize their banking system," I continue, eyes scanning the message.

Mario whistles low. "The famous Calabrese mental stability strikes again. Johnny would be so proud—keeping the family tradition of paranoid breakdowns alive."

But something about the pattern of Anthony's violence makes me uneasy. I sink into the leather sofa, trying to organize my thoughts. "It's not just random brutality anymore. He's specifically targeting anyone who suggests change or modernization. The violence is getting more ... personal." I struggle to find the right words.

He's becoming like his uncle Johnny—all cruel impulse without calculation.

"A desperate Anthony Calabrese is infinitely more dangerous than a rational one," Mario agrees, his hand finding the small of my back as he sits beside me.

My phone lights up with another report that makes my blood run cold. Anthony's called in old favors, gathering forces from families that still cling to traditional power structures. He's planning something big—I can feel it in my bones, the same instinct that's kept me alive in this world of calculated violence.

But then I watch Mario coordinate with Matteo's security teams, seeing these careful new alliances form. His voice is steady as he issues orders, seamlessly integrating his brother's men with our own protection detail.

Maybe we're finally building something stronger than Anthony can tear down.

Maybe we're creating the future I want for our daughter, one careful step at a time.

29

MARIO

The tentative truce with Matteo is testing every ounce of control Giuseppe ever beat into me. Like this morning's strategy session.

"The security rotation needs adjusting," my perfect brother announces, studying the plans like he's still the only one who knows how to run an operation. His fingers tap against the desk and the sound irritates me.

"My men know what they're doing," I respond coolly, leaning back in my chair with deliberate casualness. "Or have you forgotten who trained half of them?"

Matteo's eyes are cold. "Before or after you tried to destroy the family?"

"After. Their skills improved dramatically once they stopped following your outdated protocols." I catch the slight tick in his jaw and can't help but smirk. God, this is just too easy. "Amazing what happens when people stop blindly following big brother's orders."

"This isn't a game, Mario," my brother snaps.

"No? Could have fooled me with all your posturing."

I'm heading back from another thrilling session of brotherly bonding when Elena calls. My heart stops until I hear her voice—calm but urgent.

"You need to come home. Now."

I grip the phone tighter, my palms slick against the cool metal. "What's wrong? Is it the baby?"

"No, but—" She pauses, and something in her tone makes my skin prickle. "Siobhan's here."

What? "How the fuck did she find our safe house?" I demand, my mind whirling.

"That's really not important right now," Elena snaps with uncharacteristic impatience. "Mario, please. Just get here."

"Tell me what's happening." I fucking hate being kept in the dark.

"I can't," she insists. "Not over the phone. Just hurry."

I have my driver break several traffic laws getting us back. The elevator feels impossibly slow as scenarios race through my mind—each worse than the last. Did Seamus find us? Has Anthony made some move we didn't anticipate?

The doors finally open and I move through our safe house with urgency, every sense on high alert.

But nothing prepares me for what I find.

Elena stands in our living room, one hand protectively over her prominent bump, tears threatening to spill. Her usual calculated composure is cracking around the edges, and that scares me more than anything.

And beside her ...

Siobhan, her clothes covered in what can only be dried blood, looking more shaken than I've ever seen her. The always composed Irish princess seems smaller somehow, her usual sharp edges dulled by whatever has happened.

My blood runs cold at the devastation in both their expressions.

"What the fuck happened?" I ask, my mouth dry.

Siobhan's laugh carries venom. "My father lost his fucking mind."

Something has gone very, very wrong.

"He killed Sean Murphy," Siobhan announces. "My most loyal captain. Made an example of him for supporting 'modern ideas.'"

Her hands shake as she accepts the scotch I offer, the glass catching lamplight like tears.

I sink into the nearest chair, feeling like I could collapse. Sean Murphy *dead*?

"How?" The word comes out rough.

"Public execution. Called it a 'lesson about respect for tradition.'" Siobhan's perfect composure cracks, something raw bleeding through. "Right there in Murphy's Pub. The same place Sean's father tended bar for forty years."

Elena's hand finds mine as she lowers herself carefully onto the sofa beside me. Her fingers tremble slightly against my palm.

"That's not the worst part," Siobhan continues, downing the scotch in one swallow. "He killed Sean's boy too. Seventeen years old. The kid just made captain of his high school baseball team."

"Jesus Christ." The room spins slightly. I'd seen the boy at gatherings before. He had been Sean's clone. "Why?"

"To make a point." Siobhan snaps. "The boy begged for his life. He reminded my father that his grandfather died protecting mine." Her composure splinters further. "Seamus shot him anyway. Said modernization was a cancer that needed to be cut out."

I feel Elena's sharp intake of breath beside me as we process the implications. Sean Murphy was beloved by the younger generation, his family's loyalty to the O'Connors stretching back generations. His execution won't inspire obedience—it will ignite something far more dangerous.

"He's gone mad," Siobhan whispers, and for the first time since I've known her, she looks her age—just a young woman watching her father lose it.

"The young families won't stand for this," I say quietly. "Killing Sean was bad enough, but his boy? That crosses a line even in our world. But why are you really here?" I ask her. "This news could have come through secure channels. Why risk coming to New York?"

Her laugh is terrible—all sharp edges and barely contained rage. "I thought you'd want a front row seat to watch me burn my father's empire to the ground." She straightens her bloodstained jacket.

"Besides, I need Elena's network. And ..." She looks like she's swallowing glass. "Your help."

Part of me wants to savor this—the mighty Siobhan O'Connor asking for my assistance. But Sean Murphy's boy was innocent; Sean didn't deserve to die. Some things matter more than petty satisfaction.

"What do you need?" I finally ask.

I'm already moving as she outlines her plans—activating networks, coordinating with our allies. Elena's hands flying across her laptop as she connects with her own sources.

"You should stay here tonight," Elena offers. "Rest before—"

I shoot her a sharp look, but Siobhan's already shaking her head.

"Sweet of you to offer," she says, rising with the elegance she learned from boarding schools. "But I need to get back to Boston. I have a revolution to implement." Her smile is downright sinister. "Time to show my father exactly what his 'cancer of modernization' can do."

The moment she's gone, I'm on the phone. "Get me everything," I tell Dante, heading for our command center. "Every reaction, every whisper. I want to know exactly how this plays out."

The responses flood in within hours. Young Patrick Brady withdraws his crew's support from Seamus's dock operations. The Flaherty heir redirects three major shipments without explanation. Michael O'Brien's construction unions suddenly find reasons to delay projects that benefit the old guard.

The revolution isn't coming. It's already here.

Through surveillance feeds, we watch the younger captains gather in back rooms of pubs and social clubs across Boston. Their voices coming through clearly:

"For Sean."

"For his boy."

"Time to show these old men what real loyalty looks like."

Elena's breath catches beside me as we witness power shifting in real time. Young faces hard with purpose, pledging themselves to

Siobhan rather than Seamus. The revolution happening not with gunfire, but with whispered oaths and digital signatures.

"My father thinks he's taught them fear," Siobhan tells her gathered captains, her voice carrying that deadly calm that inspires loyalty. "He doesn't understand he's taught them hate instead."

The cheers that erupt make the surveillance audio crackle.

"For Sean Murphy!"

"For the future!"

"Death to the old guard!"

Elena works her network while I coordinate with Sean's remaining loyalists. "Get your crews in position," I tell Tommy Flynn, Sean's former second. "When Siobhan gives the word—"

"We're ready," he cuts in. "Every young captain from here to fucking Providence. We've had enough of watching our friends die for refusing to bow to outdated methods."

Elena's phone rings—Siobhan, who we put on speaker.

"The old guard's making their move tonight," she reports, her voice cool. "Against all of us who support change. My father, the conservative captains ... they're meeting Anthony in an hour to plan coordinated strikes."

But Seamus's fatal mistake was underestimating his daughter. While he clung to old methods, she built a shadow network of loyal young captains. While he demanded blind obedience, she earned genuine loyalty.

"It's time," Siobhan announces through our secure channel, her voice stripped of its usual polish—just pure, cold purpose. "Sean's execution was his last mistake. Every young captain, every modernized crew, they're all in position."

Through multiple feeds, we watch her network activate like a precisely coordinated dance. The Murphy crew—still wearing black armbands for Sean—secure the docks with military precision. The younger O'Briens lock down South Boston block by block. The Brady heir's political connections ensure police focus elsewhere tonight.

"My father always said I was too soft," Siobhan says as reports of her success flood in. "That I spent too much time with computers and cryptocurrency when I should have been learning about power." A joyless sound emerges from her. "He never understood that real power isn't about breaking bones anymore. It's about controlling systems."

Elena's intelligence confirms what we're watching unfold—Seamus remains completely oblivious, too fixated on his meeting with Anthony to notice his empire slipping through his fingers. His own security teams, carefully infiltrated by Siobhan's people months ago, are already turning.

"Your father's still got loyal captains," I warn her. "Men who remember the old ways. Who helped build his power."

"Let them remember." Her voice drips venom through our secure line. "Let them see what happens to people who choose tradition over evolution. Sean's death taught us all what loyalty to the old guard costs." A pause. "His boy was seventeen, Mario. *Seventeen*. And my father put a bullet in his head to make a point about respect."

I think of Giuseppe, of all his lessons about power and control. How none of them prepared him for a world where his sons would choose love over vengeance. Where daughters would dismantle empires their fathers built through carefully orchestrated revolution rather than brute force.

"Besides," Siobhan adds, real satisfaction coloring her tone, "Anthony's too busy hunting you and Elena to see how thoroughly we've infiltrated his operation. By the time my father realizes what's happening, it'll be too late for both of them."

We watch in awe as Siobhan's revolution unfolds with devastating precision. Her forces move like shadows through Boston's underworld, each piece falling perfectly into place. The next generation claiming their birthright not through violence, but through careful coordination and digital warfare.

"Jesus," Elena breathes beside me, watching the screens. "She's actually doing it."

I don't even have words.

"The old guard's locations are confirmed," she reports moments later, her fingers flying across her laptop. "At the Dubliner."

"They're toasting their alliance, planning how to 'handle' the modernization problem. While their own security teams ensure they can't leave," Siobhan says.

The reports flow in steadily, each one more impressive than the last: dock operations transferred seamlessly to Siobhan's crew. Digital banking systems locked down and transferred to new control. Every piece of infrastructure Siobhan built over years of careful planning now serving its true purpose.

Through the feeds, we watch young captains coordinate with military precision. The next generation of Irish leadership moving as one organism, systematically securing power centers their fathers thought impregnable.

"My God," Elena whispers, leaning against me. "She's thought of *everything*. Look—she's even got the police commissioner's son coordinating with her people. The cops won't interfere."

"It's done," Siobhan announces finally, real triumph in her voice. "The families are with us now. Every crew, every captain who matters." A pause. "Time for the old guard to learn about real power."

"Be careful," I warn her, recognizing the particular madness that comes with victory. "Cornered animals are the most dangerous."

Her laugh holds no warmth. "Oh, I'm counting on it."

30

ELENA

The aftermath of Sean Murphy's execution transforms our safe house into a war room. Encrypted communications flow between New York and Boston as we help Siobhan solidify her control. My laptop screens display real-time updates of the Irish power shift—young captains pledging allegiance, old guard supporters being systematically isolated.

"The Murphy crew just seized another of your father's warehouses," I tell Siobhan during one of our daily phone calls. Through the secure feed, I watch her navigate her father's old office like she was born to it. "No resistance. Seems your infiltration of his security teams was more thorough than even he realized."

"Sean taught me well." That raw edge remains in her voice whenever she mentions her murdered captain. "While my father focused on breaking bones, Sean showed me how to break entire systems. How to turn everyone's blind spots into weapons."

My network confirms that Seamus is practically under house arrest—his own modernized security teams ensuring he can't interfere with his daughter's takeover. The old don who once ruled through fear now watches helplessly as his empire transforms around him.

"He tried bribing his guards yesterday," Siobhan says, satisfaction coloring her tone. "Offered them triple their salaries to let him contact his old captains. They recorded the whole thing and sent it to me."

Mario smothers a laugh from beside me and I nudge his shoulder. "How's he taking the isolation?" I ask.

She laughs delightedly. "Not well. Apparently, he spent an hour ranting about ungrateful children and the death of tradition. The guards say he keeps demanding to know how I turned his own security against him."

"And did you tell him?" Mario can't help but interject.

"I told him Sean taught me everything I needed to know about loyalty." Her voice hardens. "Right before my father put a bullet in his son's head."

After hanging up with Siobhan, I lean back in my chair, rubbing my aching back. "She's a scary motherfucker."

Mario's laugh fills the room. "Finally figured that out, did you?"

"I mean it," I say, shoving him lightly. "The way she orchestrated this whole thing ..." I shake my head in admiration. "Remind me never to get on her bad side."

"Too late for that, little planner. You're already in bed with her enemies."

He has me there. "True. But at least I'm smart enough to be useful to her," I admit.

Our moment of levity shatters as my phone buzzes with new intelligence about Anthony. The reports make my skin crawl—he's gone completely erratic since the Irish families turned against him, executing suspected traitors without proof, making increasingly unstable decisions.

He shot another captain at dinner last night, my source reports. *Carlo suggested using blockchain for some transactions. Anthony put three bullets in his shoulder right there at the table. Said modernization was a disease that had to be burned out.*

I watch Mario absorb this news, seeing that dangerous focus sharpen in his eyes. The same look he gets before violence becomes necessary. We both know what this means—Anthony is becoming like his uncle Johnny, all violent impulse without strategic control.

"Men like him, when they're cornered ..." Mario's voice holds dark knowledge. "They strike at what they think they can still control."

His hand drifts to my stomach, where Stella kicks as if sensing the tension. I cover his fingers with mine, feeling the slight tremor he tries to hide. These moments of vulnerability are rare—glimpses of the man beneath the carefully constructed weapon Giuseppe created.

My phone lights up with another report from inside the Calabrese organization. Anthony's gathered his most violent supporters, the ones who still cling to his uncle Johnny's methods. They're meeting at the old warehouse where Johnny used to "handle problems."

"He's talking about bloodlines," my source writes. "About tradition and purity. About making examples of traitors."

I pull up security footage showing Anthony at his latest family dinner. The change in him is shocking—gone is the sophisticated swagger that I once knew. He reminds me too much of the Johnny who held me at gunpoint in my apartment.

I shiver at the memory. I hated feeling so helpless.

"He's obsessed with the baby," another source reports. "Keeps talking about his heir, about blood rights. About making sure his child is raised with proper values."

Mario's hands ball tight, but I catch something else in his expression—a flash of that old insecurity about the baby's paternity. Even now, after everything we've built, Anthony's words about blood and birthright hit those carefully hidden wounds Giuseppe left.

"Hey," I say softly, taking his hand. "She's ours. Biology doesn't matter."

"I know." But there's still tension in his jaw, still that shadow in his eyes that makes my heart ache. "I just ... I remember how Giuseppe treated me. His bastard son. The constant reminders that I wasn't really a DeLuca. I won't let her ever feel that."

I turn his face toward mine, making him meet my eyes. "She

won't. Because she'll have something you never did—parents who love her for exactly who she is, not what blood runs in her veins."

Stella kicks again, as if agreeing. This time, Mario's smile holds no shadows as he feels her movement beneath his palm.

～

THE NURSERY HAS BECOME my sanctuary—all soft grays and blush pinks, elegant but warm. The Hermès blanket Mario insisted on buying drapes over the custom crib, while hand-painted butterflies dance across one wall. It's feminine without being precious, chic without feeling cold. Everything chosen with careful thought, just like all my plans.

I sink into the oversized rocking chair—another of Mario's indulgences—and survey my favorite room. The mobile catches afternoon light, casting rainbow patterns across the cream carpet.

Designer stuffed animals arranged just so, books about strong women lined up on floating shelves, that ridiculously expensive French chandelier Mario said our daughter deserved.

Every detail perfect, yet somehow also purely us. The bulletproof windows hidden behind delicate curtains. The panic button disguised as a decorative switch. Beauty and danger intertwined, just like everything in our world.

"What do you think, little star?" I whisper, rubbing my belly where Stella kicks. "Did Mama do okay with your room?"

She responds with a series of movements that make me smile. "I'll take that as approval. Though your papa might add more security features when he sees the final result."

I rock slowly, imagining what it will be like to hold her here. To read her stories about queens and warriors while Mario pretends not to listen from the doorway. To watch her grow into something stronger than the violence that created her.

"You're already so loved," I tell her softly, tracing patterns on my stretched skin. "More than biology or bloodlines or any of the things the old men think matter. You're going to be extraordinary, my little star. And so, so free."

She kicks again, right against my palm, as if sealing this promise between us. I catch my reflection in the antique mirror—my hand protective over my bump, surrounded by this perfect blend of beauty and security we've created for our daughter.

The peace of the moment feels almost magical, until my phone rings.

Siobhan.

"Is your perpetual shadow hovering nearby?" she asks without preamble.

"No, Mario's handling 'business.'" Which means coordinating with Dante about security protocols while pretending not to be overprotective. "What's wrong?"

"We have a problem," Siobhan says. "Anthony's reached out to some of my father's old allies. They're talking about 'purifying' both families. About making examples of anyone who betrays tradition."

I pull up more intelligence on my tablet—bank transfers, weapons shipments, movements of known hitmen. All pointing to something big.

"He won't stop," I say quietly, watching the pieces come together. My hand drifts protectively to my stomach. "Not until he has what he thinks is his."

"Anthony's rallying every old guard faction he can find," Siobhan continues grimly. "Conservative Irish crews still loyal to Seamus, Italian families who remember Johnny's glory days, even Russian outfits that cling to Soviet methods."

The rainbow patterns from the mobile suddenly feel less magical, more like targets. I study the peaceful nursery—this sanctuary we've built—and wonder how much longer we can protect it.

When Mario gets home, I can see tension radiating from him even before I share Siobhan's news. His face darkens with each detail I relay.

"Anthony's gathering forces," I explain. "Old guard Irish crews, traditional Italian families—"

"Anyone who still worships at the altar of outdated methods," he finishes grimly, shedding his suit jacket.

"He's building an army," I say as we review the intelligence sprawling across our screens. "But not for territory or profit. This is about ideology now. About punishing everyone who chose progress over tradition."

We monitor Anthony's movements, watching his desperation grow with each passing day. Every screen shows another piece of his unraveling—bank accounts drained in rage-fueled gambling, loyal captains fleeing his increasingly violent outbursts.

"The baby makes us vulnerable," Mario says that night, after another report of Anthony ranting about his heir. The words seem to cost him something to admit. "He knows that. He'll use it."

"The baby makes us stronger," I counter, meeting his gaze steadily. "She's why we've built these alliances. Why Matteo helps protect us, why Siobhan's people guard our perimeter. She's not our weakness—she's proof that love is stronger than blood."

But that night, watching Anthony's latest surveillance footage, I see something that chills me to my core. He's in his private office, surrounded by photos of me, of Mario, of every movement we've made. His usual composure is shattered as he screams at his men about tradition and loyalty.

"Soon," he promises the photos, running his fingers over my image in a way that makes my skin crawl. "Soon we'll purify everything. Return proper order. My daughter will never know these modern corruptions."

My blood runs cold. How did he find out we're having a girl? The information was protected—encrypted medical files, trusted doctors, every precaution taken.

If he's breached that security ... what else does he know?

∼

A FEW DAYS LATER, my network explodes with urgent warnings, screens lighting up like a Christmas tree gone wrong. Anthony's forces are mobilizing—not just in New York, but in strategic positions across the East Coast. Every old guard faction answering his call to "restore traditional values."

I study the patterns emerging across our surveillance feeds, my heart racing as I recognize the formation. "He's going to try to take everything at once," I tell Siobhan through our secure channel, my voice tight with tension. "Your operations, the DeLuca alliance, everyone who's chosen modernization over tradition."

"Oh *please* let him try." Her voice holds that deadly calm that reminds me she's as dangerous as any of them. "The old guard forgets—we control their infrastructure now. Their communications, their banking, their security systems. They're fighting a modern war with outdated weapons."

But Anthony's madness makes him more dangerous, not less. Through our feeds, I watch him gather his most violent supporters at the old Calabrese warehouse. The same place where his uncle Johnny used to torture rivals, where tradition meant spilled blood and broken bones.

"He's giving them names," my source reports, voice shaking. "Targets. Everyone who needs to be 'purified' for the sake of family honor."

Mario studies the intelligence over my shoulder, his hand resting protectively on my back. The warmth of his touch contrasts sharply with the ice in his voice. "You're at the top of his list, aren't you?"

I nod, pulling up the intercepted kill order. My name heads a document that reads like a manifesto about blood purity and proper values. About making examples of those who corrupt tradition.

"He won't touch you," Mario promises, his voice holding that lethal edge that first drew me to him. "Either of you."

I lean back against him, drawing strength from his solid presence while watching Anthony's forces gather on our screens. All the familiar patterns of impending war spread across our monitors—weapons shipments, troop movements, strategic positioning.

We're past the point of prevention. All our careful plans, all our built alliances—they've brought us to this moment.

The only question is: who strikes first?

Mario's phone lights up with Siobhan's name. He raises an eyebrow, showing me the screen with exaggerated distaste.

"Oh, just answer it," I say, rolling my eyes at his dramatics. "She wouldn't call you directly unless it was important."

"Maybe I'm busy," he grumbles, but answers anyway. "What?"

I watch his body go rigid at whatever Siobhan says, my own pulse quickening in response. Even through the speaker, I can hear the dangerous satisfaction in her voice: "How would you like to come back to Boston?"

"Why?" Mario's tone is dangerous.

"Because my father's becoming a fucking nuisance. Even under house arrest, he's still causing problems. Reaching out to old allies, making promises about restoration of proper order." She pauses deliberately. "I thought you might enjoy helping me eliminate the man who spent five years treating you like his personal attack dog."

I study Mario's face, watching emotions war across his features. That muscle in his jaw ticks. His fingers tighten on the phone, his knuckles turning white.

"You have him exactly where you want him," Mario says carefully. "Why do you need my help?"

"Because I thought you'd appreciate the poetry of it." Siobhan's voice sounds bored as if discussing how to kill a parent annoys her. "The exile he tried to break, returning to put him down. Besides ..." She pauses. "You're the only one who truly understands what needs to be done. The only one who won't hesitate."

Mario's eyes meet mine, and I see the decision form. Five years of rage and pain crystallizing into purpose.

"When do you want me there?" he asks.

Siobhan's smile is audible. "Tonight. And Mario? We make sure he suffers. Like Sean's boy suffered. Like everyone who crossed the old guard suffered."

The call ends, leaving us in charged silence. I watch my dangerous, complicated man prepare for one final act of vengeance.

Some debts can only be paid in blood.

31

MARIO

Murphy's Pub rises against Boston's night sky like a fortress of old power—all weathered brick and stained glass that's witnessed generations of Irish politics. Where Sean Murphy poured drinks while orchestrating revolutions. Where his boy learned to run numbers before he could drive. Where Seamus O'Connor built his empire one brutal decision at a time.

Dante follows me inside, his silence speaking volumes. The pub's been closed since Sean's execution—the ancient wood still holding echoes of violence, the polished bar now a war room for the next generation's revenge.

Siobhan awaits in her father's old office above the bar—a space transformed from traditional power to modern warfare. Displays replace vintage whiskey bottles, surveillance feeds monitor every angle of the O'Connor compound where her father remains under house arrest.

Her crew gathers around what used to be Sean Murphy's ledger table—all young, all modernized, all burning for revenge. These aren't the muscle-bound thugs Seamus preferred. They're tech experts and tactical specialists, wearing smartwatches instead of brass knuckles.

"My father's becoming more unstable," Siobhan explains, pulling up compound schematics. "Even confined, he's dangerous—reaching out to old allies, promising restoration of 'proper values' if they help him regain control."

I study the plans, Giuseppe's lessons rising unbidden. The old bastard might have been a monster, but he taught us well. Shame he died of a heart attack before I could show him exactly how well.

"Security's already ours," Siobhan continues. "But the kill has to be meaningful. It has to send a message about the cost of clinging to outdated methods."

Siobhan outlines her strategy with precision, her young crew leaning forward with hungry attention. I study their faces—these aren't the bruisers Seamus preferred. Tommy Flynn, Sean's protégé, monitors digital security through his tablet. Sarah O'Brien, barely twenty but already legendary for her ability to hack any system. Declan Flaherty's youngest son coordinating with dock crews through encrypted channels.

"My father's daily routine is predictable," Siobhan explains, pulling up surveillance feeds. "Even under house arrest, he maintains his habits. Every evening at exactly nine, he's in his office. It's the only time he's relatively alone—just two guards who are already ours."

The plan is elegant in its simplicity. While Anthony focuses his paranoia on New York, while the old guard watches for external threats, we'll eliminate their patriarch from within. Using their own adherence to routine against them.

I outline the approach to my team—a mix of my most trusted men and the DeLuca soldiers Matteo sent as a show of support. Antonio stands slightly apart, his expression carefully blank as he absorbs the details.

"The compound's security is already compromised," I explain. "Siobhan's people control every camera, every alarm, every digital lock. We'll have exactly seven minutes between systems going dark and backup power engaging."

"When do we move?" Tommy Flynn asks, his scarred face hard

with purpose. He was there when Seamus executed his mentor, when Sean's boy begged for mercy.

Siobhan's smile is pure ice as she rises from the desk. "Now."

The word hangs in the air like smoke, like promise, like revolution written in carefully planned vengeance.

Some debts can only be paid in blood. And Seamus O'Connor's bill is finally due.

~

THE O'CONNOR COMPOUND'S architecture casts shadows perfect for our approach. Everything we've built with Siobhan, every alliance we've carefully crafted, comes down to this moment.

Seamus forced everyone's hand when he ordered Sean Murphy's execution. The video of Sean's teenage son begging spread through Irish circles like wildfire, that terrified face becoming a symbol for everything wrong with blind loyalty to tradition.

Now his men fall under precise fire as I lead the assault. Sean Murphy's loyalists move like ghosts through the east gardens while Siobhan's inside crew eliminates key positions with surgical efficiency. Every piece of her network activating at once, just like we planned.

I take down two guards with perfect shots. No wasted movement, no hesitation. A third rushes me with a knife, but I'm already inside his reach, using his momentum to drive him into the stone wall. The crack of bone is almost satisfying.

"West entrance secured," Tommy Flynn reports through our comms.

More of Seamus's traditionalists pour from the house—all muscle and outdated tactics, still fighting like it's the early eighties. They don't understand this new kind of warfare, where digital intel matters more than brute force.

I move through them easily, each motion precise and practiced. Giuseppe's lessons serving their purpose as I systematically dismantle Seamus's remaining defense. Three more go down before they can raise their weapons. A fourth loses his gun arm at the elbow.

"Inner security disabled," Siobhan's voice carries through our earpieces. "He's in the office. Right where we knew he'd be, clinging to his *precious* routine."

I advance through blood-splattered Carrara stone halls, past evidence of how thoroughly Siobhan has infiltrated her father's operation. Guards we pass don't even raise their weapons—just step aside, young faces hard with purpose as they choose the future over the past.

"Seamus has barricaded himself in the study with what's left of the conservative faction," Antonio reports through comms.

I move through corridors thick with gun smoke and spilled blood, past gilt-framed portraits of O'Connor patriarchs watching their legacy crumble. Crystal chandeliers cast fractured light across hardwood floors where I once crawled after Seamus's "lessons" in respect.

Every shadow holds memories of violence, of five years spent earning my place in Boston's underworld.

But this isn't about revenge anymore. It's about Elena at home, about our daughter who will inherit whatever world we create tonight. About ensuring they grow up where loyalty means more than blind obedience, where family is chosen rather than forced.

Siobhan appears beside me as we reach the study doors, her suit spattered with evidence of tonight's work. Her nod is barely perceptible as we take position.

Three.

Two.

One.

The doors splinter inward with explosive force. Through clearing smoke, I see Seamus standing behind his massive oak desk—the same desk where he broke men's fingers while teaching me about power. Every inch the Irish king in his crumbling domain, though his empire bleeds out around him.

The old guard who remain flank him with outdated loyalty—Sullivan with his brass knuckles, O'Brien still wearing his crucifix,

Flaherty's hands steady on his weapon. But it's the empty spaces that speak loudest—the younger captains who should be here, who would have died for him before Sean Murphy's execution.

"You really think you can destroy everything we've built?" Seamus sneers, but his knuckles are white on his weapon. "That the Irish families will follow a woman? Follow these modern ideas that corrupt everything they touch?"

The words echo off wood paneling that's witnessed generations of violence. But his voice holds something new—fear disguised as contempt.

"The families already chose," I reply conversationally. "The moment you executed a teenager to prove your point about tradition. Tell me, how many other sons are you willing to sacrifice for your pride?"

My words hit their intended marks—Seamus's remaining men flinch. They all have sons, all remember Sean's boy begging for mercy. All of them know how easily it could have been their children.

"The old ways kept us strong," Seamus insists, but doubt creeps into his voice as more explosions rock the compound. The blasts illuminate the night sky through bulletproof windows, casting strange shadows across his desperate face.

"The old ways are dead," Siobhan's voice cuts through the smoke like a blade. She stands beside me, her weapon trained on her father's heart. "Just like Sean Murphy's teenage son died. Just like every other child you'd sacrifice to maintain your control."

"You're no daughter of mine," Seamus spits, but fear finally cracks through his composed facade. Real terror bleeds through as he watches his empire crumble. "Conspiring with exiles, betraying your own blood—"

"Blood?" Siobhan's laugh holds no warmth. "You want to talk about *blood* while Sean's still stains your hands? While his son's execution video plays on every crew's phone?" Her voice shakes with barely contained fury. "That boy grew up in our house, called you 'Uncle Seamus.' And you shot him to make a point about tradition."

"You're surrounded," I tell Seamus, watching his remaining men eye the exits. "Your security teams changed sides. Your conservative allies are being systematically eliminated. Even Anthony Calabrese can't help you now."

"Anthony understands!" Seamus roars, desperation making him sloppy. "He knows what happens when you let women and bastards corrupt tradition—"

The shot comes from Sullivan's son, the bullet taking Seamus in the shoulder. "That's for Sean's boy," the young captain says quietly.

The room erupts into chaos. Old guard loyalists open fire while younger captains dive for cover. Sparkling decanters shatter, spreading whiskey and glass across imported carpets. The air fills with gun smoke and shouted orders as decades of resentment finally explode.

I move through the chaos, each motion precise and deadly. Old guard loyalists fall under methodical fire—one bullet through the throat as he tries to flank Siobhan, another catching his partner in the chest as he reaches for backup weapons.

A third man—O'Brien's oldest enforcer—comes at me with military training, his strikes fast and efficient. But Giuseppe beat better skills into me during those basement sessions. I slip inside his guard, using his weight against him before snapping his knee with a precise kick. His scream joins the symphony of gunfire and breaking glass.

Two more rush me from opposite sides, coordination showing years of partnership. The first loses teeth to my elbow while his friend's head meets the oak paneling with bone-crushing force. They drop like marionettes with cut strings, joining the growing collection of bodies proving that tradition means nothing against superior training.

Siobhan proves herself her father's daughter, though not in the way he intended. She moves with deadly efficiency, each shot finding its mark as she systematically eliminates threats. Her clothes are splattered red, her face a mask of cold purpose.

But Seamus doesn't know how to surrender. With a roar of fury, he grabs one of his fallen men's weapons and opens fire. The first shot misses Siobhan by inches as I tackle her behind an antique cabinet. Wood splinters around us as he empties the clip.

"Just like your whore of a mother," he taunts, trying to draw me out. "Another DeLuca bastard thinking he deserves power—"

I return fire, forcing him back behind his desk. Siobhan slips through like smoke to my left, her own shots pinning down the few men still foolish enough to stand with her father.

"You remember what I did to you that first year?" Seamus calls out. "How you begged? Just like Sean's boy begged—"

The rage rises in my chest—memories of chains and basement lessons in respect. But then thoughts of Elena and our baby rise unbidden and it makes me momentarily pause.

This isn't about my revenge anymore.

Through smoke and gunfire, I catch Siobhan's eye as we advance on her father's position. She moves with grace—every bit the queen she was born to be, regardless of what Seamus thinks about women in power.

When I finally have the kill shot—Seamus exposed and desperate—I lower my weapon.

"This one's yours," I tell Siobhan, stepping aside. "Consider it my one act of generosity."

She smiles at me as she raises her gun. "How unexpectedly decent of you."

"Siobhan." Seamus raises his hands, blood seeping from his shoulder wound. "Let's be reasonable. You've proven your point. I'll step back, let you implement your changes. Whatever modernization you want—"

"*Now* you want to negotiate?" Her laugh holds no warmth. "After Sean? After his boy? After every young captain you sacrificed to maintain control?"

"I'm still your father," he snarls. "Still head of this family—"

"Family?" Siobhan's smile shows teeth. "You want to talk about family after everything you've done? After what you've said to me?"

"I'll give you everything," he tries one last time. "Total control of the operation, my blessing for all your changes—"

"Go to hell." The shots are precise—one to the heart, one to the head. Just like he taught her.

Seamus falls behind his massive desk, blood spraying across the family crest carved into ancient wood. For a moment, complete silence fills the study—even the gunfire outside seems to pause, as if the whole compound holds its breath.

Then reality crashes back. Young captains flood the room, their faces a mix of triumph and disbelief. The old guard who survived drop to their knees, offering loyalty to their new leader while their former don's blood soaks into imported carpets.

"Get him out of here," Siobhan orders, and Sean's crew moves with efficient respect. They wrap Seamus's body in the Irish flag he once used to justify his brutality—a final irony he'll take to his grave.

A cheer goes up from the compound grounds as word spreads. I watch through bullet-scarred windows as decades of fear transform into celebration. Younger crews embrace, share drinks, mark this moment when everything changed.

I feel tension I didn't even know I was carrying release from my shoulders. Five years of playing Seamus's attack dog, of enduring his "lessons" in respect, finally paid in full.

Within hours, Siobhan's carefully prepared network activates. The alliance we negotiated weeks ago slides into place—her modernized Irish operation working with us rather than against us. Territory agreements are signed, digital systems transferred, power consolidated with surgical precision.

While her father's body is still warm, his daughter dismantles everything he built and replaces it with something entirely new.

"My father never understood," Siobhan says later, signing the new territory agreements in what was once Seamus's office. She uses Sean's favorite pen—a small but pointed gesture. Her eyes are hard as she looks at the spot where her father fell. "Power isn't about destruction anymore. It's about building something sustainable. Something worth protecting."

Like Elena, or our daughter. Or the future we're securing not through violence but through careful choices. "Some lessons our fathers never learned," I agree.

My phone buzzes with Elena's message: **Stella just kicked hard enough to shift my laptop. She knows her papa's winning.**

Those simple words nearly undo me—this normal moment amid our extraordinary circumstances. This chance to be more than Giuseppe's son, more than the exiled brother, more than all the dark lessons of our world.

Some debts can only be paid in blood.

But some futures can only be built with love.

32

ELENA

It's been three days since Siobhan eliminated her father, since the Irish families officially aligned with us. Three days of watching power shift through my network of carefully placed sources. But Anthony's silence makes my skin crawl.

Even at eight and a half months pregnant, I maintain my cover as New York's premier event planner. The DeLuca security teams stationed outside think they're just protecting Mario's pregnant mistress—they don't see how many strings I still pull from behind bulletproof glass.

"The governor's wife loved the centerpiece options," Kate reports through our secure line. My assistant has proven invaluable, handling the physical presence our clients expect while I coordinate remotely. "Though the mayor's daughter is being difficult about her sweet sixteen."

"Send her the pink peonies," I say, rubbing my aching hips as I review seating charts. "She'll cave once she sees them arranged with the crystal butterflies."

But while I play society planner, my other screens tell a darker story. Anthony's gone completely dark—no movement through known channels, no contact with traditional allies. Even my best sources have lost track of him.

A smart person would focus on the baby, on preparing for Stella's arrival. The nursery is ready, the hospital route secured, every detail planned with military precision. But I can't shake the feeling that Anthony's planning something. Men like him don't just disappear.

My phone buzzes with another event crisis—some socialite demanding last-minute changes to her charity gala. I handle it automatically, mind already mapping possible scenarios. Where would Anthony go? What resources does he still command?

The baby kicks hard, as if sharing my unease. "I know, little star," I murmur, running my hand over my swollen belly. "Mama's worried too."

Because Anthony's silence can only mean one thing—he's finally ready to make his move.

∽

It happens a few days later. I'm on FaceTime with Kate, reviewing floral arrangements for the children's hospital benefit, when Mario bursts into our command center. One look at his face and my heart drops.

"They're moving," he says without preamble, already pulling up surveillance feeds. "Anthony's forces, all over Manhattan. Not attacking, not yet, but—"

"Positioning themselves," I finish, recognizing the pattern instantly as I mute Kate. On our screens, red dots appear like a spreading infection—Anthony's men taking up strategic positions around our known safe houses, our allies' businesses, our entire support network.

I'm not surprised—we knew this was coming. But seeing it unfold makes my hands shake slightly as I rest them on my bump.

"He's finally doing it," I tell Mario as we review the intelligence. After Siobhan's takeover in Boston, after watching the old guard crumble, Anthony's rage has finally crystallized into action. "Every old-school faction he could gather, every traditionalist crew that resents modernization—they're all falling in line behind him."

"Kate, I'll call you back," I say, realizing that Kate was still waiting for me. I end the FaceTime call. I pull up intel on my computer. "Look—they're not just surrounding us. They're setting up around Matteo's territory too. Anyone who's chosen progress over tradition."

Mario's hand finds my shoulder as we watch Anthony's forces gather like storm clouds. "This isn't just about us anymore," he says quietly. "This is his last stand against everything that threatens his way of life."

Stella kicks again, harder this time, making me wince. Both of Mario's hands come to my belly, his touch featherlight.

Mario's phone chimes with a text from Matteo. It's a video.

"Play it," I urge him, my heart hammering.

The video quality is grainy—security footage from one of Anthony's warehouses—but what we see makes my blood run cold.

Anthony paces like a caged animal, his usual polished appearance completely shattered. His suit is wrinkled, his perfectly styled hair wild, dark circles under eyes that hold something terrifying in their intensity. This isn't the sophisticated heir who seduced me. This is something else entirely—something broken and deadly.

"My daughter will not be raised by a DeLuca bastard," he snarls at his assembled men, spittle flying from his lips. "She will know proper values, proper tradition. We will purify both families of this modern corruption."

He runs his hands through his disheveled hair, that familiar gesture now manic and uncontrolled. "The child in Elena's womb is Calabrese blood. Pure blood. Not some mongrel bastard's spawn."

Mario's hands clench into fists as we watch, his jaw tight with carefully controlled rage. But I catch something else in his expression —that shadow that crosses his face whenever Anthony claims our daughter. Those words about blood and tradition hit those carefully hidden wounds Giuseppe left.

"Hey," I say softly, taking his hand. "She's ours. Biology doesn't matter."

"I know." But there's still tension in his jaw, still that old pain in his eyes. "I just ... I remember how Giuseppe treated me. His bastard son. I won't let her ever feel that."

The video continues, showing Anthony's descent into complete madness. He rants about bloodlines and family honor while his men exchange worried glances. Even they can see their leader has crossed some line into dangerous instability.

"He's going to come for us," I say quietly, one hand protective over our daughter. "For her."

Mario's arms wrap around me from behind, his chin resting on my shoulder as we watch Anthony unravel on screen. "I dare him to."

But we both know this isn't just about us anymore. This is about two visions of the future colliding—tradition versus progress, blood versus choice, the old world dying violently as the new one struggles to be born.

And our daughter is caught in the crossfire.

Anger rises in me as I watch Anthony's ranting replay on screen. How dare he try to claim this child as his? He was nothing but a sperm donor—a means to an end while I gathered intelligence.

This baby is a DeLuca, regardless of whose blood flows through her veins.

I grab my phone, dialing Siobhan with sudden purpose. "I need a favor," I say the moment she answers.

"The Irish are at your disposal," she responds immediately, making both Mario and me pause in surprise.

"Wait, *what*?" Mario responds, leaning forward in disbelief. "Just like that?"

"Don't act so shocked," Siobhan says, affronted. "I can be generous when it serves my interests."

Mario mutters something under his breath about generous snakes, earning a smack from me.

"I need forces in New York," I tell her. "For when Anthony makes his final move."

"Delighted to help eliminate more old guard deadweight," Siobhan practically purrs. "How many men do you need?"

I glance at Mario, eyebrows raised. "As many as you can spare without compromising Boston."

"Done," Siobhan remarks. "And Elena? Make it hurt."

Within several hours, the Irish arrive in New York. I coordinate with Siobhan's forces while monitoring Anthony's movements. The Irish crews loyal to her now guard our perimeter, working seamlessly with Mario's security teams.

Even Matteo has contributed protection, our careful new alliance proving stronger than old vendettas.

"Every traditional faction that resents how the families are changing—they're all at the Calabrese mansion, swearing blood oaths about restoring proper order," Antonio tells us that evening.

My phone chimes from Antonio's intelligence, showing Calabrese movements—weapons being stockpiled, crews taking positions near our allies' businesses, old guard soldiers infiltrating places we once thought secure. Anthony is building toward something big, something that will make Sean Murphy's execution look like a warning shot.

"My guards caught three of his men trying to breach the hospital's security," Matteo tells me, his voice icy with rage. "They were placing spotters, learning shift changes. He's planning for every contingency."

My hands shake slightly as I rest them on my bump. Anthony knows I'm due soon. Knows our daughter could arrive any day. He's preparing to take what he sees as his, to rip her away from the "corruption" of our modernized world.

"He'll strike during a public event," I tell Mario. My fingers trace over the society calendar on my laptop. "Somewhere he thinks he can control the variables. Somewhere my security will be stretched thin by social obligations."

"The children's hospital benefit," Mario says, studying the schedule. A muscle ticks in his jaw as he recognizes the perfect trap. "Next week at the Plaza. He knows you won't skip it—not with your reputation for handling their annual fundraiser."

The realization settles like ice in my veins. It's perfect really—a high-profile event I can't avoid without raising suspicion.

"He's counting on my pride," I say quietly. "On my need to maintain appearances."

Mario scowls, his fingers drumming against the table. "We could send Kate—" He starts to suggest but I cut him off.

"No." I meet Mario's gaze steadily. "He wants us afraid. Wants us hiding. I won't give him that satisfaction."

The hospital relies on my connections, my ability to squeeze maximum donations from Manhattan's wealthy. Even now, eight months pregnant and being hunted, I can't abandon them. Those sick children need every dollar I can extract from society's elite. Anthony will expect that loyalty, will plan around it.

"We could use it," I suggest, my mind already mapping possibilities as I pace our command center. "Let him think he's cornered us. Meanwhile, Siobhan's crews will be in position, the DeLuca teams ready. We control more variables than he realizes."

I pull up security layouts for the Plaza with fresh eyes—seeing beyond the usual event planner concerns to every vulnerability Anthony might exploit. Each service entrance becomes a potential attack point. Every blind spot in the camera coverage offers both threat and opportunity. All the hidden routes I once used for more innocent purposes now transform into tactical considerations.

"The kitchen access here," I point out to Mario, enlarging the blueprints on our main screen. "And this service corridor that runs behind the ballroom. I used to plan escape routes through there for society wives needing breaks from their husbands' boring speeches."

"Now they'll be Anthony's attack points," Mario says grimly, already coordinating with our security teams. "He'll expect you to use those same routes when he makes his move."

Matteo's team reports roll in—Anthony gathering specific equipment that makes my skin crawl. Tactical gear designed for stealth, specialized weapons meant for close-quarters combat in crowded spaces. He's planning something precise, something that minimizes collateral damage to the society figures who'll be attending.

"He still cares about appearances," I note, watching the intelligence flow across our screens. "Even now, he wants to maintain that image of legitimacy. Of being better than Johnny."

My phone buzzes with updates from the hospital board—last-minute guest list changes, donation projections, all the normal chaos of a major fundraiser. The mundane mixed with deadly stakes.

"Dr. Cho needs the final numbers for the pediatric wing presentation," I tell Mario as I respond to emails. "And the governor's wife is threatening to pull her donation if she's not seated next to the Broadway star."

"Again, you could skip it," he says quietly. The words hold real fear beneath his usual control. "Let someone else handle it this year. Keep you both safe. Think of Stella."

I rest my hand on my stomach, feeling our daughter's restless movements. She's been more active lately, as if sensing what's going on. Her kicks feel like punctuation to our war preparations.

"No. I won't let him make me hide. Won't let him control what I can and can't do." My voice hardens with conviction born of months running from Anthony's shadow. "Besides, he'll just find another opportunity. Better to face this on our terms, with our people in position."

Mario's arms wrap around me from behind again, his hands covering mine where they rest on my bump. For a moment, we just stand there, feeling our daughter move between us. This perfect, innocent life amid all the violence and schemes.

But that night, reviewing final security protocols while Stella practices what feels like Olympic gymnastics inside me, I can't help but wonder: are we walking into his trap, or is he walking into ours?

33

MARIO

The Plaza glitters like a fortress made of gold and old money, its Beaux-Arts facade punctuating Manhattan's twilight sky. Through our surveillance feeds, I watch the grand ballroom transform under Elena's direction—light fractured through crystal fixtures across hand-selected stone, white roses and orchids arranged to conceal security positions.

I study our displays from the command center in a building across the street, every screen showing a different angle. The service entrance where Anthony's men have been spotted. The kitchen access they'll try to breach. The hidden corridors Elena once used for more innocent purposes.

Now those same routes could mean life or death.

Siobhan's teams move efficiently through the pre-event chaos, perfectly disguised as hotel staff. Irish crews fresh from Boston's revolution serve champagne and adjust place cards, while Matteo's men blend seamlessly with arriving donors in their designer suits.

"Anthony's forces confirmed at three entry points," Dante reports through our secure channel. "Exactly where Elena predicted. They're maintaining distance, trying to look like normal security."

But I catch the subtle tells that Giuseppe taught us to recognize—

how they check sight lines too precisely, the way they position themselves near key exits. They're waiting for something. For orders. For their moment to strike.

Elena moves through final preparations like this isn't a potential war zone. She's magnificent in midnight blue Valentino that makes her look like a queen, her nine-month bump somehow adding to her authority rather than diminishing it. The dress is a masterpiece of design—flowing enough to conceal the gun strapped to her thigh, elegant enough to command respect from Manhattan's elite.

Watching her work, you'd never know she was being hunted. She coordinates details effortlessly—adjusting flower arrangements that hide security cameras, directing servers who carry weapons beneath their uniforms, ensuring every element serves both beauty and tactical advantage.

My little planner, orchestrating war behind perfect manners and social graces.

But I see how she watches every person who enters, mentally noting their allegiances and possible threats. The careful way she positions herself near defensive positions we established earlier. Even heavily pregnant, she moves with a precision that would make Giuseppe proud.

"Movement at the service entrance," Dante murmurs through comms. "Two of Anthony's top lieutenants just arrived. They're carrying diplomatic pouches—weapons we can't touch without breaking social protocol."

Fuck. I adjust my feed, watching Anthony's men take their positions. They're being careful, professional—nothing that would alarm the wealthy donors arriving in their designer gowns and tuxedos. But I recognize their formation from years of planning similar operations. The way they establish overlapping fields of fire while appearing to mingle casually.

"Matteo just intercepted new orders," Antonio reports from his position near the ballroom. Through the feed, I see Matteo's second standing guard like a statue, gray hair catching the light. His face betrays nothing, but his voice holds real concern. "Anthony's coming himself. He wants to be here when ... when it happens."

My hands clench into fists, cracking knuckles that have broken too many bones to count. Of course the fucker is coming. He wants to witness his triumph personally, wants to watch as he tears our world apart.

"All teams on high alert," I order. "No one moves without my command. Let him think he has the advantage."

Anthony arrives like he owns the Plaza—perfect in Tom Ford, that Calabrese arrogance radiating from every movement. But the slight tremor in his hands as he accepts champagne gives him away. The manic edge to his smile as he greets society figures. The way his eyes constantly track Elena's position like a predator stalking prey.

He's unraveling. And that makes him infinitely more dangerous.

Because men like Anthony Calabrese are most lethal when they have nothing left to lose.

"He brought more men than we anticipated," Elena's voice comes through my earpiece, steady as a surgeon's hand. Through the feed, I watch her work the grand staircase—all marble and gilt that's witnessed a century of New York power plays. She greets donors with perfect poise, never betraying how she watches every threat. "At least twelve new faces I don't recognize. Old guard specialists, based on their positioning."

I adjust my surveillance angles, studying these new players. They move easily through the crowd—taking positions that effectively cut off our planned escape routes. One by the northwest service corridor. Two flanking the kitchen access. Three more covering the main exits. This isn't just about grabbing Elena anymore—Anthony's preparing for war.

"Siobhan's teams are tracking them," Dante reports, his usual cool professionalism cracking slightly. "But they're good. Professional. The kind of crews that specialize in extraction operations."

My throat tightens as I watch Elena through our feeds. Her pregnancy gives her an otherworldly glow as she works her magic. I watch her charm seven-figure donations from Manhattan's elite with practiced ease—a perfectly timed laugh here, a carefully placed compliment there. Every society figure who enters gravitates toward her, drawn by the grace that masks the predator beneath.

But Anthony watches her too. The possessive hunger in his eyes makes anger course through me. He tracks her every movement like a man obsessed, that polished exterior cracking to reveal something dangerous beneath. He's not just here to take our daughter—he wants to destroy everything we've built. Wants to remake both families in his image of tradition and blood purity.

"He's going to make his move soon," I tell our teams, already moving toward the building. "Everyone in position. Remember—we let him think he has control until the last possible moment."

I slip into the Plaza through channels my brother's security helped establish—maintenance corridors that bypass normal security, service elevators monitored by DeLuca men. Matteo might never forgive my past actions, but he won't let Anthony hurt Elena. Won't let him tear another family apart.

"His men are getting antsy," Elena murmurs, her voice steady in my earpiece as she works the crowd. "The ones by the service entrance keep checking their watches."

As I move, I watch Anthony carefully. He plays his role perfectly —the legitimate businessman supporting a worthy cause. But beneath that polished veneer, I see Johnny's madness waiting to break free. The same cruel edge that made men tremble at the Calabrese name.

"Latest intel from Siobhan," Dante reports, his voice tight. "Fucking hell, Mario. Anthony's got a medical team standing by at a private facility. He's planning to take Elena there when ... when it happens."

Ice spreads through my veins as I process the implication. He's not just waiting to strike—he's waiting for Elena to go into *labor*. Wants to take her at her most vulnerable moment.

"All teams hold position," I order, forcing down the panic trying to claw up my throat. "No one moves until I give the signal. Let him think his plan is working."

"Really, Mrs. Astor, your generosity is overwhelming," Elena's voice carries across the ballroom. "The pediatric wing will help so many children."

Her hand drifts to her stomach—a gesture that could be maternal pride but I recognize as checking her concealed weapon. Her other hand pulls out her phone, fingers flying across the screen with practiced efficiency.

My phone buzzes with her message: *He's getting impatient.*

I move closer to her position, every protective instinct screaming to grab her and run. Because that's what Anthony's counting on—that I'll let emotion override strategy. That I'll make the same mistakes Giuseppe always said I would.

Not this time. This time, we play it smart.

"Ready?" I ask, knowing she can hear me.

Her smile could cut glass as she accepts another champagne flute she won't drink. "Always."

I force myself to maintain position, watching as Anthony springs his trap. The bastard thinks he's so clever, so perfectly in control. Let him.

Anthony's forces move, tightening their formation like a noose. They isolate Elena from the crowd with subtle efficiency—a waiter requiring her attention near the service corridor, a donor "accidentally" blocking her path back to the main ballroom. Another of his men starts a minor scene near the east exit, drawing security's attention away from their true target.

"Target is nearly in position," one of Anthony's men murmurs into his comm, not realizing we've hacked their channel. "Medical team confirms they're ready."

Dante's voice comes through our comms: "They've got three men in the kitchen, two by the staff elevator. Whatever they're planning, it's centered around that service corridor."

The same corridor where she once helped society wives escape their boring husbands. Now it's become Anthony's trap—a choke point where he thinks he can isolate her, control every variable. Force her exactly where he wants her.

"He's moving," Dante warns as Anthony smoothly excuses himself from a group of donors. "South entrance team is mobilizing."

His men take their final positions. Each one exactly where we predicted they'd be. Each one thinking they're the hunters rather than the prey.

I move through the crowd, watching as Anthony's men systematically isolate Elena near the service corridor. They're good—using waiters and donors as unwitting pawns to cut off her escape routes, to guide her exactly where they want her.

Elena plays along perfectly, letting them think their subtle manipulation is working. But there's the slight adjustment of her stance as she's "accidentally" herded away from the main ballroom, her hand brushing her concealed weapon as she's drawn toward the service area. She's ready. We're all ready.

Anthony's smile as he approaches makes my blood run cold. He's not just confident—he's triumphant. Like he knows something we don't.

"One last chance," I murmur through our private channel. "We can still get you out."

Elena's laugh carries pure ice as she turns to greet Anthony, now effectively cornered near the service entrance. "Not a chance. Let him learn what happens when you underestimate a pregnant woman."

The next few minutes unfold with excruciating tension. From my position behind a marble column, I watch Anthony approach Elena, all polished charm on the surface. But I see the predator beneath, the way his eyes track her every movement like a hunter closing in on prey.

"Elena." His voice carries across the marble floor. "You're looking radiant. Motherhood suits you."

"Anthony." Her smile is warm but her eyes are cold. "How unexpected to see you here. I wouldn't have thought children's causes interested you."

His answering laugh holds no warmth. "Oh, I'm *very* interested in children's causes. In family. In making sure the next generation knows proper values."

I catch the subtle signal between his men—the way they shift closer, cutting off escape routes.

"Boss," Dante's voice is urgent in my ear. "New players just entered through the kitchen. At least six more. These aren't his regular crew—they're specialists."

The realization hits as I see their formation. These aren't just extraction specialists—they're the kind of professionals who handle "complicated" pregnancies. Who ensure babies are born exactly where and how their employers want.

"Whatever you're planning," Elena tells Anthony, her voice carrying a deadly softness that makes the hairs at the back of my neck rise, "you should know—I'm not the society planner you tried to control anymore."

Anthony's smile is pure Calabrese arrogance—all perfect white teeth and dead eyes, like a shark scenting blood. The same smile Johnny wore before destroying things he considered his property. Triumphant. Mocking. Sure of his victory.

"No? Then what are you, *cara*?" He moves closer, that movement making my fingers twitch. "Besides the mother of my heir?"

"I'm the woman who's about to teach you why you never underestimate a pregnant DeLuca."

The words hang in the air like a prophecy, like a promise of blood to come. Because that's what she is now—not just Elena Santiago, not just the society planner everyone overlooked. She's become something more dangerous. Something worth fighting for. Worth dying for.

My hand tightens on my weapon as I watch Anthony process her words. The way his smile freezes, then cracks around the edges as understanding dawns.

Because Elena isn't just carrying his child. She's carrying our future. Our revolution. Everything the old guard fears about the next generation.

And Anthony's about to learn exactly what that means.

34

ELENA

I've experienced bad timing before. Like getting my first period during a middle school dance. Or my heel breaking as I ran for a taxi in the rain.

But going into labor in the middle of a standoff with Anthony Calabrese? That's a special kind of terrible timing.

The first contraction hits as I'm telling Anthony I'm a DeLuca—a sharp, twisting pain that steals my breath. I maintain my composure through sheer will, not letting him see how my insides are trying to turn into outsides. Years of maintaining perfect poise while gathering intelligence finally serve a real purpose.

Another contraction rolls through me as Anthony's men tighten their formation. This one's stronger, making me grateful for the marble column at my back. The pain radiates from my spine around to my belly, lasting longer than it should.

This isn't the mild cramping I've had for days. This is the real thing. *Fuck.*

I catch Mario's eye across the room, seeing the moment he realizes something's wrong. The slight shift in his stance, the way his hand tightens on his concealed weapon. But I give him the smallest shake of my head. Not yet. We stick to the plan.

Even if our daughter has apparently decided to make her entrance at the worst possible moment.

Through the growing waves of pain, I maintain my smile. Keep playing the perfect society planner while Anthony gloats, while his men move into position, while my body prepares to bring new life at the worst fucking time.

Stella kicks hard, as if apologizing for her timing. Or maybe she's just her father's daughter—always ready for a fight.

Through my earpiece, I hear Dante's urgent warning: "Teams two and four compromised. They've got our people in the kitchen. These aren't regular soldiers—they're medical extraction specialists."

Another contraction rips through me, more violent than the last. Warm liquid trickles down my legs, soaking into my Valentino, and I fight back a wave of pure panic. Not now. Please, not now. The timing couldn't be worse—surrounded by Anthony's men, our backup compromised, my carefully planned revolution threatening to dissolve into chaos.

I force myself to breathe through the pain like my Lamaze instructor taught me, mind racing through options even as my body betrays me. Through my earpiece, I hear the coordinated chaos unfolding—Siobhan's teams engaging hostiles in the kitchen, their Irish accents sharp with urgency. DeLuca security containing the situation in the main ballroom, protecting innocent society figures from impending violence. Mario's people trying to fight their way to my position, but meeting heavy resistance.

"They've got the elevators locked down," Dante reports, real fear coloring his voice. "And their medical team is setting up in the service bay. They're ready for immediate transport."

Another contraction hits, stealing my breath. This one's stronger, making my knees weak. I brace myself against the wall, trying to maintain tactical awareness but having a difficult time doing so.

"He won't choose you," Anthony says, moving closer like a shark scenting blood. "DeLucas always choose power over love. Even Matteo would have, if Bella hadn't proved useful. Right now, your precious Mario is too far away. By the time he reaches us, you'll be gone."

But he's wrong about DeLucas and love. Because even as another contraction tears through me, I hear the distinctive sound of Mario's preferred weapon. He storms in, his tuxedo jacket discarded, dress shirt covered in blood that isn't his.

His eyes meet mine across the chaos, holding a promise of protection, of love, of everything Anthony will never understand.

"Get away from them," Mario growls, rage covering his face.

Anthony's eyes light up as he notices my stance, the way I brace against the wall through another contraction. "Ah, perfect timing," he says, triumph coloring his voice. "My daughter is already so punctual, wanting to meet her dear daddy."

"She will *never* know you," I gasp through the pain, even as fear claws up my throat at his delighted expression. "She's not yours."

"No?" His smile turns cruel. "In a few hours, you'll both be safe in my private facility. Away from this corruption, these modern ideas that poison everything they touch."

Mario's face transforms, that DeLuca restraint crumbling completely. What follows is chaos—gunfire and shouted orders mixing with my increasingly painful contractions. I'm aware of Mario shielding my body with his own, of Anthony's specialists falling under precise headshots. But they're professionals, adapting quickly to our defense.

"Second team breaching through the kitchen," Dante warns through comms. "They've got hospital scrubs and credentials. Watch for—"

His voice cuts off as an explosion rocks the building. Through security feeds, I see Siobhan's crews engaging in the main ballroom, buying us time. But Anthony's extraction team is moving with frightening efficiency, herding us exactly where they want us.

Another contraction hits, this one actually bringing me to my knees. Mario catches me, his arms steady despite the violence around us. But I see the impossible choice in his eyes—stay with me or pursue Anthony, who's retreating toward his waiting medical team.

"They're setting up a perimeter," Antonio reports. "Medical transport standing by, full surgical suite prepared. They're ready to deliver the baby themselves."

The realization hits through waves of pain—they never planned to wait. They'll take me by force, perform an emergency C-section if necessary. Anything to get Anthony's heir.

"Hospital," I manage between contractions, seeing Mario's internal struggle. "Now."

"Cover the east exit," Mario orders through comms as another contraction hits. "Dante, get that transport—"

"Negative," Dante cuts in urgently. "They've got the parking structure locked down. Medical team's set up roadblocks, checking every vehicle."

I grip Mario's arm as another contraction tears through me, the pain so intense black spots dance at the edges of my vision. "Service elevator," I gasp, fighting to stay logical even as my body betrays me. "The one they use for ... for delivering supplies. Security's lighter because ... because they think we'll go for the main exits."

Mario's already moving, practically carrying me as his teams engage Anthony's forces. The world becomes a blur of gunfire and explosions, tactical gear flashing as both sides trade fire. The specialists are terrifyingly good—methodically cutting off our escape routes while maintaining enough distance to avoid civilian casualties.

"Elena!" Anthony's voice carries over the chaos. "Think about our daughter. About giving her proper values, a real family—"

A contraction hits so hard I scream, my knees buckling. Mario catches me, but I feel him tense at Anthony's words, his worried face transforming into anger as the taunts hit their mark. For a moment, I think he'll turn back, will choose revenge over protecting us.

But then Stella kicks hard, as if reminding him what matters. His arm tightens around me as we reach the service elevator, his body shielding mine from incoming fire.

"They're in the shaft," someone shouts. "Medical team, move to—"

The service elevator becomes a nightmare. Mario keeps me

pressed against him, one arm secure around my waist while the other fires at shadows above us. Each floor we pass brings new threats—boots thundering on metal stairs, voices coordinating positions, Anthony's specialists trying to predict our exit point.

"Third floor team, they're coming down!" Someone shouts above us. "Cut them off at the service bay—"

Another contraction rips through me, and I bite my lip bloody to keep from screaming. The world narrows to pain and chaos and Mario's steady presence behind me.

"North stairwell secured!" Siobhan's crew leader calls through our comms, his Irish accent thick with adrenaline.

"They're trying to flank through the kitchen," another warns.

"Not anymore," comes a smug Irish drawl. "Area contained."

"DeLuca teams, create a diversion at the main entrance," Antonio orders. "Make them think we're going for the parking structure."

"Copy that. Moving into position."

"Two minutes to the exit point," Mario murmurs against my hair, his arm tight around me as another contraction hits.

"Brother," Matteo's voice cuts through our comms. "Your route is clear. My men will hold them."

But Anthony's forces are adapting, moving to cut us off. Through the pain, I hear them coordinating: "Target approaching basement level—"

"Remember, we need them both alive—"

I gasp, clutching Mario's shirt as pain rips through me. All the books said first-time labor would last hours, but I already feel the urge to bear down. Pure panic claws up my throat.

"I am not," I tell Mario, nearly hysterical, "giving birth in a fucking service elevator!"

Another contraction cuts through me, this one bringing another scream I can't suppress. The sound echoes through the shaft, giving away our position.

"There!" Someone shouts from above. "They're between one and two!"

Mario shoots upward without taking his supportive arm from my waist. But I see the strain in his face—trying to protect me while fighting, trying to get us out while keeping me from falling.

"The maintenance tunnel," I gasp, remembering the building layout through another wave of pain. "If we can reach ... reach the access panel on the next floor ..."

"Boss," Dante cuts in urgently. "Calabrese has multiple teams. Another medical team's set up in the tunnel. They're waiting—"

"Let them wait," I manage through gritted teeth, my mind still working despite the pain. "Siobhan's teams ... they're in position ..."

As if on cue, gunfire erupts from below—but not aimed at us. Through the open shaft, we hear Anthony's medical team shouting in surprise as Irish crews emerge from their hiding spots throughout the tunnel.

"Caught the bastards completely off guard," one of Siobhan's men reports through our comms, satisfaction clear in his voice.

"Targets engaged," Siobhan announces. "Tunnel's clear. Get her the fuck out, DeLuca."

Mario helps me swing toward the elevator doors, his movements precise despite the awkward angle. Another contraction hits just as we reach the maintenance access, making me cry out.

Our daughter is coming, whether we're ready or not.

"I'm sorry," I gasp as we navigate the dark service corridors, tears mixing with sweat on my face. Another contraction tears through me, making my vision blur. "I'm so sorry I got us into this. I should have listened to you—should have had Kate handle this—"

He cuts me off with a hard, desperate kiss, his lips fierce against mine even as his hands remain gentle supporting my weight. "Stop apologizing," he growls against my mouth. "And this is the one time I won't tell you I told you so, so you better fucking enjoy it."

A hysterical laugh bubbles up—I'm not sure if it's the adrenaline, the pain, or the complete absurdity of Mario DeLuca choosing this moment to develop a sense of humor.

Through our earpieces, we hear the chaos unfolding—Anthony's forces regrouping, trying to cut off our escape route. But our allies have been one step ahead the whole time.

"East entrance secured," Matteo's men report.

"Two more hostiles down in the stairwell," comes Siobhan, laughter clear in her voice.

"Medical team neutralized," another Irish voice confirms.

"Vehicle's waiting in the loading dock," Dante reports. "Path is clear but—"

Another contraction cuts him off as my knees buckle. This one feels different—more urgent, more demanding. Like our daughter is done waiting.

"She's coming," I gasp, gripping Mario's arm hard enough to bruise. "Stella's coming *now*."

His smile is fierce as he lifts me into his arms, cradling me against his chest even as he maintains tactical awareness. "Then let's make sure something happens next. Ready to fight for our future, little planner?"

Everything narrows to pain and motion as Mario carries me through the service corridors. Each contraction hits harder than the last, making it almost impossible to focus on the updates crackling through my earpiece.

"Anthony's mobilizing his reserve teams," Dante warns, words spilling over themselves as he tries to get them out as quickly as possible. "They're converging on the loading dock. At least twelve hostiles, heavily armed."

"Not anymore," Siobhan's taunting voice cuts in. "My people just took out their transport. They're on foot now, scattered."

Gunfire erupts ahead of us. Through waves of pain, I hear Siobhan's and Matteo's teams engaging the hostiles, buying us precious seconds. But scattered enemies are sometimes more dangerous than coordinated ones. Through the haze of pain, I hear boots on concrete, voices calling positions:

"Target spotted in the west corridor!" Someone roars.

"Don't let them reach that vehicle!"

"Mario," I repeat between contractions that are now almost continuous. "*Please.*"

Mario's already moving, his entire focus on getting us out. Behind us, Anthony's enraged voice echoes off concrete walls: "That's my heir! My blood! You can't—"

The rest is lost as another contraction rips through me. But through the pain, I witness something beautiful—our allies moving in perfect coordination.

"DeLuca teams, maintain perimeter," Antonio orders. "Irish crews, advance and eliminate threats."

The loading dock erupts in precise violence as Mario carries me toward the waiting car. Gunfire and shouts mix with my labored breathing, creating a symphony of chaos.

"Clear that corner—"

"Two more incoming—"

"Got the fucker!"

"Get them to Mount Sinai," Matteo orders through our earpiece. "Our people are already there, securing the maternity ward."

Another contraction hits, bringing a scream I can't suppress. Fuck, I'm never doing this again. I feel Stella moving lower, more urgent with each passing moment.

"Calabrese is retreating," Dante reports. "His forces are either down or scattered."

"Let him run," Siobhan responds coldly. "We'll deal with him later."

"Hold on, little planner," Mario murmurs as we reach the car. He doesn't even glance back at the chaos behind us, doesn't pause to witness Anthony's retreat. His entire focus is on getting us to safety, on protecting this child that isn't his by blood but has somehow become his in every way that matters.

"You chose us," I whisper between contractions as Mario breaks every traffic law getting to the hospital.

A sharp laugh cracks out of him as he takes another corner at dangerous speed. "I'll always choose you," he promises. "Both of you."

Mount Sinai looms ahead, its emergency entrance already secured by a mixture of Irish and DeLuca guards. The contractions are continuous now, my body demanding our daughter's arrival regardless of the danger still lurking.

Antonio meets us at the door, his usual stern expression replaced by urgent efficiency as he helps Mario get me inside. The captain's gray hair is disheveled, blood staining his clothes, but his movements are precise as medical staff swarm around us with wheelchairs and monitors.

"The floor is locked down," he reports as they rush me toward delivery. "Our people only. Every doctor, every nurse has been vetted."

The delivery room becomes a fortress within a fortress—guards outside the door, snipers on neighboring buildings, every entrance covered by people we trust. But through the haze of contractions, all I can focus on is Mario's face, the way he never looks away even when I crush his hand. His usual scowl is replaced by something softer, though tension still radiates from his shoulders as he maintains awareness.

"Christ," he says as I grip harder during another contraction. "Remind me to never let you near my weapons hand."

"I hate you," I hiss through the pain. "I hate you so much right now."

His laugh is gentle as he brushes sweat-soaked hair from my face. "No you don't, little planner."

"Security breach in the north stairwell," Dante reports through our earpiece. "Anthony's specialists trying to get through. We've got it contained."

"Forget them," Mario growls, his attention completely on me as another contraction hits and my body jerks. "Just breathe, little planner. Focus on bringing our daughter into the world."

Our daughter. Even now, in the midst of this chaos, those words make my heart clench. He's never once hesitated to claim her, to love her despite biology. Despite Anthony's taunts about blood and tradition.

She's been ours since the moment he chose us over revenge.

The pain becomes all-consuming, everything narrowing to this moment, to Mario's steady presence beside me. The doctor's instructions mix with security updates in my ear: "Push now" overlapping with "Target neutralized in the parking structure."

Mario's hand never leaves mine, his thumb rubbing gentle circles on my skin as I fight through each contraction. Through waves of pain and exhaustion, I hear Siobhan coordinating with Matteo's teams, our carefully built alliances protecting us while I labor to bring our daughter into this complicated world.

"I see the head," the doctor announces. "One more big push, Ms. Santiago."

Mario's hand tightens on mine as I bear down. His eyes never leave my face, his own transformed into something softer, something I never thought I'd see from Giuseppe DeLuca's exiled son.

"You're doing so well," he murmurs against my temple. "So strong, my little planner."

With one final, tremendous push and a final, animalistic scream, our daughter announces her arrival with healthy lungs. The sound of her first cry makes something break open in my chest—pure love flooding through me as they place her in my arms.

"She's beautiful," I whisper, tears streaming down my face as I study her perfect features. She has my coloring, thank God, but I swear there's something of Mario in the determined set of her tiny jaw. When she grips his finger with surprising strength, I watch his careful composure shatter completely.

"I love you," he tells us both, his voice rough with emotion I've never heard from him before. The words feel like freedom, like possibility, like everything we've fought for. "No matter what happens next, no matter whose blood she carries—you're mine. Both of you."

Stella's tiny hand grips his finger tighter, as if sealing this promise between us. For a moment, watching them together—this dangerous man transformed by love for our daughter—every choice that led us here feels worth it. Every risk, every betrayal, every game we played; all of it leading to this perfect moment.

Because Mario isn't just choosing to raise another man's child.

He's choosing love over blood, choosing to be better than the poison Giuseppe left in his veins. Choosing us.

And watching him hold our daughter with hands that have dealt so much death, seeing him transformed by this tiny life we'll protect together, I know we've won something more precious than any territory or power.

But through my earpiece, I hear Dante's urgent warning: "Boss, we've got movement. Multiple vehicles approaching. Anthony's here."

The perfect moment shatters as Mario's body tenses beside me, that beautiful softness transforming back into something lethal. I watch his walls slam up, the loving father replaced by Giuseppe's most dangerous son.

Stella continues to wail, unaware that her biological father has come to claim what he thinks is his. Unaware that our brief moment of peace is already dissolving as reality crashes back.

The war isn't over yet.

35

MARIO

I feel the change in my body before Dante's warning comes through—that combat-ready tension Giuseppe beat into both his sons. One moment I'm lost in my daughter's perfect face, marveling at how tightly she grips my finger. The next, I'm fighting back the urge to burn the world as Anthony's forces converge on Mount Sinai.

"Multiple teams approaching," Antonio reports through comms, his voice tight with controlled urgency. "At least twenty men, all highly trained. They've got every exit covered, and they're carrying specialized equipment—not just weapons."

"Another medical transport standing by," Dante adds grimly. "Military experience. They're prepared to take the baby by force if necessary."

Elena cradles Stella closer, exhausted from labor but her mind still razor-sharp as she processes the threat. Even after giving birth, she calculates angles and implications. "He's done playing games," she says quietly. "This is his last stand."

I study our daughter's sleeping face, memorizing every perfect feature that thankfully favors her mother. The same determined chin, the same stubbornness even in sleep. My hand drifts to my weapon as boots echo down the hospital corridor—too many sets to count.

"That's my daughter," Anthony announces as he bursts through the door, his lawyers hovering behind him like well-dressed vultures. But this isn't just a legal play—I see the violence barely contained beneath his designer suit, the way his hand keeps drifting toward his concealed weapon. The same madness that consumed his uncle Johnny bleeding through his polished facade. "My blood. My heir. And I'm done asking nicely."

I move faster than thought, placing myself between him and my family. Because that's what they are now—*my* family, chosen and claimed and protected despite blood or biology or all the poison Giuseppe left in our veins. "Touch them," I say quietly, letting that DeLuca darkness fill my voice, "and they'll never find all the pieces."

Some things are worth burning the world to protect.

"Biological rights aren't so easily dismissed," Anthony sneers, but there's something fractured in his expression now—that same madness that made his uncle Johnny infamous. "That's my blood she's holding. My heir. Every court in New York will recognize that."

His eyes keep darting to Elena and Stella, something desperate and possessive in his gaze that makes my trigger finger itch. He takes a step forward, trying to see around me. "Elena, please. Let me just see her. She's my daughter—my blood. You can't keep her from me."

Through my earpiece, I hear his forces engaging with our security teams throughout the hospital. The sounds of precise violence echo through supposedly sterile corridors as Siobhan's crews and DeLuca security work to contain the threat.

"Three hostiles neutralized in the east stairwell," Dante reports. "But they've got more coming in through the service entrance."

"We'll see about those rights," I snarl, moving to block his view completely. The urge to strangle him rises as Anthony's eyes fix hungrily on my daughter. "But right now, you're leaving. Elena just gave birth. Any legal discussions can wait."

Instead of retreating, his face transforms into something almost pitying. "You really think you can escape blood?" he asks softly. "That you can play happy family with my child? We both know what you are, Mario. What Giuseppe made you. Some darkness runs too deep to escape."

"Maybe." I let him see exactly what kind of monster lives in me now—all the violence Giuseppe carved into my bones focused on one purpose. Protecting what's mine. "But I choose to use it protecting them instead of destroying everything like you. Like my father. Like everyone who thought love was weakness."

Behind me, Stella starts to cry—a sound that makes something primal and deadly rise in my chest. Through my earpiece, I hear the coordinated chaos as our allies fight to protect us. "Two more teams breaching the fourth floor," Antonio warns. "They're trying to secure a path for transport."

I see the moment Anthony's control snaps—his eyes going wild as he lunges toward Elena's bed. But I'm faster, Giuseppe's lessons serving their true purpose as I slam him against the wall, my forearm across his throat.

"Touch them," I growl, pressing until he gasps, "and I'll show you *exactly* what kind of darkness Giuseppe created."

Because Anthony's right about one thing—there is darkness in me. But now it serves a better purpose than revenge or power.

Now it protects what matters.

"Love is weakness," Anthony spits, struggling against my grip. His carefully maintained composure shatters as Stella's cries grow louder—the sound of my daughter clearly driving him toward madness. "My uncle understood—power is the only thing that matters."

Elena's voice cuts through his rant, that steely determination never wavering even after hours of labor: "Power?" Her laughter cuts like glass as she cradles our crying daughter closer. "You want to talk about power while your empire crumbles? While every young crew chooses modernization over tradition? You're fighting a war that's already lost, Anthony."

That final thread of sanity snaps from Anthony as he breaks free, his hand moving toward his weapon. But I'm faster, my body responding without even thinking.

The gun doesn't even clear his jacket before I have him by the throat, slamming him against the wall again hard enough to crack plaster. Through my earpiece, I hear his forces being systematically eliminated throughout the hospital—our allies working in perfect coordination to protect my family.

"East stairwell clear," Dante reports. "Medical transport team neutralized."

"Perimeter secured," Antonio adds. "They're running out of options, Mario."

Anthony struggles against my grip, that polished veneer completely shattered. His eyes fix on Stella with desperate hunger, making my grip tighten until he gasps. "The baby—" he chokes out.

"Again, is mine." The words come out like a vow, like a promise written in violence. "Not by blood, but by choice. By love. By everything you're too broken to understand."

Because that's what Anthony will never comprehend—some bonds are stronger than blood. Some choices matter more than tradition.

Behind us, Elena holds Stella protectively while coordinating with our teams through her earpiece—still running operations even from her hospital bed. I catch fragments of her conversation as I focus on Anthony:

"Release everything," she orders quietly. "Every file, every document, exactly like we planned."

"Understood," Siobhan's voice carries faintly and then I hear her tell someone, "Do it now."

"Your empire is gone," I tell Anthony quietly, watching realization finally dawn in his eyes. "Your old guard allies either dead or switching sides. Even your own family is turning against you—choosing progress over your outdated traditions."

His sneer holds pure Calabrese arrogance, but fear edges his voice. "I will *never* stop coming for them. Nothing you do will prevent me from taking my child. And when I get my hands on her, we'll disappear where you'll never—"

. . .

THE THREAT DIES in his throat as I increase pressure, but I maintain perfect control. "Remember that flash drive Elena gave Sean Murphy?" I ask conversationally. "When you tried to kidnap her at her office?"

I feel him freeze, that arrogant facade cracking further.

"Funny thing about that," I continue, my grip tightening as he tries to reach for another weapon. "Every illegal operation, every connection to trafficking, every corrupt deal—it's all being released. Right now. To law enforcement, to rival families, to everyone you tried to convince you were better than your uncle."

Through comms, I hear the chaos unfolding:

"Files received by FBI."

"Interpol confirming—"

"Major news outlets running the story."

"You've been so focused on tradition," Elena adds from her bed, "you never saw us playing the long game. Everything we gathered, every piece of evidence—it was always meant for this moment."

"You're destroying everything," he gasps, real fear finally replacing the madness in his eyes. "Generations of tradition, of proper values—"

"No." My voice holds that deadly quiet Giuseppe taught us to use—the calm before violence. "You destroyed it yourself. The moment you chose power over evolution. The moment you threatened my family."

His body goes slack as the full implications hit him. Through our comms, we hear his empire collapsing in real time—forces abandoning their positions, hired specialists melting into the night, even his most loyal captains choosing survival over outdated loyalty.

"Target teams withdrawing from north entrance—"

"Medical transport crew surrendering—"

"All Calabrese forces in full retreat—"

"Sir," Antonio reports, satisfaction clear in his voice, "all hostile forces have been neutralized. The hospital is secure."

The police arrive with perfect timing—another piece in our carefully orchestrated endgame. Anthony's lawyers spring forward, their expensive suits rustling with desperate importance.

"Officer, you should be arresting him," one gestures toward me. "Mario DeLuca is the real criminal here—"

The chief of police cuts him off with a cold smile. "We have evidence of Mr. Calabrese's involvement in human trafficking, money laundering, and attempted kidnapping. Step aside."

I can't help but smirk—the NYPD has been in DeLuca pockets since before I was born.

Some traditions are worth maintaining.

Anthony's composure finally shatters completely. He lunges forward, all that polished sophistication dissolving into raw madness. "You can't do this! I am a Calabrese! That's my child—"

I glance at Elena, expecting satisfaction, but her face is pure ice as she watches Anthony unravel. In that moment, she looks more dangerous than any DeLuca—a queen watching her enemy's destruction with cold calculation.

It takes three officers to restrain Anthony as he thrashes and screams. His designer suit tears, his perfectly styled hair wild as he shrieks for his lawyers to do something, anything. The sight would be pitiful if I didn't remember his threats against my family.

When it's over, Anthony Calabrese—the heir who thought blood mattered more than love—is led away in handcuffs. His empire in ruins, his legacy destroyed, his obsession with tradition finally costing him everything.

Some men create their own destruction while claiming to protect tradition.

Some lessons can only be taught in handcuffs.

When we're finally alone, Elena's composure breaks. Tears stream down her face as months of tension release. "It's over," she whispers. "It's really over."

I gather them both into my arms, pressing a kiss to her hair. "We're safe," I promise. "All of us."

She looks up at me, those clever eyes soft with emotion I've never seen before. "Would you like to hold your daughter?" she asks gently. "Stella Maria DeLuca?"

My throat closes at the name—not just the feminine version of my own, but *DeLuca*. She's given our daughter my name, chosen my family over blood.

The gesture means more than any victory we've won tonight.

With trembling hands, I take Stella from Elena's arms. She's impossibly tiny, impossibly perfect—all dark lashes against pink cheeks, rosebud lips, and delicate fingers that somehow still manage to grip my thumb with surprising strength. A perfect angel who somehow became mine despite biology, despite tradition, despite everything the old guard claimed about blood.

"Hello, little star," I whisper, cradling her close. "I'm your papa. And I promise I'll protect you forever." I study her perfect face, already feeling myself fall completely, irrevocably in love. "In fact, I'm going to build you a tower. No one will ever be good enough for my princess—"

Elena smacks my arm, rolling her eyes. "She's not even an hour old and you're already planning to lock her away?"

"Of course." I grin, unable to take my eyes off our daughter. "Have to start early. No dating until she's thirty."

"You're impossible," Elena groans.

But watching Stella sleep in my arms, feeling Elena lean against me in exhaustion, I know we've won something more precious than any territory or power.

We've won our future.

And I'll spend the rest of my life protecting it.

Over the next few hours, our hospital room fills with allies as reports confirm Anthony's complete downfall. Siobhan arrives first, immaculate in Chanel and Christian Louboutins, not a single red hair out of place. She could have been heading to a board meeting rather than coordinating the takedown of one of the most dangerous families in New York.

"It's done," she reports, her designer suit somehow unblemished despite the night's violence. "Every extraction specialist neutralized, every old guard faction either surrendering or eliminated. We've won."

She studies Stella in my arms, her usual sharp edges softening fractionally. "Well," she says, looking like the words physically pain her, "fatherhood makes you look human, DeLuca."

I raise my eyebrows as Elena's jaw drops. "Did you just compliment Mario?"

"Don't read too much into it, Elena. It's only because there's a baby present." Siobhan waves her hand dismissively. "That's my one nice comment for the year."

Elena presses a hand to her mouth to stifle her smile. "Would you like to hold her?"

I tighten my arms protectively around Stella, horrified at the thought of handing my precious daughter to the Irish queen. "Absolutely not," I hiss to Elena.

Thankfully, Siobhan doesn't look offended. Instead, her face scrunches in distaste. "I'll pass. Children are not my area of expertise. Or interest." She leans down to kiss Elena's cheeks. "I'll be in touch. We still have work to do."

"Can I at least get maternity leave?" Elena asks hopefully.

Siobhan's laugh echoes as she heads for the door, stilettos clicking against hospital tiles.

"I was serious about the maternity leave," Elena tells me, her eyebrows furrowed as she looks at the doorway where Siobhan disappeared.

I snort, still cradling Stella like someone might snatch her. "The devil works hard, but Siobhan O'Connor works harder."

There's a knock at the door and Matteo pokes his head through—my brother looking exhausted but dangerous. His eyes linger on me holding Stella, something shifting in his expression as he watches me with his niece.

"Up for visitors?" he asks quietly, and I glance at Elena, who nods.

Matteo and Bella come into the room, Bella pushing a stroller with the twins. I hear Elena's sharp intake of breath at the sight of the nearly five-month-old babies sleeping peacefully. Her hand flies to her mouth, tears already falling as she takes in the children she helped save but never got to meet.

I hand Stella back to Elena and take up position beside her bed, every protective instinct on high alert. Even though Matteo allied with us against Anthony, I'm not sure where we stand now that the threat is eliminated. If we're back to being enemies, back to the exile and the don.

Matteo clears his throat, looking uncharacteristically awkward. "Anthony's people are turning on him completely," he tells us. "Offering up evidence of other operations, other crimes. They're desperate to prove they're not like him."

Elena relaxes against me, but I refuse to move one inch. The tension in the room could stop hearts.

Bella shifts her weight, staring at Elena and Stella with an expression I can't quite read. "You brought your babies," Elena croaks out.

Bella nods, her hazel eyes filling with tears. "I thought …" She swallows hard. "I thought the twins should meet their cousin."

The words hang in the air like possibility. Elena makes a sound somewhere between a sob and a laugh, and suddenly Bella is moving forward, careful of the babies but unable to stay away any longer.

"I missed you," she whispers, perching on Elena's bed. "God, I missed you so much."

"I'm so sorry," Elena sobs. "For everything—"

"I know." Bella carefully hugs her around Stella. "I understand now. About impossible choices. About choosing love over tradition."

Matteo and I eye each other across the hospital room, the weight of years pressing down between us. There's too much history here, too many scars that won't fade just because we fought on the same side tonight. His shoulders are tense, like he's expecting a fight even now.

I gesture toward Elena and Bella, who are still crying and hugging. "Don't worry," I tell him dryly, "I won't expect you to cry too."

His laugh is sharp, cutting through the emotional atmosphere. "I'd never expect that much humanity from you, Mario."

The words should sting, but there's something different in his tone now—less venom, more weariness. Still, I bristle. "That's rich coming from the don who exiled his own brother."

"And yet here you are." Matteo's eyes drift to Stella. "Making me an uncle."

"Yeah, well." I shift uncomfortably. "Wasn't exactly planned."

"Nothing about you ever is." But there's almost amusement in his voice now. "You always did like throwing wrenches in my carefully laid plans."

"Someone had to keep you humble," I shoot back.

We lapse into awkward silence, both watching as Elena carefully hands Stella to Bella. The moment feels fragile, like one wrong word could shatter everything we've built tonight.

"She's beautiful," Matteo says finally, his voice rough. "Looks like Elena."

I sigh with relief. "Thank God for that. I don't think I could stomach looking at a female Anthony Calabrese."

His lips twitch. "It's better looking than your face."

I stare at him in disbelief. "*That's* the comeback you have? How old are you? Twelve? Christ, Matteo, you need help."

The banter feels strange now, like putting on an old coat that doesn't quite fit anymore. We're not who we were before—before the exile, before Elena, before our children changed everything.

I watch as Bella cradles Stella, my protective instincts warring with the undeniable rightness of the moment. She leans down, studying my daughter's features with a gentle smile. "Welcome to the family, little one," she says softly, then looks up at me. "Both of you."

The words hit me harder than any bullet. This acceptance from the family I once tried to destroy—it means more than I can process. Beside me, Matteo moves to check on the twins, his movements sure and practiced as he adjusts their blankets. I remember Giuseppe's sneering voice: "Children make you weak. Family makes you vulnerable."

But watching my brother with his children, seeing how naturally he's adapted to being a new father despite Giuseppe's poison, I realize how wrong our father was. Matteo hasn't gone soft, he's never been soft—he's grown stronger, found purpose beyond power and control.

"I never thought we'd be here," Matteo says quietly, not looking at me. "You, me, our children together."

"Yeah." I clear my throat. "Guess we both learned some new tricks."

He snorts. "Like not immediately trying to kill each other?"

"Baby steps, brother." The word feels strange on my tongue—not wrong, just unpracticed. "We've got time."

Looking at Elena and our daughter, at Bella with the twins, at my brother who chose family over tradition, I finally understand what real power is. It's not about blood or territory or maintaining iron control. It's about love. About family. About being better than the darkness that created you.

Giuseppe taught us that power comes from what you're willing to destroy. But he was wrong about that, like he was wrong about so many things. Real power comes from what you choose to protect, from the family you build rather than the empire you inherit.

And watching my daughter in my sister-in-law's arms, seeing my brother's careful attention to his own children, I know we've all chosen something stronger than tradition.

We've chosen love.

EPILOGUE: ELENA

The DeLuca chapel is still as beautiful as I remember—still all old-world elegance and carefully curated power. Afternoon light streams through stained glass windows, casting jewel-toned shadows across marble floors that have witnessed generations of family ceremonies.

But this time I walk these hallowed halls with different purpose, Stella sleeping peacefully in my arms while I review the final christening arrangements.

At four months old, our daughter is pure angelic perfection. Her dark lashes fan against cherub cheeks, her rosebud mouth slightly parted in sleep. She has my eyes and nose, but there's Calabrese in her jawline—though I see only love when Mario looks at her, never a trace of the biology that could have torn us apart. Her hair has grown into wispy dark curls that refuse to be tamed, a trait that makes Mario joke she's already inherited his stubborn nature, even if not his genes.

I study the elaborate floral arrangements lining the chapel's stone walls—white roses and lilies creating a path toward the baptismal font, their perfume mixing with centuries of incense and candle wax. Delicate glass vases catch the colored light, scattering rainbows across careful arrangements of white hydrangeas and baby's breath.

Everything is exactly as I planned, each detail perfect for my daughter's special day.

"The families are confirmed," I tell Mario, shifting into event planner mode as I mentally review my checklists. "The Vituccis, the O'Connors, even the Calabreses—though Anthony's cousins sent their regrets."

Their absence speaks volumes—a public acknowledgment that any biological claim Anthony might have made from his federal prison cell holds no weight against the family we've chosen.

Mario steps closer, and I can't help but smile as I hand Stella to him. It never fails to amaze me how this dangerous man transforms completely around our daughter. His entire body softens as he cradles her, those lethal hands impossibly gentle as he adjusts her blanket. The tender look in his eyes when she snuggles closer in her sleep makes my heart ache—this man who chose to be her father in all the ways that truly matter.

"And Matteo?" he asks, though we both know his brother was the first to accept the role of godfather. The question carries weight—evidence of the careful bridge being rebuilt between them.

"Already arguing with Bella about whether the twins get to help carry the candle," I say, my smile holding real warmth now. Four months of careful reconciliation have thawed most of the ice between us, though some scars may never fully heal.

I smooth my hand over the christening gown laid out on a nearby pew—delicate white lace and silk that generations of DeLuca children have worn. The same gown that Arianna wore just months ago, though Giovanni had his own separate gown as tradition dictates for DeLuca twins. The old fabric is impossibly soft under my fingers, carrying the weight of history and family—a history that will now include our daughter, chosen and claimed by love rather than blood.

∽

Sunlight paints Stella's christening gown in jewel-toned light. The ancient lace catches fragments of ruby and sapphire, transforming my daughter into a living masterpiece. She rests in Matteo's arms, her dark eyes fixed on his face with that peculiar intensity she gets when studying someone new. Her tiny fist is crammed firmly in her mouth, drool dampening the pristine gown that's witnessed generations of DeLuca ceremonies.

Matteo holds her with unexpected gentleness, his usual stern expression softened by something I've only seen him show his own children and Bella. He looks almost regal in his hand-stitched black suit, every inch the don, but there's a tenderness in how he cradles Stella that makes me blink back tears.

"Try not to drool on your uncle Matteo, little star," Mario murmurs, and I catch the hint of a smile playing at Matteo's lips.

Bella stands beside them as godmother, radiant in pale pink silk, her eyes bright with pride. She reaches out to smooth Stella's unruly curls, and my daughter responds with a gummy smile that makes the assembled families murmur in appreciation.

"She's got your charm," Bella whispers to me, and for a moment I'm overwhelmed by how far we've come—from betrayal to this moment of pure joy.

The priest begins the blessing, his Latin rolling through the chapel like music. In the front pew, nine-month-old Giovanni sits perfectly still in Bianca's lap, his tiny suit matching his father's, already showing that innate DeLuca gravitas. Beside them, Arianna fusses with her cloth book, her spirit refusing to be contained by ceremony. She drops the book and reaches for Stella with a delighted squeal that echoes off ancient stone.

"Hush, Aria," Bianca murmurs, but she's smiling at her baby sister.

I catch Mario's eye across the marble font, seeing in his face the same fierce pride I feel. His hand rests protectively on the baptismal font's ornate rim, those lethal fingers gentle against centuries-old stone. The same gentleness he shows our daughter, biology be damned.

"Who brings this child before God?" the priest intones.

"We do," Mario answers, his voice carrying all the weight of choice rather than blood. The families shift in their pews, a ripple of acknowledgment passing through New York's most dangerous people.

Stella barely reacts as holy water touches her forehead, too busy studying the glittering crucifix hanging above the altar. "Stella Maria DeLuca," the priest pronounces, and I remember another child in another chapel—myself, years ago, watching society christenings. That girl could never have imagined this moment: standing beside Mario DeLuca, our daughter blessed by the family that once condemned him, our future secured not through games or manipulation but through honest strength.

"May God and all the saints protect her," Matteo adds formally, and there's real warmth in his voice as he hands my daughter back to Mario.

I watch my chosen family gather around us—Matteo and Bella with the twins, Siobhan looking uncomfortable but present in the back pew, Dante hovering near the back, Marco and Sofia Renaldi beaming in a middle row.

These people who fought beside us, who chose evolution over tradition.

Stella reaches for me from Mario's arms, and I gather her close, breathing in her sweet baby scent. That girl I used to be could never have imagined this happiness, this sense of belonging. This family built on choice rather than blood.

After the ceremony, I move through the crowd at the mansion with practiced ease, watching our carefully curated worlds blend together. The grand ballroom echoes with laughter and conversation, with paper-thin Venetian glasses ringing like bells when touched, their rims traced with gold.

But I'm not just the event planner anymore, not just the society girl playing power games. I've earned my place in this world, built something real from all our complicated pieces.

Mario finds me on the terrace later, Stella sleeping peacefully against his chest while the party continues inside. Her christening gown spills over his arm like frozen moonlight, her tiny fingers curled into his shirt. The sunset paints them both in gold, this dangerous man and the daughter he chose to love.

"Having regrets?" he asks quietly, but his smile says he already knows the answer. His free hand finds mine, those strong fingers intertwining with my own.

"Only that we didn't choose this sooner," I respond, leaning into his side. Because that's what we did, isn't it? Chose each other, chose family, chose to be more than our pasts or other people's expectations.

Through the glass doors, I watch Bella spinning with Arianna while Giovanni observes from Matteo's arms, his tiny face serious. The don moves easily between both sides of the family now, his previous rigid formality softening into something more natural. Even Bianca has started to thaw, her initial hostility melting each time she cradles Stella.

The gathering represents everything we've built—Irish crews mixing with DeLuca security, young leadership talking modernization with Siobhan's people. The next generation claiming their birthright not through violence, but through careful alliance.

Through choice.

Stella stirs against Mario's chest, those dark eyes blinking open to study the sunset. My daughter—*our* daughter—born into one world but claimed by another. Chosen and protected and loved.

"We did it," I whisper, watching the future unfold in the ballroom behind us. All the pieces we fought for finally falling into place.

Mario's arm tightens around me as Stella drifts back to sleep, safe in the embrace of the father who chose her. "No," he corrects gently. "We're just beginning."

And he's right. This isn't an ending—it's a foundation. Something stronger than blood or tradition or all the games I used to play. Something built on love and choice and the family we've created from broken pieces.

Something worth fighting for.

Something worth choosing.

Every single day.

EXTENDED EPILOGUE: SOFIA

I'm sprawled across my bed, scrolling through TikTok and trying not to laugh at some ridiculous dance trend. The weak evening sun streams through my windows, painting golden patterns across the cream carpet. Taylor Swift plays softly in the background, just loud enough to fill the empty silence of the house. Mom and Dad are at their charity gala—Mom probably micromanaging every detail while Dad works the room with that practiced charm that makes people forget how dangerous he can be.

Marco is ... somewhere. He's been different lately—more secretive, more intense. I catch him watching me sometimes with this worried look, like he's seeing threats I can't imagine. But tonight, I don't mind the solitude. These are rare moments when I can just be Sofia instead of a Renaldi, when I can pretend the world outside my bedroom door isn't filled with power plays and carefully maintained alliances.

My sheets rustle as I roll off my bed, heading for the bathroom. But I freeze mid-step, every muscle suddenly tense. The hairs on the back of my neck stand up—that primal warning system Marco's always telling me to trust.

Something feels wrong. A sound that shouldn't be there, like someone trying very hard to be quiet and almost succeeding.

My heart pounds against my ribs as I grab my phone, fingers trembling slightly as I check my family's locations—a safety measure Marco drilled into me until it became a habit. No one's anywhere near the house. The blue dots showing my family are scattered across the city—Mom and Dad at the Plaza, Marco somewhere in Brooklyn. I turn down the music, straining to hear ... *there*. Footsteps on the stairs, pausing every few steps as if testing whether they've been detected.

The sound sends terror galloping through me.

I rush to my window, throwing it open. The late summer air hits my face as I look down. The drop looks daunting now, though I've scaled this roof countless times sneaking out to parties. Three stories up, but there's that sturdy trellis and the garage roof below. My hands shake as I text Marco: ***Someone's in the house.***

My phone lights up instantly with his call. "What the fuck do you mean someone's in the house?" Marco demands, his voice sharp. I hear car engines revving in the background, the squeal of tires.

"I don't know," I whisper frantically, already climbing out onto the roof. The tiles are slick under my feet, still damp from an earlier rain. "But I hear them on the stairs, and Mom and Dad aren't due home for hours—"

"Where are you right now?" The edge in his voice makes my stomach drop. Marco doesn't scare easily.

"My room. I'm going out the window. Meet me at our spot?" Our childhood hideout, where we'd retreat when things got too intense at home. The old treehouse in the woods, our sanctuary since we were kids.

A floorboard creaks right outside my door—that loose board I usually avoid because it gives me away when I'm sneaking in late. My breath catches in my throat, and I can feel a panic attack starting to build.

"Sofia?" Marco's voice holds real fear now, the kind I've never heard from my unshakeable big brother. "Talk to me."

"They're here," I whisper, panic making my voice shake. The doorknob turns slowly, deliberately. "Marco, I'm sorry, I'm so—"

My bedroom door bursts open, the force sending my framed photos crashing to the floor. I scream, scrambling fully onto the roof, but strong hands grab my hair, yanking me backward. The pain brings tears to my eyes as I catch one glimpse of masked figures before a chemical-soaked rag covers my face. The scent is sharp, medicinal, wrong.

The last thing I hear is Marco screaming my name through the phone as darkness claims me.

While you wait for Sofia and Dante's story, check out Matteo and Bella's story here.

WANT MORE AJME WILLIAMS?

Join my no spam mailing list here.

You'll only be sent emails about my new releases, extended epilogues, deleted scenes and occasional FREE books.

Printed in Great Britain
by Amazon